Wayfaring at Waverly
in Silver Lake

WAYFARING AT WAVERLY IN SILVER LAKE

stories by

James McCourt

Alfred A. Knopf   New York   2002

THIS IS A BORZOI BOOK
PUBLISHED BY ALFRED A. KNOPF

Some of these stories have been previously published,
in slightly different form, in the following:
"Wayfaring at Waverly in Silver Lake" and "In Tir na nOg" in *The New Yorker*.
"A Plethora" in *The Reporter*.
"Principal Photography" in *Southwest Review*.
"Ensenada" and "New York Lit Up That Way at Night" in *The Yale Review*.

LIBRARY OF CONGRESS CATALOGING-IN-PUBLICATION DATA
McCourt, James.
Wayfaring at Waverly in Silver Lake / by James McCourt.— 1st ed.
p.   cm.
Contents: Wayfaring at Waverly in Silver Lake (Pride) — In Tir na nOg
(Covetousness) — Principal photography (Lust) — Ensenada (Anger) — New York
lit up that way at night (Envy) — A plethora (Gluttony) — Driven woman (Sloth)
ISBN 0-394-52362-8 (alk. paper)
1. Deadly sins—Fiction. I. Title.

PS3563.A266 W3 2002
813'.54—dc21   2001038265

Manufactured in the United States of America
First Edition

In memory of Veronica Geng,
originator and pattern of Kaye Wayfaring

Contents

Acknowledgments

With heartfelt gratitude to my editor, Victoria Wilson, for her patience and astute guidance in the publication of four books over two decades, and for her steadfast determination in weaving the seven separate strands of this work into a single chronicle. Also and most emphatically to my production editor, Kevin Bourke, for his astonishing close reading capabilities, his unflinching will in correcting a now-and-again errant author's renditions, and his unmistakable desire to hand over for publication a better manuscript than he was given.

Wayfaring at Waverly
in Silver Lake

As OUT BEYOND long tinted windows Los Angeles lay gleaming in the bright air, while in the studio commissary the televised women's Olympic marathon neared culmination on the multiscreen background wall, Leland de Longpré, Hyperion Pictures' controversial new chief of concept evolution, was speaking words of caution and concern to the chief of publicity over lunch.

"Vanity of vanity, all—"

"But I didn't say 'vanity,' " the chief of publicity, purposedly attuned to words, objected. "I said 'pride.' And please don't tell me they're the same thing, because even if I don't know exactly what vanity is, I do know what I think it isn't."

"True enough," the strategist allowed (managing, his lunch partner thought, to sound both affirmative and not). "The Dodgers, it must be said, brought to Los Angeles a cohesive focus, enforcing a civic pride that had never been provided by the self-serving motion-picture industry. I've even heard it said the Dodgers in effect brought to bear on their adopted city the mysterious assimilative pride of Brooklyn—never to be confused with the exploitive vanity of Manhattan—thus creating, principally, but not entirely, through the Jewish factor, the atmosphere for the construction of a new civilization in what had been a desert."

"As a matter of fact," the publicist continued, boldly staking out his own territory, conceptually speaking, "whenever I've heard the word—'vanity'—all I've thought of really is a piece of set decoration—one of those boudoir units with big round deco mirrors. Jean Harlow had one in *Dinner at Eight*."

"It would seem clear," Leland continued, relentlessly, "that vanity is not, all said and done, to be confused with devotional intensity. Devotional intensity is not vain; quite the opposite."

"Faulkner," the publicist offered, "says a character in a book must be consistent in all things, while actual man is consistent in one thing only: he is consistently vain. His vanity alone keeps his particles damp and adhering to one another, instead of like any other handful of dust which any wind that passes can disseminate."

"Faulkner gave the industry much more trouble than he was worth. Well, in all events, whatever vanity is, you can't chastise it anymore; people are proud of it."

The publicist nodded congenially. "Los Angeles certainly is. Did you read Bunny Mars today in the *Herald-Examiner*, welcoming the women over there on the wall to their marathon?"

"I'm afraid not. So, you're a Bunny Mars enthusiast. So is my lovely wife, talking of women and marathons."

"I read Bunny Mars faithfully every day."

"You know your job."

"Bunny Mars," the publicist insisted, "is currently the most out-there journalist in Los Angeles. Get this," he advised, opening up the newspaper that had been lying folded between them. " 'Like Athens, Alexandria, Florence, Paris, Vienna, London, and New York in their day, Los Angeles is at the end of history, the very end-historical hub of those creative energies that resuscitate, refashion, redefine, and reinterpret all consumer drives.

" 'Los Angeles is the home of ideated decoration. It trades and cares for as well as cheats, steals, murders, exploits, and lies. It is modern media culture. Los Angeles is America's other-world city. The city of eternity. The only city in the world that issues blanket permission for self-scripting. The industry has bequeathed that to us as our rebirthright—satellite-direct time-line redial, darlings, to the Vienna of Freud and Max Ophuls.

" 'And so in the age of the face-lift, liposuction, dentistry more expensive than psychoanalysis, bionic life-extension more expensive than both put together, miracle cosmetic surgery, and forty-, fifty-, and sixty-year Hollywood careers—appearance careers, that is—Los Angeles vouchsafes unto you these tidings. Keep them in mind, all you strong-worldwide women, when the running–jumping–javelin–shot-put days are over: a face-lift is forever, in the sense that you will always have looked better than if not.

" 'After all, only when in technology body and image so interpenetrate that all revolutionary tension becomes bodily-collective-innervation bent on revolutionary discharge, has reality transcended itself to the extent demanded by Adrian and Perc Westmore.

" 'You are made in the image and likeness of God—where is it written that on that account you are required to decline from a vision of gorgeous glory to a necessary cadaver at the very same efficient and deadening pace with which a regulation three-act Hollywood script accomplishes its terrible mission? Heed the words of one rhapsode of Los Angeles: There is a tide in the affairs of men, which taken at the flood leads on to Malibu. Ride that tide high—on endorphins, on glamour, on the Ventura Freeway!' "

"Interesting," Leland allowed, trying to decide whether or not to consolidate his power further at the studio by sending back the abalone, whose immediate provenance, he divined, was the freezer locker rather than the warmer sands off Catalina. "But what is it exactly you were saying about Wayfaring?"

"Her pride's been hurt—she's retired to the alcazar in Silver Lake like Marion Davies did to San Simeon, like Dolores Del Rio did in that Santa Monica palace Cedric Gibbons built for her."

"On Wayfaring at Waverly—alcazar indeed! It's a good Schindler house; why the compulsion to exaggerate?"

"A good Schindler house," the publicity maven stressed, " 'gloriously proportioned and sympathetically refurbished in anthologized original Southwest, augmented by mixtures of mission, modern, nouveau, and marble-bolection-molding deco, resplendent in its terraced-garden setting atop the Silver Lake hills, and caressed by feng shui.' Bunny Mars again, just last week."

Yes, the new executive thought (deciding the abalone must definitely go back—noticing meanwhile as he gestured to a waiter that in the space created by the temporary suspension of the women's marathon, viewers were being offered the distraction of an interlude feature, the cunning fuchsia-haired Beverly Hills astrologer, industry scold, civic activist— "Everything west of Doheny—it's always wise to know your limits"—Astarte. Astarte, a Kaye Wayfaring intimate, was hosting a group of visiting anthropologists from the earth's four corners). Yes, a nice house up on Wayfaring at Waverly. Unlike its principal occupant, it didn't have an enormous amount of curb appeal in today's terms; but if you got into it, it had a number of sturdy features: parquet floors in the entry hall and the bedrooms, tesselated marble elsewhere throughout; the original Tiffany windows; the long mirrors, some of smoke glass; the amethyst Venetian chandeliers in the dining room. Assortments of bergères, fauteuils, Empire divans and modular sectionals, and everywhere you looked, signed photographs in chased silver frames. Then you went out back to the patio looking out over Silver Lake, and with the water running continuously over the lip of the Lautner pool, you couldn't tell where the pool stopped and Silver Lake began.

"Yes," he allowed, as the anthropologists began pitching on-the-job impressions of their arduous exploratory week on that edge of the Pacific Rim. "Wayfaring at Waverly is enchanting, all of it—as is the much simpler and more functional Gehry Laguna beach house—but it isn't really an alcazar. Orphrey Whither's pile in Whither Park—now that, mutatis mutandis, is an alcazar."

"Yes, agreed—albeit a Regency one."

"As befits the regent Orphrey was in glorious days gone by. Nash exterior, Brighton Pavilion pillared-alcove gaga interior, all wrapped around a pool the size of Lake Hollywood. Rex Ingram gave Orphrey very big ideas, and Wallace Neff was only too glad to fulfill them, building for him the very Taj Mahal–ish pile he didn't get to build for the Dohenys. Orphrey for his part has been known to proclaim Whither Park, the result, a source of pride in an uncaring world."

"I was never there, but I always think of it as chock full of random crap like the Huntington place in Pasadena."

"Really? I've never been in Pasadena."

(The subordinate, seriously doubting Leland's sincerity, let the extraordinary declaration pass. Instead of formulating something, anything, by way of a neutral reply, he thought back to a recent discussion with the truly informed and truly formidable, often deceptively chummy Astarte, a fierce protector of everything Wayfaring, concerning the back story of Livonia de Longpré, Leland's considerably older wife, and her pivotal position vis-à-vis the husband's bold ascent to power at Hyperion.

"But who was she?" he'd inquired.

"Voni," Astarte declared, in a tone expressive of an attempt to avoid the sententious, "was Vonetta Drew—affectionately known in the industry as VD and 'the meanest dame in pictures'—not excepting Beverly Michaels, Bella Darvi, and Ann Savage. Which of course is how all the rumors got started—she was that good at being bad. But as she put it, when it came to really being rotten, 'I think maybe I was finally too vain to actually repel viewers.' "

"Bella Darvi!" the publicist erupted. "*The Egyptian.* 'I ask for nothing,' she murmurs, petting the white Persian cat, 'but if you will give me the deed to your parents' apartment in the House of the Dead, I will show you the perfection of love.' He brings her the deed; she throws him out in the rain. Years later she crawls back to him—now Pharaoh's court physician—covered with leprosy, wrapped loosely in a shroud, like the walking dead, her pride peeling off her clay-colored face. He pities her. It's heaven—and she wasn't even nominated!"

"Neither was Kaye Wayfaring for *Avenged.* But you're wondering about Voni."

"Well, yes, I was."

"A couple of cuts above Bella Darvi, to say the least, but there are marked similarities. Foxy plotter that she was, she asked for nothing either—or next to it. In campaigning for Leland, a confirmed bachelor many years her junior, she never stooped to lying—outright. And in that smart calculation one may discern both the gauge of her quite remarkable success and Leland's wisdom in not being a man too vain to profit from a spouse's wiles. Voni may come up nowadays on the elevator, but elevators do not—except in the dramatically sudden shift at the very outset from service to customer elevator at Bullocks-Wilshire—fairly represent her climb in this town.

"No, Voni has taken the cable car up Bunker Hill, and known the flats well, as well as all the sad little bungalow courts of Hollywood and all the sad, sunny little kitchens in them.

But none of that sapped her spirit, an essential product of the East Texas piney wood country, a very determined region."

So that was it.

Leland for his part was remembering a lunch—his first as a Hyperion high operative—at Whither Park the previous week. Mahi-mahi with steamed cactus, blue tortillas, and a good Pinot Grigio from the Whither vineyards up in Sonoma, goat cheese, figs, Calistoga water, all in the company of his wife and what as it turned out was a group of her old friends, Kaye Wayfaring, Orphrey Whither, kingpin of Hyperion Pictures and veteran director [of *Ominous*, *The Day That Dawns*, *The Night of the End of Time*, *Pilgrim Soul*, *Way Station*, *We Are Born*, *We Live*, *We Die*, and *Avenged*], Jameson O'Maurigan, poet, actor, playwright, and motion-picture scenarist to Hyperion Pictures, and Astarte, at which the sore topic of *Avenged* and the arcane production-financing technicalities that supposedly had denied nominations to all involved [though it was generally assumed that irredentist spite had been the chief obstacle] had inevitably come up.

"As I've told you all repeatedly," Astarte had proclaimed with ongoing finality, "you polecats were all included out for the time-honored unspoken principles relative to the sanctity of the Hollywood cabala. You simply cannot tweak these folks' collective vanity with certain divulgements. You may have been content with the notion that you were remaking *Les Dames du Bois de Boulogne*, filmed nearly in its entirety in New York and East Hampton, but do you still not realize any of you what that Elusive Drive–Bronson Canyon sequence was read as an allegory of?"

"Dorothy di Frasso and Bugsy Siegel?" Voni de Longpré drawled, as Jameson and Orphrey Whither looked away separately, in two directions, while Kaye Wayfaring wondered was there a use.

"There are things," the seer continued, "up with which they simply will not put.")

"But," Leland was now remarking, "speaking of Regency—or Brighton—don't miss this television audition. If that apparition isn't something that, did it not exist, your Miss Mars might have found it necessary to invent, you and I are both doing thirsty work in the wrong business."

The wrecking crew had torn away, Kaye Wayfaring reckoned, a little more than half of the second story of the house next door on Waverly; in another few days the demolition would be complete, the land entirely cleared, and landscaping could begin on the expanded Wayfaring property in that residential parkland in the twentieth-century Eden that was and ever would be southern California. In the haze-free sky patch bracketed by an empty window frame, the unadorned white cross on the hill at Forest Lawn seemed craftily positioned, advertising an untroubled condominium eternity. She suddenly remembered a piece of skywriting out her bedroom window on the top floor all those years ago: TOP STAR DROPS DEAD: COMING SOON TO FOREST LAWN. CONSIDER YOUR LOVED ONES. RESERVE.

Over the hill on Wayfaring, in the other direction, high above Hyperion Avenue, the reservoir lay pool-blue in the blazing August sun. Further left the high white HOLLYWOOD sign—of all place names the name, in Los Angeles—flashed in the same refulgence. "Our Father, which art in heaven," she mumbled, "Hollywood be thy name."

She looked out the new windows—the house had been taken apart and reinforced with a kind of Ray-Ban glass—remarking again on the effect of the absence of the variously colored pastel aluminum Venetian blinds that were a big feature of the house in her childhood, and with which she first imitated Marilyn's scene from *Don't Bother to Knock*, only to return the next year to find them all taken down and replaced with long curtains and outdoor shutters.

She had risen early that morning to tune in the women's Olympic marathon, now nearing completion off-camera, and was now as intent on watching Astarte's interview as on avoiding her own interrogative glance in the long *verre églomisé* mirror (1830 French, cobalt blue and clear glass with an enamel border of peacocks, it had come in her mother's, Cordelia's, dowry, and supposedly had belonged to the duchesse de Praslin—according to an entry in *Children of Pride*, the pre–Civil War diaries of citizens of Georgia, an ancestor murdered by her husband in the most notorious scandal of the Second Empire).

She remembered that like the mirror in "The Lady of Shalott" the *verre églomisé* had once cracked—or been cracked—from side to side. (Cordelia claimed it "just happened," but it seemed clear to everybody she'd thrown something at it.) Subsequently it had been sent to the attic, and only years later, after Cordelia's suicide, taken out to Los Angeles and repaired at fantastic expense.

"You avoid that mirror, don't you?" Jameson O'Maurigan had asked her.

"Just after I was married, my mother-in-law was telling me an old Czech proverb she'd gotten from Emmy Destinn: 'At twenty you have the face you inherit, at forty the face you develop, at sixty the face you deserve.' 'I'm well over sixty,' she said, 'and you're just over forty. I played my mother onscreen—presumably we deserved one another—and you've been approached to do likewise.' 'You won the Academy Award for it,' I said. 'I think it was by one vote—Bette's. You'd get it in a landslide.' 'I may never be nominated again.' 'Nonsense. You'll be nominated and you'll win. Ought to be enough for anybody, but of course it's not; how could it be?' Yes, I tend to avoid the mirror—*that* mirror."

Instead, she watched her friend and champion the psychic-astrologer Astarte, just now listening to one anthropologist-on-the-job, a Briton attempting irony, holding forth on Los Angeles.

"We, votaries all of the Hollywood myth, have been, as you like to say, checking it out—the Olympiad, held again and in our lifetime, hard by the very slopes of Mount Palomar, the new Olympus! The events, the teams, the visitors, the natives—superintendents to the only gods the world has left, let's face it.

"For my part, although I blush to say so, so conditioned is one by the most potent of all myths ever concocted that, in spite of what one knows to be the truth of the matter, in our time one fully expected to find in the purlieus this Olympus of the inner eye, this Hollywood–Los Angeles of exalted evangelical tropes signaling great consequence, a factual wonderland metropolis of celebrities actually walking the streets. Although one doesn't quite go about actually wielding a map of the stars' homes in the clutch of one fist and a blank autograph book in the other, one might as well do, on the off chance and in the demented hope that Kaye Wayfaring, for example, should suddenly be seen swirling out of Schwab's drugstore or sailing into the Roosevelt Hotel—both of which temple precincts, along with, for instance, the Egyptian Theater, one knows to have been, as it were, discontinued.

"Celebrities and palm trees are what one's been led through a lifetime of celluloid transport to expect. Well, the palm trees are everywhere, all right, but where are the stars? One can't help asking oneself this mad question. There, I'm afraid you have heard my confession."

Chuckling, the canny seer replied, "That is so true! Gosh all get-out, and yes, we know what you mean—about Los Angeles, about enchantment. But look at it this way. Celebrities, like everybody else at the moment—one anything but reckless, by the way; indeed, quite the opposite—are all at home, in Los Angeles, watching the Olympics taking place in Los Angeles! Yes, even on a Sunday morning. You can't, for instance, as you lament, see Kaye Wayfaring anywhere, but I happen to know she can see you—right this minute, as we speak. You ought to wave right into that camera and say hello."

"Oh, do you think—?"

(She's going to get him to do it, Kaye Wayfaring said to herself, amused.)

"I most certainly do, and what's more, you really ought to, because, as you may know—"

(There she goes narrowing her eyes. No mystery what's coming next. She's sublime; I love it.)

"—a lot of people right here in the greater Los Angeles area do think Kaye Wayfaring has flown the coop—for good—and retired to Laguna!"

(Imagine. How funny. Of course nobody—nobody in the industry anyway—ever thinks of Silver Lake.)

"Because of the *Avenged* scandal. Nobody nominated—on that maddening technicality!

"But I can tell you that as far as Kaye Wayfaring, at home right here in Los Angeles, is concerned, the *Avenged* outrage is very over. And I can tell you something more—and it's that the 'Womanly Girl' video by Rock Formation that the entire living planet has watched pole-vault to the top of the charts is no fantasy of Hyperion Music's publicity department, although it is without any question the stuff of myth—the enactment of a kind of incantation, a rite older than the pyramids. Kaye Wayfaring walking the walk all over town in zigzag New Wave jump cuts in fabulous song—and let me tell you, dear, she's come a long way even from her fabulous East Coast summer-stock Adelaide in *Guys and Dolls*, not too many years ago, a show that had them flying back in squadrons—anyway, produced and written respectively—'Womanly Girl,' that is—by her gorgeous, young, richly talented only husband and his equally fabulous twin, they of course being Tristan and Jacob Beltane, the twin sons of the one and only legendary Mawrdew Czgowchwz. And if you ever want to talk about a story! No longer, if ever indeed she did, need Kaye Wayfaring rely for sustenance as a performer on the massed love of strangers.

"Oh, yes, Kaye Wayfaring is right here in Los Angeles, now as we speak. And while you won't find her at Schwab's or at the Roosevelt—time was, but time is no more—or at House of Pancakes or Tacodobe, for that matter, I can tell you—"

"Oh, brother!" Kaye Wayfaring murmured.

(You will do the work, she heard a voice from the past declare, as it was meant to be done, or get out and not come back!)

"It's too bad, it really is," Astarte was telling the anthropologists, "we can't summon her to be with you. I'm sure you must remember Barbara Stanwyck charming the professors in *Ball of Fire*; I just know Kaye Wayfaring would immensely enjoy a short little remake with you."

"Oh, brother!" Kaye Wayfaring cried, right out loud.

"She's always been very drawn to intellect."

And to palm trees—even if the date palm trees all over Los Angeles, planted for the 1932 Olympics, had begun, she did feel, to reach menacing proportions. When I was a child out here, she thought, they looked friendly (then so did I). Yesterday, walking through West Hollywood, I thought, Another distortion in a city of relentless distortions. I am sounding like an anthropologist. I am not an anthropologist. I am an actor—drawn to intellect, of course—and the mother of

twins, one boy, one girl, who are with their father just now—
my gorgeous only husband—in Laguna Beach.

Kaye Wayfaring, looking away from the *verre églomisé*,
remembered. She put herself into one of her favorite mental
contraptions, the Hollywood Bowl Memory Theatre—high in
the hills, thus offering, she dreamed, a vision of the world and
of the nature of things seen from a height near to the stars
themselves.

In the house in Clayton, there were four ornamental ele-
ments in the moldings: gadroons, astragals, volutes, acanthus.
Kaye and her brother, Jack, hearing the house described by a
local expert on architecture, had made of these four races of
aliens who had invaded Warwoman Dell and set about burning little X's in the townspeople's necks, making them victims
of mind control, and together drew up the scenario for the
8-millimeter home movie *I Married an Astragal*, Kaye's first
performance on celluloid. (Then, later, Stella said, "In
Chekhov people are heartbroken all day long and live quite
normally.")

How many ways can I imagine him now? As amorous, as
tranquil, as angry, as melancholy. As leading the Los Angeles
Philharmonic and mixed choruses from Everywhere in a
volcanic performance of Mahler's Eighth Symphony, a vision
of the world seen from the supercelestial founts of Wisdom beyond the stars themselves, and as simultaneously (for
he's twins too) hawking programs up and down the amphitheater aisles. As drilling the kick line in "Womanly Girl" and
as ringing Tibetan bells on the empty stage in a winter sunrise
service. As sitting behind me like a stranger, whispering distracting information into someone else's ear, and as sitting
alone in the top row, and how as a point of pride I've got to
reach him from the footlights. As sitting next to me looking up
at the sickle moon in the starry sky—which he, being the son
of a wizard, can actually see—while the crowd pushes past us

to the parking lot—and saying nothing at all—all said and done, for the time being.

I am driving to Laguna as soon as the women's marathon is finished.

When I was young, too young, my brother, Jackson, and his Rabun County ridge-runner cronies tried the Atalanta trick on me; I threw the croquet ball across the wall into Warwoman Dell.

Here she comes now into the stadium. Atalanta. She is more the stuff of myth, if you ask me. No question.

Freedom . . . locomotion . . . love . . . exploration of the unknown. The mirror on Mount Palomar, trained on the heavens as seriously as Astarte's searching eyes. The mirror in the train that time on the way up to Manitoy—reflecting the New York skyline.

They always told us there's nothing so over as just yesterday; what all for we never knew; it was just what they said.

But the palm trees? The week before, at lunch in Whither Park, she had been quietly planning a long walk, from Whither Glen to Silver Lake, by way of Sepulveda, Wilshire, Santa Monica, Melrose, Highland, and Sunset, and as the *Avenged* discussion wound down the palm tree situation had come up.

". . . up with which they simply will not put," Astarte had insisted; "these spiritual descendants of Metro, Warners, Universal and Fox, Columbia, Paramount and Republic. Hyperion and its personnel compromise their images. They hate that. Anyway, darlings, you swept Cannes. That's something."

"Every endeavor," said Jameson O'Maurigan, "has its enthusiasts. Look at the palm trees—they have theirs."

"Not on this property," Orphrey Whither countered. "I say uproot them, one and all! They never belonged here in the first place," he growled, a little oiled on Pinot Grigio and gruff in the glow of the southern California summer afternoon.

(Kaye Wayfaring wondered: Did her host's copper beeches belong there, either, among the mesquite and eucalyptus?)

"Who the hell belonged here in the first place," Astarte demanded, "besides the Cahuenga? The progenitors, forebears, and predecessors of the rest of us came west in covered wagons, or, as film noir would have it, in broken-down buses, in search of some kind of paradise."

"And," Jameson O'Maurigan added, "an effective cure for the inferiority complex."

Sprawled to the east and south of Whither Park, Los Angeles (according to O'Maurigan "a series of locally abrupt disjunctions in search of a wider coherence") stretched to the horizon, enacting its own performance for its own information, offering no easy explanations. "The problem with the trees," the poet declared, "is that when they were young, and we were young, what never was spoken of but was nevertheless believed to be cached, secreted, folded in the fronded nests of them was, or seemed, within reach. Now here we are in later life, and like so much else—everything we cared about in the fifties—what there may have been in them is out of reach, and it's as if nothing, therefore, were ever there. And that's the nuisance.

"Now as to Whither Glen," he continued, "in Whither Glen there were never any palm trees. There were and are your native birches, linden, larch, copper and weeping beech, and immense quantities of your native yew—but no palm trees. You will find palm trees in West Cork, and in west Los Angeles, but not in Whither Glen."

"Well," Astarte declared, "so far as the rest of Los Angeles is concerned, Whither Glen is an unknown kingdom by the sea."

(The same talk echoes down the ages, Kaye thought. It's

the moods that do us in, not the talk, she told herself, watching the front-running woman in the featured event now resumed approach the Olympic stadium. We run around in circles—we sit at tables running around in circles, while they sit across from us, seeming to run counterclockwise, seeming to thwart us, and all it is in all likelihood is an elaborate watch-works of sharp-toothed gears.)

"And what," Orphrey Whither demanded, in the strange paternalistic way she'd never gotten over finding oddly comforting (wherein, she supposed, lay the explanation for her virtually exclusive association with Hyperion, right down to the new music-video undertaking that had been Leland de Longpré's startling idea), "are Miss Wayfaring's particular enthusiasms—apart, that is, from infiltrating behind the lines of popular youth culture and clocking demolition crews in that inland kingdom Silver Lake?"

"Considering the fact, Orphrey," Livonia de Longpré declared, rather boldly, Kaye Wayfaring thought, "that your studio offshoot produced it, you might as well admit that 'Womanly Girl' is not only a work of pure genius, but one that everybody in the world, it would seem, but you yourself has taken in—"

"Or," the director challenged, "been taken in by—always admitting," he added slyly, "the element of willing deception we all of us in our sometimes quite Luciferian pride take—"

"Whatever of that," Jameson O'Maurigan cut in, sharply, turning back from contemplating the Malibu coastline, "Rock Formation has gone straight to the top of the charts—not only bypassing Strumpet, Sliced Bread, and Terror Tactics with the might of an LAPD tank on Central Avenue, but knocking the last-named's 'Redondo' out of the top slot in one quick week—and under the Hyperion logo."

"Indeed," Orphrey Whither sighed. "Leave it to television to rescue an ailing studio, delivering in only eleven minutes of viewing time the real Kaye Wayfaring to America's adoring youth."

"You mean old fool!" Astarte remonstrated lightly. "She's bazooka in 'Womanly Girl.' It's a revelation, absolutely."

"Oh, to you too?" her adversary calmly queried. "Well, I must say she looks to me—lighter by the load of twins, for which I, along with America and all the world, am indeed grateful—still rather remarkably like the young woman who was brought to me—"

(Pride of ownership, she thought—identical to that generations of them have had for their racehorses.)

She stood as if at attention, declaring, "I must be off; don't stir—I'll let myself out."

"Take the Stingray down to the beach, if you like," said Jameson O'Maurigan encouragingly. "I'm off to New York."

"No thanks, I'll walk."

"Walk where?" Orphrey Whither demanded.

"Home."

"You can't walk, woman, from here to Silver Lake!" Orphrey sputtered. "This isn't a video—or the women's Olympic marathon, either. Quite apart from the desperate want of sidewalks in the area, there are hordes of Europeans, Asians, Australians, carousing from Santa Monica to downtown Los Angeles!"

"Honey, do be sensible," Astarte interposed. "Let me drop you at the Polo Lounge."

"Moreover, you've hardly et a piece of food!" her director scolded.

"Orphrey, it was delicious, really it was—even if I should feel the perverse need to swerve into Johnny Rockets on the long, winding way."

"Vixen. I'm old, and weary, and resigned to your contrary ways."

"Then buck up; we'll make another picture one of these days." She turned to Astarte. "No, not the Polo Lounge—there might be Europeans—but if you'd drop me at Westwood, I'd be grateful. It's time I dropped by again and had another chat with Norma Jean."

"Eleven minutes!" Orphrey Whither hissed into his wine.

"Less is more, more or less," Jameson O'Maurigan said, watching the backs of the heads of Astarte and Kaye Wayfaring diminish as Astarte's Porsche convertible entered the tunnel of elms on the long road down to the Whither Park gatehouse. "Or as the oul fella said, 'Isn't it a sad thing, Willie, when y' lose yer dog!'

"I'd forgotten," he added, "that it was Marilyn's anniversary—twenty-two years."

"Yes," Orphrey grunted, "and it's typically good of the creature to remember that it is and to want to go and look in at Westwood. Be that as it may, however," he growled, "less is not more; less is less. Moreover, it is a great deal less than enough, and furthermore, I'll thank you not to throw wise saws and ijit sayings in my face on top of everything. And furthermoreover, I have seen the thing—I let this man here put my money into it, after all—" Leland de Longpré nodded—

"I have seen what they're calling the new art form; I have seen the future, and it isn't on."

They drove south on Sepulveda Boulevard.

"Tell me," Kaye Wayfaring asked Astarte, "which do you think is longer, Sepulveda Boulevard or the Appian Way?"

The seer looked confused. "Isn't Appian Way that little cul-de-sac off Bellagio?"

"Tell me this then," the star inquired, "did you ever know Peg Entwhistle?"

"Honey, Peg Entwhistle was before my time—a long while before."

"They were talking about Peg Entwhistle in Silver Lake that day in '50 when Norma Jean came to take me for a spin. Thalia was there, over from Pasadena. They'd assured her Silver Lake wasn't Hollywood, that as long as you were east of Hyperion, you were safe. Thalia had known Peg Entwhistle well—worked with her in stock. The sign was in ruins back then—nobody ever thought they'd ever put it back up."

Astarte understood her friend was talking in encoded terms about anxiety.

"Look, honey, I'm all for the video thing."

"Do you remember the line 'Give me one hundred stacks of one hundred one-hundred-dollar bills'?"

"No, honey, I find it, in two words, im-possible to catch the lyrics. I go with the noise and the look and the mood—and they're all dynamite."

"They come—the lyrics—from a play I devised once. A play about a heist at a nightclub—think of the Eddie Mars joint in *The Big Sleep* or that place in the Valley in *The High Window*—the address of which was 1010101 Wayfaring, supposedly way up in the hills. The mythical Wayfaring was supposed to be longer even than the real Sepulveda, and of course miles longer than the real Wayfaring, in Silver Lake. I sometimes think the vanity came with the name—handed down like the old French gilt mirror."

"You are not vain—anyway, no more than anybody would be."

"Excuse me, Astarte, I am as vain as anybody would be, could be, or might be."

"Well?"

"That's not not vain."

"Excuse me, but out here it is—or isn't."

"Must be the reason I keep coming back for regular checkups."

"If you played your cards right, you'd never have to live anywhere else."

"Play the cards I've been dealt? I might, although I haven't as yet been able to get anybody really interested in staying in Silver Lake. They prefer Laguna. But now that we've acquired the lot next door on Waverly and we're renovating the house at last—as if to go with the sign across the gully that poor Peg jumped from. But Silver Lake is yesterday to them; I can't seem to get them to see a future in it. One result of marrying outside my generation."

"Honey, your marriage was, to coin a phrase, made in heaven—believe you me. Call me your fairy godmother and believe me."

"I believe you, I believe him. I believe the cards. We were playing just yesterday down in Laguna—the letter at the door, the party, the two duelists, sabers lowered, and on and on; revelations, reconciliations, absence, gossip."

"The agendas," Astarte declared, "affixed to divination are assay, correction, approximation, refinement, venture, return, and verdict."

Kaye nodded. "Seven in all—corrective each to a deadly sin?"

"I never thought about it—maybe I will."

"Tomorrow."

"No, if I think about it, I'll think about it tonight."

"Very California. That was Norma Jean's way too. I remember that first day she came to Silver Lake. I was listening to them from the upstairs window over the sound of Buddy

Clark on the radio singing 'Dance, ballerina, dance.' One of them—a visitor, a man—said, 'The highest men are calm, silent, and unknown.'

"Norma Jean was very concerned with divination always, as you of all people well know. I remembered that vividly yesterday, when the letter came to the door, as it were—there in the cards. We discounted fan mail. Somebody said the letter of the law comes to the house of self on any given day. Also we allowed it might mean something from back home asking to be read. Mother's diaries, more than likely."

"Of course."

"And the duelists. We laughed, because when the brothers were very young, on Manitoy where I first met them—I was just twenty-one—playing the silent role of the young Emilia Marty in *The Makropulos Secret*. They must have been . . . never mind. They had a fight over me, and I pretended I couldn't tell them apart."

"But now?"

"They never fight over anything. Which is why, I suppose, that although it was Jacob who seemed to come after me, he was doing so for his brother. It confused me at first—as if I really couldn't tell the one from the other—but when he told me how difficult it is sometimes for heterosexual men to either know for sure or to ask outright for what they want, the confusion somehow disappeared."

"A great story, really, in a Gemini life. And the duelists?"

"Well, I suppose, what does what there is of her—Cordelia—in me want from what there is of the Colonel . . . or something. What we took in was the fact that although the swords are held down while the left hands are clasped, they, the swords, are not dropped. Hence all promises, treaties, and contracts made by men . . . Do you know, Orphrey actually asked me whether we'd had a prenuptial drawn up?"

"Oh, you know him—always mad to sound alert and contemporary."

"Well, we laughed, then gathered the evidence up, reshuffled it, and put it in the box with the Ouija board, an old original Monopoly game that must have seemed very exotic to the original players, none of whom had likely ever been East, and a collection of wooden blue chips from the old casino at Avalon.

"Anyway, Silver Lake—terribly private."

"Terribly," Astarte agreed (somewhat uncertainly, Kaye thought).

"No temptation to roll out of bed and right away hit Campanile for breakfast without makeup, with the sunglasses on the table folded next to the coffee cup."

"Oh, honey, really," Astarte insisted, "that was never you."

"I guess not. I used to think it was, until that night—it was Bette's seventieth birthday party—she said, 'Don't be ridiculous, you're not like those others, the ones who beef about the necessity of—of course you can have your privacy. It's the ones who would die without it who go on and on—' "

"What a divine Bette," Astarte said. "Any drag queen would envy it to tatters. You get the essential Back Bay quality perfectly."

"Thanks. I remember answering—trying to—'Maybe they simply can't handle—' 'It isn't even that'—she was absolutely insistent. 'They would *die*!' "

"Actresses in the theater," Livonia was saying, "served their part when they were authentic, but in pictures this cannot be done in the same degree at all, and the actress serves and creates her persona. What they knew they would leave behind were composite character studies, to which any and every role was subservient. Davis and Stanwyck are the supreme examples—although Davis hated sharing the honor: one of her rare but unmistakable declensions into vanity, overcompensated for by her championing of Mary Astor and Ida Lupino. And Warners was, no question, *the* studio. And when they played the roles, they played them to the hilt, because each facet of their personas needed exact definition. They knew the only way to survive being cut up that way is to work with bullet-proof angles of self-definition."

O'Maurigan nodded agreement. "Hence Davis's valor, coming on Johnny Carson in the red dress and talking about being hacked to bits by surgeons, and still having the moral energy to overwhelm the people."

"Of course," Livonia said, "Wayfaring has the most threatening sort of stuff to work with. If acting starts with dressing up in Mama's clothes, then what that wardrobe dictated—for instance, if that story about the mother and the three fishermen is actually true, instead of some crazy Southern Gothic take on some old fable. I know she once told me that as a child she'd developed an obsession for Rumpelstiltskin, and that at Yale, she played the girl with the peg leg in that Flannery O'Connor thing."

" 'Good Country People,' " O'Maurigan interposed. "And yes, it is—it's true, the fishermen story. Gospel—or more accurately apocryphal, since the whole of it, known to that generation, only came out in the diaries. I knew Thalia Bridgewood very well, and she talked about both her sisters all the time, but I never heard the truth about Cordelia's fugue. I'll never forget the afternoon Wayfaring sat with me and read it out of the diary."

"I'm afraid," Leland admitted, "I don't know the story at all."

O'Maurigan paused, considered, and began.

"Cordelia, for years after her son's death, would sit sipping Belle Rive scuppernong wine and reading the obituary notices in the *Atlanta Constitution*, then get the Colonel's staff driver to take her all over the state to the funerals of young men under thirty, where she would invariably assume the pose of neighbor come to succor the bereaved in their tribulation in a most curious fashion: reciting aloud from the Bible passages dealing with the Sealing of the Tribes and the Genealogies, and saying things like 'There never was a happy mother—only if you count the mother of God, and only intermittently at that,' and 'You must not think the dead are prideful, or that it is hard to be at ease with them. They will speak of the unrepining dead. They are much mistaken. My son, Jack, a boy born to cause an extremity of grief to anyone unwise enough, helpless enough, so defiant of consequences or simply commanded by nature to love him . . .'

"The army psychiatrist's report started off, 'It is not unusual in cases of mental unbalance brought on by sudden bereavement for the subject to take a morbid interest in disasters and human dramas, under the sway of the delusion that attributes to themselves an active, even prominent role in the events that fill their mind.' Well put, because by way of condoling, Cordelia would tell the story of her own life and of her marriage and children and how one died and the other went into a convent.

" 'Well, Daddy said I was going to marry the Wayfaring boy no matter what I wanted, as I'd been up to West Point, got pinned, got in the society columns of all the New York newspapers plus the *Atlanta Constitution*, and that there was going to be a war and the Wayfaring boy was going to have to be in it, and I was not going to get away with deserting my country before the fact. So I got into the Duesenberg V-8 roadster with the whitewall tires and I drove down at about a hundred miles an hour in all the heat, across the Chattahoochee into Alabama, and I stopped at the first place I needed to get gas in, and down on the shore were three boys poking in the mud for flatfish with a pointed stick, right there in the shade of a big old river oak—they were all brothers. And I walked right down the slope in my white shoes and white dress and white hat, and up to them, and I said, "Whichever of the three of you boys has a decent suit of clothes to get married in and the gall to marry me right this afternoon in Phenix City can do so. My daddy has a lot of money." And the one called Jack Infinger did, and his two brothers, Barry and D.J., were the witnesses.' "

"Jack Infinger," Orphrey repeated.

"It gets better!" the poet fairly snarled. " 'It's a funny thing, but I was happy with Jack Infinger. His brothers always said he was the laziest boy in Alabama, that he was so shiftless until the sun went down and there wouldn't be a fish in his barrel, except he would haul his pecker out of his britches and then the bottom fish would be jumpin' all right, up out of that muddy ol' Chattahoochee right into his lap. And they sure knew something, those brothers of his, because he sure could *fuck*'—it's underlined. 'But of course Daddy caught up with the whole deal, and had the marriage annulled—Daddy's might and power, people said, extended throughout the whole of Georgia, Alabama, Mississippi, and Louisiana, and if you went outside that country after crossing him, he'd find you through agents and get your tail feathers rearranged real pretty. And so he roared at me as to how those boys were lucky to get away with their lives, never mind any such thing as a payoff of money.

" 'And I was happy in another way, and for a time, with the Wayfaring boy, especially when he was far away in the Pacific. They say there is nothing so exhilarating to a woman with small children as the idea that she may at any time find herself a widow and the cynosure of all eyes.

" 'But the Wayfaring boy never was sure was he the first-born's father, as I insisted on the name Jack. No more was I—and I found that right handy.' "

"Can you beat it?" Livonia wondered.

"No," O'Maurigan replied, "but I certainly can use it to advantage—and she could play it to a fare-thee-well and win the Academy Award. You know, once, when Cordelia was really off the wall, she told Kaye the Wayfaring boy—by then of course a war hero and a colonel—had never been able to—that periodically she'd had to go back to find the Infinger boys, fishing on that same riverbank, and that her only daughter, the very light of her supposed daddy's eyes, was the product of one of them—she couldn't remember which. Nice, huh?

" 'I earned my run of lying cheating tramps,' she told me once, 'in pictures about the dirty deals and low maneuvers that keep this corrupt world going.' I said her lying cheating tramps had been the envy of the industry, from Paramount right down to the Factory.

"Cordelia had her own handmade Ouija and a crystal ball from the conjur woman of Dismal Swamp. She would often refer to 'a terrible night atmosphere' and say, 'Children are all children together; parents are lonely.' It was a sign she was about to go under. Then she'd quote Blake, 'Give me my bottle of salvation.' What really did her in was television: it brought into the home all her projections, and when she turned it on, her defenses stopped functioning."

"Every time I sit quiet in Westwood with Norma Jean," Kaye Wayfaring told Astarte, as they turned left off Sepulveda onto Wilshire, "it's like it's just yesterday and we're together on that hot June day in 1950 just after our birthdays, just after *All About Eve* had wrapped.

"I never remember her more full of life. She knew exactly

what she'd done on *Eve*. Johnny Hyde had just driven us down from her place on North Palm Drive to Schwab's, where she bought a bottle of Sortilege, and we were sitting openmouthed at the counter, eyes riveted on the counter mirror, while the ice melted in our vanilla Cokes, watching the ruby-red-lipsticked woman in the white dress, white gloves, shiny black straw picture hat, and spectator pumps, sitting at the bend of the counter devouring a glass gondola dish of vanilla ice cream covered with Pepto-Bismol.

"I got a very serious shorthand concept lesson that afternoon from Norma Jean: You can never tell—you'll never be able to. I never knew what she really wanted—in the acting sense, I mean, according to the Third Question, or the way Stella made you know yourself—but nobody ever went at lines the way she did, with that expression. Nobody ever really wrote what she said. When she looked in the mirror at Dick Widmark in *Don't Bother to Knock*—'You came here to flirt. I don't mind, as long as you aren't grouchy about it'—that was her talking."

"So you don't—tell," Astarte said, "you sit still."

"Then, years later—Norma Jean was long dead—I remember talking to Bette about Old Hollywood and *What Ever Happened to Baby Jane*, and Bette saying, 'I hadn't the slightest idea what to do with Jane—until I saw the wardrobe.' I connected it right away with Norma Jean and me watching that woman at Schwab's.

" 'You know, Wyoming,' Norma Jean said—I was calling myself Wyoming that summer—'all you ever read about Hollywood is the girl who gets discovered, waiting tables or something like that, and gets to be a big star, like in *A Star Is Born*. Well, that was a good picture, and one day they'll probably make it again, and maybe it was somewhat of a true story, but it was *not* the true story, if you know what I mean—whereas I know you don't, exactly, but I bet you've heard rumors. And true stories too without knowing the difference, such as they were testifying to back there in Silver Lake about one Peg Entwhistle.'

"I admitted, yes, I'd heard rumors. 'Well,' she said, 'everybody has secret demons—even celebrities, I guess. I don't know yet.' Then she told me the Peg Entwhistle story and how she herself would never do that, she didn't think. 'But be that as it may, and even if I should happen to wind up back in the bungalow court, in a manner of speaking—'

" ' 'Cause somethin' you trusted done rusted and busted? Mama would say that.'

" 'In a manner of speaking—with nothing but a lot of memories and the habit of coming back here to Schwab's to buy Sortilege, there is one thing you can be sure I will never say about Hollywood, and that is I should have stayed home.'

"Yes, wonderment and sympathy, Norma Jean insisted, for as long as you can manage to are all you can do. When she said it at first—you never can tell—I said, 'that's what Mama says.' But of course what she meant was, you daren't ever reveal anything."

"Southern."

"Southern. You should have heard her when after her breakdown they said she ought to confide in her doctors. 'A Southern woman has her pride. It behooves the soul, perhaps, to confess her transgressions to the Almighty—but to betray her own confidence to a strangeuh? Nevuh!' "

"That's rather wonderful, really, in its proud way," Astarte said, as she pulled over to the right and stopped directly in front of the unprepossessing gate of Westwood Cemetery.

"Norma Jean thought that was very peculiar, and troubling. 'Whereas you have to confide in the doctor to get anywhere,' she insisted, while we kept staring in the counter mirror at the woman in the white dress, black hat, white gloves, and spectator pumps eating the pink-and-white ice cream. And then she said, 'In that we both have mothers who are crazy, we have to learn certain things—upwardly important ones mothers are supposed to teach their daughters other ways.' I was exactly nine years old."

"Whereas she was what—twenty-three, twenty-four?"

"Imagine. Sitting there at the counter at Schwab's, she then started talking about the New York theater and Gray's Drugstore, Times Square—she hadn't yet been to New York."

"Whereas you had."

"Yes, to visit Thalia and see her in summer stock, as Peter Pan. But Norma Jean knew all about Gray's, where the theater extras went and you got cheap tickets to the shows in the basement. She had researched it all for her part in the picture. Miss Caswell, Claudia, she said, was really cleverer than Eve Harrington, and Norma Jean—Marilyn then—had walked up that staircase at Margo Channing's and right into a two-shot as if she belonged, and the dialogue had been no problem, either, even if half the men in Hollywood—and Bette too, until she went to the premiere at the Roxy and very quickly outright changed her mind—thought she didn't know what she was saying when she spoke the words."

"Whereas she did."

"Better than anybody before or since. Do you know what she said then? 'There aren't but two ways to play the game out here, Wyoming, and most girls play it stuck-up, whereas stuck-up is the very worst way to play it. You really shouldn't say "worst" whereas "worse" is correct for only two ways, but in that stuck-up is so stupid it *is* the worst, absolutely.' "

As she sat quietly in the garden of the Westwood mausoleum, in front of the plaque reading MARILYN MONROE: 1926–1962, she remembered all the notes she'd taken in Psychology and Religion at UCLA.

Pride is entirely narcissistic and therefore in its euphoria the fountainhead of all the other deadly sins. The various outcomes of the narcissistic agon determine the courses of the events of the other six, which are based on the ego's stimulation by the object in one of six ways.

Sensationally. The ego, astonishing itself, says, "I must have that or I'll kill myself." Equals covetousness.

Structurally. The ego, having acquired whatever it has, says, "I must examine every luxurious inch of what I already possess." Equals lust.

Conceptually. The ego vents its growing rage over the temporal incompleteness of its forensic investigations, seeking to carve out an everlasting concept. Its failure bespeaks its dissatisfaction. Unwilling to admit it is the investigation—its own activity—which is tragically faulty, it imputes further fault to its object. Equals anger.

Symbolically. Equals envy.

Mnemonically. Equals gluttony.

Inversely. Despair equals sloth.

Then she remembered going to the vault in Clayton some years after Cordelia's suicide and taking out her diary, in which were repeated all her sayings and doings, as first overheard in Silver Lake, such as, "Mama always said only good girls keep diaries, bad girls don't have the time. Well, lost girls keep them too—and leave pages behind on the path through the swamp, or at the boat landing, hoping someone will discover them, and follow on."

Remembering when, sometime back in the forties, Jack was named Peoples Department Store's Most Beautiful Child, and his picture put in the window. Cordelia, when asked how it had come about, said, "On account of the war—there were shortages."

Then telling Norma Jean all about Diana's peacocks. When she found out about them, she wrote to Miss Flannery O'Connor on the subject, and finally went over to Milledgeville (which Cordelia was always spooked by, because it was the site of the insane asylum). She got two birds from the Colonel, but their screaming drove poor Cordelia madder— and she would sit by the hour looking at herself as a madwoman in the *verre églomisé* French mirror.

And about the letter her cousin Gabriel sent her in 1957, in which he said there were two kinds of people trying to influence the young, those who read Tolstoy and those who read Dostoyevsky, and the thing to know about the Tolstoy crowd was they were all hiding something. True, the Dostoyevsky crowd tended to be more dimwitted, but the Tolstoy crowd were worse: they were lying. Take that opening sentence in *Anna Karenina*. There are no happy families, so the way in which they are happy is the same way as the nonway: they are lying.

About playing the movie game with Jack back in Clayton, doing the scene from *Out of the Past*.

"That's not the way to win."

"Is there a way to win?"

"There's a way to lose more slowly."

"Show me."

And then,

"I hate him—I wish he was dead."

"Give him some time."

She walked along Wilshire to Santa Monica, then along Santa Monica to La Brea, then up La Brea to Melrose, then along Melrose to Fairfax, then up Fairfax to Hollywood Boulevard. (In the window of one of the terrible little souvenir shops wormed into the space once occupied by a quality emporium to which important stars had given their custom, she saw a placard of a type become familiar: "There are four animals necessary in a smart woman's life. The sable on her back, the Jaguar in her garage, the tiger in her bed, and the dumb sonofabitch that pays for it all.") Then past the Roosevelt Hotel, where, in the Blossom Room, the first Oscars had been presented over half a century before, to the Chinese Theater.

She stopped to look at her footprints in the cement (at the lower left of a rhomboid cluster the other corners of which were impressed with those of Shirley Temple, Bette Davis, and Donald Duck), put there in the Grauman days, in 1969, the year of *We Are Born, We Live, We Die*. Then, walking along, she looked up at a billboard for Rock Formation's "Womanly Girl." There she was, at some fantastic size.

> *Give me one hundred stacks of*
> *One hun-dred one-hun-dred-dollar bills!*
> *She's not a casual girl,*
> *Not a frivolous girl—*
> *She's a complicated, sentimental,*
> *Independent, stylish*
> *Womanly girl . . .*
> *Womanly girl.*

She was standing at number 6774, just east of Highland Avenue, looking down at Marilyn Monroe's star, when Jameson O'Maurigan drove up in the Stingray.

"I stopped off at Johnny Rockets, Tacodobe, and House of Pancakes. Nobody at either place has seen you since before the nominations. They're getting worried."

"Oh? I worry myself. Do you think this town has a good story for itself anymore?"

"Get in, and I'll tell you what the story's all about."

They drove south on Cahuenga to Sunset, passing the

international newsstand. She remembered suddenly the embarrassment of the national tabloids—her first appearance in them since the troubled seventies. NOT EVEN NOMINATED! the screaming headlines had accused. Looking back, she admitted she almost had to hand it to them. They'd chosen four frame enlargements from *Avenged*, each of them a perfect emblem of vanity, narcissism, vainglory, and contempt, as the face of the feature's cruel heroine accused the Academy of Motion Picture Arts and Sciences of mortal lowlife treachery in the calculated oversight that had become the talk of the industry.

At Sunset and Western, she broke the silence. "I know what the story's all about—it's about driving. Driving—searching for that off-ramp to happiness. The way I used to dream it, I'd start out on the big H and sail out into the night sky, swooping like a condor over the blanket of twinkling lights, under the canopy of stars like the roof of Paradise, which I pretended belonged to me, and interrupted by brother Jack on Pegasus from the gas-station sign, who'd take me back riding pillion behind him from Silver Lake to Clayton. And when I heard Jo Stafford sing 'Arms you have taken possession of,' I thought, No man is ever going to rip the arms off me! Because I'd heard them say that very afternoon, 'If you love a thing, let it go; if it doesn't come back . . . hunt it down and kill it.' And I knew they were serious, laughing. The first thing I remember saying to my husband as a grown man was, 'Your method of approach is soothing to a woman's dignity.' He didn't laugh. He hardly ever did in the beginning."

"No, neither did his brother—as a grown man."

"Poor lonely Peg Entwhistle. Poor Butterfly. You know, I can make him laugh like a loon these days. There's vanity for instance.

"Drive up to the observatory, will you? A zigzag ramble should end on a zag."

. . .

They stood in silence on a parapet of the Griffith Park Observatory, until finally Jameson O'Maurigan said, "Know what I miss most about you from the earlier pages of your life? The way you used to sit still and smoke and worry creation along. Always put me in mind of the Cahuenga—those still, deliberate smokers."

"I started out in the early fifties trying to devise ways to get Erskine Johnson and Coy Watson to pilot that convertible and camera of theirs into our driveway at Wayfaring on Waverly. What would I say to them, they'd ask me—to the viewing audience of that ugly little medium emanating from New York—once I'd snared them? 'Welcome to California,' I answered. 'Like in *War of the Worlds*.' I knew by then that L.A. is to New York a backyard where kids' shows are put on, just as New York is to Los Angeles a back lot."

"Then television came to Los Angeles."

"Yes, to televise the mud slides. I was marooned up at Ralph Von Gelsen's, and we sat there looking out the window down at Nichols Canyon. There were all these coffins floating down the avenue like Sunday-morning traffic on the way to the Hollywood Bowl—as if all on their way to a reunion at the Roosevelt Hotel. Television didn't exactly think that up, but it was the only medium to make it work—spontaneously, as it were. I suppose it will be the same for the earthquake, unless . . . well, unless not."

"Word on the street is the earthquake's been called off."

"Looking down from here, as evening comes, I'll try hard to believe you."

As soon as the winning woman had crossed the finish line in the Olympic stadium, Kaye Wayfaring first looked directly into the mirror—wondering again about *verre églomisé,* about the duchesse de Praslin, about the Lady of Shalott, about her mother, Cordelia, and about the conflict between running the race and stopping to pick up the golden apples—and then looked out the window to see the second story of the house next door had been completely torn away. She picked up the telephone and dialed Laguna Beach.

"It's over—she's won it, whoever she is. The sun is climbing to the yardarm, and the house next door is now half torn down. I'll be there soon."

"Good. Can't say can't wait—been waiting."

On the San Diego Freeway to Laguna, there was next to no traffic. Behind her, Union Station, the pueblo, the view toward Bunker Hill . . . Raymond Chandler, *The High Window.*

No, not the high window; the stage door.

Talk about a woman's marathon . . . and why not?

All because of a house they built back when, on Wayfaring at Waverly, in Silver Lake.

What's important after all? The off-ramp to happiness. To hang on to the house. Wayfaring at Waverly in Silver Lake. The house will stand; the house stays put—and we'll expand the garden beyond the pool. We owe life that, don't we? I'd say we do.

Los Angeles lay gleaming in the bright air.

In Tir na nOg

OF THE TWO PUBLICATIONS, it was the second the twins finally opted for—*The La Brea Story*, a picture book on "the Death Trap of the Ages," the Pleistocene asphalt pools ("commonly and incorrectly called tar pits") just off Wilshire Boulevard, in Los Angeles. They had put aside the first, a pop-up-icon assemblage of immortal motion-picture moments—from *King Kong, Gone With the Wind, The Seven Year Itch,* and *Casablanca*—having delighted in its two New York scenes. (They had themselves in real life stood with their mother, Kaye Wayfaring, atop the Empire State Building and astride a grating's corner as the subway rumbled temblor-like beneath them.) Moreover, they knew that Marilyn Monroe had been their mother's dear friend, but had died "decades ago, when your father was your age"; and after a time they had asked to be read to on the theme of the days before anyone was alive, by their grandmother, Mawrdew Czgowchwz.

"The *tar* pits—the *tar* pits!" they commenced in unison. "The *ass*-fault pits! The *ass*-fault pits!" they continued in descant, gyrating, correcting each other, rescinding and affirming the smoke-screen words "tar pits" and "asphalt."

"Jack Benny called them the tar pits," Mawrdew Czgowchwz remarked.

"Who was Jack Benny, Grandmother—*your* old friend?"

"Well, yes, he was. He used to let me on his radio show. He'd play his violin and I'd sing something funny."

"Like what?"

"Sing Eartha, Grandmother. You were *supposed* to sing Eartha in See-addle, but there isn't any money."

"Not 'Eartha,' dear ones—Erda," Mawrdew Czgowchwz replied. "Erda is a German lady—a goddess—who comes up out of the earth and sings."

"Does she come out of the tar pits, Grandmother? The *ass*-fault pits, does she? Does she?"

"Well, now, there's an interesting idea. Now they've canceled the Seattle *Ring*, perhaps Los Angeles would do one here in the tar pits."

"If she comes from the earth, Grandmother, what does she *want*? What does the goddess *want*? Where is she going?"

"She doesn't seem to want anything but to talk. You see, she knows everything, poor creature."

"She knows *everything*, Grandmother?"

"Well, yes, at first—but it's a long show, and she forgets. She takes a great nap for herself while everyone else is singing, and when she wakes up she's changed her mind. 'Dazed am I since I woke,' she says. 'The world seems wild and strange to me.'"

"*Is* the world wild and strange, Grandmother? *Is* it? *Is* it?"

"Betimes."

"It's *not*—it's *not*!"

"It's not, is it? Why'd you ask, then, if it's not?"

"It's not bedtimes!"

"Oh! No, no—only for Erda. It's always bedtime for Erda. She's taken everything she's got into the bed with her, you see, and if she were ever to get up again, she'd lose it. You've got to lose a little contentment—give a little away—to live, is the moral of the story—her story."

"Grandmother, when may we go and interrupt mother and Uncle Dee?"

"Any minute now. Come look a little longer at these prehistoric things—wild horses, for example."

"*Swan Song?*"

"*Swan Song.*"

"Sounds ridiculous," the scenarist declared.

"It is," the actress admitted.

" 'That's all, folks!' You did say French."

"They've all got French names. They flew over on Air France. They're staying at the Chateau Marmont. And the play she's rocking Paris in—besides *Phèdre*: she's also this seismic Phèdre; clearly the one French play they're told one's heard of—is called *Le Chant du cygne*."

"What's the package—yourself and a French ventriloquist?"

"Turning . . . *turning!*"

Jameson O'Maurigan, who had walked to the edge of the terrace to look at the sun starting to set over the Pacific, turned back to rejoin Kaye Wayfaring, his partner in the Yeatsian board game Great Wheel, who, having thrown the dice and landed on Phase Sixteen, turned a card and read it.

Phase Sixteen has a dream thrust upon it and finds within itself an aimless excitement. If it use its intellect to disengage the aimless child, it finds the soul's most radiant expression and surrounds itself with some fairyland, some mythology of wisdom. If it subordinate the intellect to the Body of Fate, all the cruelty and narrowness of that intellect are displayed in the service of preposterous purpose after purpose until there is

nothing left but the fixed idea and some hysterical hatred.
Examples: William Blake, Rabelais, Paracelsus, some beautiful
women.

"I've turned back, so tell me the rest."

"Why *am* I telling you all this?"

"Because it's preposterous. Because you mustn't do it. So where are you now?"

"Sixteen. What have you done to these dice? No, I won't do it, even if the pitch *was* high concept, and delivered at Hors Gabarit in Laguna Niguel. As I advised the spokesman, 'Jean-Loup, you could outline the plot of this opus in squid ink in the white space on your plate, between the steamed cactus, the blue polenta chevrons, and the scorched riz-de-veau?' And you yourself do not, then, envision a future screen-classic pop-up book of *Swan Song*?"

"I don't envision the *picture* itself, *Phèdre* boom-bah notwithstanding, so I do not. Some *beau mec* flamboyantly and literally stampeded to death by all the wild horses on the Camargue while you yourself, stampeded—only figuratively, of course—by *tout Paris*, hold forth onstage at the Babylone in *Le Chant du Cygne*, the show that must go on. The prospect of any of it is unnerving, entirely; to be summarily struck from the mind."

"Consider it struck, forthwith. Meanwhile, a propos stampedes, you might wish to take cover—here come your fans: but two in number, yet scarcely less ardent than tout Paris."

"They are my imps, my lucky dice. I deny them naught. On the contrary, I shall put them in pictures—they *ought* to be in pictures; it's high time."

"In the new extravaganza?"

"Absolutely—with your permission. It's actually in the story of Granuaile. There's only the one, a boy, but we can easily improve on that. She captures both from the earl of

Howth and prizes them more than all her fabulous horde. With the parents' permission, of course."

"If they're captured, they're captured—no part of the parents' permission."

The twins had come less than halfway across the terrace and, stopping there, had set about rehearsing (Kaye thought, remembering her own childhood maneuvers) some cunning yet mannerly approach. It was Jameson's habit, having schooled them thoroughly in the four questions "Who am I?," "Where do I come from?," "What do I want?," and "Where am I going?," to demand of them at each approach "Where to?" When he called, they were that ready.

"The *tar* pits—the *ass*-fault pits!"

"Jack Benny always called them the tar pits," Kaye Wayfaring recalled.

"Commonly and incorrectly," Jameson countered. "The Death Trap of the Ages."

"Los Angeles?" Kaye Wayfaring challenged, while the children, forgetting their anthem, looked back and forth between their mother and the comical visitor.

"Los Angeles. La Brea. The tar—rather asphalt—pits of La Brea, in the Wilshire district of the City of Angels. Where we are not now—being as we speak, in the best place, some say, in the state of California, if not on earth: Laguna Beach."

"I'll bet you anything you like," Kaye Wayfaring advised the poet, as the children came closer, "she's been sitting over there talking to them about Erda—how she used to go on Jack Benny's show and be Erda, down in the vaults where he kept his money, always trying to tempt him to a game of blackjack with a bit of the Rhinegold she'd scavenged. He'd play the violin and she'd sing 'My Heart at Thy Sweet Voice.' Somebody would always then butt in with 'Wrong opera! Wrong opera!' Your grandmother," Kaye advised her children, "can be a very funny lady."

45

"Is Eartha in the tar pits, Uncle Dee? Is King Kong? Is Frankenstein?"

"Not 'Eartha,' darlings—Erda. You must ask your grandmother. Your grandmother knows all about it."

"She says ask you can we go see."

"To the pits—the *ass*-fault pits! Can we go, Mother?"

"Yes, yes. Go ask your grandmother when, OK?"

As they marched back across the terrace, their shadows lengthening in the sunset, she thought, Stop again, stand, stay, thou art fair. (When they'd opened the pop-up book to *Casablanca* and a microchip mechanism had begun playing the first few bars of "As Time Goes By," she'd flipped the pages back to *King Kong*, thinking, This is no time for "As Time Goes By.")

"Grandmother can go anytime," said O'Maurigan. "She's out of work."

"Aren't we all," Kaye Wayfaring answered. "Well, not you—there's always work for you, isn't there?"

"Isn't there—for me and my sort. Where there's life—"

"I wish you did horoscopes," the actress declared in earnest, picking up the magazine she'd started grazing at breakfast and had kept in reserve all day. "I'd so much rather read you on life's free-loop spaces than—well, you know I met Astarte all those years ago through Norma Jean, when she was still operating out of that little shack on Kilkea, and took to her. And she does often come up with the stuff, but sometimes when I read her in the trades—I mean, how can this message be for every Gemini in the industry?"

O'Maurigan reached for *Company Town* and read the column "Ask Astarte."

When the war was over, you blasted off like a rocket headed for a different planet. You moved from the old home town to a mecca of madness. Come spring, a weird series of coincidences will push you into the same situation again, but this time you're likely to head for a foreign country with dreams of becoming an international operator. Before the excitement begins, fast from fantasy for three months. Face the reality you're ready to leave behind.

"Should I call her—Astarte—for the full line?"

"Aren't you overlooking someone rather more cunning even than your Astarte—and rather closer to home?"

"Here they come back. What did she say?"

"Grandmother says tomorrow, so—"

"She said see if that's OK."

"It's OK. Are you inviting your father, and your uncle Jacob as well?"

"Yes."

"Yes."

"Good. OK. Go tell Grandmother it's a deal."

(Moreover, she thought, he's right. She knows as much as Erda—and walks the earth besides.)

As the sun set, and Mawrdew Czgowchwz ushered her grandchildren in to supper, Kaye Wayfaring watched Jameson O'Maurigan looking at the Pacific.

What does he want? He wants me to play the White Sea Horse, his Irish pirate queen. He wants the older woman, herself indoors, to play Elizabeth, the English queen. What do I want? Where am I going? I want the answers to a few simple questions—a preposterous demand. So I'm going along to the La Brea Tar Pits. Tomorrow. Isn't information gathering a function of covetousness? Yes, tomorrow.

Kaye Wayfaring sat alone in the atrium garden of the Page Museum of La Brea Discoveries, under a lush canopy of white-belled Sierra laurel "of neat and sturdy habit." "Herself indoors," she muttered, thinking again, with feelings of inadequacy, of her mother-in-law, the diva Mawrdew Czgowchwz.

Herself indoors. Outdoors, in late February, Los Angeles itself, the entity, at its yearly greenest, cleansed by strong Santa Ana winds (unusually free, because of the welcome early rains, of the freight of desert pollen), rose effulgent from the new eighties metropolis, tier upon tier, open-fanned, from Silver Lake, across Bunker Hill, up the Wilshire Corridor, past the Beverly Center to Century City, across San Vicente and out to the Pacific Palisades.

All afternoon, in the beyond, out at the beach, from Malibu down to Redondo, from Marina del Rey to Bolsa Chica, the Pacific, energetic-to-squally, a kabala-gemstone azurite, had sped hundreds of sailboats northwest-southeast along the coast and southwest to Catalina and San Gabriel. Then, suddenly, on Santa Monica Beach, and simultaneously at several spots in the San Fernando Valley, a snowfall.

"Snow at the beach! Snow in the Valley!" the twins had cried out, their attention decisively diverted from the La Brea discoveries.

"It's on the *television*! Snow at the beach—snow in the Valley! Snowmen—there'll be *snowmen*!"

"Neither of them, you realize, has ever seen a snowman," the twins' father, Tristan Beltane, had advised his twin brother, Jacob, and their mother, Mawrdew Czgowchwz, over the commotion.

"Now, where do you suppose I'd have been," Mawrdew Czgowchwz had replied, "that I wouldn't know that kind of thing about them? I've only been in New York all these years, I haven't been in Tir na nOg."

"Where's that?" the twins had cried out simultaneously, in

case something beyond the San Fernando Valley and beyond snowmen had been revealed.

"Tir na nOg? Oh, Tir na nOg's the Land of Nod. Well, not exactly. It's the Country of the Young. It's Irish."

"*We're* young!"

"We're *Irish* too—three-*quarters*!"

"You're young—but you're not going to stay that way forever, are you?"

"No!"

"No!"

"Not on a dare. Well, you see, in Tir na nOg, that's the way. The indigenes stay young forever. Impossible place altogether."

"What kind of indijuns, Grandmother? Apaches? Comanches? The Sioux? The Cahuenga?"

"Don't tease your old grandmother, now: you know what indigenes are—we looked them up yesterday."

"Can we go—"

"—to see the snow?"

"Can we go? Now, that I don't know. You must take that up with the authorities."

Tristan Beltane had turned to his brother. "Hah!"

"The authorities," Mawrdew Czgowchwz remarked, "one of them anyway, says 'Hah!' "

"Mother!"

"Mother!"

What a setup. What was I supposed to say then—no? No, under no circumstances, young lady, young man. Impossible, young ones.

They've gone. They've gone. To Tir na nOg.

All our parodies of Chekhov exercises started like that.

Somebody in the wings calling out "Goodbye! Goodbye!" and then coming onstage, bewildered always, saying, "They've gone! They've gone!"

I let them go without me. I was suddenly captivated by the glass-box image of the La Brea Girl: she keeps turning into her own skeleton—the facsimile of the one diggers found here in the pits—and then back into herself in the flesh again, looking like a Gauguin girl in Tahiti, in Tir na nOg. (Here is no Tahiti; here is no Tir na nOg. Here is the Death Trap of the Ages. And here am I.)

What am I doing—that interview I wouldn't do last weekend? Informed the caller I only ever do them on the job.

That is obviously just what I'm doing. Listen, I don't do anything over the phone but order refreshments in, and neither do you want to come all the way down to Laguna, or even over to Silver Lake. Nor am I free to meet you at the Polo Lounge, or by the Hockney pool in the new Roosevelt, or at any restaurant on La Cienega, so meet me at the old reliable La Brea Tar Pits. We'll walk around. Meet me in the atrium garden of the new museum. There are no unnerving attractions in the garden. I'll arrange for my mother-in-law to remove my husband and children—she'll spirit them away to chase rainbows and build snowmen in the Valley.

How would he start? Let's play solitaire interview pinochle on a snowy afternoon.

Miss Wayfaring, why have you declined to be interviewed or photographed by *Life* and the rest to celebrate Hollywood's hundredth birthday?

Declined? I haven't. It's manners to wait till you're asked. I've not been.

Why—or why not?

You'd better ask Hollywood.

You haven't made a picture since *Avenged*. Do you think maybe the town's forgotten you?

Well, they sent you—or did they? Look, I live here—part of the time permanently. In Silver Lake, at the other end of Sunset Boulevard. Also in Laguna Beach. Happily.

Methinks he thinks this lady doth . . . She doth; she always did. "The untold want, by life and land ne'er granted, / Now, Voyager, sail thou forth, to seek and find." The untold want wasn't hers. She told hers—she told them all. Next question.

On safe ground, how did you begin your day in Silver Lake—or was it Laguna?

Laguna—or, as the children call it, Labeena Gooch. With the *I Ching*—I threw my age. I threw "Gathering Together," hexagram forty-six, the fourth line changing, yielding "Holding Together"—do you love it?

When? Oh, I took up the *I Ching* years ago, years ago. As a matter of fact, talking consequences, as the upshot of an invitation to impress my shoe prints in cement over in Sid Grauman's sidewalk on the occasion of the premiere of *We Are Born, We Live, We Die.* You know what lines went right next to the footprints? They were my first throw. You can still go and look at them—"Fellowship with Men." Whoever said publicity is meant to deceive the populace? I was sincere.

Time out of mind it was—*fado, fado,* the Irish say—that night in Tir na nOg. Yes, *We Are Born, We Live, We Die* was the second nomination. I don't like to talk about the Oscars. Consequence perhaps of my brother's gift to me of a Nehi cola bottle spray-painted gold, which I, in a rage, all too soon after broke into bits against the rocks on Warwoman Dell. Interpretation is no solace, however, and as a result I came to turn against it. I never try to interpret anything, least of all a part in a play or picture.

My brother and I used to play La Brea Tar Pits at the end of the stagnant mud pond in Warwoman Dell. Warwoman Dell was a wild place, situated in Clayton, Georgia—still is;

you could look it up. I tell myself I'm never going back, not even with the children. I tell myself wild horses—

" 'We wait for a small herd of horses to pass by as they slowly graze at the foot of a hill.' "

From across the garden, a docent voice, reading from the same book Mawrdew Czgowchwz had been reading from to her grandchildren the day before, addressed its young audience, any and all passersby, Kaye Wayfaring and her imaginary collocutor.

" 'Suddenly, nervous and alert, they move away and break into a run. From nearby bushes a tawny lioness streaks towards a young horse, lunges at its head, and knocks it to the ground. A short, wild struggle ensues in a cloud of dust—' "

"And a hearty 'Hiyo, Silver!' "

"Excuse me, Desirée, but I am your moderator, reading at the moment out loud, for your entertainment and, hopefully, edification from this book, *The La Brea Story*, published by the Division of Education in cooperation with the Earth Sciences Division, Los Angeles County Museum of Natural History. May I continue?"

"Everyone knows there are no lions left anymore anywhere near Los Angeles. Only coyotes. For lions, you go to San Diego."

"This book—in fact, this place—isn't about now. It's about the past, the remote past."

"Well, it's stupid—violent."

" 'A short wild struggle ensues in a cloud of dust and all is quiet. A larger male lion proudly joins her, and she moves back as he satisfies his hunger on the warm body.' "

"This is making me sick. I'm going to be sick—in the tar pits."

"You stay away from those tar pits! They dug a dead woman out of one of them."

(Goodness, that child is Ralph Von Gelsen's precocious daughter, Desirée. My interlocutor is invisible. Am I invisible?)

" 'Shaken and shocked at the quick and violent action, we cover the short distance to the stream. Resting in the shade of a tree, we watch the activity—' *Desirée!*"

"I'll be right back. I have to say hello to somebody I know."

(I am not invisible. It's just as well. I was getting tired talking to this nobody.)

"Hello, Miss Wayfaring. Long time no see. I notice you too are resting in the shade of a tree, watching the activity."

"Hello, Desirée. How's everything? How's your father?"

"Not so bad, Miss Wayfaring—not so bad as it was. Only my father isn't everything—my father only *thinks* he's everything."

"Hmm—you look well, I must say. You're growing like—"

"Well, I've got a chance at last. I finally convinced him to stop sending me to all those dubious intergalactic schools—that it was either Hollywood High or the Rubber Room at Camarillo. Of course, being an adolescent, I am terrified of the earthquake, but unlike most of the clientele at that last luxury lockdown I skipped through, I'm not a multiple, and as I'm learning fast how to push all the energies into the third eye, if I do go under, at least I won't have to spend eternity haunting the astral. How are *you*? I *loved* 'Womanly Girl.' It put me in such a renovated *up* head. It was my favorite video for a *year*, even after Desperate World came out with 'Why Can't I Make You Love Me?' Radical work!"

"Thank you. Well, as you may know, I've got twins—I had them not long after we last met. They were just here, but they've gone off with their father, their uncle, and their grandmother looking for a snowman in the Valley."

"I was wondering what brought you here alone. Of course, you're *never* alone, are you, truly."

"What do you mean?"

"*Desirée!* We're leaving now!"

"Oh, nothing bad—nothing about multiples or so many people loitering about, or anything at all like that. I just mean that, well, needless to say . . . oh, never mind. I've got to go. Take care of yourself, and of the twins. Don't fall into the pits—promise!"

Heard that for years about everything. Skirt the edge; don't get too close, you'll fall in.

As you're back—and I do apologize, you're clearly not nobody—shall we continue? Last night my mother-in-law was reading to the children, as I've told you, from that book we just heard from. It's a grim thing. There's a passage in it about vultures—how they'd swoop down on the quadrupeds. The children love to regress and imitate the quadrupeds, while their various male relations and honorary relations play predators—prehistoric predators. How the vultures, the *Teratornis* vultures, would get the tips of their wings caught in the bubbling asphalt and, weighted down, would suffer the same fate as those they preyed on. And on and on as she read it . . . "There are no more territory vultures in Los Angeles, are there, Uncle Dee?" the boy asked O'Maurigan with great confidence. "Oh, but there are, there are indeed," the clown insisted. "Only not in Silver Lake. We've spotted them on the other side of the river, but if they try to fly across, the Lorelei of the Los Angeles River wails like a civil defense siren, and we bag the monstrous things. We've also got patrols. We've got the Silver Lake–Los Feliz Territory Vulture Vigilante—"

"Would you *stop*, you!" I finally spoke up. I'm the one they come to, of course, for night prayers and talismans against territory vultures in their sleep. Not to mention questions about the Lorelei, who has been definitively identified by certain

Silver Lake crazies they overhear on their tricycle rides in the neighborhood as who else but Norma Jean's ghost. Would it do any good to tell them that for years, before Norma Jean ever became Marilyn, my "they" told me that when poor Peg Entwhistle jumped off the big HOLLYWOODLAND H what she did was take a long swan dive into the La Brea Tar Pits? And that if they were alive today to tell the children the-truth-the-whole-truth-and-nothing-but-the-truth about Hollywood, that they'd without question peg as Peg the girl whose bones the searchers have dredged up and assembled over there? No good in the world.

Anyway, he kept on at them like that, at the openmouthed pair of them. "And beyond Los Feliz, above Whitley Heights in old Hollywood, just beyond the lush recesses of Hyperion Canyon itself—perched in fact on the H, the L's, the Y, and the W of the renovated HOLLYWOOD sign—there may be seen for your amazement and instruction in the ways of the increasingly complex and worrying world in which you live, on any given occasion, never fewer than *eight* Hollywood territory vultures, the very latest evolutionary specimens, hatched full-size. They come that way now as a result of radiation fallout from the Utah, New Mexico, Arizona, and Nevada deserts, where secret testing of weapons of untold destructive capacity goes on unabated in terrifying tunnels the like of which did never lead to Oz, under the flag of the United States of America, in defense of the Republic for which it stands."

By which time the twins were in fits and starts both, deciding from then on to be themselves the vultures pursuing their elders, camel, wolf, sabertooth, and ground sloth, trapped in the tar pits. And I, to join the game, would have been called upon to impersonate the Lorelei—Marilyn's ghost—*and* subsequently the ghost of poor Peg Entwhistle. But I refrained. I came to the edge, but I did not fall in.

Who was she anyway, the woman, the girl—the womanly

girl—whose bones they found there? The Chosen Maiden? Hollywood Hopeful? Fashion Victim?

I've been taking pictures of them lately. They got wind of the Indian superstition about the camera capturing their souls—for *ransom*, they decided—and turning them into inhabitants of *Night of the Living Dead*. "Weren't you in that picture, Mom—the first one, in black and white?"

"No, I was *not*! Who told you that?"

"Never mind!"

Chilling things they come up with. Ransom. Likely they're thinking of what they've heard of the pirate picture they're to be in.

"You could put our pictures on the backs of milk cartons—'souls extra!' "

"They'd be worth their weight in uranium."

"Neptunium!"

"Plutonium!"

"And who told you what was the weight of your souls?"

Suddenly I heard my mother's voice in my own. My mother kept the rooms of the house in Clayton dark and cool, and especially the kitchen in the morning—into which no light from unshaded windows was admitted. She had been to Atlanta to hear *Madame Butterfly* and came back with a translation of some lines from the last act that suited her prevailing mood: "Too much light and too much springtime, spilling in from outdoors." And of course she would never allow bottles or cartons on the kitchen table, only ceramic pitchers; and no cereal boxes, newspapers, magazines, or radios. "No information is necessary at breakfast," she informed the household—as Cookie, the housekeeper, rolled her eyes to heaven—"to avid connoisseurs of morning except the news that you are alive and kickin' and rightly covetous of the day that has dawned. Sittin' up, takin' nourishment. Sufficiency is the Lord's name; the name of the beast is What Else?" My brother and I would routinely sass back, "Don't touch that dial!" and she'd rejoin, "Oh, *really*, Miss Defiant? Oh, *really*, Mister Brass? Well, I declare right in front of Cookie here that I've a strong mind to trade you both *back* to the Cherokee Indians and repossess my cat's-eye brooch, my Russian sables, *and* my peace of mind—*no change!*" I feel that defectively springlocked apparatus in my own voice, ready anytime to—Cherokee? Cahuenga.

Of course they've both decided—on their own, they've let people know, presenting a united front—to go into the business. I was sitting reading Bruno Bettelheim's latest on child's play, and fretting over the question of guns, which has not yet come up, and the two of them *tangoed* right past me, *chanting*, in thick accents, "Vot did you do before?" "Before vot?" "Before ze jools?" "I *vahnted* them!" Just like that. I said to myself, Such behavior clearly does not erupt unbidden.

"You ran away, didn't you, Mom, in *Way Station*? But you came back."

"What is all this about pictures on milk containers and *Way Station* and the jewels and *Night of the Living Dead*? I can't keep track of you—together or separately."

"Nothing, Mom, only frolicking."

"Did their father and their uncle talk like that?" I asked their grandmother.

"Well, yes, I'm afraid they did—took it from their father. I supposed then it was a kind of Brit-elfish. Then by the time they were these children's age, he was dead. They employed it less frequently thereafter, but they've never quite given it up, as you well know. Apples don't fall far, do they?"

Two of the things she said terrified me. The fact of her husband's early death terrified me, although I'd known about it since the very summer it happened, the next summer after Norma Jean's death. And the utterly irrational threat that my children might turn into British elves—in which case they would no longer belong to me. They'd be as if traded back to the Cahuenga, something more or less Tir na nOgish.

I find I go in for these fears. They erupt from day to day as the children outgrow early childhood—a kind of idle luxury that prevents my calculating something far worse. It's so much easier to admit to being possessive—to admit to covetousness. It's a sanctioned obsession, after all. Suppose I didn't (or suppose I was forced to blaspheme, to say I didn't) care. Nobody would believe me? I wouldn't believe myself? See, if you let the reins slip—

"You ran away in *Way Station*. But you came back." The next thing you know, the informers will be treating them both to their mother's total disintegration in *Avenged*. Stay, infants! Stay, thou art fair! No, it's no use. There's no such place as Tir na nOg. There's California, where they'll grow up. California: fair enough.

Actually, I think we have sufficiently absorbed both the atmosphere and the deep significance of the tar—or asphalt—pits. I've got a little browsing to do, and then it's home to Silver Lake. Let's continue this on a nice long walk down the Miracle Mile, up Fairfax, past the Farmer's Market, and then along Melrose.

As Kaye Wayfaring walked out of the atrium garden, toward the museum exit, she passed by the student group from Hollywood High at the end of their field trip. Their proctor was summing up *The La Brea Story*.

"We have completed our journey back forty thousand years. Today the skeletons have been returned to Hancock Park and stand to greet the awe and wonder of millions of visitors. La Brea pits are surrounded by a lovely park in which replicas of the ancient animals gather near the pits, depicting the scenes of their life."

Indeed. Ciro's. Mocambo. The Trocadero. The Cocoanut Grove. The Brown Derby.

Forty thousand years ago. We've enough to do going back forty. "Old, unhappy, far-off things and battles long ago," quoth O'Maurigan. *There's* covetousness. We covet childhood memories, even the terrible ones, and we rehearse and re-rehearse the old stories as if they were our best expensive clothes—the things they promised down at Peoples Department Store wouldn't ever wear out. Of course they will, of course they do, and of course they have. We patch them and restitch them, and finally we send them back to Wardrobe overnight, and Warbrobe sends us replicas one uneventful morning—copies, rethought, recast, and reinforced. *Those* are the ones we won't wear out. Those are the ones they'll bury us in: not the first ones, not the true ones, but the replicas. Replicas of the ancient animals all decked out in facsimile drag gather on sound stages, in replicated interiors depicting the scenes of their life. Admission free.

In a way it's surprising that when they redid the HOLLY-WOODLAND sign, for instance, reducing it to HOLLYWOOD, they didn't bother to create a mechanical Peg Entwhistle replica that would jump off the H once a day, at noon, accompanied by a civil defense siren. Whereas, for instance, I thought for a long, long time that I would never stop feeling the stab of pain, or be able to look away before it registered, at the sight—everywhere-but-everywhere—of Norma Jean's astounding smile, the one that says "I got it—they *gave* it to me!" It's always surprised me they haven't yet matched the image with a voice-over of something she actually said. That's exploitation of a kind she'd have understood perfectly—definitely endorsed. "Sure, go ahead."

We had a lecture at Yale—by then she'd been dead how-ever long—comparing her to the *Mona Lisa*. Comparing their smiles. I remember somebody read a poem. I don't remember who—O'Maurigan would; he was there; he'd come up to New Haven to catch me in *Twelfth Night*, the last show of the season. "However long?" What do I mean by "however long"? She had been dead nine months, exactly. The poem went with the *Mona Lisa*. With the photograph of Norma Jean—that one—went something she'd written, something O'Maurigan said scanned. (I remember resenting that.) It was a wonderful statement about waiting and wanting.

> *It's night outside.*
> *Automobiles*
> *roll down Sunset Boulevard*
> *like an endless string of beetles.*
> *Their rubber tires make a purring high-class noise . . .*
> *There must be thousands of girls sitting alone*
> *like me dreaming of becoming a movie star.*
> *But I'm not going to worry about them.*

I kept my lips zippered after the lecture, but later I told O'Maurigan—I had to. She had said those very words to me one afternoon at the La Brea Tar Pits. "You're going to be a big star," I told her—"I heard the talk!" "And you are too—I heard the very same talk. So don't you worry either—see what I mean?" And then—this was the part that made me crazy at the lecture—she started singing: "Many dreams have been brought to your doorstep / They just lie there, and they die there." Then she turned to me and said, "Not yours, not mine. We're Gemini; we're insured!" Then she finished singing, "Are you warm, are you real, Mona Lisa / Or just a cold and lonely, lovely work of art?"

People ask, "Do you remember where you were when you heard?" I do. I was at Sunday-morning breakfast at the Manitoy Yacht Club in the company of most of the actors playing on the island in *Ah, Wilderness!* at the Mawrdew Czgowchwz

Theater. I'd been playing Muriel McComber, the ingenue. I was having acute subtext difficulties—probably because while they were playing *Ah, Wilderness!* I was projecting *Strange Interlude.*

"I don't want to listen! Let me go! If you don't, I'll bite your hand!" They were repeating that, kidding me mercilessly. Lead Boy was telling them all to be careful of me—feigning pulling back a Band-Aid, showing teeth marks—that I was "Method," that I'd drawn blood, and would again, when somebody came running up the gangplank with a radio broadcasting the news: she was dead.

"I don't want to listen! Let me go! If you don't . . . I don't want to listen! Let me go . . . I don't want—" I sat there and stopped hearing everything—everything happening. I heard her voice saying, "It's night outside. / Automobiles / roll down Sunset Boulevard . . ." I felt happy.

The neon in the windows on Melrose flashed in the gray light of the chilly afternoon. She looked into vitrine universes of art deco fixtures and fittings, of contemporary toys, and of up-to-the-second cosmetology's Egyptian mud regime (too reminiscent of the La Brea Girl, she thought, redolent of that February afternoon of death, not renovation). She gazed for a long while at a display of forties getups, remembering climbing into her mother's cast-off clothes for Thanksgiving begging, equipped with a postwar clutch bag for loot (old junk jewelry, mostly, and IOUs).

A few blocks beyond Kilkea, she stopped in front of CHOC'L.A.TESSEN (lit up in the banner colors of the 1984 Olympics, still decor-prevalent in the metropolis: the L, the A, and their two periods in torrid fuchsia, the remaining letters in cool aqua) and entered purposefully.

"I was attracted by those fresh strawberries dipped in white chocolate," she informed the slender young Hispanic assistant (eyeing his ceramic name tag: fuchsia letters on an aqua background) in an easy confidential tone, as if speaking to someone in whose company she'd spent a substantial part of the afternoon. "They're enormous, aren't they? Irresistible, really."

"How many would you care for, Miss Wayfaring?"

"Huh? Oh—well, let's see. Let's say about four dozen— thank you, Plácido."

There's a great story about Garbo going into a nut shop.

"We'd be happier to dip those fresh for you, Miss Wayfaring, if you wouldn't mind waiting."

"I'd be delighted, Plácido."

In New York, somewhere on the East Side. Back when. Flabbergasted young nut salesman—definitely no Plácido. "I vant some nuts," Garbo says. Flabbergasted opens mouth, looks down at display cases as if he's never before seen anything like them, or what's in them. "I vant some of those . . . and some of those . . . and some of those." He starts to shovel assorted nuts into a paper bag; he doesn't stop. Garbo reaches across, puts her hand on top of his, and says, "Dot's enough nuts." She gives him ten dollars; she takes her change. He never closes his mouth, and he never utters a syllable. Struck dumb for life was the cackle. I don't know how the story ever got out, but it's a favorite of my mother-in-law's.

Looking up, Kaye Wayfaring saw her face on a television screen, hovering over the empty out-front of CHOC'L.A.-TESSEN's premises, and at the same time watched a large-framed, heavyset, black-mustachioed, grinning man come out through double porthole-windowed swinging doors from the candy kitchen at the back.

"Kaye Wayfaring! We knew your whole family back in New York from before the Second World War! Did a lot of business—catering—with your aunt, Miss Bridgewood. So, we're fixing you four dozen strawberries. *Forty* dozen strawberries dipped in chocolate would just about make a dent in the kind of order we used to fill. We sent *truckloads* of delicatessen over there to Sutton Place, or in the train we'd ship a carload of it on the Central up to—what was the name of your aunt's place up there?"

"Willows."

"Yeah, Willows. I remember once your aunt was leaving on one of those cross-country tours. Must have been '47, '48."

" 'Forty-eight. She was touring *Hedda Gabler* and stumping for Harry Truman."

"Yeah. Well, we stocked her up good that time. God, the beluga alone. You couldn't do that today—well, maybe *you* could, being the rock star you are."

"Me, a rock star?" She laughed. "Get a grip, Mr.—"

"Vartanessian. Vartan Vartanessian, of CHOC'L.A.-TESSEN, proprietor. Welcome to my place, to my little bailiwick, to my creative world, to my television screen."

"Thank you, Mr.—Mr. Vartanessian, I *remember* you!"

"Of course you do. You were on that Westchester platform in '48, correct?"

"But you look the *same*—exactly the same. No difference whatever."

"Well, listen, that's the way it goes. I should practice California gallantry and say the same about you, but frankly, I can't."

"Mr. Vartanessian, have I gone mad? Look up there on the screen and tell me frankly."

"Miss Wayfaring, it's your turn to get a grip. All I've done is turn into my father—from the platform in Westchester."

"Oh, yes—yes, of course. I see. Could I sit down?"

"Chair coming up—also strong coffee. It's time to close up and switch to the news. Plácido, hola! Una silla para Miss Wayfaring, y después dos cafés armenianos, por favor. All children turn into their parents, don't they, eventually?"

"I wish I knew."

I feel like I just woke up. "Dazed am I since I woke, wild and strange seems the world." I hear you.

On the television screen, on a Greater Los Angeles metropolitan news feature, the big story was the snow.

"Look at that snow!" cried CHOC'L.A.TESSEN's proprietor, warming his hand with the cup of Armenian coffee. "They've never seen snow you don't spray out of cans on the poinsettias at Christmas. They don't ever go north of Oxnard, these people." Chuckling, he gestured with his free hand out the window in the general direction of West Hollywood. "They've never *heard* of snow not wrapped up in a Ben Franklin!" He looked across at his celebrated guest, sipping strong coffee, and smiled a broad smile. "Not you, of course—you're a different breed of cat altogether."

"Mr. Vartanessian, do you go north of Oxnard that much?"

"Me? Not that much. No, not 'not that much'—never. Confidentially, Miss Wayfaring, I never go north of Sunset. I send Plácido. We live at the beach, you see."

She nodded, and looked up again at the screen.

"Mr. Vartanessian, I'd say you'd probably recognize my husband, my children, and my mother-in-law, wouldn't you?"

"Well, your mother-in-law, Miss Wayfaring. At one time everybody in the civilized *world* recognized her. She was a great international—"

"Operator?"

"International star. Opera star, movie star, winner of the Academy Award."

"Indeed."

"I don't know whether or not I would recognize her now."

"Well, would you mind looking up at the television screen and telling me if you see anybody there resembling my mother-in-law, standing in a group with two small children next to a snowman?"

Vartan Vartanessian looked up.

"That's Mawrdew Czgowchwz, all right—or at least it's a woman answering to her famous hair. Darker, and shorter, but still amazing."

"She doesn't resemble anybody who just rose up from the bowels of the earth, does she?"

"She resembles, if this is what you mean to say—she resembles in style and bearing—she *represents* in point of fact—that whole generation of people gone. Of legendary artists and their audiences no longer mutually engaged."

"I suppose that is what I mean. What made you switch from caviar to chocolate, anyway?"

"It's a complicated story."

"Mr. Vartanessian, the thing I find most interesting about life in Los Angeles is that everybody has a complicated story—and the time to tell it, too. Usually in the car, often on public transport—on the way out to the beach, for instance—or sometimes just sitting around waiting for chocolate-dipped strawberries to arrive."

"Miss Wayfaring, in view of our families' connected histories and shared experiences, my story is yours for the asking. My conversion took place in Paris, many years ago, in the neighborhood of the Faubourg–Saint-Honoré. For the exact details, however, I must ask you to wait until I have finished supervising Plácido and the strawberries. Plácido is a boy with a warm and generous heart, and a tendency—which I am afraid in the light of your presence in the shop he would be unable to contain—to double-dip, which is not good confectionery practice. While there should be no question of *stinting*, you understand, it is every bit as incorrect to overwhelm the fruit with the chocolate as to be skimpy. In any event, you should at this very moment be watching what is happening up there on the television. What beautiful children: how *alive*! You just sit back, now, and relax with them."

On the news, replayed from somewhere in the San Fernando Valley, Kaye Wayfaring watched her children, their father, their uncle, and their grandmother, Mawrdew Czgowchwz, enlisted in a work force of combined adults and children, building a snowman.

What do they think they're doing, my alive and beautiful children? Something extraordinary—something they've never done before. How much will they remember? Who said one must have a mind of winter and have been cold a long time? They'll recall the freak chill of an afternoon.

What happens in "The Snow Queen"? Kay is the boy. The Snow Queen carries him off to the northernmost reach. . . .

On screen, celebrations in the Valley, edited, seemed drawn to a memorable conclusion.

Eternity—that was it. She promised Kay the whole world and a new pair of skates could he discover the meaning of the word "eternity." Turns out the meaning of eternity is television—or is found on television. Stay, thou art fair. Play it back—nothing ever lost anymore. It won't be necessary for them to remember anything; they'll replay the program— unless, amid life's hurry, nobody ever reminds them to replay the program.

In "The Snow Queen," there aren't any parents. The little girl tracks Kay down, melts his frozen heart with her tears, and brings him back home. At the end of it all, they've both grown up—what else?

Vartan Vartanessian reentered from the kitchen bearing on a china tray a construction in meringue studded with coal-lump bosses of black licorice, dusted with confectioner's sugar, and standing a foot high. "Michelangelo, they say, you know, made snowmen for the Medici children. In his off hours; in his spare time, so to speak. This is for you—you and yours. I have, you know, in my time been called—in print—the Michelangelo of confectioners."

"How . . . nice."

A silence fell. Breaking it, Vartan Vartanessian declared, "Something is striking you so funny, you're scared to start laughing."

"Guilty as charged, I'm afraid. Sorry."

"Afraid? Nonsense. No charge. On the house, same as the snowman."

"Which is a beautiful—"

"—thing, but not the thing that is making you laugh."

"No. Suddenly I pictured the Last Judgment in swirls of candy—"

"You are, as a matter of fact, in spiritual conjunction with the story of my conversion—a result of the declension in the immortal Renoir family from painting to chocolateering in the Faubourg–Saint-Honoré."

"I see—but was there not in that same declension a celebrated term of filmmaking?"

"Indeed so—and considering the amount of chocolate eaten in movie theaters all over the world during the run of a typical feature, perhaps a valid metaphysical consideration. But, concerning Michelangelo, you must you must think of Michelangelo the sculptor and architect. I did, for example, in the old days, Sid Grauman's Chinese Theatre in brilliantly sculpted multihued spun sugars. And the sidewalk—before your lovely imprint was included—in pure white chocolate."

"Could you do the La Brea Tar Pits the way they used to be, with the little white round deco observatory?"

"From memory. A piece of—excuse me—cake."

"I can see it, decorated with miniature sugar skulls—the kind Mexican children eat on the Day of the Dead."

"I did the Colleen Moore Fairy Castle—worked day and night for weeks. That was my masterpiece—there I did work to challenge the Sistine Chapel; the Cinderella mural in the drawing room. Too good to be—to be permitted in this town . . . in this terrible world."

Kaye Wayfaring looked alarmed. "Oh, *you* did that?"

"For the little Von Gelsen girl. Obviously you know what happened. That wife—number eight? Off the platinum trolley, into the pool. 'Now you can play Atlantis, dearie!' What a witch."

"I saw the original on tour once, in Atlanta. It—she killed herself."

"People said about that outrage that night that it was very Hollywood. Imagine! The wife, you mean? Number eight?"

"She was number four. In the same pool. I ran into Desirée herself, before, in the Tar Pits museum."

"People laughed. Not me. It was my masterpiece. The Von Gelsen girl—really? How's she doing?"

"Breathing normally, I'd say. Walking around standing up. She's something altogether, if you're interested in miracles."

Vartan Vartanessian nodded gravely. "I can dig them."

Kaye Wayfaring smiled the smile that had enchanted viewers for decades. "You're so New York! Why did you come to Los Angeles?"

"Many Armenians came to California, many relatives, of course, among them. They kept calling it the Land of Youth and Beauty. My father never took the bait; I did."

"Tir na nOg."

"What's that?"

"The Land of Youth and Beauty—in Irish. Actually, just youth; I added beauty because—well, you know. The camellia never freezes and the snowman never melts. 'Stay, thou art fair!' "

"Los Angeles is that—is all that. But it's also the Last Stop. Remember Miss Winwood?"

"Estelle Winwood? Yes, of course. She was my aunt's great pal."

"I used to make for her great plates of white chocolate asparagus, with pale green tips streaked with violet. One afternoon we sat looking out the window—she could make you think she saw things, you know. She was sitting there, humming that old song 'Only a Bird in a Gilded Cage'—and you know, she did seem enclosed in a cage of gold light. 'Miss Winwood, is there anything else you want?' 'I want to die.' 'Do you really? Or are you just being Estelle Winwood talking offbeat talk?' 'No, I *mean* it; I want to die. It would be a *chaynge!*' And so she did."

So do we all. "And on that note—"

Plácido had come out of the kitchen, carrying a carton of fresh-dipped strawberries.

"Oh, thank you," Kaye Wayfaring exclaimed, "they look irresistible! They are. If you would put just one—that one—in a piece of tissue paper, I'll feast on it in the taxi. May I use your telephone to call—"

"You may not!" Vartan Vartanessian declared, with a sweeping gesture. "My guests never go home in a taxi—and as for the meringue snowman, his nerves couldn't stand it. Plácido will deliver you. Plácido, por favor, el Bentley."

"This really is unnecessarily kind of you."

"Nothing of the kind—nothing could be more necessary, if only because in this time and place, you understand, it makes a change."

"Well, all the same . . ."

"Your family," Vartan Vartanessian instructed, "will certainly by now be coming home from the winter carnival. You yourself have had a busy day and likely have not had time to instruct the cook as to dinner; you will therefore order in from Chasen's—but you will order no dessert; dessert you have already taken care of."

Vartan Vartanessian led Kaye Wayfaring back through the porthole swinging doors, through CHOC'L.A.TESSEN's stainless-steel and white-marble kitchen, into the alley running parallel to Melrose Avenue, where, under a spreading chestnut tree, Plácido sat revving the engine of a vintage Bentley while looking at the Los Angeles street atlas to determine exactly the route to Wayfaring at Waverly in Silver Lake.

"It's a straight line down Sunset," she offered, "then left on Silver Lake around the reservoir."

"If you draw the line in red," the driver replied, "I would cherish it—a souvenir."

"Of course," she said, and accepted the marker.

While drawing the red line on the street map, from left to right, west to east, she suddenly saw Marilyn Monroe, in *Bus Stop*, showing Eileen Heckart the red line on Cherie's map of the United States—the line of her ambition from right to left, from her hometown in the Ozarks, buried under floodwater, straight to Hollywood, no turns whatever to the north or south.

Turns out, from Reno, she took a turn to the right, north through Utah, past the Great Salt Lake, and into the wilds of Montana to get home—whereas I take a left off Sunset, up around the reservoir and into the Umbrian hills of Silver Lake.

The interior of the car was heated against the cold snap. Cruising east along Sunset, biting into the strawberry, Kaye Wayfaring considered the meaning of Cinderella.

Every girl believes at some point in her life that because of her secret wishes, if not also her clandestine actions, she deserves to be degraded, banished from the presence of others, relegated to the netherworld of smut.

Crucified on the H. Taken down at sunset and thrown into the La Brea Tar Pits. Born to be bad, as her mother had attested, she'd wanted: the jewels, the dress, the carriage, her father's love, a night on the town, the prince. She'd coveted the works.

And now the motion-picture "resurrection" version. She was having her footprints taken at Grauman's Chinese when the horn blew at midnight; her time in the spotlight was up. She ran away from her Venetian-blown size fours, but not before panicking and cutting her foot, thus leaving a trail of blood along Hollywood Boulevard—streaked across the star they'd welded her name onto, and across (as it turned out) half a dozen of her handsomest leading men's. She wrote a book about it; she was brought back.

They'll be on their way back now from Tir na nOg, led by the all-wise one, Herself, Immortal She, Great Mother. They called her that, Immortal She, during her ascendancy.

While the other mother, this good enough one, who stayed behind, generously, is bringing home dessert. Ought to be enough for anyone. Sufficient. What more could the creatures want? What more should I?

Principal Photography

Keeping a practiced distance, Mairead Shortt, the young documentary filmmaker from Dun Laoghaire, turned her Sharp VHS-C8X zoom camcorder on the actress Kaye Wayfaring and the poet S. D. Jameson O'Maurigan, star and scriptwriter, respectively, of *The White Sea Horse* (Orphrey Whither's first Hyperion Pictures venture since the already legendary early-eighties "neon-realist" feature *Avenged*), billed in preproduction broadsides fired in *Variety* and the *Hollywood Reporter* as "The Life and Times of Grace O'Malley (1530–1603), called 'Granuaile,' a Notorious Woman."

After signing to do the picture, Kaye Wayfaring had worked on Granuaile for a year at home in Laguna and Silver Lake. She was to portray as many years, exactly, of the Hibernian pirate's life as she had lived of her own, ending up a woman—a notorious woman—of seventy-plus. The diva Mawrdew Czgowchwz, absent from the screen since her Academy Award–winning debut in Orphrey Whither's *Pilgrim Soul* more than three decades earlier, had signed to play Granuaile's adversary, Elizabeth I, Queen of England. Principal photography on *The White Sea Horse* was set to commence that day at Malin Beg, Glencolumbkille, in County Donegal.

(They had come up from Dublin only the day before, but look, Mairead Shortt besought her lone assistant, Cathal, what

75

they'd done to the place: pavilions erected, marquees hung, banners streaming, pennants volant. The Silver Strand had been enhanced with multicolored stones, all wetted down to gleam like gems, blanketing the brilliant sand. The cliff's emerald ferns and velvet mosses, its wild rhododendrons and furze, its butterwort, samphire, lupines, and thrift had been similarly drenched—as if there weren't rain enough per diem in the Irish weather scheme—to bear the heat of intense artificial light. It was, in the documentarian's severe things-left-as-is esthetic terms, unnerving, delirious, like feigned lust and folderol.

"Well," Cathal had protested, "don't you dress up to have your photo taken? Or didn't y'used to, before y'woke up so *puri*-fied, so *evolved* that fatal mornin' and decided t'turn your life t'this?")

Having no brief to record off-set conversations, and unable, upwind, to catch the drift, Mairead Shortt attempted making a good fist of the job by inventing (casting herself and her sidekick as celebrity pass-remarkables on the qui vive) the discourse the conspirators were about.

"Look at this card," Kaye Wayfaring entreated Jameson O'Maurigan, leaning across the reach between their collapsible chairs and handing it to him. The poet, scanning the missive, scrutinized the painting reproduced on it and, impersonating Orphrey Whither, replied in his gruff rhetorical bass:

"Telling. The very brief and abstract storyboard of the entire undertaking!"

"But isn't it uncanny?"

"A ferocious good omen on day one of principal photography. Oh, I don't know," he continued, resuming his own register and melody. "Not really; not in your mail. D. K. Synchronicity Wayfaring, when and where she's at home."

Kaye Wayfaring took the card back, and, turning it over, reread the message, printed neatly at the base of a hand-drawn musical staff, scored in the treble-clef key of C and peppered with a few quarter-notes: ". . . a talking picture of you-oo . . ."

"Although Skip's always had a direct line to me."

"Poor devil."

"What?"

"You say that of all the best boys. They live to hear it; they'd perish—ecstatically—in the lists to prove it."

"I don't—they don't—they wouldn't. And anyway, please don't rag me; I'm in character makeup."

"Sheathed in the part. Only waiting for the light—in Donegal."

"I shouldn't be talking to you at all; I shouldn't be looking at postcards. I shouldn't be myself; I should be she."

"Herself. In that case, return your fan mail for safekeeping, tilt up the chin, so, dispose your parts, and cast her two too-cold eyes out to sea. Will you do all that, for me?"

"I might. But tell me this: what would I ever—"

"Do without me? Something else. Something unrecorded. Something undertaken out of sheer lust."

The postcard, a four-inch-by-seven-inch reduced photographic reproduction by Ashcraft, Inc., Kansas City, Missouri, of Thomas Hart Benton's *Hollywood* (1937) from the Nelson-Atkins Museum of Art, depicted a fantasy sound-stage triptych of klieg lights, wind machine, platforms, tower scaffolding, the matte painting backdrop of a city in flames and refugee rowboats afloat in a great indoor tank; cameras, booms, sound recorders, bulb-ring mirrored makeup tables, all arrayed in sectional perspective around the central figure of a scantily clad (pink brassiere, silver-spangled blue panties, silver helmet, pink shoes) proletarian-goddessy bottle blonde standing right-hand-on-hip and left-leg-bent-forward under the half-hoop of a white two-columned arch, and holding a staff surmounted by a silver sphere. It did indeed, Kaye Wayfaring decided (what was that expression, she asked herself, the men always used back then? Yes, *mutatis mutandis:* always sounded like some extinct specimen). It did indeed—that expression, somehow—in spite of the star's "authenticated" sixteenth-century Connaught pirate queen costume, and in spite of the fact that they were shooting, as Orphrey Whither had always (with the single, still-rankling exception of *Pilgrim's Soul*) shot his features, entirely on location. ("Echt location," Mawrdew Czgowchwz had remarked when advised of the director's intention to reconstruct the Great Hall at Nonsuch in situ.) It did indeed, somehow by coincidence—as if the sender, a poet as gifted in irony as in devotion, had read through the secret minutes of Hyperion Pictures' preproduction pow-wows, and decided—it did somehow sum the whole arrangement up. All the same (the thought flew in) and all the while, the communication she held in her hand was something else entirely—an entirely different story, really, come to think of it.

Sends me a dirty postcard; I'm such a gay old shoe.

It's not a—you're talking crazy.

It's a dirty postcard, like you send from the boardwalk at the honky-tonk seaside resort.

Why do I pretend to understand what men mean, what they're up to when they send me dirty postcards?

Oh, please.

It isn't, in fact, a dirty postcard. The message is forthright: it says, clearly, "a talking picture of you-oo."

So, why do I think it's a dirty postcard?

Grace's men. Would they have sent her a dirty postcard? That one from Ocracoke: the sailor sitting on the jetty looking out to sea: "It's hard waiting for you." Whatever was so funny about that, nobody let me in on it. The sailor looked unhappy; he was lonely.

Joan of Arc's men would definitely never—but then, she never left them; she almost never let them out of her sight.

One of the boys: a very different story.

Professor Mullein said woman is to men three things in succession in life: the maiden, the mother, and the crone. He didn't say, or forgot to say, the crony, by which they mean the whore, the love-goddess pal.

In Spain it's the whore and the nun . . . all women. . . . In England the two came to mean the same thing—wouldn't they!

Remember when I did *'Tis Pity*, my mother wouldn't come up. The title.

So, OK, it isn't a dirty postcard.

My husband, for example, wouldn't have sent—and that's why I'm sitting here telling him this.

She handed the postcard over to her colloquist.

Sheer lust. They'll excuse me maybe if I doubt they have the faintest—

Telling. Always one of my favorite remarks of theirs. Threatening, although they'd never admit it was. "You did it, and I'm telling. . . ."

This kind of thing always makes me think I'm back on the front page of the *Enquirer*, being hawked at supermarket checkouts. So, what's the difference anyway between that and this, only lighting and location—oh, no, not that played-out tune again: it's like little boys relentlessly going to confession to recite the kind of thing no smart little girl would ever tell a priest.

Waiting for the light in Donegal is only—no, it isn't even the beginning. Does he think I've forgotten Orphrey always lights the light? Cast two too-cold. . . .

The water was freezing cold that summer on the Outer Banks. "It warms up in September." "How do you make it

September?" Is that what made me do it? That and "September Morn" in the hotel bathroom. "Whut did you think you were doin'?" The beginning of that long period of days punctuated with—"Wait until she finds out" and "Wait until he gets home."

They'd sent me my supper on a tray. Finally the sound of his car on the gravel drive; distinctive sound, that car. Why? He came into the room, a little tanked, looked at me, and went over to the window. He sat there, smoking, looking out at the Atlantic. Usually he never shut up; I thought that night he'd never speak. He did at last. "A woman . . . a woman . . . a woman is a vessel—a vessel."

"The first day of principal photography," said Jameson, "is the day of all days on a picture when lust—rapacious lust: the ravenous raptor's screech demanding information—know what I mean?"

"Orphrey always lights the light; did you think I'd somehow forgotten?"

"On the contrary, I think I've always, somehow, realized you'd remember—and return."

"To? Where are we?"

"I believe, according to your woman's scene board over there, Malin Beg, Glencolumbkille, in Donegal."

Return. Raptor. Humoring me. Or, rather, humoring her. Herself, a Notorious Woman.

"Who the hell was she, honey?" the matey astro-seer, social columnist, and New Age talk-show host Astarte had demanded the week before, of her long-term acquaintance Kaye Wayfaring, over Avocado Avalon at Zitronen on West Hollywood's Melrose Avenue. "I mean, with those dates inserted purposely like that, was she actually historically real, or was she more of a mythical beast?"

"Darling, at this stage in my career, what would I be doing playing a mythical beast?"

"Answers question with question; very Irish. Because stars startle, honey; it's their function. Eat up. 'Authentic locations.' When's it start? Soon, hopefully. Nobody's ready for another Orphrey Whither marathon."

"As soon as we can get there. We're packing as I'm talking to you. Pray for sunshine, would you?"

"And the children are in it, right?"

"Yes, they are. She kidnaps them and transports them to her pirate cove."

"And your legendary mother-in-law in her screen return? They're certainly downplaying that one."

"It's a short scene."

"You'll deal with it. Don't let me put words in your mouth, honey, but any other—"

"—actor in the business would be—I know. Anyway, they talk about the laundry. Very metaphysical."

"They—who?"

"The Irish pirate queen and the English queen. Although, as Orphrey and Jameson both delight in pointing out, the English queen was actually, patrilineally, Welsh."

"Laundry."

"Yes. It seems that when Granuaile, the Irish—"

"I've got that part."

"—went to see Elizabeth, the English queen—"

"—actually Welsh. To talk about the laundry."

"No, not at first. About gold—you couldn't possibly be interested in this."

"Hey, there, remember me—in one ear and in the other? Try me. This is the Information Age, honey; the people want their information sitting on their couches around the monitor. Details, details. You know, honey, it isn't—it really isn't that discourse in Los Angeles isn't about anything, the way they say; it's that it isn't about anything else. That they can't assimilate; that they can't admit into the mezzanine."

Went on like that. Drive you right out of your mind. Laundry. Lust. No, not laundry lust, laundry list. Drive you absolutely crazy like that, waiting. Fritz you to Tilt. Return? Never been to Donegal.

Oh, but she has; this is her territory. She's the raptor; she's one of those territory vultures Jameson invented in Silver Lake to terrify the children.

That Welsh thing—strange. Orphrey yesterday bellowing away about the rain. "Drive you mad! Country deluges you in rain!" Then, "Ah, well, could be worse: we might all have been Welsh."

She was lusty, I suppose. The Welsh Queen. Lust itself, some said, despite—her father's daughter.

Last night, in front of the peat fire, O'Maurigan told the children all about both women.

"Are you dissented from Granny Whale, Uncle Darragh? Mr. Whither says you are, says ask—see if you're not."

"Well, yes, I am."

"Are you! He'll tell you anything, you realize," I said. "Your uncle Sean Darragh Jameson O'Maurigan was, it may interest you to know, the only child on his block regularly sent to bed without his carrageen for telling the truth. He soon shaped up."

"What's 'cat-o-green'?"

"Carra-geen. It's seaweed. Real Irish people eat it for dessert, the same way people in California eat tapioca."

"Yuck!"

"Yuck!"

"It's hallucinogenic," I said. "You see things—wild things—when you eat it." Out of character—my own. I'd never say that at home. I was already on location, becoming her.

"We didn't live on a block. Not in those days, anyway."

"Nobody around here tells the truth about anything! Uncle Darragh, are you really—"

"Indeed I am, and not à la any mode de Bretagne, either, but directly, on the bias. She's my thirteenth great-grandmother. And while you're at it, you may thank Herself directly through me for not only the words that will be put into your dear little recorded mouths—which incidentally I get directly from automatic writing through the patient medium of this brilliant lustful woman here, your mother, on her carrageen breaks—but in point of fact for your salaries themselves—and those ain't, as you probably realize, seaweed—which are being paid to your business manager more or less directly—"

"Directly on the bypass!"

"You got it—as it were, directly from the coffers of Herself, the Ancestress, in a sort of transfiguration, y'see, of the hoard of Armada gold ingots—as many as the bricks of turf you observed cut out of the bogs of the Curraun Peninsula on Saturday in County May-o. Those ingots she stashed away four hundred years ago nearly exactly in that very cave we're going on location in tomorrow."

"Although it does provide a key script element," I said, "there was no gold-bearing ship I ever heard of in the Armada."

"Oh, but there was," the heir replied. "You bet your unit publicity there was. Whereas it is regularly given out that there were, in that fabled conglomeration of dreadnoughts under the command of the duke of Medina-Sidonia ferrying the army of the duke of Parma back from the Netherlands, one hundred and twenty-four ships, there were in point of fact one hundred and twenty-five: one hundred and twenty-four as mentioned returning from et cetera, aboard which all profanity, gambling, profligacy, and lust were, as the French would've said, had they been involved and their commander Joan of Arc, *formellement interdit*, and one more, *una más*. She was called the *Califia*, and she was on her maiden voyage—to Seville, from what was then reckoned as the island kingdom of California, northwest of Mexico, at the Very Edge of Night, where in fact she had been built—in six days, history informs us, hewn out of a single sequoia by the mescal-driven slaves of her namesake Califia, the island's ageless Amazon queen."

"You got Califia out of that pet epic romance of yours," I intercut, "the book that drove Don Quixote crazy, where California's an island—and from the restaurant in Baja on the way to Ensenada. When they charted Baja, they reckoned it as an island, and called it California. There are no sequoias in Baja."

"So there are not, but it is recorded that your woman Califia was a tremendous trading monarch—not unlike Granuaile. She traded lustily with the Ultima Thule of those climes and regions, the Sequoia Snow Country—known to us in our time, as it happens, as northern California, Wayfaring Country—divine mescal for great numbers of divine redwoods. They'd take the mescal up to Ultima and distribute it to the indigenes—from some of whom, we've heard, certain illustrious Wayfarings bypass-derive—who, thus empowered, would then virtually gnaw the great beasts of trees out of the red earth with their bare teeth, and, hoisting masts and sails on them, voyage down to what we now know as Baja."

I gave up then. After all, if I was really going to be she— Granuaile, Califia, or another (and who knew, or could, in an Orphrey Whither picture?), then he, the narrator, was—what? Hell-or-high-water, bent-demented, putting words into my mouth as well as into everybody else's, and so, *fado, fado*.

"On her way to Seville, via Cádiz, bearing a cargo of gold ingots, in exchange for numbers of Valencia orange trees alive in clay pots, and the secret receipt for *horchata de chufa*, the fabled Catalonian milk of youth, along with a consignment of condensed samples of same: the very formula and calcified stuff that centuries later Califia's descendants and inheritors of moxie in Pasadena unearthed and made the basis of that billion-dollar cosmetic line—

"But I digress, for you see, as a result of the Armada storm, the gold never reached Seville. It never got any further into Europe than this very cove, where Granny Whale herself—"

"Granny Whale made the storm happen, didn't she, Uncle Darragh? To get the gold from Kelly."

(That shut him up for a minute anyway.)

"You're very close, and in fact some—Donegal folk— would say 'bang on.' "

"Bang on!"

"Bang on!"

"But evidence—good English evidence—says otherwise, which is where your grandmother comes—any minute—into the picture."

"Grandmother's in Dublin—negotiating."

"She is indeed, in that very way she has: the way of divas, queens, and lusty wizards everywhere in the revolving world."

"Is grandmother a wizard?"

"Your grandmother has contracted to impersonate a wizard in this picture. Y'see, this Elizabeth, this Welsh Queen, well, what we now know is that she, advised by her famous Chaldaic-Scottish wizard chamberlain John Dee his confederate, one Chaldaic-Hibernian called Kelly, and a few companion witches—later infamously immortalized after the Welsh Queen's death by her posthumous enemy the earl of Oxford in his melodrama *Macbeth*—succeeded by means of incantations and a scrying glass in raising from a millennial sleep and transporting from his abode under the earth at Tintagel, in North Cornwall, nobody else but your man Merlin, the wizard *capo di tutti capi*, mind out of time, who, he himself, raised the storm that wrecked the Armada. The word that went out from Nonsuch, of course, was 'God breathed.' Cover story. Metaphor—like the laundry. Point is, the Spaniard went under, and we got the gold!"

"Bang on! What about the laundry, Uncle Dee?"

"The laundry. Oh, you mean the metaphysical altercation."

"Was it about which product to use?"

"Did they have products back then? Did they have product lunches? Industrial receptions? Ceremonies?"

"Don't talk to me about receptions, about ceremonies. Did they have products? They had *horchata de chufa*, didn't they?"

"Whatever that is. What is it, Uncle Dee? And what's a crying glass?"

"Didn't I just—listen, about the laundry—"

("The uncanny thing," Astarte had marveled, "is the resemblance you showed me between you and the figurehead on that Irish what's-that—"

"On the coast guard's brigantine. Doesn't it? When O'Maurigan showed me that photograph last year, I thought Orphrey's had only the decorated prow of the supposed boat built, but it's real, all right."

"It looks like alabaster, though, and you don't, thanks be."

"Yes, well, that's where the selective in Orphrey's selective realism intervened. 'I don't care if she was bathed in butter-milk three times a day for seventy-three years. If she was out in the wind—and she had to be out in the wind, unless, and I'd disbelieve it if I was told it, she ruled like Mae West, from the bed—then she was rubicund to a degree.' And anyway, the scene with Gloriana is indoors in winter, with great open fires blazing everywhere, and the poet's got her makeup—the old decaying queen's—actually melting off her face into the hand-kerchief, like something out of *House of Wax*."

"Very timely. Did you hear? Another big time Beverly

Hills plastic surgeon's checked out on cyanide over the silicone face-slide epidemic."

"I did. I tell you, I never did understand those operations."

"God gave you bones. So, what about the laundry?"

"Oh, well, the old queen keeps using up handkerchiefs—Irish linen, produced by Lady-in-Waiting A. Then Lady-in-Waiting B keeps taking them from her and discreetly pocketing them. Each time this routine is played, Granuaile looks bewildered. At length, with the heat, and amid the preamble to the politics on the agenda, she, Granuaile, sneezes on a whiff of soot, is given a handkerchief, blows her nose, and, unblinking, ignoring B, steps over to the hearth and tosses it into the flames. Reprimanded by Gloriana herself, who, as Jameson likes saying, gives out to her, she receives a lecture on laundry. Professing shock at the—shall we say anal-retentive—behavior rampant in Albion, she launches into a comic aside on the impracticality of turning her buccaneers into launderers, and tries to imagine herself and her band allowing hold space wasted on dirty linen. It's a very funny scene."

"Under light—Whither light.")

"Here's the light now," O'Maurigan declared. "Betraying your memories—memories of—"

"Diapers."

"Diapers. Whyever not. What comes to mind—"

"They had diaper service. My mother's Milledgeville family. Hannah's Savannah Stork Pickup and Delivery Diaper Service. Like white on rice."

"You remember."

"Remembering or lying. Lighting the light, like Orphrey."

"In Milledgeville, the truck had a big white stork painted on its side. 'That seyvuhce was nevuh availuble heah in Clayton,' my mother told us, 'only theah in the civulahzed part of Goahgia. Ah used to think—Ah used to say, if only that pictyuh of the stoak carryin' that babeh in the diapuh sling represented—if onleh Hannuh's would take away the babehs f'three days at a stretch instead of—they'd alweys be the chayunce that in sum provu-denshl confusion, Ah'd get back two wun'uful, diff'unt—' We, of course, we contemporaries, threw away the—"

"Threw away the diapers and kept the children. Aren't you glad?"

"Glad? Sure."

"Even happy?"

"Before I get what I think you mean by 'happy,' I'm going to have to know much, much more."

"Aristotle says knowledge is the outcome of our union with all being, finite and infinite."

"Aristotle who? There have been a lot of Aristotles; a lot of moderators."

"But only one Orphrey Whither, and only two children of yours—three more creatures for light to fall on, and so they appear, the two helping the one out of the rear of the company saloon motor, a prewar Armstrong Siddeley."

"Doesn't that look like a stork painted on the side door?"

"That is Hyperion himself."

"Pickup and delivery. I must deliver now; I must be she."

"You must be she. She Who Must Be Obeyed."

"All right—get lost."

"The first day of principal photography," O'Maurigan intoned, walking away, "is that day of all days on a picture—"

Kaye Wayfaring watched Mairead Shortt turn her attention to Orphrey Whither's grand entrance.

What does she make of that? What comes to mind?

Introibo. Wonder if she—ought to. Very like. Very? Exactly like.

She watched the quartet advance in a procession, shadowed by the filmmaker and her assistant, and attended by a small phalanx of crew attending the director's opening remarks.

Look at that: action in everyone's separate, intersecting circles. Of light? Uncanny, really, exactly like—must write, no, call Skip. It wasn't, after all, a dirty postcard. This afternoon on the satellite walkie-talkie.

Just look at him. No workaday celebrant; Orphrey Cardinal Whither, Archbishop of—he's talking. Can't hear: the wind. Just as well, absolutely.

He's got them talking bits of Irish, though, and sounding into the bargain as authentic as—I'll say that for the old—

I remember the first day on *Way Station.* "One of the first things we're going to have to do about you, Miss Wayfaring, is put the South back in your mouth." "What, the whole thing?"

What possessed me? I still remember—the exercise to get it, the South, out of the mouth. It was Aunt Thalia's decision to give me lines from Norma Shearer's speech in *Marie Antoinette,* heaping scorn on the duke of Orleans. "Everything serves him: the deficit, the hard winter, the failure of the crops!" "She's comin' along just fahn, Thu-lyah," my mother said to her one afternoon in Milledgeville, "but have you noticed that the bettuh she sez the *weyds,* the closuh tugethuh huh *ayhs* seem t'get?"

(Why did Roman mythology make Venus slightly cross-eyed, like Norma Shearer? To do with lust: no point in looking before you leap.)

Orphrey Whither walked to the edge of the cliff and, raising his arms, raised his voice:

> "O my Dark Rosaleen,
> Do not sigh, do not weep!
> The priests are on the ocean green,
> They march along the deep.

There's wine from the royal Pope,
Upon the ocean green,
And Spanish ale shall give you hope,
My Dark Rosaleen."

"We don't drink Spanish ale, do we, Uncle Dee?"

"No, we do not. We do, however, drink *horchata de chufa*."

"Who's Dark Rosaleen, Uncle Dee? Where does she come from? What does she want? Where is—"

"Never mind that—your director is merely addressing the weather in bardic vowels. Do concentrate on your characters, both."

"The world began this morning," Orphrey Whither continued, in rhetorical crescendo, "God-dreamt and full of birds!"

Heard that all right. Voice of the—got to hand it to him: he dispels air. What birds? White crows? Ravenous raptors?

Must concentrate on herself. Always the same distraction waiting to go on: voices in the vestibule. "Do not sigh, do not weep. You are in competition with nobody but yourself. Do the work as it was meant to be done, or get out and don't come back."

The competition at Peoples Department Store: Act Out an Ad.

"I dreamed I was First Lady in my Bosom Buddy bra." Picture, as I remember it, something very like the Jean on the p.c. Made the Atlanta papers; became "a scandal to the buzzards." I shouldn't have worn the pillbox hat with the veil on, and I shouldn't have started hiccoughing. It was from fright. Sat there hiccoughing, looking like I was playing drunk, and everything contrived jiggling with each hiccough. Went on like that all afternoon—covered up, disqualified, dismissed, and bundled home—and into the night, when he got home. I was sitting there smoking when he knocked and walked in.

"Cigarette?" I asked him. "This time," he said, when I lit it for him, "this time I just don't know. I don't." "I do," I said. "I've got it figured out. A woman is a vessel, right? Well, I reckon I'm out to be a tramp steamer." There's nothing like a laughing jag to cut off hiccoughs. He was all right, when you think about it.

Orphrey was addressing the twins, his captives, as in the past he had addressed their mother.

"The performance is the actor's circumference; the actor can only reach his circumference through the radius of his experience. He-and-she must know that it will be his-and-her care to come to terms with his-and-her experience, at the center; that it will be his-and-her chief hope to establish and maintain an equilibrium between his-and-her temperament and his-and-her milieu."

Or hers-and-hers. Look at them. Do they love it? Do they lust? Do they—

"An equilibrium." Between love and lust? The second day on *Way Station*, he said, in front of everybody—cast, crew— "Play the *scene*, Miss Wayfaring; don't play the *mood*!" All my beautiful wickedness! We worked it out, I remember: love is the scene; lust is the mood.

"An equilibrium that can only otherwise be described as his-or-her histrionic persona. His personality as a man—or hers as a woman—is of no interest to anybody except the people who have to live with—"

Equilibrium? Tell that to the *Enquirer*, to the *Globe*. Standoff is more like it. Standoff, standstill: waiting for the kindly light—which, now it's come, must, it turns out, be addressed, dressed, lit. Go figure. Go figure? Go crazy is more like it: blow your stack.

Last night Orphrey said to everybody in the room, "To be dead is to stop believing in the masterpieces we will begin tomorrow. Sure, fillimmaking isn't anything only coitus interruptus; that's entirely what fillimmaking is now." O'Maurigan, pretending to repeat the words in a whisper of religious awe, translated—nicely, I thought—for the children. "Sure, fillimmaking isn't anything, only creatures in eruption. That is untidily what fillimmaking is now." They, suitably armed, gave back to Orphrey, "Fillimmaking. . . ."

"And lastly," Orphrey Whither was saying, straight into Mairead Shortt's camcorder lens, "let us remember what fillimmaking is. Out of the mouths of children we have heard it. 'Fillimmaking is only craytures in eruption!' As the immortal Confucian Book of Wisdom says, 'That which is bright riseth twice.' Or, as Granuaile, Witch of the West, declared as she snatched the wee pair from off the Hill of Howth—"

Actually, history—or legend—relates she snatched the one called Christopher, the heir, not a pair. Only to accommodate the pair of—he wanted to: to have them in the picture.

Was she? Is she like me? Why did she really kidnap the boy—now the pair? Was it just so their father would follow her? Just so. Like me. I must have him, their father; explode otherwise; go something called temperamental . . . or would I?

"Pardon me, Miss Wayfaring, here are your cards."

Would I? "My what?"

"Your cards," said the best boy, standing in front of her, blocking out the sun. "Did y'not say y'wanted them to carry wit' you, in character, onto the ship?"

I did. "Thank you, Declan." God, look at him, backlit like that. Beautiful. Irish kids; drive you—

"The wild goose draws near the cloud heights," Orphrey Whither declared. "Its feathers can be used for the sacred dance. Good fortune."

(Which feathers—the tail? How can it then fly down again?)

"Mr. Whither, the O'Maurigan, Miss Wayfaring, Master Tristan Beltane, Miss Maev Beltane, Miss Shortt, and assistant

aboard the conveyance—come along, please," a voice commanded through a bullhorn.

"Uncle Dee?" whispered Tristan Beltane. "Is God breathing us out to the ship in this balloon?"

"You bet she is."

"I still don't understand," Kaye Wayfaring's younger twin
protested, between exhilaration and fear, in what she decided
he imagined a businesslike tone, "why we must go in a balloon
to the ship anyway. Why we couldn't just be on, sleeping
aboard, overnight? Why, we're playing the whole story
backwards!"

"Because," his sister rejoined, calmly, "'the wild geese draw
near the cloud heights.' You never pay attention. Mr. Whither
borrowed this conveyance from the Living Planet producers,
especially. I like it."

(Or because the witch, her captives netted, flies through
the air—but never in the afternoon; only at night. Only
dreaming—what?)

"But I still don't understand," Maev whispered to her
mother in confidence, "what Mr. Whither means by 'the
radios of experience.' "

"Let's wait, shall we, and ask him at supper," Kaye Way-
faring whispered back. Looking down at the ship, a hermaph-
rodite brig of Basque design, she thought not of Grace
O'Malley's pirates, or character work, but of sailing, between
Laguna and the private Orphrey Whither island paradise San
Gabriel, where—

"O.W.," said Jameson to young Tristan (attempting, he decided in his Irish persona, the O'Maurigan, to mollify, in this
singular untoward instance of the mother's role distraction,
the slight he detected to the child), "stands time and again in
this business for Orphrey Wizard—whose balloon gets you
places. This is real life. You can't be transported over turbulent
currents swirling around rocky cliffs by clicking your boot

heels together three times. Where you can get doing that is only back in your bed in Laguna."

Aboard the brigantine, Cathal relieved her of the weight of the zoom camcorder as Mairead Shortt turned her attention from Orphrey Whither, rehearsing the Beltane twins on the fore-deck, to Kaye Wayfaring, stationed high up in the prow, push-ing buttons on a Novatel cellular telephone. Again frustrated by her inability to overhear anything pregnant, neither pause nor exchange, she soldiered on, directing her assistant to set the zoom for close-up, all the while mulling over two dis-tinctly tantalizing options: intertitles, as employed in silent films (a bold bit of documentary *trucage*, she told herself, as she con-sidered the opportunities for improvised, comedic "wild analy-sis" scripting), and the undoubtedly more devious, detailed, and fulfilling eavesdropper's protocol, redolent of schemer's genius: bringing the footage to a lip reader. No, there was no such thing anymore as who cares? Everybody, and not only in Ireland, was only desperate, as the saying had gone for gen-erations in and around that environ and milieu called Dub-lin 4 (whereto she was bound and no mistake).

Unaware of the epistemological impasse besetting Mairead Shortt, and innocent of the upshots, forged and contrived, it might spawn, Kaye Wayfaring, having failed to get through to her husband, Tristan Beltane, in Laguna, had reached her brother-in-law, Jacob Beltane, Tristan's twin, in Silver Lake.

"Any news? What's happening? If you happen to have heard, or overheard, any scrap of—"

"There was a message here on the tape from the Cahuenga cabala woman, Astarte, when we got in. I wrote it down . . . here. 'You have the potential to achieve a great deal this month. A pet scheme can be carried out through friendly per-

suasion. Lucky letter, S.' Hermosa, no? About your husband—
you've probably been wondering."

"I don't want to make noises like an imploring wife. The
thing is, I've been reporting to him anyway since morning—
like doing an analysis. I wondered the girl hawkeye doing this
Aosdána documentary on the picture might detect a serious
disturbance, but decided after all she'd be more likely to credit
the rapid-fire lip movement to exemplary industry, or California meditation."

"I think he got your message. We were down at the beach,
asleep, as you probably realized when you flashed it, and it
so happened I was getting some of it, then static. So I interrupted him in the middle of the night. He's on his way."

"Where?"

"There."

"Here?"

"There. He's bringing the new song—called 'Run Around
the Reservoir.' Perhaps I needn't tell you that in your absence,
he's commandeered somebody else to run around the reservoir
with him."

"You."

"Myself. It's not my stuff, although I did sort of miss it this
morning. Now it's my turn; how is my friend?"

"Well, he's—well, you certainly can tell he's back home in
Ireland."

"You certainly can—especially if you're me between last
night and this morning."

"Don't talk to me, as they say here. Eretz Eireann is what
he calls it—Ireland—but you probably—I'm jabbering on."

"It is your dime, and anyway, as usual, I much prefer to
listen."

"About the shoot? It is that I was calling home to talk
about."

"Talk. You know how I love the first day of principal photography."

"Well, your friend does, doesn't he, have the habit of throwing the protagonist in at the deep end of the scene. Remember, she kidnaps the children, not because of the famous insult, on the Hill of Howth, to the great tradition of Irish hospitality, but because she wants to lure the father away to the West. 'Yes, I will, yes,' Orphrey keeps repeating, but as the O'Maurigan knows, I prefer, as determination articulated, the West herself—'You can be had.'

"The children, meanwhile, are very worried—or at any rate your godson is—that the story is being recorded out of sequence. 'Good training in memory,' the O' advises him. 'Makes you real-*ize* that the next thing that's going to happen in your head is going to be something that's already happened you're remembering. So if we're not shooting until next week something that happens in the script in the beginning—' whereupon your goddaughter pulled him by the sleeve and said, 'Don't stir, Uncle Dee—would y' mind? Stirrin' makes me nervous.'

"We're in the middle of the tarot card game sequence. He plans to use up the light and then corrugate moompix time to telescope the action of the father's pursuit, y'see. I know now, finally, from within, what grand opera is: the chorus in the rigging doing chanteys in Gaelic; the hundreds of dress extras behaving all over the cliffs and the strand; the wind machine; the conductor. Not to confuse the last two, but this time Orphrey really—'Does he have to wave his arms around the place like that all the time?' your goddaughter whispered to me. 'Sssh,' I whispered back through the teeth of that old standby Irene Dunne smile, the one out of *The Awful Truth* your friend is always charging me with, the one I'm flashing right this minute at the Aosdána girl videotaping us at our labors. Anyway, Herself does the seven-card Star spread and pulls—I pulled the Queen of Pentacles. Conscious Desires, remember? 'A woman who takes great pride and pleasure in sensual comforts,' blah, blah, blah, blah, and all the rest of it. No disrespect to this script, and anyway 'blah, blah, blah, blah' is a good voice warmup. 'Blah, blah, blah,' until the girl child points to and overturns the Knight of Wands, Unconscious Desires, the handsome, daring young man astride a splendid silver steed, carrying a quiver of arrows, startling her—me—the White Sea Horse. 'Our sire!' she cries. 'Our sire sits a mount that flies! On his winged steed he will pursue!' To which Granuaile, remember, turning her gaze out onto the Atlantic, replies—and here comes the brogue, or, as your friend does insist, 'That's not a brogue, my dear, that's a lilt.' 'I have seen these winged steeds. I have seen them charging, white, in the foaming crests of the waves, in the clouds unfurling in the West. I am called the White Sea Horse. I know these myths; I am one!' How's it all sound?"

"It sounds—don't tell them this, but you've just brought back radio drama. If you can still do that horse whinny you taught us backstage on Manitoy a hundred years ago, and if you can get ahold of that wind machine, a clopper, and a mallet, there'll be no need to put the thing up on the screen at all. We can all just sit around in circles in the dark the world over, hold hands, and be swept away. Meanwhile, speaking of sound effects, you can probably hear there's somebody terribly determined on call harrowing. Possibly some handsome, daring—who's looking to run around the—can I put you on hold? Perhaps you'd like to work up another scene."

"No," said Kaye Wayfaring. "Tell you what, call you later, as soon as—"

"He arrives—just like in the picture—to recapture his children."

"I thought of that. Isn't erotic life just—"

"Isn't it a riot; isn't it a scream? Whoever this is better have a winged horse—or a very different story. Bye."

Young Master Tristan Beltane was looking past Mairead Shortt, videorecording him, at his mother, talking on the telephone again (she was looking, it seemed to him, all the way across the Atlantic), reiterating the words he was to—Orphrey Whither said "declaim"—in a few minutes in the next scene, and all the while wondering how she kept her concentration. He wondered to whom she was talking now, wondered how well Mairead Shortt understood the terms of the California Celebrity Protection Rights Act, and wondered then, looking up (because he had been advised by his director to connect the text with something happening just then in the silent thought pictures of 1988—"What does he want?"), would he be able to see the airplane his father was flying in over the North Pole descending in the west to Shannon?

"I want to thank you for the card," Kaye Wayfaring said to her younger poet friend. "It's put me in a reflective and confessional mood, conducive to heavy give. Thanks for holding the mirror up to my nature."

"Don't mention it, except to *The Irish Times*. Confessional? How invigorating to be assured one's vatic functions—function. Happen there's a career in it. Subsidized travel to museums, monuments, and places of worship the world over, plus a living wage. One might spend years—one might spend a life—globetrotting, perpetually invoking, perpetually on the get for just those postcards. Things like Christ's feet off the Via Appia, and the Mouth of Truth in Santa Maria in Cosmedìn. It could be a new kind of location scouting, a new wrinkle in oracular propagation: information—"

"Talking mouth, yours is in great working order."

"That's because there's nobody here just at the moment to throw the cloth over my cage."

"Listen, Astarte says my lucky letter of the week is S."

"For what?"

"Could be for Skip?"

"Hold that thought. Maybe it's for sex—or maybe skip sex."

"Don't talk to me. But isn't it coincidental that the script—uh-oh, the scene bell."

The falling light, partitioned into oblique footlighting, elapsed the narrative time. They resumed, dovetailing the action with the repetition of Granuaile's declaration.

"I know these myths: I am one—"

Unbidden, Christopher, *tawaiste* of the earl of Howth, overturned the card in the seventh position in the Star, "the Top of the Matter," revealing the Chariot. Young Tristan Beltane took a deep breath and launched into his declamation.

"Our sire's no myth. He is a ferocious warrior, more notorious than yourself. He commands retainers and their chariots that seem to fly, leading them in his own, drawn by two stallions. One roan Rage by name, one speckled argent called Laughter. Rage rears north toward the Kingdom of the Red Oak; Laughter rears west, toward his home above the Silver Strand. Together they will lead our sire's cavalry, thundering across the plains of Meath, beyond the rising of the Shannon, here to the shores of the Western Sea, indeed, to the very cliffs! Look you draw the center card—for wasn't I born with the science of this chase in me? Call yourself Pirate Queen of Iar Connacht; call yourself Queen of Pentacles, Swords, Cups, and Wands together. Call yourself Empress of the Western Isles, High Seer of the Sea of Dreams. You are but what you are the same, a Gypsy woman with no lasting home on

Eireann's sod. In days to come a song will tell the generations of your craggy nest of stones."

They heard the helmsman's chantey high above them in the rigging:

> *A gray old tower by storms and sea-wave beat,*
> *Perched on a cliff of yore, a fit retreat*
> *For pirates' galleys. Now you nought will meet*
> *But the sea and the wild gull. . . . And beneath*
> *Yawns wide a cave. . . . A hundred steps lead your feet*
> *Upward unto a lonely chamber. Bold, fleet*
> *And brave is he who climbs that stair to greet—*

"You have no devotion to the hearth," the young lord continued, "no children but are raised only to hang upon a scaffold. Unfortunate, intemperate, desperate queen, look now to the Heart of the Matter!"

Kaye Wayfaring, stunned nearly to distraction from her immediate scene goal by the fluent vehemence of her actor son's delivery, reining in, regained herself in Granuaile and turned over the card in the Major Arcana called the Lovers.

"As you come to study the Lovers in more detail," she had read, in preparation for the role, "bear in mind what the previous exercises concerning mother and father have revealed. Try to connect your own romantic choices with your experience of—"

"I'd rather tackle this one from the outside in," she'd announced during rehearsals. "You're obviously angling here for Garbo's omniscience at the fade-out of *Queen Christina*, coupled with Crawford's stupor at the climax of *Humoresque*."

"What about Wayfaring's own—"

"Taco sauce? There's no such brand; at least not yet. You'll have to be content to go with this until such time—"

Negative way. There was no way I was between that time and this about to bear in mind, with the children life-cast as the children, mine, the previous exercise concerning—my experience—connecting my own romantic choices—

Soaring? Spitfire?

Sluttish? Serene?

("You're not serene, you're depressed," she'd been advised, often enough, in Emotional Recall.)

So I'll do this . . . ought to be enough for anybody.

"I couldn't get it," Mairead Shortt said later into the phone at the roadside call box to a crony back in Dublin. "The best feckin' stuff of the afternoon, and I couldn't have it; it wasn't mine, it was Orphrey Whither's. The poundin' waves, the startled lust: Wayfaring going flappin'-bat-wing, barkin' demented in an instant, right before everybody's eyes, without movin' a muscle. God only knows what she'd invoked; if she'd spewed shamrock green, I'd not have been more devas-*ta*ted."

"I look," Mawrdew Czgowchwz declared, as she unbuckled her seat belt and let herself out of the sedan rental, "like something dragged through the hedge backwards. Ten years older than Jesus, creasing *pli selon pli*, like She. I noticed it in the rearview mirror coming across Roscommon. Now I've just had a gaze into this," she said, displaying an open mirrored face compact. "Same info."

"Every day we live," said Jameson O'Maurigan, "both lengthens and shortens our lives. Your grandson would tell you that you'd been looking into your crying glass."

"Or else yesterday lengthened them and today shortens—anyway, it started out that way this morning, at Dolphin's Barn, when I picked this motor up. 'Wouldn't you'd be Mardagh Gorgeous,' asks your man, 'in her later years?' After that I murmured—to myself, sole passenger—what Neri murmured towards the end: 'I've been everything, and what's the use!' I had the windows down and the sun roof open the whole way, so. A spell's been cast—there was never such sun in Ireland. Is it real, or is it himself F.X.?"

"We are, in fact," said Jameson, "expecting a late shower. Orphrey's with the unit, still, over at Malin Beg, shooting a cover sunset, and insists on a rainbow, arching from behind the cliff onto the ship's deck, to close out the card scene."

"He's kept the children with him," said Kaye Wayfaring.

"We've just been wondering how far he'd go—"

"There was a time," Mawrdew Czgowchwz replied, looking toward the sunset, "in the annals of Orphrey Whither's rarified esthetic lust—but the question that answers itself these days is what is the Atlantic esthetic *for*, now we no longer sail in boats across it? Only to appear as a leading player—alongside the Pacific—in Orphrey Whither's films. In the light—rainbows and all included—of that revelation, what fright can there be in us? We are like the lemmings to the cliffs, all right, but Orphrey Whither and Hyperion Pictures have us so strung—and so heavily insured—that not a foot shall dash upon a rock, not a toe shall stub a pebble.

"I've had nobody to talk to all afternoon, y'see—nor a bite since the Mullingar pub lunch: and since when is prawns and cress on a plate a meal? There wouldn't be such a thing would there as a cooked tea available in the parish?"

As the remnants of the tea were being cleared, Mawrdew Czgowchwz sat discussing the palavers she had been delegated to participate in with the Baile Atha Cliath Millennium Committee, concerning Hyperion Pictures' participation in the capital's one-thousandth birthday party, set for early in July.

" 'What we'd loike is . . . What we'd loike is . . .'—they kept on saying that. Finally I advised them, 'What you'd like and what you're likely to get is two very different stories.' "

"The one shot through the other," said Jameson O'Maurigan. "On the bias, subplot-like."

"For example," said Mawrdew Czgowchwz, "I did volunteer the opinion that I considered it just possible that Mr. Whither, and Hyperion Pictures—in the light of the many past, present, and likely future cordialities obtaining variously between and among themselves, the Dublin Corporation, and the city council, not least in the long-standing friendship between himself, themselves, and herself the Lord Mayor— and leaving aside the ancient, best forgotten thwarts to *Pilgrim Soul*—would see their way clear as indicated in the leak to *The Irish Times* to the participation of the company and its vessel in an appropriate way in the Millennium Liffey Sail, but that I frankly did not, myself, envision, in the light of my knowledge of and profound respect for her method of work, Miss Wayfaring's sailing, herself, up the river, in the prow of the vessel, in the character of Granuaile, a Notorious Woman."

"No policy in the industry would cover it," Kaye Wayfaring declared.

" 'As to the likelihood,' I said to them, 'of Miss Wayfaring's appearing, while shooting *The White Sea Horse* for Hyperion, with Rock Formation in the Phoenix Park—' "

"I'll do it in a shot, if he lets me; like a subplot, on the bias."

"Remember Eden, before the Fall," the O'Maurigan wondered, "when we did as we liked, one and all?"

"Not remotely," Kaye Wayfaring rejoined. "What I remember is *East of Eden*, at the Paradise Mountain Drive-in, in the summer of 'fifty-four."

"Thanking you. And would you care to tell us what else— anything else at all—you remember about that summer, Miss Wayfaring?"

"I might."

"Some snowy night in front of the fire."

"Thank you," said Kaye Wayfaring to Mawrdew Czgowchwz, "for negotiating with the front office."

"Not at all, it's all bound to—and look: here comes the magus with his hostages."

"And how," Mawrdew Czgowchwz asked Orphrey Whither, "did the sunset go?"

"In a word," the O'Maurigan whispered confidingly to Kaye Wayfaring, "down."

"In the light of the setting sun," Orphrey Whither sighed (while Mairead Shortt aimed her camcorder past him out the window at the station island across the narrow inlet, over which the last few streaks of alizarin orange gleamed in the last sky of Europe), "men either beat the pot and sing, or loudly bewail the approach of old age."

" 'If music could boil the pot.' Didn't they always used to caution that in County Mayo?" asked Mawrdew Czgowchwz.

"Damn the fools of County Mayo-God-help-us," said Jameson O'Maurigan. "Men ten thousand years older than Jesus, dragged through the hedges backwards, who view it all through glasses darkly. Bad cess to them."

"Men in sunglasses, like in California?" wondered young Tristan Beltane. "Do we get tea—and cookies?"

"It's not like California here," Maev Beltane protested, "it's different! I prefer it."

"How can one wish," Orphrey Whither continued, "to hold for long the light of the setting sun?"

"Anyway," said the O'Maurigan, "what you want and what you'll get is always two fundamentally different stories."

"Of course you may have cookies," Mawrdew Czgowchwz assured her grandchildren. "I've organized the cookies—come here to me and get this."

"Not, apparently, in Donegal," Kaye Wayfaring said to the O'Maurigan.

"They're rune cookies," Mawrdew Czgowchwz announced. "Here's how you arrange them."

Rune cookies. Whatever happened to animal crackers? Extinct. Mutatis mutandis.

Mawrdew Czgowchwz set out the cookies, made of flour, sugar, lard, and milk, in five rows on a plate, telling their insignia.

"The Self, Partnership, Signals, Separation, Strength; Initiation, Constraint, Fertility, Defense, Protection; Possessions, Joy, Harvest, Opening, Warrior; Growth, Movement, Flow, Disruption, Journey; Gateway, Breakthrough, Standstill, Wholeness, the Unknowable: he's blank."

"Where's Getaway—can I have Getaway?" Tristan asked.

"Not 'Getaway'—Gateway," Maev corrected. "This one, right, Grandma? Looks like a nose."

("He always bites the nose off the elephant." "It isn't a nose, moron; it's a trunk! Elephants don't have noses. Here, go bite the nose off this: it's a girl baboon!" Funny the things you—they're so much better, kinder, to one another than we ever were.)

"Yes, that's right," said Mawrdew Czgowchwz, "Gateway. The game works better—it's more fun—if you choose at random, by the signs."

"Then I'll take the arrow—and the bow tie, both."

"All right, that's Warrior and Breakthrough for you. And you, miss?"

"I'd like the M, please, and the B; they're my initials."

"That's Movement and Growth. Now we're getting somewhere. Let's pass the plate around, so, shall we?"

What is this, propaganda? "I've lived too long," my mother would say in a situation like this. She meant each time a new—the threat. She killed herself. Or is that "So, she killed herself"? Was it only and ever the difference—between what she wanted and what she got: the two fundamentally different stories? When something new—the reminder?

"Mother, have a cookie."

"What?"

"Pick one!"

"Oh, all right. Give me—um—that one, with the S on it."

Steadfast? Sentimental?

"You may have two."

"No, just one, thanks."

"What does it mean, Grandmother? What does the S stand for?"

"It stands for Wholeness, the Sum."

"Better not break it in pieces, then," declared Tristan.

"Grandmother, we do get to eat these things, don't we?"

"We do—as soon as they're all distributed."

"And what about the stories that go with them?" asked Maev.

"The stories," Mawrdew Czgowchwz replied, "will be made intelligible in dreams. Stories to be swapped around tomorrow evening's fire, or perhaps sooner, in the tiresome intervals—or refreshment breaks—between filming successive scenes of *The White Sea Horse.*"

"In the interests of which enterprise," Orphrey Whither declared, as the cookie plate was passed to him, "I choose the single significant morsel scored Journey."

"Mr. Whither's played this game before," said the O'Maurigan to Tristan and Maev.

"About these stories," Maev questioned, "couldn't we keep them to ourselves?"

"You could," Mawrdew Czgowchwz replied. "You could, so. There has ever been kept, even among the busy and the driven, an honored place for the contemplative."

"Two for me, please," the O'Maurigan requested. "The fella called Signals and his great pal Possessions."

"Scrutiny," Mawrdew Czgowchwz continued, "being as it is even for the professed performer—Miss Shortt?" she asked, passing the plate from Jameson to Hyperion's guest.

"Oh, I don't know—that one, with the X on it. It might reveal buried treasure."

"Partnership. Presents from the gods—or from chiefs to loyal followers. Lovely choice. Tea all around?"

"Which cookies are you taking, Grandmother?" Tristan asked.

"Let's see, I usually pick with my eyes closed."

"Can you see with your eyes closed?" inquired Maev.

"Well, no, I can't," Mawrdew Czgowchwz replied, closing her eyes and reaching toward the plate. "Tell you what—you pick for me."

"Me too!" Tristan insisted.

"Of course you too. Come on then, both—let's not make a high mass of it."

(Now she tells them. Double message. What the hell. Saves time.)

"Here, Grandmother."

"Thank you. Hm. Constraint and Defense. I hope I can get to sleep tonight after this picnic."

"Grandmother, what happens to leftovers?" asked Tristan.

"Tomorrow's tea," Mawrdew Czgowchwz replied, "and another whole array of propositions for dreaming. Then, at the weekend, as I'm the one on holiday, I shall engineer another batch, and we'll begin again—that time, perhaps, with all eyes closed."

"Better engineer two batches at least," Jameson interposed. "The O'Dolmens and the McBurrens are stopping over. They're on holiday in the vicinity, inspecting sites."

"The who?"

"You don't know them? Des and Fidelma O'Dolmen, of Galway; Rosc and Aosdana McBurren, of Clare. The brother and the sister married to the brother and the sister, or vice versa. Masses of offspring among them, all the same ages, crosshatched. They are the ultimate Irish Family Romance.

Let's see, there's Emer and Eoin, the twins; then there's little Dessie and little Rosc, little Fidelma—Fiddles, she's called—and little Aosdana. Then there's Ardara, Moya, Nuala, Fintan, Finbar—"

"Who are these people, and why ever are they stopping here?" Orphrey Whither thundered. "It's out of the question!"

"I have an idea," Mawrdew Czgowchwz whispered to the O'Maurigan, "you're making this up—to terrify people."

"People ought to be terrified," he whispered back, dunking Possessions in his tea. "The sun has set. It may shine again tomorrow, or if not, and we're deluged, or turned Welsh, we shall all be left alone, with our fundamentally different stories, lusting, contemplative."

Allowing Orphrey Whither to construe for her children the scope, thrust, and drift of the term "radios of experience," Kaye Wayfaring joined Mawrdew Czgowchwz for a walk out under the stars.

"See how the sky looks at dawn," she said, "at midday; at midnight. That was exercise number twenty-two, the shortest one in the book—and the longest."

"Like 'Love God, and do what you will,' " said Mawrdew Czgowchwz, looking up at the heavens. "Or, perhaps more like"—and she mimicked to perfection the bruised soprano of the Polish comedienne Lyda Roberti—" 'Peck a number from vun to tan; dobble it and edd a meyllion—' "

"Exactly!" exclaimed Kaye Wayfaring, looking up. "That. Coming down the mezzanine staircase singing that, sheathed in bias-cut backless black satin covered with as many silver sequins as—what were those lyrics Orphrey was bullfrogging that night in Laguna, about the stars? Astarte quoted them in her book."

"Gieroglifici eterni!" Mawrdew Czgowchwz suddenly erupted into the night, in her sepulchral contralto.

> *"Che in ciffre luminose ogn'or splendete—*
> *Ah! ch'alla mente umana*
> *Altro che belle oscurità non siete!*

Truer words, as the usher said, you don't hear on Sunday."

"They've always been just that, hieroglyphics to me," Kaye Wayfaring admitted. "I can pick out the Big Dipper, and that's about it—that's how the sky looks to me at midnight."

"In the West of Ireland," Mawrdew Czgowchwz replied, "the Big Dipper—there it is—is called King David's Wain."

"King David was a singer, wasn't he—apart from everything else?"

"He's pictured as such in certain stained-glass windows. Apart from everything else."

" 'An expression,' my father used to say. 'Ah reckanize an expreshun when Ah heah wun,' my mother would fire back. 'Wut Ah wannuh know is, whut is it an expreshun *uv*?' I was thinking earlier of what happened when she found out, and what happened as a result when he got home. Not much has changed; now it's when you find out, when I tell you, and soon it will be when—"

" 'Only two topics can be of the least interest,' Yeats wrote, 'to a serious and studious mind—sex and the dead.' "

" 'Apart from everything else' was a pet expression with us at school. 'Play that scene from *Apart from Everything Else,*' we'd say, 'where she's left at the altar.' I was thinking when you said the Big Dipper was King David's Wain: we start the chariot scene tomorrow. 'Thundering across the plains of Meath.' The sire. When he gets home—my husband, the singer."

"You're a singer."

"Oh, no I'm not. He's the—you're the—I'm—well, let's not get into name calling. If that's the chariot," she continued, looking up, "then where's King David?"

"The singer? Well, he wouldn't be pictured. It's rather like—if we were to hear the plane your husband—and look up now and see the lights, we wouldn't expect to see him—well, you might, after all, the way you do your exercises."

"I would want to—I certainly am in the mood to."

"Well, you see, the Irish wouldn't figure their saints in the apparent stars. They wouldn't station them in First Heaven—they'd shoo them on up to Seventh. It isn't the stars in the roles here, if you like, but the stars in their vehicles—or rather, vice versa, the vehicles figured in the stars. Vehicles and implements: such as the plow in the stars, the old flag of the Republic, yet another name for the dipper. To put the saints or the heroes in the stars would be Greek, or Roman—it would be idolatrous."

"Like lust—the mood."

"I don't understand that."

"The mood and the scene. The vehicle conveys the scene, you see. Those constellated personnel of antiquity, both the fortunate and the unfortunate—like Cassiopeia, like Phaëton—convey only the mood. Something like that."

Kaye Wayfaring looked up again at the constellations. "If you were going to chart a character among them, from the famous radius of your experience, where would you stick the compass? Orphrey would probably have an answer ready—something like 'the possibilities are infinite.' "

" 'Only infinite,' " Mawrdew Czgowchwz corrected, mimicking Orphrey Whither. She continued, in her own speaking voice. " 'If the universe is infinite, and uniformly sprinkled with stars, then there should be no night.' "

"Is that Irish? Did some Irishman say that?"

"No, some German."

"Thank God. It sounds like the argument for another Orphrey Whither lighting scheme."

"You mentioned Phaëton—you're not worried, are you?"

"You know," Kaye Wayfaring admitted, a little worriedly, "when I asked your son, my husband, the singer, when he'd fallen in love with me, he said, 'It was in *Way Station*, when you shot the evangelist dead. I knew you didn't mean to do it. I knew she did mean to, and I could see you show that, but I knew you didn't. All you meant to do was—' "

"Play the scene," said Mawrdew Czgowchwz, looking up.

" 'I loved the part,' I assured him, as if—what? 'It was some part,' he said, as if reprimanding—'but it's not you.' I wondered, Does he want to marry an actor?"

"He certainly must have, because you didn't want to marry *him*."

"No, I certainly didn't. Now it can be told, huh?"

"It was told then—when you told him."

"That was the mood I was in; what a close call. No, I'm not worried. I'm not—really not—a femme fatale."

The stories will be made intelligible in dreams. Who can sleep? "Love is a beast you feed all through the night," said Garbo, in *Romance*. With rune cookies.

When we ran around the reservoirs, in Silver Lake and Central Park, we'd start in opposite directions and, I don't know, pretend, or something, to be meeting cute passing one another. Sometimes a tree would loom up as I'd be running, and I'd say to myself, Yesterday I met him passing here, now where—and there he'd be, looming, on the circumference. Passing, he'd say something—"Shazam" or something. Later, he said about the reservoirs: "Don't you ever want to break through the fences and dive in, just the two of us?" I think maybe the reservoirs are what love is—just there, fenced around, protected from us, for us, something.

In her dream she was the ship's figurehead, affixed face-down, looking at the fabric of the Liffey rip as they sailed into Dublin harbor escorted by the Spanish Armada. She could hear them all on deck, clearly make out their agitated declarations. Her twins, experts in demarcation and native to the place, were enumerating points of interest for the benefit of the O'Dolmen and McBurren offspring. "That's the Statue of Liberty on your left, and there on your right the Brooklyn Bridge." Straining her peripheral vision, she could just make out, in the place she reckoned Poolbeg Light ought to be, Mae West standing swathed in the tricolor of the Irish Republic, left hand on hip, right leg and pink-shod foot thrust forward, holding Liberty's torch in hand, aloft. On her right, swarming over the Brooklyn Bridge, from the Hill of Howth, the Lord Mayor and innumerable citizens of the capital, risen from the dead or dressed historically—and what's the difference anyway, she said to herself: they'll tell you anything, for as long a while as you'll listen to them.

Straining to hear, she caught details of negotiations on deck, among the adults, negotiations formalizing the nuptials, forthwith, of her children, one with an O'Dolmen and one with a McBurren, she couldn't make out which to which. "Yes, we prefer Ireland to California," Maev and Tristan were saying, in forced, stilted readings, as the brigantine approached O'Connell Bridge and landing ropes were thrown down to the quays, "and mean to make our lives here. Mr. Whither is giving us away."

The gangplank was thrown down, and the party on board disembarked, caught up in the millennial parade, which then wound up the hill toward the Liberties and Christ Church, all the while Mairead Shortt, behind an immense Panaflex, kept calling out "More light! More light!" as the sky clouded over.

There was nothing Kaye Wayfaring, stationary, affixed to the brig's prow, could do to prevent what was going to happen happening; neither the O'Maurigan nor Mawrdew Czgowchwz, both in attendance, in spectacular bejeweled Elizabethan getups, seemed alarmed.

As the procession snaked up Parliament Hill, under a canopy of artificial sunlight, and the quayside was drenched in rain, she saw the best boy, Declan, descend from O'Connell Bridge. Fanning the tarot deck in great anguish, he sat down on a wet step, turned a card, looked at it, then up at her. "There you are, with the rain rollin' down the alabaster face on you, weepin' like, and I can't read these runes at all. What'll we *do*?"

The sound of car wheels on the wet gravel driveway tore through the fabric of sleep.

Is that—yes, here he comes. Shazam.

Ensenada

OUTSIDE UNION STATION, Kaye Wayfaring decided to leave Plácido with the Bentley. He refused.

"You'll take a *bus*! You know what Mae West said about a nun getting on a bus? Same goes for you—exactly."

"But Plácido, Mae West said a nun gives her whole life to God; I don't do that at all."

"You give the best part of your life to the only religion that still works wonders. That's good enough for me—*para mí es el mismo. Claro?* No bus."

She knew she could take a bus up Sunset to Hyperion, get out and walk to Wayfaring at Waverly in Silver Lake unrecognized: that she was possessed of the ability Norma Jean had—had Norma Jean in fact, making her up, taught her how?—to disappear as herself. Schizophrenic? A question like religion. Just a very good actress—as Norma Jean, when she was Marilyn, was.

"Your husband told me I should look after you; you're a lost lamb in a jungle."

"Plácido, that's a line from a *movie*."

"I know the line—and the movie. *Variety* says it's playing to packed houses in New York right now. Also in the same issue of *Spin* where Rock Formation got put on the Twenty-five Best Albums of All Time list with *Womanly Girl*, and you made the Hundred Greatest Singles list? It got on the Twenty Coolest Movies list. Didn't I say 'religion'? Now you want an argument? What your husband told me, that's like 'deliver us from evil'—so just call me El Buen Pastor—that's the Good Shepherd."

"I know. He lays down his life for his sheep—but despite my performance in 'Ensenada,' and unlike the Cobra Woman, I don't covet men's lives. And I do trust you. El Buen Pastor would have told me before release if 'Ensenada' was insulting to Mexico, yes?"

"*Claro.* No way insulting—and you sound good when you say, 'No sé, lo conseguí en Ensenada.' But now you're you again; you need major down time, Miss Wayfaring."

They compromised; she took a long walk downtown, while he followed her at a slow crawl in the Bentley—past City Hall, the library, Pershing Square, and the Biltmore.

She'd come upon the placards at Pershing Square.

The Scene Machine Presents

DAY OF THE DEAD BALL

featuring exclusive engagement from San Francisco

"DEAD MARILYN . . . 30 YEARS OF TEARS"

Shaken, she hurried along into the concrete canyons of downtown Los Angeles, stopping at Seventh and Grand to look in the windows of the J. W. Robinson Company. She stood there, clearing her eyes, thinking how one of the mannequins resembled Norma Jean (was something going *on*? likely not, outside her head), then walked on until she reached the Clifton Cafeteria, on Second and Olive.

She sat at a window table, having coffee, watching passersby (there was Plácido in the Bentley, circling the block), thinking of the girl in Hopper's *Automat* and of the character she'd created in Rock Formation's current smash, "Ensenada."

("I'm not playing any more lost girls," she'd insisted, barely a half hour earlier, at Union Station, just before the train carrying her husband and his twin back east pulled out. "This dame in 'Ensenada' is my last."

"We don't think of her as lost—only driven."

"She is a witch."

"I married a witch," Tristan Beltane replied, smiling. "My mother married a witch, and I've done exactly the same.")

I'm not really a witch, Kaye Wayfaring thought. True, I did once run away to the Southern Spiritualists' Walpurgis Night Camp Meeting in Cassadaga, Florida, to try to get hold of my brother, Jack—bolted, something like their driven woman does in "Ensenada." But if he thinks . . .

Now I'm remembering Norma Jean telling me about Phyllis Dietrichson in *Double Indemnity*, and making me up to look bad, saying she couldn't wait to play somebody as bad as that—really bad. I'm thinking now of her—Marilyn—in *Niagara*—and of me in *Way Station*. Bad girls got it in the gut back then . . . now they only go crazy, like I did in *Avenged*, or even get away with it. I think this one in "Ensenada" gets away—but in a video, how can you *tell*?

Looking out disconsolately at downtown Los Angeles, she recalled the brightly painted shop facades of Clifton, in Connemara, a world away—pictured the vivid posters in the windows, advertising amateur theatricals, sessions of traditional Irish music, and walking trips through the flowering, wild Atlantic verge.

"Should I take the Hollywood Freeway," Plácido asked, "and double back through Los Feliz, take the Golden State and double back on Glendale, or go surface . . . Sunset to Hyperion?"

"Oh, go surface, I suppose . . . Sunset straight to Hyperion."

"You looked funny sitting in there—in that window in that place. Not like yourself at all. Just like that lost lamb."

"Strong direction—and Plácido, would you flick on the radio, please?"

As she sat back, the zesty voice of KBYZ took over.

"Don't touch that *dial*—it's time for KBYZ's *Radio Ga Ga!*"

(What ever happened, Kaye Wayfaring wondered, to Oxydol's own Ma Perkins?)

"They have already started dressing up for Halloween on the West Side. In Santa Monica, at the Bonzoburger stand, we found the Pacific Palisades Animalibertarian Alliance pickets chorus line, dressed as sheep. One woman—a woman you'd recognize, who prefers to remain in this cause anonymous: it is, she maintained, principles here above personalities—is dressed as a cow, carrying a cross. From the crossbar hang plastic re-creations of grills and roasts. They are chanting 'Dead meat . . . dead meat,' and are beginning as we withdraw to upset people."

(We know what happened to Helen Trent. She married Gil Whitney. In Mexico, at Honeymoon Hacienda, they walked out onto a balcony under a full moon. Sudden earthquake. Blackout.)

"And so we withdraw downtown, where, behind the hoardings in Pershing Square—former scene of so much squalor: seismic epicenter of old Los Angeles Nickel-Odeon despair—we encounter the personnel of San Francisco's Scene Machine—milling about between the statues of old Black Jack—who remembers when we used to win 'em singing, and hang out our washing on the Siegfried Line—and old forlorn beetle-browed Beethoven. (Beethoven is looking glad to be deaf, and as if he wouldn't mind a blindfold either. What does he know that we don't—or need we ask?—and is he telling us?) Rehearsing in bright sunshine some pretty macabre things, we think, for their performance tonight at the Park Plaza of *Dead Marilyn*. If 'rehearsing' is the word— because frankly what we have to say first off is that *either* this crowd is *actually* some kind of self-help group for adult casualties of attention deficit disorder, or they give to the word 'aimless' a new configuration . . . and you *know* how sensitive we are ourselves, particularly here on the West Side, to charges of pointlessness—as opposed, say, to the soubriquet 'random.' What they were doing looked to us pretty much like slam dancing on Thorazine up in old Camarillo—

" 'You only think they're freaky,' we are assured by the press agent, 'because they're rehearsing in sunlight. They're a little freaked themselves; we don't get much sunlight in San Francisco; we work in mist. When you see them tonight under light and with the Resuscitator Overlay, you'll get the whole point.' We took five to form an opinion . . . and, because you asked, here it is."

(Did Lamont Cranston ever tell Margo . . . what?)

"Some of the stuff they send down from the Bay Area, its silicon satellite burbs, and outposts like Redwood City, we endorse—and adapt. Other concepts—virtual reality, for instance—well . . . pending. Frankly, we're getting more than a little whiff of *po-mo* boodle. To the word, for instance, that Japanese consumers have already responded favorably to using VR goggles and glove systems to preview kitchen arrangements of Matsushita appliances—that's Matsushita, parent company of Universal Studios (er, *1941*, anybody?)—we say, 'Who says that means the industry—what with more sophisticated cybernetic F/X, with laser disc, with coming high-definition television and promises of more creative multicultural programming—has totally exhausted the possibilities of the feature release and the miniseries as definitive stress-free analgesics against sinusitis and the vasocontractor tension generated by logarithmic linearity and book-brain mind bondage?' Are we talking? Are *they* listening?

"Anyway, some of the stuff, yo—but to certain other ideas offloaded by the City of the Winding Mists we firmly say *'Include us out.'* Such as The Big One, for one; and for two, scenarios like *Dead Marilyn*, appearing tonight at the Park Plaza, direct from the Folsom. We call this bombinating negatively into Voidsville. We have a stunning Live Marilyn of our own right here in the City of the Angels. You've all seen her act: she jumps out of her limo at malls all over the West Side, her boom box playing the Fox fanfare. At gallery openings, premieres, and valet-parking-restaurant parties the guests thought were hush-hush. Even in the Valley. She is known to have made many forays into the Sherman Oaks Galleria in search of cosmetics, and has been sighted recently at kiddie matinees in Encino. (Informed rumor: she lives in a mobile home off Yolanda, in Tarzana.) We love her, and her idea of the year 2000 as the start of the Marilyn Millennium—say, you *do* get it. We love her the way we love all things truly positive, such as sunshine, navel oranges, drive-in car-shame therapy workshops, affirmative-supportive day-care centers for the child within . . . we could go on."

(What evil lurks in the hearts of men, of course. Miscreants on the lam, bombinating negatively into the void . . .)

"So really, go out trick-or-treating to your Halloweeny's content, and have a blast at whichever parade—Hollywood Boulevard or Santa Monica Boulevard, or both. But for ringing doorbells west of La Brea, a few ground rules. Beverly Hills Talking T's are back big time, especially the '84 Olympic originals; but for full rig-out, no Mommie Dearests, no Baby Janes, no Dead Marilyns, and—really—*no* mutilated Jimmy Deans! Ask yourself: Do I, simply to validate my nerve, need to risk putting myself through predawn roundup and interrogation by the Rites-of-Passage-and-Ritual-Abuse Task Force?"

(And what was the address on Wistful Vista?)

"And remember, tricksters, you won't boff in the treat yield unless you tell them *how you got there*, dig? We didn't just *arrive* in paradise; there was a *purpose*—maybe even a *destiny*.

"And this is why, when we tell where we've come from on any given occasion, we *always* tell *how we got there*.

"And every time we talk about our route, enumerating the names of our highways and byways, our thruways, boulevards, streets, drives and avenues, we *resonate* with *purpose.* Automotive and directive purpose, dig? Remember, *how you got there says who you are today!* You heard it here."

(4711? No.)

"So, here from *Radio Ga-Ga* is your Guide to Trick-or-Treating, West Side style."

(Sound of a doorbell:) *Ring*

VOICE ON THE INTERCOM: Who *is* it?

VOICE OF TRICK-OR-TREATERS: *Trick or treat!*

SOUND OF INTERCOM BUZZER: *Bzzz*

VOICE: Well, *hi!* C'mon—*in!* How'd you *ever get here*?

POLYPHONIC CHORUS:

We took Letitia to Glenhiccup to Glen Gould to Bellinzona . . . then Bellhop to Alka-Seltzer . . .	*We* took Califia to Lalapalooza to Sunstroke . . . then Taco to Scaramouche . . .	We took Sepulchre through Mantrap Canyon then Flight Deck Lomotil and Travesty.

(Why does this make me think *only* of driving through Topanga Canyon at 110 MPH with a tail wind? Of how in Clayton, according to Mother, I'd be playing at some nonsense and the next minute be tearing someone's hair out . . . what is it O'Maurigan and the Irish always say? *Eating the face off him.*

Why is this litany so . . . Everybody who comes to Los Angeles—everybody except New Yorkers masking their anxieties by calling themselves bicoastal—seems to comes from somewhere so far away that the story of their arrival and the stops they made along the route are crucial to the upkeep of their self-image.)

Melo . . . Paso	Ex-Lax . . .	Vigilante . . .
Doble . . .	Alimony . . .	Varathane . . .
Avalanche . . .	Focaccia . . .	Vacuum . . .
Inkwell.	Albatross.	Vendetta.

(Anybody who thinks like Cherie did in *Bus Stop* that they're going in one straight line is likely if not certain to wind up in Montana—with or without their one true love. Norma Jean certainly knew that.)

"We came through the Valley on Vendetta to Varathane, then, up Vacuum to Vigilante. . . ."

(People who come to New York cover their tracks. You'd hear them in bars saying where they came from—mostly made up—but never telling how they got there. Nobody has time to listen in New York, even to themselves; they're on the crowded subway trying to figure out the route. But in Los Angeles, alone in the mobile bubble, you have nothing but time. You can either go in for channeling—if you're on your way to your psychic or your massage—back to when you were somebody else, or you can review your case again on your way to group encounter. So you get into word games based on street names. . . . That song Steve Carey taught me, that Doby and his cronies in the Ford gang loved singing.

Three girls down on Fountain,
Each one brings me happiness—
Three girls that I'm mountin'
Down on Fountain and Van Ness . . .

"*That* I'm mountin'," of course.

It's always three. Why so? Three wishes, the three fates. Three sheets to the wind. Three men on a horse, the Trinity. That dirty joke I didn't get and couldn't get explained in Clayton. What are the three main parts of a stove? *Lifter, leg,* and *poker.*)

"And *now what?* This. Nostradamus is back. Remember him? No, not Orson Welles in *Black Magic;* that was Cagliostro. Right church, wrong drive-in window. Nostradamus, the French ventriloquist—who told Norma Shearer as Marie Antoinette . . . no, that's not right, either. Whatever. Nostradamus, whoever he was, said:

Sol vingt de Taurus si fort terre trembler
Le grand théâtre remply ruinerà,
L'air, ciel et terre obscurcir et troubler
Lors l'infidèle Dieu et saincts voguerà.

"*So?* So this. Announcement of discovery of new faults, that's what—from seventy-year-old maps. Under Wilshire Boulevard at the Hollywood Freeway intersection cloverleaf. Connecting with the Elysian Park fault. And there you have it. The biz in ruins, the troubled air turned darker still, and the unfaithful vogueing God and the saints. Well, we at *Radio Ga-Ga* always did feel—and did say—that vogueing was Big Earth Trouble. Who listened?

"The *only* excuse you have for staying on—with us—is you know all this has already come down. In *Day of the Locust,* the motion picture. In the burning of Los Angeles, in the looting of Frederick's of Hollywood, under Taurus, on April 29th, 1992."

(79 Wistful Vista. Fibber McGee and Molly had no children.)

"As for *Lost Angeles—mala noche.* From Malibu and Santa Monica down to Laguna, *adios,* Beach Boys. Catalina will survive.

"But *why* worry about all that *now?* Instead, in the spirit of both Live Forever and Live Today, KBYZ and *Radio Ga-Ga* salute Rock Formation and its Kaye Wayfaring—wherever they are, together or separately. And lately, with Miss Wayfaring warbling those solos with Democratic Presidential nominee and charts favorite Bill Clinton—Elvis, to his intimates . . . and have you ever seen them together, or lately? No innuendo, just checking. This *is* the late twentieth century—speaking-while-we're-talking of Fox—and what with cryonics and *very advanced plastic surgery.* Well, we know the Arkansan isn't Disney, anyway—not with *that* platform! Playing for your enjoyment the new Rock Formation mega-hit video title song, 'Ensenada'!

"Like it says in *Pollstar,* Biz-Zorros, with their crossover mix of skirt-edge Sunset Strip ersatz film noir, grand opera, Grand Ole Opry, and Fox musicals, Rock Formation with Kaye Wayfaring on vocals cannot miss on tour. What *Radio Ga-Ga* says is, '*Witch-girl,* what you have *done,* you have *mailed* this song!' "

"Plácido, if you wouldn't mind?"

"*Never* mind, Miss Wayfaring—here's the driveway."

At home, on Wayfaring at Waverly, in Silver Lake, she found a tape cassette from her twins, in New York (having decided after the spring riots to leave Los Angeles—afraid, they said, in unison, of turning into racial phobiacs. How would that—after everything she'd—she'd decided to *listen to what they were saying*. Environment can be fatal. And they'd chosen New York over the one-room school on Manitoy, where their father and uncle had been educated—and where they were returning, to vote—so something cosmopolitan certainly. . . . They'd entered the eighth grade at Friends and were living with their grandmother, Mawrdew Czgowchwz, in Gramercy Park. The girl, Maev, was best at grammar and geography, the boy, Tristan, at trigonometry and counterpoint, but they knew they could never tell any of their California friends about any of it. They'd be laughed at. "*Grammar? Trigonometry?* Who cares about *storing* information like *that*? That's what *computers* are for!"). The subject of the current missive was their adjustment to New York, as reflected in a discussion at the Meeting House on Stuyvesant Square about getting along with people of different backgrounds.

Listening, she marveled at the phenomenon that would soon pass—their sounding, boy and girl in early adolescence, almost exactly alike. (As had, she remembered, their grandparents, contralto and countertenor, the oltrani, who sang, nearly in another millennium, that modal descant and those French art songs. Where had the time . . . where would it—but what had *Radio Ga-Ga* advised? Live Forever—Live Today.)

"I suppose that proves," Tristan was saying, "Uncle Dee is right in insisting that of the three constituents of altercation, grammar, rhetoric, and logic, the one that's never trivial is rhetoric. Uncle Dee has a palatial mind. So, if—or as he says, 'if and when: this is New York'—some differently advantaged male from a neighborhood with fewer trees . . . and those mainly ailanthus—some ruffian, some pale and loitering dweebezoid Goth—you know, *un tipo suave*, chunky, but stunted, and not exactly verbal . . . consequence of attachment from birth to Joe Camels cut and rerolled with *really* good sin-semilla . . . if he calls your pet twin sister 'Retail Slutburger,' what do you do? Stuff his smelly Jack Purcell—"

MAEV: Converse All-Stars . . .

TRISTAN: Whatever. Stuff his grody—

MAEV: Barfogenic . . .

TRISTAN: Right—footwear down his clueless throat? (Being not the little guy in the grunge cap he took you for, but a chis-eled, coiled-spring male adolescent whose loose garments do not reveal the sinews you've been cultivating running around the reservoir in Silver Lake and doing laps in your Olympic pool in Laguna—routines you've continued in Central Park and at the Yale Club.) Or simply, suavely, trip him to the cement? (You're still up on the tai chi chuan you learned in Bronson Canyon: now you do it in front of the statue of Edwin Booth in Gramercy Park.) Placing one of your own Doc Martens air-cushion-sole Na-Na brogans athwart his neck, symbolistically, so as not to bruise the tendons? Or do you just stand there coolly dissing him in an ugly personal way? *Knowing* as you do he's never been west of the West Side Highway, and so has been put up to this seemingly ultra-cool Melrose Avenue putdown by some spineless sneak, likely female.

Get this: It turns out you do neither—in fact you do nada, unless you feel you must. Then what you do is, you use *verbal judo*. This *doesn't* mean you talk down to him. As one of the *ninth* graders put it, "*Condensation* doesn't go over big in New York." You do not say anything like, "Sis here is named for an extremely powerful Irish witch queen. If she *did* decide to pay you so much as a nanosec's attention—choosing to ignore the fact that you are undoubtedly that variety of New York abo-rigine who thinks a freeway is some kind of athletic scholar-ship to a trade school—that attention would definitely put you through multiple changes into a robotic trance. You would end up carrying her books home from school—and as you may have noticed, you don't even go to her school. If word of that got across town, you could find yourself at a severe disadvantage in your peer group." You do not say anything *like* that. Instead, out of your mouth comes something *reasonable*, like, "If my sister has hurt your feelings in some way, by walking past you without noticing you, it's probably because she was concentrating, for an important test, on her state capitals. Maybe you'd like to come with us to our grandmother's place for some hot chocolate and spend an hour discussing your feelings there . . . in the kitchen." Can you dig it?

I tried it out last week at school. In a contest to coin a new word to replace both "awesome" and "radical," which by consensus are now—as you said once about us two: you were angry—worse than one another. I proposed "fab-ine." Somebody said, "That sounds faggot, are you gay?" Notice the suave random shift: ugly to hip—this is New York. I said nothing at first—I didn't want to flex my wild Irish tongue, sensing this a test moment for a newcomer to the eighth grade—and come out with some dumb thing like, "No, but some of my best friends are," so I kept silent.

MAEV: Uncle Dee says, "Of that which we cannot speak we must perforce remain silent."

TRISTAN: Yeah, perforce. I thought of the Attracta joke too—about virginity—and I almost said, "Not yet." Instead I didn't say anything for a long while. . . . Then it came to me; so when the girl next to the guy asked me again—*"well?"*—I said, "I'm *thinking*, I'm *thinking*." It worked . . . it also made me think: it *was* like being asked for your money or your life, wasn't it—in a way? And while I was thinking, I realized I wasn't afraid . . . and since you took the trouble to schlepp us to the analyst practically as soon as we could talk, and we found out that anger is the flip side of fear, and vice versa, it turned out I wasn't angry either.

Speaking of footwear, the local place seems to be out of my particular item—you know, the abovementioned; they are definitely still my faves; they are most radically expo-random, but of course they have gotten a much more thoroughgoing workout in two months on the streets of mid- and downtown Manhattan than ever they got in the whole of the Greater Los Angeles area.

MAEV: That could be because he never takes them off.

TRISTAN: True. I never do remove them—except to change my socks; I do change my socks—tube, one size fits all—occasionally. And of course to put on my Rollerblade in-lines—50 MPH downhill, watch for sewage grating and hecklers, see above . . . not allowed in places of business or museums, avoid dancing—because this is what "having wheels" means in Manhattan, and roller hockey is *intensely* in. I was only wondering if, since you are coming back east after the elections for the big tour, and you might find yourself with a little extra time on your hands at the beach on Monday, could you possibly check out the Laguna store—or maybe, if you come home that way, the totally exemplary one in South Central that's reopened? Needless to say this is not some kind of *priority*. I might say—but then Creature, here, might then interject "Oh, *brother*"—or even *"barfo-genic"* . . . and once is enough—I've got the love; I don't, so to speak, need the Reeboks. Even if sometimes I get the feeling my sibling here looks at me as if I've turned into some cyberspace actor system without a receptionist. Anyway, not that it *is* Reeboks that I'm after . . . but you knew that—

The telephone rang. Just like them, she thought, to call from Yuma or someplace. Surprised they didn't call the car phone . . . but before she could pick up, she heard Plácido from the patio engaging the caller, and that switched her back to her son.

TRISTAN: And there's something else I haven't been able to find here either; it's a computer game called Dactyl Nightmare.

MAEV: Speaking of stores, there's one on Fifth Avenue—

TRISTAN: Oh, God, Mother, it's—

MAEV: Excuse me, this is my story—

TRISTAN: Anyway, it wasn't even a *store*, just a store *window*, on Fifty-second Street.

MAEV: Unless he lets me tell *this* story, I may be forced to leak the information that he is seriously considering having business cards printed up—with a New York address, an L.A. address, and two fax numbers—to make meeting girls easier. Is that verbal judo? Anyway, whoever put that window up must have rocks in his head. It's *supposedly* a *tribute* to Marilyn.

TRISTAN: Wait—how do we know it's a *he*, anyway?

MAEV: It's a *he* all right. A he with rocks in his—

Plácido opened the patio doors. "Miss Wayfaring, it's Mr. O'Maurigan from New York. He says you'd want to know."

"He's right," she answered, stepping outside. "Plácido, would you put that machine on call waiting, or whatever? Thank you. Here, I'll take the phone."

She sat down in late sunlight on a chaise longue.

"I was just listening to my children going on about you; they both think you have a palatial mind."

"You won't tell them," the poet, scripter, and rock theorist snapped, "at their age, that it's become Castle Rackrent?"

"They really have settled in. Tristan refers to my coming 'back east' next week. He'd like to take me to the South Street Seaport, where they have installed a new thing called Virtuality. He's taken to a game called Dactyl Nightmare. You heard of it?"

"*Heard* of? I *have* them. *'This is the forest primeval, the whispering pines and the hemlock'* . . . particularly the hemlock."

"You deserve them. Obviously what he's remembering, unconsciously, is you in Laguna, going on about those *raptors*—those *Teratornis* vulture things. Remember?"

"Yes, dearie, I remember. I'm very much older than you. Like the *Teratornis*, older than the rocks I sit among—in the back yard, in my head. But you *are* behind the times! Besides here in Gotham, there are Virtuality theaters in St. Louis, in San Francisco—but you never have been to San Francisco, have you?"

"I've *been* there—just don't happen to like the place."

"And you just don't try to kid yourself, that's all."

"I may just start."

"Whatever. In any case, I myself have accompanied your son to play both Dactyl Nightmare and its companion terror Exorex at the aforementioned waterfront suckers' bazaar, losing in consequence a full night's sleep. I may add the thing costs a buck a minute; he's plainly inherited your instinctive costic tastes. I'm thinking seriously of approaching Virtuality, Inc., with a scheme called Specimen Days. I could use the steady income in these spare times."

"Speaking of which—specimen days, that is—and of the rocks in *somebody's* head, what about that storefront display at Fifty-second and Fifth? Some kind of Marilyn *tribute?*"

"Unfortunate. Obviously some lunatic on a mission rented the space—one can't even remember what it was—here, you realize, we don't torch, we merely disremember. Rented the space and constructed a papier-mâché effigy of your old pal as she appeared among us in the golden fifties, before the turn, before the studio altercations, when we still thought of her as ours. Married to Joe, going to Actors Studio . . . turning back and forth from Norma Jean to Marilyn to Norma Jean at will. Standing over a subway grating on Lexington Avenue . . . a lovely moment in a terrible picture. Unfortunate reminder."

"It's worse here. Do you know what's happening here?"

"Yes, I do. My friend told me only yesterday, as they were packing to depart in all that rain. They'd hoped the weather might continue, shielding your eyes from the promotion of the event. I see it didn't."

"I see now what Plácido was getting at."

"Oh?"

"Never mind; there's no point in shielding people."

"Oh, I don't know, considering what the relentlessly deranged manage to—listen, what are you going to Ralph's as tonight?"

"The Morrigan."

"The Morrigan; I approve."

"I feel like going instead as Good Marilyn, but I couldn't co-opt anybody's work—especially not anybody's good work."

"The misappropriation of the discourse of the Other; not your MO."

"I wish I could find her all the same—whoever she is, or he is, or whatever they are together in the one head—and take her with me."

"She might get there on her own steam—anybody in the world and time might, with that cable car Ralph's had put in to run up from Hyperion Canyon."

"I mustn't go into upset. You know what Promotions told them? 'Her going into upset will solve nada—as in *Ense*-nada!' They're going for wit—next we'll have *metaphors!*"

"Well, speaking metaphorically, why did you slam the dressing-room door?"

"Speaking metaphorically, I didn't slam it, I *closed* it."

"So far so good. Why did you? Was the hinge loose?"

"No."

"So, you needed the stone that was keeping it open, right?"

"Not exactly."

"You were keeping out the music of the rehearsal. You were changing, and were determined to surprise the people— knock 'em dead—with your new costume."

"To quote your protégé, what good are they to me dead?"

"It's true, the old questions are the great questions. So Promotions interrogated you through the closed door . . . no, wait, interrogated *them*. You heard them talking over the transom. Talking about the possibility of talking. Being complicit. 'You want to renegotiate this? We'll take a meeting. Get your girl to call my girl—calendar Tuesday, get this settled.' Have I got it right, the essentials, anyway?"

"You write scripts, don't you? What are *you* going out as?"

"Not, I think, the script of your life. I'm staying home."

"Smart. Tell me this: why are my children so much better able to fend off anger than their mother is?"

"Easy. Unlike their ma-*ma*, they've been well reared by their ma-*ma*."

"Thank you. That *was* a compliment, wasn't it?"

"Of sorts. There are disadvantages. I suspect neither of them is ever likely to become something called a Temperament."

"Norma Jean used to take me to the cosmetics department at Bullocks-Wilshire. Free samples and makeup tips. It was there she narrated *Double Indemnity* for me. Today I was at J. W. Robinson, downtown. One of the mannequins resembled her from then. How she still was when she played Miss Caswell. How at Bette Davis's party at Trader Vic's in San Francisco she drank nothing but milk. All the men thought she was nothing, but Bette said, 'I don't know why, but I think you're all quite wrong.' And they all went to the premiere at the Roxy, and saw the truth."

"Bette was always right—even at the end, about getting up and going to the window in *The Whales of August*. The old resemblances resemble the old stories; they're the trustworthi-est, the . . . The Morrigan, eh?"

"The Morrigan."

"Going out on Halloween as the Morrigan, under the Samhain cradle crescent moon, and the creature feigns igno-rance of what good they are to her dead at all. On this of all nights, when barriers come down, granting transit between this world and the very next, providing hospitality to dead ancestors. Why, in olden days, were not the burial caves left open so the spirits of the heroes could come out and drink buttermilk? Were not the laws of space, time, and society sus-pended, and was not all manner of reverse and bold behavior indulged in? Samhain. *Trinoux Samonia:* the Three Nights at Summer's End—pluvial resumption of the growth cycle—Celtic New Year. Makes a lot of sense in November Los Angeles—especially in the rain. Which somehow reminds me that poor Jim Morrison actually did once say something about Nature assuming a terrifying mask before—you know, some mirific marshmallow version of 'Whom the gods wish to destroy they first send out shopping.' But do be careful as those barriers come down. At Ralph's the walls have ears, even if it is one of the few safe houses, where you won't actually be bugged. Therefore go with Goddess, and give the old *hoor* my best, and regrets, but they also serve who merely lie in at home on the eastern seaboard and watch old horror movies colorized on television."

"The walls had ears in *Hedda Gabler.* In the first scene I was enraged before the fact. They'd done that to me in *Rain* too—onstage at that age, half-dressed, shaking with fear and rage, telling the Reverend, 'I have the right to stand here and say to *hell* with you . . . and be damned!' *You've* earned the right to lie in state with Bela Lugosi. Call you tomorrow."

．　．　．

She sat at the vanity table looking into the mirror. Having put on the indigo silk robe, emblazoned with black ravens outlined in silver lamé, gathered it with a wide black leather belt and placed the gold, skull-knobbed torc around her neck, she was all but ready. There was no makeup; the three-faced mask, the Morrigan, Irish goddess of death and battles, glowered on top of the wig case. She switched on the children's tape again, to listen to the P.S.

"We ended up inviting the Goth to the Halloween party here. I'm going as Wolf Man; Creature is the Bride of Frankenstein. Grandmother's idea was Beauty and the Beast, but we said 'Grandmother, we *can't* go to our own New York Halloween party as two *Disney* characters. Every dweeb in Los Angeles goes out as a Disney character on Halloween.' She said, 'Disney? I was thinking of the Jean Cocteau film—don't you remember how you loved it?' It seems we dimly recalled . . . being four years old or something and Grandmother's *friend* was the Beast, and he turned out to be terribly handsome . . . but this year it's a Disney movie, so no. And anyway, passably pretty Creature evidently takes after the histrionic mother."

"Ha," Maev interjected. "Passably pretty Creature would much rather do something interesting with herself at the makeup mirror than throw on some old piece of pink tulle and play pretty. And if you ask me—and I remember well seeing that French movie—pretty dumb. I think maybe that story embodies an uplifting idea whose time ran out. Which is just what I feel that a real man would do to that girl, and soon. Call me hard-edged, but if you do, you ought to know I think I felt the same way at four. Anyway, have a great time at Ralph's. I can't wait to hear who all he let in—not to mention who crashed. Kiss-kiss."

(She's what I'd call something called a Temperament. Takes after the mother indeed.)

I remember my justification in *Rain*. I was talking to the producers, on a Sunday morning in the rain in Los Angeles, saying to hell with you, for Norma Jean, who never got the right to stand there . . . never even got a chance to talk until it was too late. Whereas I talked that way to Orphrey Whither from the beginning, and got away with it—got encouragement. "The more she vents at me, before she embraces psychoanalysis, the less likely she is ever to compromise herself by venting at the police, or turning on herself and doing herself an injury."

The Wolf Man. He means, of course, the Werewolf. Let me tell myself I'm sure that when he looks out the window tonight all he'll see is the trees lit up by streetlights, and maybe in the trees the sleeping birds, or at most a city cat.

(Beyond the patio the cradle moon rose over downtown Los Angeles.)

What will I see; what all do I . . . envision? The dead. Him; her; Aunt Thalia, who never crossed into Hollywood; Jack; cousin Gabriel; my husband's father; and Norma Jean—all sitting around the house here while I'm at Ralph's.

Hilltop graves splitting open in the mud slides . . .

Better to imagine Good Marilyn, wherever she shows up tonight. So what if she sounds a bit too Billie Burke in *The Wizard of Oz?* "There's no place like home?" I much preferred Norma Jean's formula. "There's no place like Mocambo— except Ciro's."

Justification, in Stella's class.

In the doctor's office. You turn out the lights. You are studying the x-rays.

I was studying the x-rays, all right—prognosis negative, large order.

The phone rang; this time she picked it up herself.

"Hello?"

"It's us—we're in Yuma."

"We're not getting off."

"You sound exactly alike."

"But so do *you*!"

"Very funny. Don't get off. Tonight is death night. People die in the desert."

"Dying is easy—"

"It's comedy that's hard."

"I'll remember—I'm on my way to Ralph's now."

"So knock 'em dead."

"I've been very seriously considering it. Justification's been on my mind."

Alone again, she heard Plácido calling from outside, telling her the car was ready. She regarded her three heads glowering now in the vanity mirror, commanding herself, Let's go.

Schloss Von Gelsen (industry martinets had started in calling Ralph's new home that, and one dubbed it "po-mo curvilinear Case Study Castle Dracula," although there was fairly no resemblance between it and a fantasy Mitteleuropa pile) was cantilevered on a precipice over Hyperion Canyon Road, nearby the HOLLYWOOD sign. (Another corrected, "Lautner. *Radical* mo—no po about it. The biggest Googie's ever. The apotheosis of Googie's.") Ralph resolutely said "my place." "Come on up to my place for drinks and so forth; it's in the hills."

" 'It's in the hills'!" they snapped. "*Does* anybody not on a *resuscitator* need briefing? It's the ship from *This Island Earth*; hard not to notice. All that's missing is the lime-green aura. When you board that trolley, pack a duffel for Metaluna!" (Seemingly unique access was provided not by sci-fi beam, but by cable car modeled on the Pacific Electric red cars of the 1920s from the loop on Hyperion Canyon Drive: Ralph's ambitious recreation of the "Rubio" cable car Thaddeus S. C. Lowe had run up Echo Mountain in the 1890s, lost in the

1933 earthquake and fire.) Alternate access, granted A-list friends, led down from a hidden driveway off Mulholland Drive to what Ralph called the "back lot," and it was there that Kaye Wayfaring, getting out of the Bentley, encountered her friend the astrologer, columnist, and broadcaster Astarte, costumed as the Witch of Endor, directing the Von Gelsen help in the garaging of her silver Stingray convertible, fenders ablaze with those vivid red-and-orange ornamentations called nosebleeds.

Astarte remarked, without preamble, "That goddamn cable car! Just what we need in Hollywood—a Gay Nineties notion perpetuated by San Francisco. What are *automobiles* for? What does he want to do, bring on another earthquake? Anyway, I love your getup. What *are* you, yesterday, today, and tomorrow or the three fates?"

Seeing the vehicle start its ascent from the station there below, Kaye Wayfaring suddenly wondered: What if the bodies from Bronson Canyon . . . as in *Night of the Living Dead . . . ?*

"The Morrigan."

"Oh—yeah."

"You're not just another pretty face yourself."

"Thanks. You make a little effort, you know. Even if I never have liked Halloween much, not even at Ralph's. With everybody masked, nobody's anybody you . . . you can't tell even the usual suspects. Not *nearly* chief unit enough, not for yours truly! I *know* some of these people have arrived from the Dress Extras Ball at the Hollywood Women's Club, down on Yucca and Franklin—although that couple over there is kinda cute, no?"

Kaye looked. A nearly naked green man, festooned in wet seaweed, carrying a trident, and somebody—male or female?—down on all fours, held on a leash, and wearing a mask of Disney's dog Pluto. She felt stupid.

"It's Neptune conjunct Pluto."

"Oh."

"And look—just off the cable car. The Three Blind Mice in aviator Ray-Bans, carrying their cut-off tails. *Cute*-cute!"

There was no cropped lawn, but rather a little savannah of many grasses, through which an alley had been cut and bordered with patulous cactus and coral trees. These for the occasion had been garlanded with gardenias; their extreme posturings looked, people were saying, like orgiastic sex. (Yes, the well-traveled noted, at the Diwali Festival.) Or like some late modern dance idea. Under bewhiskered eucalyptus and blue Jaipur jacarandas, dampened shrub grass of juniper, rosemary, heather, and myrtle grew in boxed borders along the flagstone terrace, in sandy patches among the Corsican maquis, the sagebrush, and the loosened rocks. A fountain of the four rivers of Eden plashed.

Inside, the Blend-Aire High Velocity air system counterpointed the rumble of various games: pinball, Pachinko, a game called Freeway, and the young guests' favorite, Virtuality ("A dollar a *minute* in the Third Street Arcade in Santa Monica!").

The Three Blind Mice, surveying the picturesque assembly and pointing fingers with their severed tails, concentrated on Kaye Wayfaring.

"Who the hell is she supposed to *be*, the Three Faces of Disgraced Eve? Don't tell, I got it. She's the Gypsy vampire Supremes in the Coppola *Dracula*, right?"

"The Bonfire of the Vampires."

"Don't be so Hollywood, it's a masterpiece. Actually, she's the Morrigan."

"*O'Maurigan!*" You mean O'Maurigan as the Holy Trinity. Or is it O'Maurigan's tormented soul in triplicate?"

"Not *O'*Maurigan, *the* Morrigan. The Irish Medusa: goddess of battle. Always three-headed—don't know why, maybe for 'as it was in the beginning, is now, and ever shall. . . .' Maybe Wayfaring has come as her own embattled soul."

"Last year she came as her own body—supposedly Nell Gwynn; one head, two tits, all of 'em gorgeous."

"Last year, if you remember, was the 1991 Is 1661 party. This year suddenly it's reality time. The election. Come as your intent. This war goddess is Wayfaring's intent."

"Well, if it's about intent, she should've come with her victims The Morrigan is supposed to have dead naked men strewn about her feet—with their heads lopped off."

"Dead, naked California Republicans."

"Sounds like Salome. She's a little old for Salome—except in the Norma Desmond reading. But in that video—and on that billboard on Sunset—she looks like she could decapitate or castrate any number of male contestants."

"Women too. Celtic women went into battle. They chanced their arms. The effect Wayfaring makes in 'Ensenada' is stunning. *She* got it, all right, and seeing her stalk around as the three witches, you are reminded of Stanwyck's triple turn: Phyllis Dietrichson, Martha Ivers, and Thelma Jordon."

"She's isn't stalking around; she's sitting there on the sofa. But whatever that drag is, it certainly does represent one angry woman."

"Ostensibly in repose, but you can see her demeanor in 'Ensenada.' A wild mix of Isadora at the wheel of the Bugatti, Ruth St. Denis waving her flame pots under a full moon, and Martha Graham breathing fire—remember?—in *Cave of the Heart.*"

"Thrilling—so long as it's kept allegorical. So long as she doesn't go around decapitating men—or women, either. Actual demonstrations of anger are taboo on the West Side."

"*Cave of the Heart.* That was about Medea."

"Yes."

"You go too far. Medea kills her kids; Wayfaring could never kill her kids."

"On the screen it's all kept allegorical."

"If she ever did actually do something desperate, you'd surely sympathize. Got a head on her shoulders worth any three in the industry—and everyone's *fixated* on the shoulders."

"Out here anyway. But listen, she's absolutely crazy about those kids."

"You heard what happened on the overlay issue. Earth go boom! *That* industry subaltern nearly got *something* cut off!"

"Come *on*! A computer-generated image changing from Wayfaring to Jim Morrison to Marilyn and *back*?"

"Cut! Really, kids, no wonder earth go boom."

"It's been happening more lately, as of old, like acid flashback. After all those years of getting used to—what, her tranquility? Happiness, or something like. Her being, you know, *exemplary*—we'd almost forgotten her inclination, if that's the way to put it, to the low drop."

"*Hell hath* no et cetera like whatever."

"But they *dropped* the idea—ostensibly."

"Something's burning—I dunno."

"No sé . . . lo conseguí en Ensenada."

"Hombre, claro—y caramba!"

"What's burning is Atlanta. Sometimes it's enough just to be Southern."

"Southern Californian. The line drawn at San Luis Obispo—No Callers."

"Whatever. She's waving *some* kind of red rag."

"It's hard work being happy and having fun."

"You'd better live up to it. No giving the game away."

"No bitterness, no resentment."

"You alienate everyone. Vilma Banky died alone."

"Vilma Banky, Louise Brooks . . ."

"Mary Miles Minter . . . so many. Too many."

"What is life?"

"Remember when we first saw Rock Formation at Gazzarri's, on Sunset? We started calling them Orchestral Manoeuvres in Klieg. Feared they might be, after the fanfares and despite the drafting of Girl Wayfaring, just another eighties haircut band. We weren't long deceived. They're true Silver Lake originals—even if 'Ensenada' owes a little something to Blondie."

"Not to mention the Ramones—and the Velvets."

"Even so, they're more than a little unique."

"They're very unique tonight—she's the only one of them here."

"All three of her. Unless maybe she's supposed to stand in for the two of them."

"Her presence certainly does dominate a room."

"Truly. So does her absence; figure *that*."

"Her power focus is random on the grid."

Across the room, the Hollywood Boulevard and Santa Monica Boulevard Halloween parades flashed on the giant wall screen. On Hollywood Boulevard, in front of the ruined Egyptian Theater, a woman claiming to be the ghost of Bella Darvi still suffering from leprosy was forecasting Hollywood's bad end. "The Big One? *The Day of the Locust?* Don't make me *laugh*! I'm talking the plagues of Egypt in requital for the sins of Babylon. And *soon*!"

"They ought to remake *The Egyptian*, you know?" one viewer declared. "With Kaye Wayfaring in the Bella Darvi role—getting leprosy in all the new F/X."

"Getting leprosy," said another, "and getting cured of leprosy this time. Suffering and renewal in the age of Clinton."

"You *could* wait till after Tuesday with that pitch."

"Well, come on—get *real*. Anyway, I like it, Clinton raising his hand and curing people. You could almost feel something like that going on at the fund-raiser."

"Are we talking politics? What you could feel at that fund-raiser was raised eyebrows ripping open the fault lines of third-time facelifts at the vision of Wayfaring, downstage from that Ozark Lochinvar and his off-key sax, singing 'The Man I Love.' *Especially* when she got to 'Tuesday may be my good news day.' "

"And following on, and speaking of remakes, concerned people are talking everywhere about Wayfaring and Clinton and Marilyn and the Kennedy brothers. Why is she here all alone tonight?"

"It was in the *Hollywood Reporter.* The Beltanes are on the train going back to their little red schoolhouse in Massachusetts to vote."

"Anyway, stuff like Marilyn and the Kennedys, it is no more."

"True, we don't need the likes of Marilyn doing that for us anymore. Or Dietrich either. Foreign intrigue, sex with the President, Mafia violence. We'll be doing it ourselves—in Virtuality. In the consensual hallucination that is the matrix. You put on a pair of gloves. . . ."

"That's the sign when you come off the plane at LAX. It says *Welcome to the Consensual*—"

"It sure looks," Kaye Wayfaring remarked, "in this UFO set, like the cantina scene in *Star Wars*, don't you think?"

Astarte looked around and across toward the television.

"The extras go all out on Halloween to dress the set."

("Ensenada," on the television screen, was reflected in the window across from the couch on which Astarte and Kaye

Wayfaring were sitting. The star watched herself stalk through blue smoke across an empty lot in Culver City, saw her husband's figure approach her, heard him whisper indistinctly into her ear, and as nearly simultaneously an encaustic flash of light exposed her famous features, she heard herself replying in spent tones, "I don't know—I got it in Ensenada" followed by an eerie echo: her brother-in-law's voice, burlesquing her own. "No sé, lo conseguí en Ensenada." And then dropping an octave and intoning first, "Who knows what evil lurks in the hearts of men?" And then, "You're beautiful—*exciting*—when you're angry!")

"It really is good, you know that, honey?" Astarte declared. "Can you see it under there?"

"As through dark glasses. Like in *Revelations*."

"Never cared for that property. *Too* De Mille."

"What I always liked about De Mille," Kaye Wayfaring mused, "was that the women got to lie on couches wearing fantastic gowns and enormous jewels, *provoking* the men to demolish temples or God to rain down plagues. I've always been made to do the dirty deeds myself—that's to say the women I've been assigned have."

(Like her, she thought, looking at the video. There she is wasting away in a Mexican jail for carving up a lover.

At the song's bridge, an adroit inversion of Gershwin's "Lady Be Good," and both men crooning low against the mariachis: "She never *could* be *good*—She *had* to be *bad*. . . ." Newsreel footage of South Central Los Angeles in flames, segueing to a mon-tage of aerial reconnaissance shots and Technicolor home movies of the Rosarita Beach Hotel, famous asylum of yesteryear, and then to a procession, circa 1947, through the streets of Ensenada on the Day of the Dead.)

. . .

"Never mind 'Lady, Be Good!' " said the first of the Three Blind Mice, "that's a red herring. It's Rock Formation's *hommage* to *Lady from Shanghai*, with the Rosarita Beach Hotel instead of Acapulco as the *locus solus*, and Ensenada subbing for the San Francisco Chinatown funhouse."

"I think it's simpler than that," said the second. "More like *The Lady from the Shanghai Gardens*."

"I agree," said the third. "The Shanghai Gardens takeout. She comes in for the egg roll. They're there, sharing a red herring. Twin One makes pass. 'Get lost.' Twin Two follows suit. 'Tell your face in the mirror I said get *lost*.' They advance together; she's a black belt in karate. Chop-chop—like that."

"In any case," said Number One, removing his dark glasses, "they were *demented* to suggest transforming her image even a *nanosec* into Jim Morrison. As for Marilyn, if Wayfaring's life means *anything*, it's as lived free of *any* Marilyn resemblance."

Number Two nodded, looking across the room toward Kaye Wayfaring. "This is known. And if Marilyn, dead, stalks her . . ."

Number Three summed up the case. "There's that black belt."

As she sat with Astarte on the big white couch, two virtually identical projections of Kaye Wayfaring bore down—from the wall opposite, and from the long window: at the wheel of the red Maserati at dawn out near the airport, hair blowing in the wind ("Whatever this thing *is* talking about, it *isn't* talking about *gridlock*!"), barreling down to Baja on the San Diego Freeway. Yet not quite identical: on the wall, she could see only herself—her head, and hands gripping the wheel—the road and ubiquitous syncopated oil derricks, whereas in the window, as she hummed the words, not of "Ensenada," but of the old Bill Martin song she'd sung with Steve Carey years ago,

I drove my ole car down the dusty streets of that ole border town.
Didn't know I'd get stuck such a long, long time,

she could make out, incorporated in her features, figures moving, and then another head, another face approaching. (Virtuality, she thought. What of it? I did not spend all those years couch-casting myself merely to recapitulate now to crummy teledildonic interface with some burned-out speed freak's alleged mind.

Bordertown. They Drive by Night. The Doors Made Me Jim Morrison into Marilyn . . . Hilarious. Hilarity, close to rage. In borderline . . . What was that fifties diagnosis?—*revolving doors.*)

The figure came up the flagstone path into the window frame.

"As I feared," Astarte said to Jameson O'Maurigan in New York over the telephone in the master bedroom, "an alarming party—tone set earlier by the intruder barred from entry below in Hyperion Canyon. 'This *is* my costume. I'm a homicidal maniac. They look like everybody else.' "

"Tell me the worst."

"As we were sitting there together on the big white couch—you know, in that living area that's approximately the size of the Taper Forum—'Ensenada' came on from somewhere across the floor, and the way we were positioned we could see it reflected in the windows. The place is all windows. Anyway, our girl, serene on the couch in the Morrigan mask, saw coming into the moving image in the glass something else—something, as it turned out, from the West Hollywood parade. Something that had made its way into Hyperion Canyon and gotten on the trolley and come up and gotten itself admitted as a Halloween trick. Something wearing, I give you, a mask made out of the coroner's photos of Marilyn dead—remember? And in a long chain of gestures—the first link purely abstract, purely musical, but obviously in close connection to her subconscious creative impulses, the last not histrionic at all; a seeming gesture of everyday life: concrete and naturalistically true—she approached the apparition and tore the hideous face off, revealing a man. You know who he looked like? Trixie Revenge—but Trixie Revenge *then*. I thought, that's just not possible. It cannot be—can it? Well, the false Trixie Revenge then reached over, lifted the Morrigan mask off Wayfaring's head, and *tossed* it down the ravine, like the three heads in the Coppola *Dracula*—then realized who was under it. Crazed, obviously, with mixed feelings: the chance at fame, probable adoration of Wayfaring on the screen versus shame and thwarted narcissistic rage—as if Mother had taken his pants down in public to spank his bottom blue. They'll be dishing it at Rage on San Vicente till the Big One."

" 'On Mimetic Violence and the Victim.' Also 'On Mimesis and Alterity.' "

"Exactly; the northwest corner. I had a sudden vision—thank God, one that didn't actualize. I was absolutely sure for an instant she was going to pull a Stella Adler—she's done it once before, remember—rip open her bodice and say, 'You don't know what these *are*; you know *nothing* of life!' But she didn't. I realized she couldn't; she didn't have both hands free. What she did do was, she stalked into the meditation room, still carrying the Dead Marilyn mask, and threw it into the central fireplace—utterly freaking out the whole assembly. They'd been mellowing out, listening to a Tibetan Singing Bowl Ensemble CD of music for the Samhain moon, and sharing the overtone vibrations. She turned then and, returning to the scene where the unmasked perpetrator stood trembling still, she walked up to him and said, 'forgive me.'

"The resurrected Trixie Revenge hung stooped, then reared up—what had just been said about *Star Wars?*—declaring—now *get* this—'De nada, sister. We are both wicked women, deceivers. Save California, star soul, and I'll pray for you until my dying day!' Then, flashbulbs popping and camcorders rolling, swooped in for the close-up. And De Mille was ready—the invaders were a *news team*, in low drag, and *I*—dolt that I am; pray for *me*—had pegged them as Hollywood dress extras on Halloween call!"

"What did anybody say? What did they *do?*"

"Well, you might say each guest's return to self-possession was characterized by oddly personal mood rhythms and reactions."

"I might. I must say I like 'star soul.' What then?"

"Wayfaring, evading Plácido, jumped into yours truly's Stingray. Remember, I told you that after I bought it, one or another of the Beltanes—your one, I think—said it ought to have red-and-orange flame nosebleeds painted on, and in a moment of madness I crossed over into the Barrio and had it done? God love them, it got me through a couple of sticky moments in the riots . . . another story. Anyway, she jumped in—saying, as she handed me her scarf and took the keys, agreeing to return the wheels and herself to my place on Glenhaven, 'As long as it's not a Bugatti!'—revved up, and exited—the pebble driveway spraying like surf cut by a board—toward Mulholland Drive."

The Three Blind Mice were developing their report.

"Nothing virtual about it—she *wasn't* wearing gloves!"

"It was as if she had committed a murder."

"If she *had* committed murder, with today's sentences, she'd be out of Tehachapi in less than ten years. Her family would wait for her, and when she got out the kids would be all grown up."

"So would the husband."

Cresting on Mulholland Drive, the Stingray sped skifflike, while below stretched the immense pinpoint-light, transistor-grid Everglades, the gangliated, freeze-frame shoals of illumination called Los Angeles. (And beyond, the Mexican border. Ensenada. Getaway. *Out of the Past.* And she as alluring and as rotten as Jane Greer—or as Marilyn courting her annihilation up at the other border, in *Niagara.* The border . . . the borderline. But before the border, the police alarm . . . and finally, before the fade-out, and the long credit crawl, death itself, in no new form.)

Past the Hollywood Bowl, at the entrance ramp to the Hollywood Freeway, she saw a sign, THE BEACH BOYS SAVE. *(If you save California . . .)* She sped downtown, singing,

> *And all that's left is*
> *A girl who's*
> *Loved by her*
> *Mother and father . . .*

(If the LAPD stops—STAR BOLTS FOR BORDER—I'll say, "This, boys, is *not* the little old lady from Pasadena; this is the *bruja loca* from Silver Lake, living her self-assertive tendency.")

Exiting the freeway, she drove back into the now-deserted downtown streets, as Walter Neff, having put a revolver bullet through Phyllis Dietrichson—"Bye, baby"—had done at dawn in the opening (and finale) of *Double Indemnity*. She parked the

Stingray at a curb and walked around, looking undomesti-cated, like Joan Crawford in *Possessed*, and like herself in the finale of her own first knock-'em-dead feature, *We Are Born, We Live, We Die.* (Orphrey Whither had insisted downtown Los Angeles—the Pershing Square–City Hall–Union Station area and the old Raymond Chandler streets like North Ala-meda and South Figueroa late at night after the moon was down—was to B pictures from 1940 to 1968 what Monument Valley was to John Ford, what the Mediterranean was to Racine: the *site*, the *habitat* of the tragedy. A ready-made back lot routinely employed to represent in the depiction of crises the washed-out innards of any sizable demoralized, decaying American city.)

The hour of the wolf passed at the Clifton Cafe. In another Hopper now, she thought, *Nightbirds*. But she couldn't imag-ine herself the girl in it; she was Kaye Wayfaring on Hallow-een, in a gown covered with black ravens outlined in silver lamé, drinking a cup of coffee. Kaye Wayfaring sitting at a window table of a nearly empty cafeteria in downtown Los Angeles, having just been served by a pretty waitress. Fin-gering the cubes in the sugar bowl and remembering the sugar skulls in Mexico on the Day of the Dead.

She glanced across at the Mexican waitress smoking behind the coffee urn and remembered reading something written by a Mexican-American journalist from San Francisco—describing itinerant Mexican laborers returning in fancy dress to their villages once a year for major saints' feast days, occasions when "expressed fragments of memory flow outward like cigarette smoke to tumble the dust of the dead. Every night is carnival. . . . Women working as waitresses in California put on high heels and evening gowns. The promenade under Mexican stars becomes a celebration of American desire." She wondered, sipping coffee, if Plácido, assuring her "Ensenada" was no offense, could speak for the waitress, wearing flat shoes and a plain white uniform, who'd smiled at her easily, asking no questions, or if the waitress would be angry at the video. Or did she think, for instance, that Rita Hayworth—would she remember Rita Hayworth?—was exalted rather than exploited by Hollywood?

As the sky was breaking into gray streaks behind the Hollywood Hills, she drove along Wilshire Boulevard to Fairfax, up Fairfax to Beverly Boulevard, and past the Beverly Center through West Hollywood. Then as the tops of the canyons turned pink, she switched on KBYZ to find the Sunday-morning discussion focused on the six-month anniversary of the riots.

Some auctorial voice intoned:

"Man is capable of anger because endowed with memory; experience of events persists—with the faculty of symbolization. Even so, no fits of temper in real life are as interesting as those of Lear or Medea."

(Maybe not to you, Sonny. And Medea was a woman—one with a long memory. Or is he talking about the actor behind the mask in the amphitheater, at dawn, having memorized the text?)

"While everyone is proud in the same way, each of us is angry in his or her own way."

(Something about happy and unhappy families. Anyway, that's better. Each finds his—or her—own truth. Looking at the x-rays, at the large orders of Prognosis Negative.)

"We do not want others to conform to our wishes because they must, but because they choose to; we want devoted *slaves."*

(". . . I wanted you to *mean* it." Or, "I ask for nothing; men in their foolishness . . ." Great lines; great readings in great landmark performances. Histrionics; then the head count. "We want them to . . . not because they must; because they choose." As if we could ever know—as if free will made any . . .)

"Sometimes harmless, unattractive, helpless people arouse in me the desire to ill-treat them. Ideal victims who won't fight back, upon whom I can vent all my resentments, real or imagined, against life. I realize it is that very element of helplessness which excites my ill will."

(What a definition of the performing arts. But what good *are* they dead, with all their heads lopped off?)

The program announcer was calling her name.

". . . To our faithful listener and favorite star—the truth, Miss Wayfaring, we counsel fence-mending. For California—and the Wayfarings are an old California family. We've got to hold firm—in the face of the Big One. Wherever you are now—and you're not home—why not go into a church, any church."

As she moved along slowly on Elevado, in Beverly Hills, the morning sky cleared to turquoise and the first church bells rang. She recalled her dead friend's reminiscence of the Sunday-morning casting couches and the way church bells rang back then. "I used to lie there wondering what denominations they were." She started humming the Men's hit number, "Church of Logic, Sin and Love."

Suddenly she caught herself going through more than one of the stop signs at each corner of Elevado (My *God*, she thought, I might run down a *kid*), but not before the flashing light flagged her over to the curb to face two officers, one male, one female, of the Beverly Hills Police. (She looked at them approaching and thought, They can't be much older than my twins!)

"Critical car, Miss Wayfaring; outrageous nosebleeds. Yours?"

"No. My astrologer's. I'm returning it to her in Beverly Glen. She's on Scenario Way."

"Registration—and your license, if we may?"

"I'm afraid I've left my license at home—in Silver Lake."

(And they *sound* alike—*am* I going crazy?)

"And you're not wearing your seat belt either. Haven't you seen the new signs—there's one forty times life size on Sunset, right next to you, as a matter of fact, in the new video, the same size. It says DON'T DO WINDOWS, BUCKLE YOUR SEAT BELT."

"Missed it. Do I have to take an attitude test?"

"No. The word is you wasted some gate crasher last night at the Von Gelsen bash."

"*Wasted?* Nosebleed?"

"Emphatically treated to your point of view. Like the club headliner suddenly turned bouncer is the noise. No physical injury reported. The word is he got in your face—they said '*all three of 'em.*' Nobody at headquarters got that part. We've heard of being called two-faced, but whatever else they might say about you, *that*, no. In your three faces, nobody got."

"You had to be there. Tell me this, is there an APB?"

"A *what*?"

"A bulletin—a dragnet—is there one out?"

"Doubtful, Miss Wayfaring. They may call Silver Lake, for

a comment. Thing is, though, we can't let you drive out of Beverly Hills without a license; we'd feel responsible."

"This isn't a choke point, a roadblock, a border station. All I did was jump a stop sign, right?"

"Overlooking the license thing, that's the deal."

"The LAPD won't come and get me?"

"They don't have the jurisdiction. You neutralized a West Hollywoodian. No West Hollywood police. That's on the ballot Tuesday. Hollywood's under the Los Angeles County sheriff."

"Well, I didn't shoot the sheriff; I didn't even shoot at him. But I don't like being on the wrong side of a citizen of—"

"Boys Town?"

(Actually, some of my best friends are boys.)

"San Francisco, actually; a West Hollywood house guest."

"San Francisco? Oh, well, it's sure to blow over. Anyway, it happened on Halloween."

"In the old days, you realize," Kaye Wayfaring said, "when scandal hit, you skidded out of town down to Baja in the black Packard, Derringer in the glove compartment."

"Or got on the train back east. There is no gun—"

"No, there isn't. Right, at Union Station, in a sealed compartment, under an alias. I was only heading for the Westwood Mausoleum."

"Oh . . . yes, you go there from time to time to see . . . San Francisco . . . it'll blow over—it was Halloween. If worse comes to worst, they'll call a spin doctor."

"I presume you do *not* mean any one of the *band* of that name. They have specialists, I suppose, for tail spins, advertised in the back pages of *Spin*."

"It won't come to that. San Francisco. And it was Halloween. Look, my colleague will get the Stingray back to Scenario Way. Astarte—your astrologer's—address is getting famous itself nowadays. If you care to get in with me, I'll run you over to Westwood; you can have a visit, then we'll see you get home."

She sat again facing the plaque in the garden at Westwood. (George Cukor had cracked, "Poor dear, on the wrong side of Wilshire, behind a used car dealership."

No more. Besides, out this far there's no wrong side.)

The sun had risen higher on a brilliant Pacific November morning. The bells of Westwood Presbyterian Church rang clearly.

"Star soul," she asked, "did you really drink nothing but milk at Trader Vic's? That rings so very true. I remember how you made plans. Thought you were nothing . . . well, they got theirs."

Now would be the right time for Good Marilyn. Dame Kind, in Cherie's *Bus Stop* tights and glitzy bangles. We'd sing "Old Black Magic" and she'd do the monologue—heading for Montana. Maybe if I close my eyes . . .

She closed her eyes. *(In the doctor's office. You turn out the lights. You are studying the x-rays.)*

Opening her eyes, she saw she was alone.

New York Lit Up That Way at Night

As THE AIRCRAFT leveled off at cruising altitude, the seat belt sign went off, and the serious conversation begun before takeoff resumed.

"Envy? Every sentence fragment."

"Take us—as sentence fragments, as signal, or signatory attractions, or if you will, as moving targets sitting pretty. It is not so much that the wish to see us—the likes of us—go down in flames gets itself articulated, as such, as that—"

"What *are* you two talking about?" the astrologer Astarte demanded of Kaye Wayfaring and Jameson O'Maurigan.

"Envy," the poet declared.

"*Deciding* anything?"

"That's the thing about envy," he observed; "it can never decide. Indecisive remarks are its hallmarks, and passion, not action, its process. It's actually one of the reaction formations."

"Oh, *dear*," the diviner fretted, "ever since Mawrdew Czgowchwz retired from singing and became a psychoanalyst, all you people do is talk Freudian. Very clinical, very global, very New York."

"A hedge then," Jameson continued, solicitously, "against narcissistic terror. Before envy, we don't want anything that's out there—in point of fact we needn't even *know* what's out there."

"Particularly not at this altitude," Kaye Wayfaring remarked.

(In acting you never do a life study from the point of view of either envy or contempt; the derived goals would be groundless.)

"It is often mistakenly put out," the poet continued, "that envy leads to anger, comes out of it, but it's become quite clear that it's quite the other way around."

On board the Hyperion Pictures company jet night flight from New York to Los Angeles, they were eleven, a short enough roster, who after takeoff kept changing places to talk to one another in various combinations (as if conversational greener grass were always just another plot away). Besides Kaye Wayfaring, Jameson O'Maurigan, and the astrologer-seer Astarte, the pilot, the copilot, and the attentive flight steward, Kaye's twins, Tristan and Maev Beltane, Hyperion's renowned chief of production, Leland de Longpré, and his formidable wife, Livonia (artist and star of a former Hollywood they all frankly envied), and, as something like an afterthought (although such an unenviable designation would scarcely have satisfied either his amour propre or his keenly honed sense of professional commitment), the French cineast, correspondent of *Quoique* (a rumpled but by no means unattractive specimen, Kaye Wayfaring had decided), whose most recent work, *Chagrin d'Amour: The Politics of Shame from "Back Street" to "Avenged,"* had caused semiotic stirs at UCLA and USC. His brief it was to cover in depth the progress of the American film star most highly regarded by the serious-minded of his native country.

Moving targets sitting pretty, headed home following the induction of Rock Formation into the Rock and Roll Hall of Fame at the Waldorf-Astoria Hotel. (Departing New York, leaving behind her husband, Tristan Beltane, and his twin brother, Jacob, who with the versatile star made up the band,

Kaye, remembering the Waldorf's now defunct Starlight Roof, declared she'd rather be headlining there, like Sarah Vaughan singing "Poor Butterfly" in the revue *Calypso Carnival* in summer 1957, than leaving them there in the entertainment universe's engine room to make further plans for them all to run around the world once again on tour.)

A combination of musical chairs and octet bridge, the French cineast heard Maev declare, was what the revolving disposition of passengers reminded her of, and forced by his innate French sense of fairness to concur, he did so with a knowing smile and a brisk nod (in a frankly contradictory wash of feelings, of which he was able to assure himself the *signature* was frank esteem, if not unmixed delight—for enough was enough, surely, in the line of surrender. It was after all unenviable to be studiously trumped at the outset by a fourteen-year-old girl becoming, apart from anything else, and like her brother, eccentrically and dangerously pretty).

In two thoroughly unstable groups of four, exchanging keen remarks from opposite sides of a sparsely appointed main cabin: part po-mo Rancho Deluxe suite, part futuristic spaceship interior (mission fauteuils equipped with regulation seat belts; oxygen masks cunningly concealed in the covered cavities of the acoustic-panel ceiling).

Musical chairs set to an old tune he didn't know, in a sprightly rhythm he couldn't count. Octet bridge with him cast as one of the dummies. Yet consequently, the cineast reassured himself, the better able, could he keep the clever girl, his partner, bidding (opening one heart, you raise to two; partner shows game interest; since you have a sound raise you can accept, setting the trump suit quickly and defining your strength), the better able to indulge in the *volupté cérébrale* of quiet observation: in this case, quiet observation of two vibrant and terribly commanding women, Livonia de Longpré, paramount social arbiter of the new Hollywood, and his principal quarry, the star of Orphrey Whither's universally acknowledged masterpiece *Avenged*.

As Tristan walked up to the cockpit, back to the tail section, then back to his seat among the elders, Maev advised the French cineast, "My brother is an interesting study, really. I keep wondering, does he want to be the copilot or the tail gunner? Of course there isn't a tail gunner on the flight, is there—there's only a steward—almost certainly an aspiring actor studying my brother. Meanwhile, does my brother, I wonder, *aspire*, to stewardship—of anything—to adulthood, for example, or is he content just now with the lot of the adolescent boy—sometimes disguised as hero worship—which is envy, pure and simple. Envy of the fully developed male— whatever *that* is."

Tristan sat looking out the window on his side, then suddenly turned to the others and declared, "In the morning, in art class, they trumpet the beauty of contrapposto; then, after lunch, in ethics, comes the solemn injunction against getting bent out of shape. Who's kidding who?"

"The vogue for channeling," Kaye Wayfaring remarked, sorting through her thoughts as the plane broke through high cloud, "must have something to do with it—with envy, that is."

Astarte bristled. "Don't *talk* to me about channeling. These hordes lately going in for it. If you ask me, California should put aside one of the Channel Islands and send them all out there to do it together."

"We ask you everything," Kaye Wayfaring assured her. "And surely some ask how you do divination?"

Astarte shrugged. "When they ask me, I tell them it's calculus and logarithms. It satisfies them."

"Yes," Jameson continued, across the divide, "envy—sin that it is—is, according to late opinions canvassed, the result of the first attempt to reach out. *Hedda Gabler*, for example, is all about envy, and women who play Hedda as merely restless or narcissistic go under completely."

"Nobody *we* know," Kaye Wayfaring announced.

"It was your greatest role, honey," Astarte declared. "You gave me the *creeps*—and I don't get the creeps."

(I remember, Kaye told herself, when I decided I had to play Hedda. I'd been told by the neighbors in Clayton that Aunt Thalia was up there *beyond the bewilderness* in *New Yawk* making herself the town talk in a *teh'ble* play, written by a Mr. Henry Gibson—same name as that man down at the garage who writes poetry in the *Clayton Weekly Sentinel*. A play about a colonel's demon daughter who shoots herself in the head. "And huhself a colonel's daughter . . . and you, too, Miss Diana, so don't you go—doin' anythin' like that out in the yawl. But *you*, we unnerstand, are goin' to be a *movin' picture* actress—an envious thing." And then they laughed, in delight, not derision.)

"Narration," Jameson continued, "is, in respect of envy, problematic. Of course, if the characters *could* have their way—their *say*—there would be none. There might well be *commentary*."

"On?"

"On the great American dilemma, the urge to travel versus the need to reside. Adventure and domesticity. Abroad and stateside. Excursiveness and nesting. Outward-bound and home-as-found."

"Los Angeles is hardly abroad," Kaye Wayfaring protested.

"Los Angeles," Astarte declared, "is, in its own estimation, the cosmos."

"Indeed, the cosmos," Jameson mused, "home of the stars. Valéry says the stars fascinate because they mirror the state of human consciousness: flickering points of energy, intense, isolate. What was it *Spin*—or was it *Buzz*—said? 'No other band in the recording industry cosmos seems to wield as much power over its own fate as Rock Formation.' "

"That was in *Edge*," Astarte informed them both. "And the stars, properly understood, are no more isolated than nerve ends."

"So you think," Kaye Wayfaring asked the poet, "we can each make up our own story?"

"Within reason, and upon due consideration, we must, lest we succumb to envy of one another, and, worse yet, of the narrator, fearing what he might try to accomplish to his own end. And since the story would be one about our flight—to Los Angeles, that is, which is hardly abroad—we would try to finesse the narration question by doing away entirely with 'he said,' 'she said,' and 'as the bystander remarked.' "

"There are," Astarte remarked, with authority, "no bystanders on this flight. And what *Edge* had to say was hardly to the point. 'Perhaps the reason Wayfaring is the envy of Hollywood is that her career at Hyperion has been one endless green light meeting.' That's a lot of hogwash. Your career, as I happen to know very well, has been one long embrace of your obstacles, which you have always realized are your material."

"So," Kaye Wayfaring concluded, unresigned, "Rock Formation is envied. I thought you both told me that envy was out in Los Angeles."

Astarte brightened, stirring Essence of Life mineral complex into her Pellegrino and warming to her subject, the New Tolerance and the efficacy of the herb compounds Balanced Woman and Re-Charge (to help the soul to catch up, when the body is flying coast to coast across American geography, through American history).

"The *admission* of envy is out in L.A., hon, but *completely*."

"An important distinction," Jameson declared. "It helps to

single Los Angeles out as living, working proof that plotless improvisation isn't necessarily random."

"We study war no more either," said the seer. "Refusing to be overstimulated by global aggravation, we've taken on road-kill, and have done something about it, becoming the nation's best drivers."

"What about," asked Kaye, "the overwhelming presence in Orange County of the defense—excuse me—the *aerospace* industry? Do you allow yourself to be overstimulated by it?"

"No. I think aerospace is healthy competition—like the Weather Channel; they keep Astral on its toes, so to speak."

"So Rock Formation is *not* envied," Maev interjected.

"More ironically observed," Astarte declared. "Rock 'n' roll without sex or drugs."

"How can they say no sex?" Maev objected. "There are progeny."

"You may be progeny—although you couldn't call yourself that; not in the business. There's already a band called that. They come to me. But Rock Formation as such—"

"—has progeny without sex," Maev cut in. "That's what you're saying. It has Adam Bomb or Adolescence or whatever it is brother and friend are calling themselves this week."

"Well, yes."

"Yes, well, you needn't think one's feeling left out; one's not. Let's put it this way. South took the ace of diamonds and cashed a high trump. He was safe if trumps broke 2–2 or if hearts broke 4–3. When West showed out, South tried the hearts, hoping to discard his losing diamonds. Alas, East ruffed the third heart, and South was left with an unavoidable loser."

(The French cineast beamed. The child was becoming more interesting every minute—more interesting even than— a voice clicked on, in English, in his head. *Do not go there.*)

I'm getting the picture, Kaye Wayfaring decided, looking

out the window as if there was something going on in the sky. Nothing but instructions—producers', interviewers', flight personnel's . . . all narrators. What happens to the identities of—oh, hell.

"Somebody has just written," Maev then informed the French cineast (as if, Kaye thought immediately and for some time after, she were reading her mother's mind), "that identity novelists, out of the postmodern loop, are still working overtime to shore up superannuated stories about the outmoded self."

"You know," Kaye declared, looking askance, lowering her voice and confiding to Astarte, as Maev and the French cineast continued talking around one another, "speaking of working overtime, of shedding outmoded selves—I suppose we really must call it 'renewal'—it's still amazing to me about Leland."

"I know," Astarte agreed. "One always liked him, but to imagine back in '84 that he would pull *this* off. I understand the new technology diversity move, in principle. He is after all a graduate of Stanford—knew the Silicon Valley people as children—whereas no one of the other industry broncos ever looked at anything happening north of Oxnard. Even so, how *is* it he's managed to double Hyperion's assets every year for eleven years?"

"Clearly," Maev, breaking off her own conversation with the French cineast to interrupt, declared with authority, "he read a book on the subject and decided. It appears people do."

Coincidentally, across the aisle, that same moment found Livonia de Longpré, bluffing her way through a characteristic anxiety, explaining to Jameson the couple's recent move to the Wilshire Corridor.

"Now that, thanks to the off-loaded perquisites of turbo-capitalism, any industrious Brentwood dentist can jump from his starter unit off San Vicente into something newly vacated in Mandeville Canyon, drive a red Lexus, stock up on buffet lamps in espresso finish, and eat lotuses out of his own lotus pond—"

"Like a character," Leland declared, "out of that Aldous Huxley book."

"Aldous *Huxley*," Livonia declared, "was a hateful wiseass shit, *reeking* of *eau de lavande*. I knew him well in his dotage."

"Hollywood careers," declared Leland, "are, like Balkan politics, determined by a hostile, treacherous topography—like Los Angeles's own. Crossed by canyon-like invaders' corridors, their open flat expanses—"

" 'L.A. is a great big freeway,' " Livonia crooned jauntily.

"—quick communication, relentless product array, and dispersed fan populations contribute to a highly volatile environment, in the arid topography of which satrapies form with ease, only to survive with struggle and actually thrive with rarity."

" 'And all the stars that never were / Are parking cars and pumping gas.' "

"So be it," the executive declared. "Fame favors seeming-vast, but fragile, expensive empires, built on supple, but shifting, foundations—"

" 'Dreams turn into dust and blow away.' Tell me," Livonia, converting registers abruptly, snapped, "about shifting foundations. You want to know what fame is in this day and age? Karim Rashid designs a *wastebasket* and calls it *Garbo*. Outrageous!"

"Catabolic worlds," Leland continued, "seeking to legitimate themselves by miscalling what is actually an elementary naked territoriality the sophisticated interplay of idiosyncratic personality, fiscal imperative, and esthetic consideration.

"Where are the snowed-in, turned up noses of yesteryear? Replaced by the new Hollywood's new and unrecognizable actors who despite their penchant for scumbag chic and the dictates of sexually explicit position papers tend to have funny American Harmonial ideas about themselves, especially when they've played attractive or important people."

"It can no longer," his wife interrupted, "be the pleasure it formerly was being either attractive or important—indeed, it must add a new terror to death to imagine oneself reincarnated by these—"

"An expression," the provocateur continued, "of the relation of status. A symbolic pantomime of mastery on the one hand and of subservience on the other. No creature on earth betrays more anguish than the player gridlocked in the force field of opposites: acute awareness and deep denial of the awful fact that nothing he does increases by a jot either the sum, the product, or even the quotient of syntactical value in the world he idiotically assures himself—alone in his car, alone in his bed, alone in his head—he represents.

"Or, having reached a certain media-slut plateau—each his own little capitalist engine driving in deluded triumph, great distances, daily, in expensive and intimidating machines over what he imagines is his own turf-strip of that socially and environmentally cognizant mutual-fund world. Clay pigeons cruising relentlessly, valiantly combatting their several vexing toe-in and camber problems, along the freeways and the flats, gonzo rack and pinion whizzing fuck-me *zoom*, with pink furry dice dangling from the rearview mirror, eyes forever looking left or right at the high hills, scheming, taking margin calls on the car cell phone and dreaming big in Technicolor of heated turquoise pools and round beds blanketed with Madagascan orchids. Wondering if ever *anyone* will take them to the top of one of those hills and offer them even a sliver of the mansion-creep kingdom built on sand, strewn with tinsel, and mired in filth."

(Recreational Zyprexa, Maev decided; it's got to be.)

"For some reason," Livonia mused, "that reminds me of the '84 Olympics. The riots too. We were at up at Trancas, of course, so not even a trail of smoke—"

"I remember the '84 Olympics," Maev announced.

"Mary Miles Minter," Livonia declared, "died in the hills watching them."

"You and Mary Miles Minter!" Kaye Wayfaring chided.

"Mary Miles Minter's," Livonia insisted, "is one of the saddest and most terrifying stories in Hollywood history. Sadder than the story of Vilma Banky, of Ann Dvorak, sadder even than the story of Helen Twelvetrees. The pert yet undeniably raunchy little thing who made millions—and in those days millions was millions—out of a puckered simper and a naughty toss of golden ringlets ended up a crazy, fat old slag, bitter, angry, and flailing—or, considering the size of her, more likely *thudding*—in the parched, enervated Hollywood Hills. And all because of a dirty guy and an angry mama.

"The two worst things you can be in America are alone and out of date, and Mary was both for sixty years. She was like Sleeping Beauty in the castle overgrown with vines—only who came to cut the vines away and kiss her was not Prince Charming, but Mr. Death."

Silence ensued; Livonia continued. "And I don't know what you mean by 'You and Mary Miles Minter.' I did not die up in the hills. I went up into—over them, to Lake Arrowhead—with Leland, where he proposed. I had a plan, you understand—I see no reason not to admit it: a woman with a plan is, after all, less susceptible to the awful corrosion of envy than a woman with none."

(That may be the trouble, Maev considered. I have no plan.)

"Stardom," Leland continued grandly, "once encompassed

everything you could find on the ride—the invasion, competition, succession and symbiosis of all the drives. More interesting surely, to our generation at any rate, than the narcissistic Xerox acting of today's twentysomething freeze-dried-sock-puppet airheads untempted by any articulated form of knowledge, who in deep-stall idiot bliss make pizza-boy eyes into the Steadicam lens and whisper 'Eat me.' "

"If only," Livonia countered. "What *I* hear them whisper is 'I'm alluring, mysterious, and completely out of your league; only *dream* of eating me.' Cases of prior restraint, pure and simple, no possibility of anything that goes to make up ordinary life is of any interest to them. Agreeable, accommodating, and absent—same size, same brand, same look, same fame as product; true believers all in modern adhesives as they go about their work of counterfeit obligation.

"They will go on confusing revelation with display, spin with spread, hidden resources and energy reserves with unexploded ordnance. Shadows slide across their empty eyes; their only thoughts come as they put aside their asset-bubble blowpipes and sit down to make up. And, of course, out on what they dumbly consider their singular, unique and custom-built career catwalks, intersecting like L.A. freeways, they ride the clutch."

"Godard says," the French cineast interposed, "that merely because they have been chosen, they already feel with great satisfaction the envy of all their peers, and they think that is enough to fuel their performances."

(His mission was to instruct Americans in what to his French mind was the most crucial of the so-called deadly sins, envy, which necessarily arose, he had been assured by the *normaliens* he'd hung out with at La Coupole in the tumultuous period following the événements of '68, because of the forced separation in the birth of thought between sign, or designa-

tion, signifier, or designator, and signified, or designated—
weakly mirrored in now-defunct Christian theology as the
Trinity. Envy, he would point out to the Americans, as the *normaliens* had pointed out to him, and with comparable verve, is,
in the only usable modern terms, the post-Freudian, man's
most valuable instinctual weaponry, the management of
which—the quality of its discharge—is the single most important task to learn in the leading of a successful life. As, for
example, all animals must learn to lie in order to survive.
Americans, as puritans, still refused to acknowledge and harness the power of envy—which is to anger what atomic fusion
is to atomic fission. Yes, the French had much to teach these
Anglo-Saxon derivatives still, would they but heed.)

"That fantasy," Leland interposed, "is undoubtedly the result of both the collective delusion of their envious peers and,
at root, the estimation in which the industry, quite correctly
from its point of view—that of an a elite having taken on a
higher polish and a more mundane seeming—holds them. So
interchangeable, so replaceable, that they must know that even
as they are being paid their inflated salaries to front for
scenery, real estate, burnished objects, and incalculably expensive special effects, they are, in effect, already living on sever-
ance pay."

"But they *don't* live," Livonia protested. "They have no
goals. The only thing you *ever* hear them say with conviction is
'I don't think so.' Do you know what Martha Graham did at
the Neighborhood Playhouse? She held up a blank piece of
paper, tore it in half, and announced, 'That is the tragedy of a
piece of paper.' I want to do that to them—but they wouldn't
get it."

"They would perhaps," Leland offered, "if what you held
up to them was a contract, or an eight-by-ten glossy.
Otherwise—"

"One of them actually talked back to me," Livonia persisted—adding for the general information of the interviewer, "I give classes now, you know."

(And the husband, Maev advised herself, a run for his money.)

"Saying, 'Lady, it's the motion of the *ocean*'! I had to tell him, 'Darling, get a day life. You're a little out of scale for the motion of the ocean; better to stick to the drool of the pool.

" 'Explanation is just *not* identical to close description of the particulars. Possibly you view your behavior as a proleptic enactment of—something interesting? Some kind of existential but-for reimbursement claim? Some symbolically encoded critique of current power arrangements? Make a *wish*, will you, darling, if you're not too worried it will mess your look.'

"To which he responded, truly put out, 'The way you say things, so confrontational, so unaffirming; it makes me feel so completely *violated*. I have to tell you it torques my jaws.'

" 'You go in for affirmations?' I challenged. 'I certainly *do*—and for a combination of personal values, supportive friends, and expressive outlets.' "

(Ah, those, Maev wondered anew; what about them?)

" 'How nice for you,' I persisted—I was of course at my wits' end—'and your greatest ambition in life must undoubtedly be to harness all that guy energy and be cast in one of the many pictures the new Hollywood has dedicated itself to producing dealing with the universal themes of friendship, confessional identity, romance, and commitment.'

" 'What if it is?' he snapped. 'Then you must *stress* all that,' I advised, 'when talking to your career coach next time you calendar lunch at Maple Drive and by way of a concept to-do list, she furthers the idea of turning you from a featureless need machine into an ultra-yummy, intrinsic-charisma strip-search hot boy in a Lincoln jeep, expressive of some historic junction of man and moment.

" 'Because as it comes off now, darling, your show reel exposes a very low-caliber bullet in the world, a doe-eyed dearie deeply entrenched in the idea of life as a chain of pause-inducing events, each enabling you to dispense in that evenly inflected timbre of yours great info-dumps of personal history, largely having to do with having found your center.'

" 'What if I *have*—what if I *have* found my center?' He was snarling now, like something cornered, staring into a flashlight beam in a back alley off Fountain."

(I'm almost on his side, Maev told the window.)

" 'Then you're too late; it's an idea, darling, that in itself is *over*—it's *done;* stick a fork in it. You can't even summon the energy to be arrogant.

" 'You aren't a person, darling, you're a one-boy split-screen talk show, a kiosk clad in generic self-advertising. Your male body is neither your rocket nor your whirlpool—it is at the very best your flagpole, your hot tub.' "

(What must it be like, Maev considered, to have that *warrant.*)

" 'Your narrative, susceptible of neither thick description nor dense citation, is a petrified event; your circumstances seek to mitigate themselves; too strange.

" 'Moreover, your grasp of the world outside Los Angeles must be terribly limited when you think, as you seem to, that the CIA is a rival agency to ICM. There is in you an apparent incident-trajectory disconnect, darling, the likely result of some low-baseline subcortical frequency glitch in the template mainframe.

" 'And I'll tell you something else. You'd be much better off, should you stay in Los Angeles, doing a UCLA seminar in chorus-line dancing than paying out all that money to a power witch who promises to plant the seeds of wonder, but who at the end of it all will only tell you how low on the tone scale you are, what little reason there really is for you to own a cell phone, and how personally disappointed she is in you—and in the same hissing whisper in a public place berate you for subordination syndrome more severely and lastingly than you can ever berate yourself at home as you scream at your image in the bathroom mirror for not aspiring more forcefully to become something greater than the nothing you have never ceased to be.

" 'And now instead of doing what I probably ought to do—telling you to get out—I'm going to take a chance and go further.

" 'I know you better than you know yourself, darling—just let me tell you what I know. You are your own creation—the product of your own greatest desire. You're crazy about yourself. You'd be wildly jealous of yourself if you knew how—but that's just it, you don't. I can teach you how—and it will make all the difference, I promise you, to your performances and to your career.' That got him."

(Not surprisingly, Maev allowed; it's got me.)

"Jealousy of self was Brando's secret—I was with him on *The Wild One*—and the reason he so loathed publicity: it interfered with his self-appraisal. *There* was self-absorption—a self-absorption that reached such a degree of white heat that the whole world was drawn into it."

"I identify with Brando, monsieur," she then testified (riveting the cineast with the alarming exophthalmic gaze that had brought her fame), "because of the calumnies he has suffered. I have suffered them myself. Why, do you know that at the time Leland and I were courting, certain notoriously wicked people in Los Angeles actually went to him to try to convince him the licentious rumors about me were *true*?"

"*Licentious*, madame?"

"Licentious, monsieur. In Los Angeles, rumor falls into categories, like French verse. In ascending order, feeble, sufficient, rich, and licentious. These rumors were licentious—

affronts irréperables, to which I did not take kindly, and which, had my husband been willing, I would have very much enjoyed prosecuting in a court of law—for I am, you must understand, not just another haunted woman from the past too hungry for a present; not some leftover, wide-eyed fifties-B-picture-hash-slinger bitch who careened through life leaving a trail of empty bottles, discarded men, and broken dreams. Not some hard-boiled cantankerous *vestige* with a voice composed of equal parts of honey and sand, but, speaking of *ces émotions qui nous fabriquent,* a principled woman, alive to outrage.

"Rumors that I had, for instance, blackmailed my first husband, the director, into paying a huge alimony in return for my silence over his dealings with the CPA—*and* that I had, for another, *suffocated* my second husband—my *first* producer, is how the gossips denominated the poor bastard—while he lay in a drunken stupor at the beach house in the Malibu Colony."

"Madame!"

"Oh, yes, monsieur. Many were the remarks concerning that particular *veuvage précoce,* and of course, it was all terribly simple really. The dumb sonofabitch simply choked to death on a corn dog. He was not, I'm afraid, very well brought up— *pas de la vraie souche*—and anyway, drunks have notoriously bad gag. Hence, I believe in correction, and in some type of obedience."

"As in Tehachapi," Leland interposed.

("Leland's little joke," Astarte explained later, when the de Longprés had both gone to sleep and the cineast had retired with the seer to the back of the plane. "Voni was nominated back in the fifties, in black-and-white, for screaming her way through *Fall Girl*—though it must be said that screaming back then was a highly developed art."

The cineast's secret bewilderment was not greatly ameliorated [for, strangely, considering his origins and formation, he had never seen *Fall Girl* and was in fact just young enough to wonder, apropos the anagram CPA, what all the fuss could have been over Voni's first husband and his dealings with the certified public accountant—although he had been informed by astute historians of the industry that Hollywood stars have time out of mind indeed been famously entrammeled both by vexing tax problems and by complicated secret sexual histories, from William Desmond Taylor, Mary Miles Minter, and Fatty Arbuckle down through Randy Scott, Cary Grant, and Gary Cooper, to Lizabeth Scott, Rock Hudson, and the purge at Universal in the fifties, right to "you-know-who and you-know-who-else" today]. He nodded knowingly nevertheless, instinctively realizing that not only was discretion, in Los Angeles as in Paris, the better part of valor, but in fact the most efficacious reusable meal ticket of all.

"Voni," Astarte assured the French cineast, "would have been nominated a second time for *Avenged*, but for the disgraceful boycott of the picture by the Academy—which of course rebounded famously, breaking the old insider power forever."

"But," the cineast demanded, amazed, "was Madame de Longpré in *Avenged*?"

"Indeed she was, monsieur," the seer advised, lowering her voice, thereby advising him to do likewise. "Surely you recall the older woman?"

"*Merde alors*—but that was she?"

"The very she. Audiences, particularly at Cannes, were not soon to forget her coming up behind Wayfaring in the mirror and hissing, 'Face it, my dear, you can't risk turning into me; you simply couldn't handle it. Wiser by far to kill yourself, soon.' ")

"But," Livonia had continued to the cineast, with an air of a summing up, "all this talk of one's self is not intended to throw the discussion off the main track. We were—we *are*—all of us, essentially talking about Kaye Wayfaring. I am not and never was anything like a great actress, whereas she unquestionably is, but for all that difference there are some essential qualities we share, and I daresay that by studying them up close in me you will not be wasting your time in assessing the star she is. Neither of us ever played the gamine—we say tomboy now—neither of us was ever devoted to the various species of lapdogs and thugs proliferate in the industry; neither of us Southerners has ever been at all sentimental about respectability; neither put any trust at all in fame, and very little, either, in our managers; and as a consequence I daresay neither of us is terribly likely to die either broke or disillusioned.

"Of course," Livonia declared, "it means nothing to say all this when to say 'I like her work' doesn't have anything to do with acting, but only with cosmetic surgery."

(Whereupon the determined cineast, taking some minutes, had examined the older woman carefully. Apart from the suspicion of a corner lift and, he thought, a little excavation here and there to forestall gaunting, he detected no stark surgical procedure; her work was quite as good as that.)

In the cockpit, while computers monitored the controls and the aircraft was drawn in a wide arc across the clear and spacious sky, the pair were deep in conversation.

"Read me that last part again?" the pilot asked. "It had a definite aerodynamic thrust."

" 'The aptly named Rock Formation's song melodramas,' " the copilot began, " ' "Ensenada" and "Womanly Girl"—' "

" 'Ensenada,' " the pilot interrupted, "was blast-off—it was stealth bomber."

" '—With their devastating critique,' " the copilot continued, " 'of corporate America's high-roller sector-fund exploitation of unhinged female sexuality—' "

"All sexuality. Jealousy, perfume . . . the works."

" ' "Rock Star" and "Lost Angeles" with their encoded meanings relative to crack addiction, narcissism, the New Age and the adrenalized glam rock of two decades ago—' "

"Yeah."

" '—have studiously avoided the folly either of composing musically naive rock-candy songs with psychobilly bossa-nova overtones to go with string quartets *or* imitating Superchunk's garage rock's smeary guitar noise or Southern Culture on the Skids' "too much pork for just one fork" and "eight-piece box"–style innuendo. *"Ensenada"* means "the creek" '—did you know that?"

"Yeah—it's crucial."

"Hm. '—and the genius of the Wayfaring signature is that of the *only rock performer today* capable of powering the scenario of the girl up shit's creek without a paddle—' "

"Exactly."

" '—who flips open her purse, extracts an outboard motor disguised as a blow dryer, and makes a flash getaway—*without mussing a hair.*' "

"Virtually."

" 'And this is why she embodies the *symbology of transformation* that the movies have spitefully abandoned in favor of big face-acting and *the symbology of assimilation* to the small-load-boom greed of consumer culture.' "

"Getting there."

" 'Rock Formation's work, then, focuses on the overall social process through which a dominant culture and its alienated challengers contend back and forth among texts and contexts.' "

"Intense. Mach two."

" 'Their songs are fields of force, places of dissension and shifting interests, occasion for the jostling of orthodox and subversive interests.' And now their offspring, Adam Bomb, has been highlighted in the advanced press as 'a two-faced dude,' and their big hits, 'Other Than Love' and 'Transplanted Heart,' cited as backtalk replies to Rock Formation's 'Womanly Girl.' In what was called the 'unambiguous, non-transgressive depth of their rapport,' the critic stated flatly, 'They are the phenomenal success they are simply because people love to look and listen to two young men who love one another work together and be together and aspire.' You have become strangely silent; what's up?"

"I was just thinking."

"Of what—liminality, structure, anti-structure, and distorted bar chords in contemporary adolescent discourse?"

"No, of automatic pilot . . . and of hair. And of envy in the business. R.E.M., Rock Formation's chief rival, comes from someplace in Georgia, right?"

"Athens."

"And Wayfaring comes from someplace in Georgia called Clinton."

"*Clayton.*"

"Close enough."

"So, you mean if she eats peanuts, maybe she had a thing with Jimmy Carter? Next you'll be saying you *believe* Chelsea Clinton recorded those revenge rock songs in the White House basement accusing her father, our President, of porking Wayfaring, among others. Or that Wayfaring's left Hyperion and signed with Fox for a fash remake of *Orchestra Wives* called *Band Girls.* Sex, drugs, rock 'n' roll, or low-down love and longing in bizarro locations worldwide."

"No I won't. That was a stupid rumor—unworthy of them."

"To their minds *nothing* is unworthy of them."

"Did she ever say 'R.E.M. is emotionally asleep'?"

"Never. A total fabrication of some mean-spirited begrudger of Method acting."

"*I* heard there was something she said that was like that."

"What she said was, 'I think they're dreamboats.' "

"Oh."

"A lot of what she says gets twisted around, or bends people out of shape. When she said she learned to sing in Georgia off old Blue Lou Barker records—said the way Blue Lou said 'You ain't got no blues till some other woman takes your man' so it sounded like 'some mother woman' spoke to her condition—*that* raised a few eyebrows."

"Unplucked ones, of those jealous of her candor."

"Well . . ."

"It's true she had some mother—Wayfaring did."

"And now she's got mother*hood*. Is that kid coming back for a look at the controls, or what?"

"He is. Did you pick up the interview he gave on *New York Kids?*"

"I did not—but then I'm not a New York kid."

"Well, he is—and a brilliant one. Maybe a little bizarre, but *fluent*—the Irish influence."

The musical-chairs realignments had by this time wrung several variations.

"So," Jameson resumed, "in fiction if the functional presence of envy is evident in the getting of a *purchase* on the events attributed to others, then the traditional voyage stories, featuring the outmoded self, of course, are understandable."

"I always like stories on trains," Astarte added, "like on *The Mysterious Traveler*. Remember him? 'I take this same train every week.' "

"Aren't we all," Kaye Wayfaring remarked, "mysterious travelers."

"If you remember," Jameson advised his stellar friend, "the one time you played the Mysterious Traveler—as Artemis Grey—you couldn't keep still in your compartment. Envy of the real world drove you to mix with the other passengers, and be unmasked."

"I must have thought," Kaye Wayfaring mused, "I was playing *Twentieth Century*."

"I like train stories too," Jameson allowed, "even if the speed of the train tended to make them farcical."

"Planes are faster than trains," Astarte remarked.

"Still are we trapped," Jameson continued, "not only in our cabin, but in our story, and not merely because envy battens on gossip shall we be scored for writing *the story is there is no story—eat your heart out*. Few can admit their hearts are— comestible. We shall be scored, because the worse suspicion will be aroused that the story we say isn't here *is*, if only because we all know we all lie. And whether there is or not an end to our stories, there is certainly an end to our *telling*—or at least a stop put to it."

"We are born, we live, we die," Kaye Wayfaring observed.

Astarte brightened. "*We Are Born, We Live, We Die*—your first nomination."

"But do we—die?"

"Yes, dear, we die," Jameson assured Kaye Wayfaring. "Of course there is rather more to it than that bald statement. As Robert Mitchum assured Jane Greer in *Out of the Past*, 'I don't want to either, baby, but if I've got to, I'm gonna make sure I'm last'—which everyone is, from his own point of view. You could call it playing the intention."

"And a picture about envy?" Astarte asked, diverting her attention from a sudden tilt in the cabin. "What about that?"

"All pictures are about envy nowadays," Jameson decreed. "That's all pictures are. Television replaced auditions with commercials and motion pictures replaced performance with casting—casting calculated to make audiences feel deprived and enraged. The only redress is to seize the screen—the subjective camera, which has been tried and has failed. No sane

viewer can more endure a passive camera's attempt to impersonate a talent subject to whims than any reader can an auctorial vogue voice doing ditto. Oddly, the reader feels less
deprived by the omniscient narrator than by the current vogue
voice droning on in the perpetual present."

"Speaking of scenarios," Kaye advised the seer, "this one's
devised a new kind of Monopoly to play with the children. A
board of the world's cities. Los Angeles is Park Place and New
York is the Boardwalk."

"They demanded something as sophisticated," Jameson
avowed, "as the Monopoly played by theorists of quantum
chromodynamics. I think I've succeeded. I've got them more
interested in it than in SimCity, or even SimEarth, although,
in spite of the fact that Tristan claims the inspiration for his
'This Town' is unified field theory, I think it's more likely
SimCity."

"Boys are boastful at that age," Astarte agreed, "and lax in
covering their tracks."

"The trick, I think, is the board game breaks the isolation
that the computer fosters. In any event, the utilities are giant
multinationals, the railroads are the airlines. Bank error in
your favor is now computer-generated currency killing, and
Chance features a lot of restaurant information."

"What's jail?" Astarte wondered.

"Problematic," Jameson said. "I say jail's still jail. They say
nobody goes to jail anymore, they go to Betty Ford's."

"And New York is the Boardwalk," Astarte mused.

"New York lit up that way at night," Kaye Wayfaring said.

"Is that what you were glued to at the window?" Jameson
asked.

"It was."

"Talking of penis envy," he mused.

The copilot, passing up the aisle, smiled at the company.

"I've invited the boy to join us up at the controls."

(And why not the girl? Kaye Wayfaring, mute, asked.)

"Thank you. Roger; he'll get a kick out of that."

(Penis envy indeed, she thought. Norma Jean used to say penis envy was *nothing* compared to what men wanted to do and couldn't. She learned all there was to learn about envy early—not to mention playing the intention—way before she became Artichoke Queen of the Salinas Valley in 1949.

My mother felt deprived and enraged without ever going to the picture show. People said she was completely crazy—the only woman they'd ever heard of who was jealous of herself. If—I guess it's now *when*—I do play her, using my fabulous Southern gift for personalization, indeed, and not to mention the intention again, I'll be concentrating on envy to start with. Mother's envy of Thalia's involvement with the Trumans, to begin with, and how she pooh-poohed it, preferring to recall her own days at the governors' balls in Atlanta.

Our self-styled narrator—he whose figments—figments including himself on this outing—we all might well be, flashing across his computer screen as its flight engines purr. He did once tell me that like Ovid's Envy, I wanted sometimes to go and live in a cave in Warwoman Dell. It's true, I would look in the mirror every day when I came home from school, and suck in my cheeks to *make* my face look lean and mean; it was the look.)

She caught herself looking at her reflection.

"But hon," Astarte said, "you *keep* looking out the window. We left New York behind two hours ago. We must be over Denver, at least, by now."

"The afterimage," Kaye Wayfaring explained, "or whatever it is, persists."

"Los Angeles is lit up at night," Astarte objected.

"Is it ever," Jameson concurred. "But not that way."

"That's terribly chauvinistic," the astrologer objected.

"The New York skyline," Jameson continued, "erectile,

versus the splayed grid of supine Los Angeles . . . replicating the splayed grid of everything seen from the air since leaving erectile New York to its own devices—the lights strung across the continent below twinkling, like stars, so that we looking down resemble them on the ground looking up."

"Stars, or jewelry," Kaye Wayfaring added. "Palm Springs seen from the air at night always looks to me like necklaces and bracelets of diamonds, emeralds, rubies, and sapphires displayed for purchase on black velvet."

"New York," Jameson proposed, "is time—time rearranged—and Los Angeles is conceived space. New York is High Stakes, Los Angeles is High Concept. New York's candid message is that in the future everybody will be world famous for fifteen minutes; Los Angeles's fanciful one that everybody will be famous forever within a radius of fifteen yards."

"I think we've passed Denver," Kaye Wayfaring said, looking out the window again.

"I'd rather talk," Astarte declared, "about people than about places. I'm not one of those who do charts for cities. I think," she advised Kaye Wayfaring, "you know the effect you have on people, for which they both love and respect *and* possibly envy you—a little."

"We stars."

"I know it's trashy and overstated, but it is the truth. What do we tell them to calm their distress—do we tell them the truth? That stars, as it happens, only *seem* to flicker? Rays of light reaching our eyes from space pass through an atmosphere which is in constant motion—layers of air whose density changes incessantly, from second to second, and these changes cause the rays of light from a star to follow an erratic and inconstant zigzag path?"

"You might," Jameson advised.

"I tried—in the middle of the '92 campaign, and they came

at me with the show business–politics question, and the astrology factor. In ancient times men looked up at the stars and read them, and a shooting star, or a fast-moving one, caused a stir. Nowadays, down there in the heartland, somebody steps out at night and among the stars are the white-and-red tail-lights of transcontinental flights such as ours. And inside the planes on some of these are the journeys being taken of today's stars, who influence the populace in much the same way—if for shorter terms—as the anthropomorphic configurations of heavenly bodies once did. Metro may have been exaggerating terribly when it said it had more stars in captivity than there were shining in the heavens, but in terms of the *effect* those stars had—and the effect their successors *continue* to have—they were rhetorically justified."

"Hear, hear," Jameson exclaimed.

"With a spectrum," the seer continued, buoyed by encouragement, "the collective motions of the stars that make up a galaxy can be measured. The ages and types in the stellar population, and the rate of star formation, can be inferred as well. Chardin says some things fall under knowledge yet cannot be exactly known, and some are neither known nor can be known—such as the complete commixtures and distinct virtues of the stars."

"There's been a lot more talk about the old studio days," Kaye Wayfaring noted. "I think it must be all the remakes."

"Not to mention," Jameson added, "all the remaking of the past."

"*That* is the truth, honey," Astarte concurred.

The pilot and the copilot kept talking.

" 'New York lit up that way at night'?"

"That's what she said."

"I guess that's the thing that makes her interesting."

" 'New York lit up that way at night' makes her interesting?"

"The fact that she notices it—probably every time."

"Every time a first, like good sex."

"More like a good takeoff in my opinion."

"Far out. They sure pinned the wings on the right guy."

"She hasn't lost that Debbie Harry aftermath quality."

"I call that her Beverly Michaels quality."

"Beverly Michaels?"

"Definitely. Beverly Michaels singing 'Long Ago Guy': 'You haven't forgotten how / You haven't forgotten when.' Remember that? It's a tar-roof-lean-to-by-the-tracks . . . a *Wicked Woman* quality."

"You always do get the undeniable impression that she's envious of the past—put *out* not to have been born and reared into the era that started with Prohibition, went into the Depression, and ended at Pearl Harbor, rather than the one that started during the War, went through the War, went through film noir and *This Island Earth*, and ended with the assassinations of Marilyn and Jack Kennedy. No wonder then she gets nuts from time to time."

"Back to the admission of envy?" Kaye Wayfaring began again in earnest.

"Yes," Astarte continued. "Well, ever since the reformed Trixie Revenge, styling herself your protégée, brought New York–style cable activism to Los Angeles, becoming the KBYZ public scold Beverly Boulevard."

"Why my protégée—*was* she Trixie Revenge?"

"We never knew; she never said. She said you showed her by way of the Halloween incident at Ralph Von Gelsen's that her conduct had become so unbecoming that whoever she'd been she'd better unbecome it. That done, she decided to become Beverly Boulevard. Very L.A., really. As she put it herself, 'Darlings, you are looking at a *fundamental solution* to category crisis.' "

"And to think," Kaye said wistfully, "when I was single, and studying philosophy at UCLA, I did that A paper on decision theory. Of course," she nodded toward Jameson, "many assumed you wrote it for me."

"I think," Astarte said, "both Beverly and KBYZ are trying to downplay New York just now, and everything to do with its wiles and ways. There was a quantity of discomposure after last month's flare-up on the show about Max's, when Greta Garbage and Holly Woodlawn nearly re-created an old Factory cat fight over the smoky mirrors in the front room versus the orange neon in the back room."

"More than that, was the word," Jameson interjected. "A whole spectrum of estimation, it was said, on that culture versus this one—civilized to primitive, decline and fall, one to ten, then and now . . . all that. Happily, nobody mentioned the wallpaper."

"Disgusting," Astarte concurred. "But the crux was room tone downstairs versus room tone upstairs affecting the working girl's operative goals. 'I *was* my operative goal!' snarled Garbage; 'still *am!*' 'Oh, *honey!*' Holly cut in, rolling huge dark luminescent eyes, and tempers flared."

"Heavy-give Boricua that she's always been," Jameson interposed. "The muzzle velocity has yet to be measured that can impact on that girl's free speech."

"She finessed the situation," Astarte continued, "with a story about her role model Dolores Del Rio."

"I remember," Kaye mused, "Holly always wanted to come to Hollywood—where the real people were—and live in the Santa Monica house Cedric Gibbons and Douglas Honnold built for Dolores Del Rio, and give fabulous parties in the sunken tennis court."

"Holly identified closely with Dolores," Jameson affirmed.

"It seems Dolores used to get *furious* at her mother, who would go to the market and trade in her daughter's old shoes for vegetables."

"My mother," Kaye Wayfaring said, "often threatened to take *us*, old shoes and all, back to the cabbage patch for a refund in collards."

"Beverly," Astarte continued, "then invited recall of Candy and Jackie, and Holly, lisping divinely, proclaimed, 'Honey, those girls discovered *cyberspace* in the *ladies' room*!' This initiated the topics Penis Envy, Narcissistic Déjà-vu, and the Earthquake, all swirling like a game of whisper-down-the-wind around the campfire. Garbage, addressing the question 'Is a wish more an impulse or an intention—the libidinal uptick of instinctual narcissistic drives, or does it imply rational object goals?' 'That *word* again!' Garbage shrieked. 'Nobody even *knows* what it *means*!' "

"What word?" Jameson asked. " 'Rational'? "

" 'Narcissistic.' Rounding on caller and camera, she demanded 'Does Being envy Knowing? Not *this* woman's! Penis envy, my ass! Let Wayne Gretzky worry about the goals; I'll take the goalie, thank you. And remember, in Los Angeles, the fickle finger of fate wears nail polish: Malibu Blood Orange!' It all made for a more vivid and stimulating exchange than recycled snap-diva rap and discussions like 'Those Bad Hair Days and What to Do About Them.' "

"High life-evolution concept. All the same," Jameson submitted, "nostalgia's not what it was. You know," he continued, "When Babylon and Nineveh entered into a protracted struggle for supremacy, Nineveh did not take Babylon seriously at all: it thought it a town where people made up ridiculous stories and built shaky towers on shifting ground. Who won?"

"How *can* you talk that way," Kaye remonstrated, "you, a native New Yorker?"

"I deal in information; do not slay the messenger. This

may even be the secret meaning of the Judgment of Paris: the sinking into the spell of the sea-borne, irresponsible Aphrodite—which the goddesses of Wisdom and Progeny could not abide, and against which they sent their mortal sons to war."

(Every goddess, Kaye Wayfaring thought, was envious of Aphrodite, calling her vacant, vain, frivolous. Every star except Bette was jealous of Marilyn. They agreed with the men Bette tried to correct at the *All About Eve* wrap party; thought she was nothing underneath, nothing but sheer libido—envious of envy itself.

Maybe envy is just what men call it. I do know that like the characters Marilyn habitually portrayed—characters like Aphrodite, the deal maker—I've never so much wanted to go and get something as to stay where I am and have it brought to me. "Oh, butler . . ." To *attract* it. And unless that's just language category indoctrination, it means I want something I don't grow—I want it *imported;* whereas my experience of men is that they go after more of what's already theirs. To convince them to go and get something they don't have a piece of or a clue about is so bewildering to them, they get fidgety and weak. If anybody wants to *typify* this as reaction formation resulting from underlying penis envy, I really don't think I can just say that's ridiculous—or ask what woman would want to have a thing hanging off her that gets stiff and looks terrible in a tight dress. It certainly doesn't look so terrible in Jockey shorts. And as a mother I've found it pretty on my son, and have said so—in confidence.)

"I suppose," Kaye Wayfaring said, "I didn't even realize Greta Garbage was still alive, but I'm glad to hear it. Talk about envy—the first time I saw her in *Flotsam* and *Jet Set*—"

"Both Jean Harlow remakes," Jameson remarked. "Odd you should say you were envious when your bad-girl portrayals were the envy of the Factory."

"Remember," said Kaye Wayfaring, "the Empire State Building flickering for eight hours?"

"It's flickering still, along with everything else left over from the Factory days—everything, that is, but Max's and the abounding dead."

"Well," said Kaye Wayfaring, "if somebody put the whole night skyline on screen, I could look at it all day long. There's nothing like it on the planet—New York lit up that way at night."

"Envy is the motor of our story," Jameson declared.

"At least," Astarte offered brightly, "until we cross the Continental Divide?"

"At which time," the poet countered, "chasing the moon in its flight across the continental sky, we change over from apprehension to anxiety, as from Mountain to Pacific time."

"Oh."

"It's the same every time we say goodbye to New York. Were the grass not greener in the other yard—watered by the Colorado River—we'd not be four miles up in the air, where there's scant pride, little anger, no lust. There is an aura of timelessness in flight—day, month, and year become so unspecific, which is the *atonement* for envy: our bargain with destiny to let us land. And having said that, we are perhaps at the midpoint of our story."

"Oh, not *already*," Astarte objected.

"At the first turn, perhaps?" Kaye Wayfaring bid.

"No," Jameson insisted, "at the single turning point. You are confusing sonnet form—our story—with three-act script form. We can't afford to indulge ourselves, set in our ways, with second-act problems, so we dispense with the second act."

"As I remember sonnets," Astarte said, "the second half was some kind of answer; it talked back to the first part. Can we expect an answer before we land?"

"I hesitate to say a dusty one," Jameson answered, "but if you hold my hand and sit real still, you can hear the grass as it grows—even over the bourdon of the engines."

"I liked it," Kaye Wayfaring remarked, "when there was an aura of timelessness on the ground. When the children were children—a time I'm beginning to envy."

"Before adolescence," Astarte offered.

"Exactly."

"They were darling kids," Astarte offered, "but kids grow up—and they're *very interesting* as adolescents. Most adolescents are so *taciturn*—not them!"

"I think," Jameson advised, "she is less worried by small-'a' adolescence than by big-'A' Adolescence, the band—Tristan and his friend Steve. Maev wasn't encouraged to join in."

"Is *that* what they're calling it—Adolescence?"

"We talked them out of Adam Bomb," Kaye Wayfaring reported. "There was Adam Ant, and now there's Adam Duritz of Counting Crows, and then inevitably the Adam-and-Steve issue came up. They finessed that, but it's all starting to tell on their nerves. They haven't even gone into the studio, and already they're worrying about being 'ranked out,' as Steve puts it, by Beavis and Butthead on MTV."

"And the thing is called—what—'Our Town'?"

"No—'This Town,' " Kaye Wayfaring corrected.

"And it's about the earthquake."

"Sort of. It's a chase fantasy, really. They did *ask* Maev, but in such a way as to include her out—by telling her they were doing a seven-minute remake of *I Wake Up Screaming*."

"They thought," Jameson added, "another trio would too much resemble Rock Formation, causing varieties of comment on the platform."

"Also," said Kaye Wayfaring, "the two of them are clearly crazy about one another in the manner of young teenage boys. I remember it well; no girls need apply."

"Is it a *chaste* fantasy?" Astarte asked.

"Chastened by adolescent anxiety," Jameson replied. "The New York and Los Angeles locales dovetail—consequence of the earthquake—reducing the Viper Room to a pile of rubble."

"Tristan believes," Kaye Wayfaring said sadly, "that it was the *place* that killed River Phoenix."

"Oh?"

"Yes, and that the earthquake was . . . You see," she continued, "on the morning of the earthquake, at exactly 7:11 New York time, he fell out of bed from a dream of Los Angeles lying serene under a blanket of snow . . . and then the glass ball was shaken and the snow swirled, and he landed on the floor with a thud. That was the very hour the temblor hit Northridge. Uncanny, really."

"Both kids," Astarte replied calmly, "are adept."

"Yes, well, 'This Town' is an action montage on New York and Los Angeles intercut."

"All about," Jameson continued, "what every young boy wants to be-do-have-get. Tristan says, adolescents don't worry about sex, they worry about territory and control; he says they—Adolescence—are looking for something beyond Bing-Bong, bang and blame."

"Especially blame that hits the papers like this."

They looked up to see Tristan standing, looking at a clipping. "Enter the prince, reading," Jameson declared. "Trying to make sense out of life."

"On his back way to the cockpit," Tristan replied, dramatically, "to investigate the controls. Making sense out of life is easy. It's trying to make sense out of show business that's hard. You do your best to be spank to the elders, and some invidious tightass Nazi bastard rants at you about finding his salvation on the Big Rock that does not roll."

"What did he rant?" Astarte asked. "I missed the story at the ceremony—indeed, I missed most of the evening; I was in the ladies' room, doing a nervous client's chart."

Striking an attitude, Tristan commenced reciting in a pronounced Georgia twang.

" 'Is anyone ennobled by the *poetry* of these young people, who speak almost exclusively of unreflective animal sexuality and their lust for guns and violence? Do they know how *common* lust is, and how more profound virtue?' "

"Imagine," Astarte commented, "*contrasting* the commonplace and the profound?"

"Exactly," Tristan agreed, continuing. " 'To the degree that art successfully captures our darker shadows, it does so *only* to contrast the *difference* between beauty and ugliness.' Emphases mine."

"Well chosen," Kaye Wayfaring nodded.

"Thanks. 'So we might desire beauty and grow in humility.' "

"Always nice," Astarte mused.

"Especially at this altitude," Jameson added.

"Is that why we're flying in this old tin can instead of a *real* corporate jet? I read just yesterday that Madonna's plane looks like a flying bordello. 'One need not await,' " he continued, " 'the winged chariots trumpeting the coming storm. They are already here. And you can hear them roar on CD for $15.99.' Sonofabitch never shelled out a *nickel* for a CD or any other piece of art!"

"Temper, temper," Kaye Wayfaring counseled him.

"An artist needs his temper, dear," Astarte counseled. "You know that."

"Thank you for that," Tristan replied. "Do you speak professionally, or off the cuff?"

"I don't wear cuffs."

"Cool. Anyway, as we leveled off, Sister Woman starts in with the remarks—such as how penis envy is male projection. *I never brought up* penis envy."

"Good boy."

"I brought up castration anxiety; not the same thing—not by a long shot. 'To cut a long story short,' she tried to say, and I said I could never in my life do such a thing—a bald admission, I allowed, of castration anxiety. Like that.

"Anyway, we've hardly leveled off, and she's on full toot like Delirium railing at Desire about how the *real* envy is the men's of the continuous female orgasm. Frankly, I was embarrassed. I said I'd been reading Kierkegaard, who says there are two despairs, the lesser and the greater. The lesser is occasioned by failure to become oneself, the greater by success in doing so. The continuous female orgasm sounds to me dangerously like the greater despair—something like free fall, or earthquake. Her *answer*—all arched eyebrows and go-to-hell expression—was that everybody's treating me gingerly since I fell out of bed the morning of the earthquake was a late start, since somebody obviously carelessly dropped me on my head much earlier on. I felt like slugging her, but I guess we've been at Friends too long, and anyway we'd just taken off, so I said, 'I'm screaming with rage and pain—but you better get more gun, unless you're just thinking of bees.' You know what she did then? She *laughed in my face*. Don't you just *hate* it when people laugh in your face? Have the *decency* to laugh at me behind my *back*! And speaking of *temper*, does *she* have one! 'Your map is about to go nova,' I advised. 'Cool it down. Up your scale.' 'Up *yours!*' she snapped back."

"Really?"

"Really. That tore it—and this is the same demure thing who refused to cue me in preparation for 'This Town' simply because of that La Cienega reference. 'Coming from you,' I retorted, 'that's bitter.' And then I walked away, with downcast eyes. A kid trick, but once in a while it will work, especially after a lot of smart conversation, full of worldliness and sly wit. Your eyes are greener, Mother, off the ground."

"It's the altitude."

"And the Balanced Woman," Astarte offered.

"No problem—just so you know. Check you later."

"The performer," Kaye Wayfaring sighed, as her son went toward the flight deck.

"Performers' envies," said Jameson, "are soothed and dead in them when they're performing, since no one present is more alive than they are for a while."

Kaye Wayfaring sighed. "They were getting along so well before. I understand her, though. No girls need apply. I faced the same thing at Clayton High."

"Clayton High?" Astarte protested. "I thought you went to *convent school.*"

"In Atlanta," Kaye Wayfaring nodded, "for a year. It didn't take. And I just know," she continued in a worried voice, "he's got that sequence memorized for inclusion in 'This Town'— probably under the heading of white rap. Can you get away with that kind of thing?"

"Of course you can," Astarte insisted, "or rather they can; they're fourteen apiece. Anyway, what are lawyers for?"

"I wouldn't be at all surprised," Jameson proposed, "if his sister was thinking along the same lines."

"What do you mean?" Kaye Wayfaring asked. "Planning out her divorces, or what?"

"I was thinking," Jameson countered, "of her thinking about law school."

"Oh. I wonder—perhaps I ought to ask her."

"Ask me what?"

"Oh, hello," Kaye Wayfaring said. "We hear there have been ructions."

"Somewhat," Maev admitted. "I'm being ratty to him

about 'This Town'—but I don't like the tone of 'the sticky
doings in La Cienega, that marshy venereal bog, that fetid
maw full of stench that typifies Los Angeles. La Cienega,
where *Dionaea muscipula* closes the spined hinges of pudendal
lips.' Just squeamish, I guess; they say girls are."

"As I understand it," Jameson said, "the passage concerns
the rivalry between the paramecium, Manhattan, with its radiating piers, and the amoeba, Los Angeles."

"That passage," Maev corrected him, placidly, "concerns
the Los Angeles grid compared to the female pudenda, always
quaking, the hole opening and closing at whim—each time in
a different place. *Dionaea muscipula* is the Venus's-flytrap. A
bad pun; I didn't care for it."

"Oh," the poet replied. "Do I detect a cynical irony in that
response?"

"That cynical irony you refer to it is something I've been
trying to hold in check since the day I discovered I was different from little boys."

"I see."

"You know we are," Maev declared, "for what it's worth,
a boy and a girl—although in that silly interview he and the
boyfriend gave he referred to us as his first joint venture. Can
you believe it? I mean, really, it's one thing for one's publicity
to be generated in an office far out on Wilshire Boulevard, but
one would like to think of *oneself*—Kierkegaard or no
Kierkegaard—as something a little more interesting. More interesting surely than just something the camera loves. Still, I
suppose we must—the truth is, he takes after you, Mother, the
camera *does* love him, and I don't even know what that means."

"Nobody does," Kaye assured her smart daughter.

"Yes. Well, someday somebody will interview me, and
until then I guess I'm just a protected thing living with the
lesser despair in reflected glory, and he is the media star, so I
mustn't stoop to criticizing him for doing publicity. I must try

to remember *Cahuenga* is after all a growing boys' magazine—
and girls have long since stopped being growing boys by
the time boys are just getting into it. By the way, Mother,"
she continued, "do we really have a relative called Bama who
carved rosary beads out of peach pits?"

"My old great aunt Bama Eula Bridgewood. She's over a
hundred. She'd sit on the porch and carve rosary beads out of
peach pits."

"Rosary beads?" Jameson coughed.

"Yes, she carved them for the Grey Nuns in Atlanta—
becoming a county talk, as if she hadn't been before. People
accused her of making little fetishes for the mambos down in
Savannah. Georgia hill people are both envious and fearful of
the shore's ways."

"Sticky doings in venereal bogs, huh?" Maev put in.

"That kind of thing."

"That is certainly true in Los Angeles," Astarte affirmed.
"You can't get people in any of the canyons to even *go* to the
beach. And as for the Valley, well, what can there possibly be
left to say, or not to say, by anybody, about the Valley?"

A certain silence ensued.

"For my own part," Jameson suddenly exclaimed, as if
gripped by an idea, "I am free to confess my almost entire inability to gratify any curiosity that may be felt with regard to
the theology of the Valley! I doubt whether the inhabitants
themselves could do so."

"The Grey Nuns," Kaye Wayfaring continued, "said envy
was the worst of the seven deadly sins. The sin of the fifth
day, Friday, the day of the Crucifixion. Gluttony and sloth,
of Saturday and Sunday, were nothing in comparison: no trouble at all for the Holy Ghost to forgive. But the sin of the
Crucifixion, Friday, was cyanide—an ugly death. The Bosch
picture in the Prado of Envy snooping is certainly the ugliest
representation on that tabletop."

"Like all the ugly pictures of Hedda and Louella," Jameson remarked.

"The general opinion in Los Angeles," Astarte remarked, "is that grievance address has improved since the days of that Reign of Terror."

"He told *Cahuenga*," Maev interjected, "they kept Bama in a box. Is that true?"

Kaye Wayfaring nodded again. "There's a picture of her sitting in some kind of shipping crate, taken around 1920. When I asked about it, I was told, 'They just said to old Bama, "Bama, we're gonna get your picture; now you be sweet, you be pretty, throw on that old lace crazy Jane was in your trousseau and go and get in that big old box you came in that we saved." ' Bama may have been the product of a closer union than there ought to have been. She never felt envy—not in Clayton, anyway. 'Ah nevuh met ennybodeh *ordin'ry* till Ah came up heah from Atlanta. These ole people, they just live *foa-ehvuh*—there is *nuthin'* else t' *do*!' "

"When I first asked you where I came from," Maev commented, "you said, 'A big old box.' "

"I never said any such thing—and neither did your grandmother!"

"I know—but it does make a neat story, no? I must have dreamed it—like Little Brother dreamed the earthquake—which was no dream, really, so maybe you *thought* of saying it, and then thought better? Or maybe not. But it makes a fetching story. I believe one ought to be prepared."

"Are you bound for up front?" Kaye Wayfaring asked.

"No, I am not. It's manners to wait till you're asked, and I haven't been asked. I'm more likely to be invited to see how Roger microwaves savories in the galley."

"Aren't you overreacting?"

"Oh, I don't know, Mother; after all, it's a Hyperion flight. I'd undoubtedly do better on United."

"Oh?"

"Yes. In all the years you've worked for Orphrey Whither, and all the money you've made for him, and all the time you've spent flying around in this archaic rattletrap that looks like a troop transport plane when every other producer's aircraft looks like a Central Park West duplex with wings—"

"Or a bordello," Jameson commented.

"Whatever—do you think it ever once occurred to him to offer you a picture of your own—to direct?"

"I never asked; he gave me profit sharing."

(Manners, Maev decided. Southern. Guess I inherited them. Little Brother too. He said the trait resembles the winner's envy for the secret knowledge of the loser, the undercurrent of the world's major religions.)

Tristan was seen returning at that moment.

"Do me the justice," he declared, terribly sincerely, "to believe that these ephemeral successes, these triumphs of the hour, are neither overestimated by me, nor do they tend to lure my time and thoughts from efforts toward those attainments and that sterling efficacy of character which forms the only true basis of deserved and lasting success."

"I'll try," Maev answered, even more terribly sincerely.

Tristan and Maev walked together to the rear of the aircraft.

The adults continued their discussion.

"Regard the tension," Jameson remarked, "that exists between agnates of the same generation: a complex interplay of processes and forces governing behavior between members of a single kinship category."

"The Pomo Indians," Kaye Wayfaring declared, "solved the problem of envy in twins by killing both."

" 'Agnates,' " Astarte wondered. "Would that be the same thing as siblings?"

"It would. Kinship status may be only *phenotypical*, as in

being Angelenos, or in the biz, and *genotypical* may be membership in opposed factions in struggles between the sexes."

"Well, honey," the astrologer confided, "as Gloria Grahame said in *The Big Heat*, 'We're all sisters under the mink.'"

"Or beyond genders," Jameson continued blithely, "in the same family, struggling over inheritance. Or beyond families, struggles for land—Beverly Hills, Holmby Hills, Brentwood, and Whither Park real estate. Or the East Side–West Side melodrama—Los Angeles wearing some of New York's old battle hair—which has now superseded in the popular civic mind all previous antagonisms such as those of the Cold War, Republicans and Democrats, or the rivalry between Los Angeles itself and San Francisco for the assumption of hegemony in post-earthquake secessionist California."

"Keep it down, will you?" Kaye Wayfaring whispered. "You'll wake the de Longprés and the French cineast. The only thing about it all that worries me right now is whether there's anything telling under his rambunctious restlessness— or for that matter her poise. Any sign one ought to—"

Suddenly, from the rear of the cabin, they heard the twins singing in unison.

> "*O moon of Ala-baa*-ma
> *We now must say goodbye.*
> *We've lost our dear old* Maa-*ma*
> *And must have whiskey, or we must* die!'"

"That sounds beautiful—really!" Astarte said.

"They've always liked Kurt Weill," Kaye Wayfaring rejoined. "When he was very young, Tristan would walk around singing, 'Oh, it's a long, long while from me to December.'"

"And they haven't woken the sleepers, either."

.   .   .

The steward had returned to the cockpit.

"How are they back there—quieted down by now?"

"They're fine: they've been fed, they've closed their books, they've settled the major questions of life and love, or so it seems. Is that Lake Arrowhead down there—already?"

"Pointing the way down. Did they ever settle the skyline question?"

"For me the L.A. skyline is much to be preferred—all ground lights. No aircraft ever plowed into City Hall on the way down. Let's wrap this one."

"The descent seems uncomplicated," Astarte remarked, soothingly, as the aircraft broke through the noctilucent cloud cover on its approach to LAX.

"Yes," Kaye Wayfaring replied, taking in the vastness of Los Angeles.

"If every cloud bank has a silver lining," Jameson added, "then descending in this silver ship, we're it."

"The thing I *do* hate," Astarte admitted, "is circling in overcast sky out over the Pacific and Catalina."

"And the Channel Islands," Jameson added, "where you'd like them to sequester the amateurs."

"No, no more—what was it?—uptick of my narcissistic drive. I'm in a forgiving mood."

"Always wisest when descending."

(Catalina, thought Kaye Wayfaring, mortal creature in a settled mood, approaching the earthlights as the streetlights and moving vehicles along the Harbor Freeway came clearly into focus below . . . Catalina.)

A Plethora

PROFILED THAT WAY against the unhorizoned wash of sky and sea, the silhouette of the one they called El Sabio, lit from beneath by dying embers of the open-pit mesquite fire, most resembled (the boy decided) that of Goya's El Cabron hanging in spectral bivouac in the Prado. He'd been lecturing on everything in material creation all the night long, from the rising of the moon to moonset and after.

"I have been striving in the dark to give you an elementary demonstration. Without light I could draw no pictures in the sand."

"Why not?" a second voice, belonging to the one they called Shadrach, objected. "*They* have."

"*They*," sneered El Sabio's lieutenant, the one they called Crystalman, "draw maps of the *world* and *sand mandalas* by the scraped light of the stars. El Sabio draws no maps or *sand mandalas*—builds no sand castles that can't last out the incoming tide."

"That I do not," El Sabio repeated. "There are already far too many ill-defined things in view around here at once. But now we have the light, and in the *anpta nia*, the first vapors of the morning as the heat of the sun begins to lift the marine layer, more will be revealed."

The boy looked away toward the builders. With the

ground fog's burr dispelled, the mezzotint scene developing in daylight revealed perhaps too many things, but they were, he thought, hardly ill defined. Ocher sand replicas of the Pyramid Temple of Kukulcan and the Temple of the Warriors in Chichén Itzá at the tideline, and further up the beach near another blazing pit one crew had been excavating through the night, re-creating Monument Valley, peopling it with match-stick Indians on bluffs and a wagon train moving through, while across a negotiated reave boundary another had gone back to work on a tract of double-wide adobes with two-car ports, while a querulous voice among the wilderness advocates protested, "What with women and children and wire fences, this country will not long be a country for men!"

Closer in to the fire circle the cartographers worked. Crystalman was advising them.

"My advice is to either hang with straight Mercator or go for broke on an Albers conic equal area. Cone secant on two parallels with no areal deformation."

"Mercator," the mapmaker declared, "is only good for equatorial regions."

"There should only *be* equatorial regions!" Shadrach cried. "Only regions where surfers crest the lip are real. Baja is real; Hawaii—*amphibious* man blessed by the Ali'i. Those hard, splendid bodies, those bruised and bruising arms and knees! 'Here is the sea, the wind, the wave. In the maze and chaos of the conflict of these it is for me to thread my precarious way. It is good to ride the tempest and feel godlike.' It's all about stoke apex, man!"

"To resume the discourse," El Sabio declared. "By ele-mentary demonstration I do not mean something for all comers, easy to understand—*ordo et connexio idearum*—like Schrödinger's negative entropy flow—"

"*Yeah*," Crystalman crooned, picking up a fistful of sintered sand and letting it run slowly through his fingers.

"Or the frictionless pendulum. Such knowledge is the simple product of magnetic gravity. I *mean* something like the spectral representation of the operator U, which demands small knowledge ahead of time but for which an infinite amount of *intelligence* is required that the *inner* light may come. Such intelligence is electric; it alone may either attract or repel, decide or undecide. *But*," he cautioned, "it is possible to become engorged and plethoric with it, as with emotion, self-extending the ego, leading to thrombosis and freak-out. If you add something to itself enough times it will exceed any other number in magnitude.

"Time, Bergson declared, is either redemptive invention or it is nothing at all."

The boy was talking on a cellular phone held loosely to his ear, making the conversation easy to overhear.

"I've been calling 1-800-INNOCENT. At first it seemed as if their phone was off the hook, but then somebody here said they'd called once, and a man answered, with hangups. So I thought of trying you."

"I see—I hear."

"As at Deja.com, huh? It's been a while. I've had people run out on me, certainly, but not when I was being both brilliant and charming."

"I got your card from Albuquerque. Thanks."

"Don't mention it. You know America's greatest expert on suicide notes says they're usually as banal as postcards from the Grand Canyon or Niagara Falls. Doesn't mention Albuquerque."

"Where are you now?"

"At the Hotel de Dream on Baile's Strand, somewhere in the fourth sector, up Soochow Creek. 'Sometimes I go down to the port, splashing sand with my stiff foot at the end of my stiff leg locked in my stiff hip, to drink in the dives with cronies, feeling old and sorry for myself, laughing louder and louder. Then when the gold fog blurs the morning I go down to the beach and tramp barefoot in the wet sea edge, searching for driftglass.'

"On Bolsa Chica, actually. You should come out; spit rats make an interesting group interaction module, illustrative of copia-element genome reshuffling and combined resource autonomy; a fetching cross between Gilligan's Island and the Forward Zone Dense Pack game station, reinforcing the Manichean notion that the material world is formed from the debris of rejected sins.

"This guy called Shadrach has the place dialed into the Internet from the utility pole—franchised out by Berkeley to track intelligent space transmissions and massage the scan data. The Internet never forgets."

"Unlike certain individual people."

"Interested in coming out?"

"I don't think so—that isn't my kind of place."

"OK, we'll go someplace else—*in Los Angeles der dritten Stadt der Reise—oder zurück in unser kleines Haus in Louisiana.*"

"You're already someplace else—with Shadrach in Samuel L. Delany's gold fog."

"On Away Team maneuvers. I-S-O the meaning of the universe. I do; Shadrach says according to Rumi we are all naked pilgrims beached on a fragile spit off the mass shell whose only raiment is sunlight, and that you must not try to clothe us."

"I wouldn't dream of it. You mention the Internet; you've been tracked on it by some vigilantes. They say you got on the bus in Dallas, and off in El Paso, and onto a bike with a stranger."

"That was Operator U—from Hilbert Space."

"We don't think so. You know you've been gone a month?"

"Listen, talking of grouped interaction modules and salient voluntary communities of passion, interest, and identity, how's the shoot going down in Georgia?"

"They wrapped. We didn't tell Mother right away that you'd disappeared."

"I hadn't—didn't; every exit is an entrance somewhere else. All I did was run out on you—but you ran out on me first, and that, I admit, threw me. I don't know why you resist me so, as I whisper come-hithers into this worm-empty can. I'm beginning to think you're either a lesbian or a replicant snake charmer."

"To be pursued and killed in the expedition of your duties?"

"Certainly not. My duties expedited, I am at rest, though harassed by skegging gunsels and by duns—by domain-server button men and their little search engines that can.

"I keep hearing a little assassin droid voice saying, 'Wake up, it's time to die.' Why don't you come out here and plug this repo man through the back of the head? Also there's this apocalyptic guy features a Relief Pitcher mullet and a triskelion of penises for a shoulder tattoo. Calls himself Niels Bohr; says he's waiting for the javelin he threw into deep space to bounce back. Sits here sorting through his chew toys, communicating with Shelby, his interactive clam. Shelby has an eighty-word vocabulary, which is more than can be said for Niels in his down phase."

"Poor Niels."

"Truly. He'd been in one of those for the last few days, apparently. All he said when I first met him was, 'I do not speak English, please do not kiss me,' and 'Number 6 on the top and don't cut it whack, Jack.' Last night, however, he listened to me talk around the fire, and that seemed to perk him up. All morning now he's been fondling what looks to be a toy hand grenade, repeating 'In-A-Gadda-Da-Vida Elugelab' and 'Play me, don't stop: chaos is perfect order.' You should come out and meet him—and Shelby."

"Derelict surfers storming at a foam rave? I don't think so."

(But it was so: under the full moon they'd begun.

"Astronomy's dots don't connect on a single plane like in the comic pages, but across the multidimensional space-time continuum, as the Egyptians and the Stonehenge builders knew."

"When they finish reconstructing the Egyptian Theater," Shadrach declared solemnly, "I'm going back to Hollywood.")

Now, in the light, El Sabio taxed the boy.

"Yours, young man, is an ill-starred situation—that can be determined with the naked eye—but I can't quite make you out as one of the vagrant-homeless young already halfway down the vortex of oblivion. You might well be in the middle of an acting exercise, or merely slumming. But appearances do indicate that it is *love* that has brought you here to this lazaretto—love, that stranger in the convertible with the top pulled down who's waiting around every corner to lure the unwary in with candy, money, trinkets, picture shows, picnics, and what not, and drive them very far away.

"Why does the ego fall in love? Because otherwise, engorged on its own delight, it would choke to death. But was it El Amor Brujo that nabbed you, not in a convertible but on that infernal machine, and brought you here, and with whom you talked on through the night of azimuths and lunar standstills on the Salisbury Plain, the while he, transmuting your deep-structured and latreutic desires into shredded-nerve-end lust, cooked up a mess of paregoric shit—probably Afghani— in a bright silver spoon, loaded it into a platinum syringe the size of something a *veterinarian* would use, and, whispering a litany of treacherous endearments, shot it first into the vein in his pretty foot, then into the vein in yours, making quite a lustrous ceremony of it, quite a sacramental little *toilette des pieds*? Was it the left foot, by the way, or the right?"

"Why?" the boy asked in a counterfeited voice.

"Much may depend on it. In esoteric thought the sole of the right foot is concerned with profitable journeys; that of the left, with unprofitable ones. In any case, if that was love, then he has flown away, taking your guitar with him and leaving you his pistol case full of works. The lovely flame dies: you are *dedechado*—"

"And you think I'll fit in here?" the boy cut in.

"I do, with each here his own foredoomed precursor, his own dedicated page and self-addressed stamped envelope, his own praepositor of the Remove, his own chief blab— disavowing the frequentative and the contortions of spiraling organization for the serenity of relief in a few main planes—"

"El Sabio," yelped Shadrach, "rides the *word wave!*"

"—each *loco centrale* in his own mind, now that the night is far gone and the day, with its multiple agendas, is once again upon us. Each restitutor of his own depraved vastations, his own martyr under his own altar, awaiting comfort in the breaking of the fifth seal. Yet all amingle, ardent, if autoplastic, defensive, misprised, and mad to be saved. Yes, I think you'll serve; you hardly qualify, as do the majority present, as yet another unemployable and obsessed casualty of the demographic wasted-generation bulge, but in your ageless ill-starred situation you fit right in on this beach, itself in the gravest jeopardy."

"True," Crystalman declared, "what with El Niño."

"He fits," Shadrach seconded, "right in on this planet."

"That is all *kinds* of true," the first continued, as the sun rose higher over Palos Verdes. "What with global warming, sea-level rise, the hole in the ozone layer, ubiquitous plumes of polluted ground water, unsafe storage of nuclear wastes, and asteroidal impact hazard—it's a plethora."

"Oh, I don't know," El Sabio objected. "Some feel that which is not yet everything is nothing—an important possible position on the mind-body problem. The first affirmation of the world is an intermediate aim on the way to its negation."

"You people and your *words*," a figure unpacking model

cars from a big box at the building site called down. "*Plethora* indeed! Are there too many stars? Are there too many grains of *sand*?"

"Why don't you dig a hole," Shadrach taunted, "climb into it, and as we start filling it up, you can answer that for yourself."

"He has a point all the same," El Sabio mused. "Kant found only two things *wunderlich*, the starry firmament above and the moral law within."

"Are there too many dots in dot-com?" the remonstrant continued. "Too many fleeting blooms in the California desert? Are the twenty-five thousand species of wild orchids alive in the world too many? If less is more is *nothing most*? You may kill me, but you can never kill what I've experienced. I've seen things—"

"Yeah," Shadrach snarled, "attack ships on fire off the shoulder of Orion. Corposants on the mothership yardarm. Here on flat earth, who knows the color of your hallucinated asymmetrical experience in the galaxy? Before the mast, hauling foresheet to aft to tally and belay, beating bow-wave into the solar wind, then easing the titanium blades to take it on the beam."

"Nor," El Sabio interposed, "will nothing come of nothing—windfall and offset laws notwithstanding. Wanting will, and from wanting motive, and from motive mischief, mind games and quizzes."

"Then all that flight-characteristic ballsass chemistry fled, gutted and spatchcocked in a triple-head-rig-split-wide-club topsail, guy ropes hung slack, rudder bound, stall-buffet stern sheets shredded to shit in the solar wind, ship yawed left to nowhere, to the cutting-room floor. And now you sit there sleepless through the earthbound night, clutching a telegram from the governor that reads, 'All of California aches with you.'

"You were somebody once; now you want to be somebody twice. Sad to say, you won't live on, but who does? Settle down with your toys—no one accuses you of having too many—and join the rest here in a few light saber exercises before sitting down to watch the Trident submarine races."

"God lives on," El Sabio continued. "And it's not true that it is lost; it is not. The mind of God is infinite; we are the reflections of the infinite being called God—whose voice, though it is heard everywhere in the universe, and may even in a certain sense be captured on certain very sophisticated tape recordings—such as those, for instance, of the songs of whales—but whereas God's one single thought suffices him, humans manufacture, in elongated strings of repeated motifs, more meaning than they know what to do with.

"As Synesius declares, everything is signified by everything, since all things in the world are related, like letters of every shape, signed in the universe as in a book—some Phoenician, some Egyptian, some Assyrian. Bifurcations are the manifestations of an intrinsic differentiation between parts of the system itself and the system and its environment."

"Oh, not *that* sermon again!" a figure cried. "I'm sick of sitting here listening to story after story, assertion after assertion, history after history empty of all probative textual support. When I was learning things, there were *set standards!*—appraisive ascriptors such that what was identified evoked responses in its interpreters which were signified as required."

"There *were* set standards," Shadrach, nodding, agreed. "Like the studio system—like sonata form—and they were *held to*. For example, Bertrand Russell destroyed Frege's entire mathematics in one night by declaring, 'It seemed to me that a class sometimes is and sometimes is not a member of itself.' "

(How often, the boy thought wistfully, had he heard his mother and grandmother each referred to as in a class by herself.)

"You wanna talk *standards*," Crystalman countered, snorting from his stash. "About evoked responses signified as required? This is *impeccable smack*, inducing beautiful thoughts, of which there can never be held too many. About *filth* and *degeneration;* then talk about the *poison algae*, like the billions that formed a net across the Sea of Cortez, killing hundreds of dolphins, or washed up in Monterey, killing *thousands* of brown pelicans. Interpret *that!*"

Shadrach nodded. "The Pomos claimed they were the souls of the unborn children of their U.S. government— sterilized loins."

El Sabio picked up the polished silver teaspoon lying with a set of works in the antique Spanish pistol case lying open on a heap of bleached driftwood.

"The class of teaspoon, for example, is not another tea-spoon, nor is the class of pretty boy it was used to minister to—this kidnap victim seeking to learn where he *really* is and how he *really* got here—just another pretty boy—but the class of things that are not teaspoons is one of the things that are not teaspoons."

"Imagine how many things are not teaspoons," Shadrach offered.

"As many," marveled Crystalman, "as there are stars in the heavens, or grains of sand on Bolsa Chica, or poppies in Normandy."

"The poppies are in *Flanders!*" a frantic voice called out.

"The red poppies are in Flanders," Crystalman countered. "Poppies, *Papaver somniferum*, like camellias, like sand in Turkey—" he took up another fistful and let it seep through his fingers—"may be red or white, and from the soot-blue seeds of Smyrna poppies first laudanum, then morphine, then heroin, are cooked to luscious syrups. As for the yellow California poppy—"

"Gluttony," Shadrach declared, "is the mark of the end times. The heroic dead . . . the heroin dead . . . what was I going to say? Now I've lost my train of thought."

"Spinoza held," El Sabio announced, "that incomplete thoughts bespeak a soul in bondage to splintering passion. *So,* the class of things-not-teaspoons is myriad: the number of particles in the universe—ten to the power of eighty-seven—minus everything that is a teaspoon. Now we have the light, I shall demonstrate."

He began writing in the sand with the handle of the teaspoon: ten-to-the-tenth-power-to-the-power-of-one followed by one zero after another after another.

"If you were to play chess with all the universe's particles, the gambit being the interchange of any two of them, then the number of possible games—called Skew's number—would be this."

"That depends," Crystalman snarled, "on what you call a particle and what a wave."

"How many *waves*," asked Shadrach idly, "are there in the universe?"

"Pipeline, Maverick's, Black Hole . . . a plethora."

"And how many surfers?"

"A concomitant number—and increasing."

"And the class of things that are not pretty boys, such as pretty, or ugly, girls. Sometimes a clever ugly girl will pass—"

"—as a pretty boy. In Shakespeare—or surfing."

"Chess problems," Shadrach then observed, "are difficult to tackle in the same way that administrative problems and children are difficult. You decide on a move, which is difficult enough, but then the next move depends upon what somebody else does, and then the next and the next. Talk about waves, about plethoras!"

"In mathematics," El Sabio intoned, as he kept on drawing zeros, "the patterns, ideas, must be beautiful. There is no place either in this world or the next for ugly mathematics, in spite of the fact that Pythagoras is said to have starved to death. In the beginning there was the ratio, and the ratio was with God—it *was* God!"

When El Sabio put the spoon down, Crystalman took it up. " 'I have measured out my life in coffee spoons.' In double doses of premeasured granular chlorinating shock."

"A coffee spoon," El Sabio declared, "is not a teaspoon—case there of the narcissism of near-sameness, in which the rage increases in inverse proportion to the closeness of the entities. By the way," he asked Tristan, "what is your scent?"

"Aramis," he replied dreamily, "like the musketeer."

"Wicked. Let us attend to this boy," El Sabio declared. "He is here among us. Made in his mind by mishap unimmortal, he seems to say, 'Turn your eyes away, leave me a little joy.' But we shall disobey, and care for him."

The waves' incessant thudding (thud, thud, thud, thud).

"Talk, talk, talk, *talk!*" a disgruntled voice accused.

"Talking has its own importance," El Sabio insisted, "altogether apart from content. It means the talker is alive, alert, and willing to—"

Suddenly somebody stood up. "Listen, you morons, cut the shit—this kid is *nodding out!*"

A day went by; the boy slept and woke again.

"He's awake now," the doctor said, "and he'd like to know if his uncle is available."

"Available," Jacob Beltane repeated, as the patient's mother, Kaye Wayfaring; his grandmother, Mawrdew Czgowchwz; and his father, Jacob's twin brother, Tristan Beltane, looked on.

"That was the word."

"Did he say anything else?" the father asked. (Like what, Kaye wondered—postsynchronized replacement dialogue?)

"Yes, he looked toward the window, around the room, and

back at me, asked where he was, and when told Hollywood Community Hospital, said, 'I was born here. Listen, feeling the way I feel is deeply uncool—is this the new place where the kids are hip?' "

Just then, Astarte, the astrologer-psychic, arrived. As Jacob went toward the boy's room, she approached Mawrdew Czgowchwz.

"So far, so good on the info grid—nothing on the Internet, in the press. He's going to make it, isn't he?"

"Yes," Mawrdew Czgowchwz said. "It appears that when they injected him with sea water, they put on Nusrat Fatah Ali Khan singing 'Don't Go Back to Sleep' in the old Persian and the sand-mandala crowd came over and started in doing Rai-ku and chanting. Still, if it hadn't been for you, they'd not have found him in time to revive him without brain damage."

"Thank Isis for the heat of that brain," the psychic declared. "It was like a signal from Mount Palomar, or even Stonehenge."

"Speaking of brains," the boy's father continued, addressing his mother, Mawrdew Czgowchwz, "and of inanity, the idiot resident wonders how much—not even *if*, but how much—conflict there is between you and the boy's mother!"

"Tell him," Mawrdew Czgowchwz advised, "to read Melanie Klein."

"The Introverted / Intuitive Promethean Temperament," the doctor's report read,

is angular. While for the others, abilities are means which set them free to perform, for them performance is only a means to enable them to store up their abilities. It is the most self critical of all the temperamental styles. He badgers himself about his errors, taxes himself with the resolve to improve, and ruthlessly monitors his own progress. He continually checks the pulse of his skills and takes his conceptual temperature every hour on the hour. He must master understanding of all objects and events, whether human or extrahuman, physical or metaphysical.

Territoriality, Concentration, Internal, Depth, Intensive, Limited relationships, Conservation of energies, Interest in internal reaction, hunches, future, speculative, inspiration, possible, fantasy, fiction, ingenuity, imaginative, objective, principles, policy, laws, criterion, firmness, impersonal, justice, categories, standards, critique, analysis, allocation, pending. Gather more data, adapt as you go, let life happen, open options, Treasure hunting. Emergent, tentative. Something will turn up, there's plenty of time. What deadline? Let's wait and see.

"I see," declared Kaye Wayfaring. (She didn't.) As the doctor withdrew discreetly, she turned to Mawrdew Czgowchwz.
"Why didn't you tell us?"
"If you mean anything in that litany—"
"Anything—anything he said."
"You don't tell *anyone*, dear, what the patient reveals; you don't tell *him*."

The boy was sitting up in bed looking out the window.
"Thinning the herd." He turned back to the room. "Bolsa Chica," he said; "remember it?"
"Yes, of course," his uncle said. "Where your father and I used to go scuba diving."
"Well, the stragglers go there now, in hiding from the other beaches, which have all become wanna-bump Web sites. Alas, the aftermath of a shattering halt is no time for chat-room gaming."
"Yes, go on."
"It seems I can't stop. Have they put me on speed?"
"Unlikely."
The boy kept looking out the window while continuing to

talk. "Good, because silence and sleep are the same as running away. Yet, I feel I've been awakened too suddenly. The Chinese say the spirit is set free in dreams, and if the dreamer is awakened too suddenly, it may not be able to return to the body in time. In time for what they didn't say. 'Sleep rose and spread through him like some soft music.' Heroin is some soft music.

" 'That I would all my pilgrimage dilate . . .' Do you want to hear my dream?"

"Sure."

"I dreamed I was asleep and woke up with nothing on. I was looking up at Mae West's old beach house in Santa Monica and suddenly Debbie Harry came out and sat on the veranda. She blew me a kiss and sat down to meditate. 'Let such silence sound for her,' I heard myself say; 'I need my noise.'

"I noticed a group of silent workers building a sand model of Stonehenge as it was in the year 1997 B.C., and all along the shore line mounds, barrows with chamfered inner edges from the Wessex sites of Lambourne, Skendleby, Avebury, and Drizzlecombe and ring-ditch urn fields from a place called the Eight Beatitudes, near Eindhoven, in Brabant. Brabant was important; fairy tales mother and grandmother told us as children took place there. I realized I'd been *sent* to the builders, and that the big box I was carrying had something in it for them. Naked as morning, my raiment the sun, I reached the bounding edges of the revetment trenches and spilled out onto the sand dozens of toy soldiers—they made up the congregation—trackers of sun and moon, Arcturus and Aldebaran, Betelgeuse and Bellatrix. Meanwhile, throwing up the earthworks had unearthed the victim of an earlier human sacrifice—a female crouched burial, like the girl in the La Brea Tar Pits—but it turned out to be Maev—*garroted.*"

He turned his gaze from the window back to Jacob and the room. "What can I say?"

"Don't say anything at all, just tell me more."

"You take the right tack—interpretation has been overdone—as El Sabio might put it, there's a plethora. A truth ceases to be true when more than one person believes in it—even a geometrical one."

"El Sabio must be the one who sent the message with the rescue squad—saying he realized you had an exquisite soul when you explained that the crux of Stonehenge ritual was the viewing not of the summer solstice sunrise but of the winter solstice sunset."

"How much more satisfactory," Tristan declared, "is immersion in the study of long barrow, curses, avenue, and row—providing evidence of artificial horizons for crosswise viewing from both sides of a single mound—read bicoastal life—and lengthwise viewing directed over a *contrescarpe* burial chamber, extending cosmic symbolism into the realm of personal liturgy: read one's career. Meanwhile the dream's crouched burial is so clearly the womb, and Maev being found dead in it all these years after seemingly we were both born—"

"Not seemingly born—born, both."

"Right—not to mention the fact she was born first. Well, I went up into the dunes then and found a single poppy growing. I plucked it; it turned into a compass rose. I brought it back to the empty box. The box had been turned upside down to make a table, and across it a parchment map unfurled and pinned down—a map of California as an island—inscribed, 'It is he that sitteth upon the circle of the earth.' I set the compass rose on top, where it melted, inking itself into the parchment. Then, as I was looking at it, there was a commotion from inside the box. I thought, Here it comes, the Big One, and as I did the top of the box rattled, the map tore in the middle, and up through the hole—like the trapdoor under the car in the circus—crawled another whole catalogue of little figures: surfers, with their boards.

"The needle in the compass rose started spinning like a clock hand out of control, which made me spin to face north. It was getting dark, the sun was setting, but again on my left, so I knew the beach was now Santa Monica. I looked up and saw Mae West come out on the veranda of the beach house and sit on a chaise longue. I realized she had come out to watch Venus rise and to commune with the dead, one of which it seemed to me I was about to be.

"Then I was cycling down the beach, between Ocean Park and Venice, in bright sunshine, on the concrete bike path that runs down to Laguna—and off to my left the palm trees, all the emblematic sisters of Adam lining the Pacific Coast Highway, were swaying, like multiple Mariko Moris in her *Burning Desire* installation, to a strange music in the Santa Ana.

"Just as I reached Muscle Beach, where all the boys were playing a game of miniature golf, it started to snow and everything got switched around, and suddenly I was on a flatcar somewhere near Point Concepcion, steering it—do you, on rails?—swept forward on a Mavericks wave of exhilaration toward the Gnostic threshold of the Beyond. Maybe I was Nietzsche seeking the Pure Land, the geographic location of the true climate corresponding to the inner same of the thinker: not that of the Sherman Oaks Galleria or the Beverly Center.

"As I careened through the preceptorial-bumper-sticker country Wayfarings once owned—lands, islands, soils, rivers, harbors, mines, minerals, quarries, woods, marshes, waters, lakes, fishing, hawking, hunting, and fowling—I was another Rimbaud crying, 'Comme je descendais des Fleuves impassibles, / Je ne me sentias plus guidé par les haleurs,' except that what I was crying was, 'Terror, obscurity, power, privation; vastness, infinity, scale, difficulty; magnificence, light, loudness, suddenness; pain, darkness, solitude, silence!' Good thing I was on rails; on wheels I'd've ended up roadkill.

"Maybe I was on my way to hear the northern lights, or to make a record with Steve at the Cistern Chapel up in Washington State, or maybe I was just some character in a story by that pederast Horatio Alger. The sense of speed, the illusion of power: wheel flanges screaming on the curves and the countryside streaming by on one side as it were vertically while the Pacific cut in, pounding on the countervalent horizontal. Good stick—and freedom from the fear of hostile conspecifics.

"Dozens of telegraph poles lay flattened and unstrung along the cliffside, making me realize *nobody could get to me*. It seemed that wherever-whenever this sequence was set, cellular phones had not yet been invented. I smiled a smile composed in equal parts of haughty triumph and mistrustful amazement.

"Suddenly I was flagged down by a gang on the tracks. All in bathing suits, they looked like denizens of Muscle Beach. 'We are the ballast gang,' they barked. 'Track-lifting, ballast-tamping, Big Dig mean-mouth motherfuckers. We need no anabolic supplements to prevent the conversion of testosterone into estrogen; we chew nails, and the cortisol concentration in our spit is zip—and as for you, the situation you are smack dab in the middle of right now has got itself one bad ass. This is all new grade up here, and if you don't get off it, we will macerate your body parts and spit your vital organs, then roast you in succulent sections over the slow-burning fire of longing.'

"I felt, well, conspicuous. I don't think, I said to myself, I've faced up to the reality of the situation. And I woke up— with the two words 'smack dab' running over and over in my head. What would a Horatio Alger hero have done, or do you know?

"So, after how many years of monitoring conditions in outer space—time lags in passing with a slowness born of studied insolence—they have discovered that astronauts snore *and* that they dream and that the characters in their dreams float around!

"Meanwhile, in reality, things must be the same this morning on Bolsa Chica beach as they were yesterday, but just before you came in I was daydreaming, and in my daydream, the surfers were collecting themselves to depart for their chosen waves: to Puerto Escondido in Baja, to La Jolla's Big Rock, to Waimea on the north shore of Hawaii, to Half Moon Bay, to Bahia—to Ireland, South Africa, Sri Lanka, Australia. They all split, and there alone on the beach was the Mex, El Matador, the one who dropped me there like Ariadne. In my daydream, he'd come back, to find me gone.

"Fully awake, I realize, of course, that the experience of him was, as El Sabio rather memorably put it, manifestly diriment to the already fragile accommodation with the world of men I and myself had made, caught up as we were in the hopes of youth, the thrill of being alive, and life's many lost moments. Although how he could've known just the kind of sitting duck I was, panting for almost any man with a pulse!"

"Who knew, the Mexican?"

"No, El Sabio. El Matador, I realize, neither knew nor cared, which is . . . well, the *crust*!

"Anyway, the dream fades, and as the sun moves inexorably towards its daily setting in the west, a voice intones, 'The time is now—it always was.' And I am awake on the flight deck, with the remains of a life story—a story of gluttony that's gone and devoured other stories; a story replete with humor, heart, intelligence and irony, hope, movement, volition and color, laughter, melancholy and promises. One that asks the question 'Do we know more than we can tell, or just tell more than we can know?' *Soul of Sex* meets *Day of Wrath* meets *Tears of Rage*; suitable for immediate publication."

"As a paperback original, no doubt."

"Quite—to be read by all the tarts of the moment. Not for you a novel listening experience."

"You'll make it new."

"Thank you. *So*, back to the life."

"On the day before you ran away from same."

"Check. Well, it was this way, your honor. Steve and I are at Tower Records on Broadway and Sixty-sixth, signing *Hostage Situation*; and they're playing the 'Guess What?' cut over and over. You remember *Rolling Stone*. 'What *is* Adolescence, the Children's Hour replay of Steely Dan? Or some coy Boy Division?' "

"I remember."

"They're starting to call us remote and withholding, but I mean *really*, somebody who looks like Steve should *stage dive*? Fuck 'em—and feed 'em beans.

"Anyway, Steve has just answered the question 'What exactly is *Hostage Situation*?' by saying 'It's, well, sort of reflecting on not exactly being present—but we're just starting out on life's rocky road, so maybe it's a bit soon to be issuing statements.' Really.

"Thus delivered of a pregnant text, he has sidled over to the display corner to sit it out in the warm glow of possibility, leaving the distribution of the remaining talking points to me, and I—while not reflecting too hard on why exactly we *are* present *or* who is this 'we'—find myself discoursing on such diverse topics as country and Pantera and on the mission central to our musical process relative to a recent study from the University of Florida that after seventeen minutes of headbanger heavy metal, *excitation transference* affecting attitudes towards women takes place. Also parrying inquiries concerning our supposed feud with New Medicines for Depression and Civic Uplift.

" 'Just because one passed up the opportunity of being

born in the backseat of a taxi in a Los Angeles parking lot, may not one so much as refer to junkie hookers, maudlin barflies, pressures put upon us to utilize esthetic accoutrements while engaging in sustained forms of affectionate interaction, and even the melodrama of rock stars nabbed by Vice in Beverly Hills recreation-area toilets, without being accused of condescending, of Scritti Politti posturing, or of bottom feeding for a buck?'

"Then, declaring 'Shanti in Old Shantytown' an attempt to show how vaulting ambition and fuzz-rick stomps can be reconciled with spiritual values, 'The words-in-music,' I said, 'constitute an axis that, in the spirit of the Velvet Underground, preserves the image of happiness by forever postponing its occurrence.

" 'Two Gentleman of Corona' I called a heartfelt tribute to the seminal genius of the Ramones. 'An album,' I declared, 'must not only be generously furnished, but must always expand its gifts in terms of memorable arrangements. You must put down what your heart wants and your memory holds in high regard. And yet, simplicity must never be banished, nor modesty proscribed, lest it should fall out that instead of being the minister of truth, the purifier of affections, the revealer of the beauty of God, our art should be degraded to the service of ambition and caprice, of luxury and pomp, becoming utterly corrupt, politically correct and false.'

"Steve just sits there throughout, an überglossy headshot with a stub of yellow pencil stuck behind his ear, the three middle fingers of the left hand clamped in the fist of the right, sometimes punctuating the moment with the complicitous chick-magnet nod, and the startled Phil Ochs 'Who me transgressive?' smile. Bright blues clicking into high beam, the smile that—who was it said?—'you can read so much into: a shared joke, a certain skepticism, beauty tips.' And looking so demure, so voomy, so money, like such a prince—most emphatically not an unpronounceable hieroglyph—he should have a docket number pinned on: too seriously beautiful to operate as anything but Alpha Guy in some Supermodels-Runway-Effect-in-Labels contest.

"So, as I can't very well stand up and scream, 'I *love* this G—long to be with him, as Rumi was with his beloved, prostrate in a timeless place!' I segue to a panegyric on Steve Earle followed by a polemic against the bogus use of border-ballad Appalachian rock to sing about Down East: how Norfolk sea chantey and the Myxolydian are the cool determinants . . . like that.

"Maev and the Friends crowd were there, and a scattering of the Juilliards, praising our ambient chords with their long reverb trails. I kept referring to Maev as Orfamay Quest, the Little Sister—it's the glasses made me do it—and saying, 'The man in the *other* magazine said we'd go far.' That'd be *Spin*—they knew as much. We were then asked to join the masses for mug and mow at Señor Swanky's on Columbus Avenue and Seventy-fourth, but Steve said the limo was pointed in the wrong direction and so we split, rumbling down Columbus, all the way down Ninth, across Fourteenth Street, headed for the Tower Records on Broadway and Fourth. We got stalled in traffic in front of the old Eagle Tavern—it's now the Village Idiot, where I'd first taken Steve to listen to Irish music, yet another life ago. There was still the sign in the window of the flea pit a little further along Fourteenth: FREE CRABS EVERY TUESDAY."

"These are the cards," Maev said, "he sent from Albuquerque."

The doctor looked at the cards, eleven in all, which pictured land formations on the Colorado Plateau; then, turning them over, read the message.

Hermione, my sweet,

Whatever its origins the Rio Grande Rift produced an arbitrary cut in the continent's interior. With the onset of volcanism, crevasse tension slowly pulled the land apart.

As for the subject, before heading off, in a passing moment of aspiration to higher ideals on a pilgrimage from the Burning Man Festival in the Nevada desert to the four sacred mountains to the Confusion range of Western Utah, to investigate ramifications in the case of the Eurasian cheatgrass introduced at the end of the last century that by weakening the native bunchgrasses and occupying millions of acres in the Great Basin has in the late nineties fundamentally altered the normal brush fire timetable, he did a little comparative geology.

And so, having spent a long and eventful day among experts measuring the strain of the laccoliths and the distribution of the diatremes, he spent an even longer, more eventful night looking into the campfire, pondering gravity anomalies, upwarps, swells, continued Pacific subduction, the Ogallala aquifer, mantle plumes, interactions between volcanic and sedimentary rock ("marble has ideas, however confused"), bulimia, the accelerated unfolding within (sink rate) and to sum it all up, the following two vexing questions: Do denials set in brackets quite occur? And did rain ever follow the plow? Whence much was gleaned, though the diatremes I think would not interest you. Unlike those of South Africa, which ovulated diamonds aplenty into the pipeline, these spat out nothing but peridotite. No depth. (As Proust says, "In order to delve for the dazzling stone, which can alone match the fire in a woman's eyes, one must descend to strange depths in the dark realm.")

Regards to interested parties, not least your little Shazaam buddy Harry.

Yours in the work, the way and the undoing of both,

Draco Malfoy

"We have been very concerned," the doctor persisted, "by his reference to his sister of the Away Team. It's what the Heaven's Gate participants called themselves."

Mawrdew Czgowchwz nodded gravely. "Yes, of course."

"Then," Maev concluded, "at the party, just before he bolted—it was after I left, but they told me—he stood at the door, turned back and said, 'All those I might have helped. Helped! Saved. Saved! The place was crawling with them.' That's Hamm, in *Endgame*. He's very big on Beckett."

"Beckett?" the doctor interrupted. "Wasn't he essentially nihilistic, and suicidal?"

"Not really," Mawrdew Czgowchwz replied coolly, "merely, it seems, irretrievably Christian."

"FREE CRABS EVERY TUESDAY. One evening in that other life we'd stood outside pointing to it and carrying on: 'Every *Tuesday*. Why only *Tuesday*?' 'Cawse Wednesday *morning* is when they come and hose the joint *down*. Then it takes a full week to build up the conditions for the crabs to *flourish* again.' 'But all the crabs you can *eat*?' 'It takes all kinds; what are you, politically *correct*?'

"We seemed stalled forever, and there was a new sign in the Village Idiot: OH, JUST GET IN HERE AND DRINK! So we got out of the limo and went in. The bartender eyed us and shrugged. I remember that when the drinking law in New York changed from eighteen to twenty-one, I heard somebody declare, 'It won't make all that much difference in the Village; there are bars down there where they'd serve the Infant of Prague.' So Steve said to the bartender, 'Drink what?' 'Straight shots.' 'Straight shots,' Steve asked me, 'do they work?' 'In nine cases out of ten they work.' 'Do they work in ten cases out of eleven?' The bartender actually laughed. Remember the tree oracle?"

"Yes."

"I worried Steve with it in Gramercy Park—the sycamore. The hiding-place tree. It was later the same night after we'd gotten back into the limo and gone to Tower Records on Broadway and Fourth, done a quick stint, lost the limo, and come up Broadway past Union Square and the old Max's Kansas City site, gone into California Burrito for take-out and over to Madison Square to eat. On the way Steve said it seemed to him I was preoccupied about something."

"And you couldn't so easily then and there go into Rumi—"

"And the beloved, prostrate, no. So I told him what I wasn't supposed to let out, about mother being down in Georgia on a location shoot, and then about the picture—that it was called *The Undertow*, and dealt with her mother, my other grandmother, on the last day of her life, hallucinating death's heads, black birds, and saints from all eternity, going about the house covering mirror after mirror with sheets and then at twilight going down to Tallulah Gorge, to the bridge over the Chattahoochee, and throwing herself in where the Indians said the door to the underworld was left ajar.

" 'She was trying to join her son,' I explained, 'my uncle, drowned in the army many years earlier.' 'That's heavy, Whizzer,' he said. I could have cried. Instead I said it could be worse: I could be like Konstantin in *The Sea Gull*, whose self-obsessed actress mother drove him to suicide, whereas mine had put me in a picture with her—although nobody was talking about repeating the gesture with *The Undertow*, 'Ah, the Sorrows of Young Wear-and-Tear,' I quipped.

"It was indeed getting heavy. Fortunately then and there, crossing Twenty-third Street into Madison Square, we came upon *Twelfth Night*, in one of those awfully valiant little productions, in rehearsal right next to the dog run, being watched by curious onlookers, including a group of Hell's Angels. The Viola, leaning against a great elm for support, had just reached

'My father had a daughter loved a man / As it might be, perhaps, were I a woman, / I should your lordship,' and I'm afraid
I was terribly rude—but she was really awful—I mean, the *tree*
was better than she was. Anyway, I stood up and brayed 'The
calla lilies are in bloom a-gayne—such a strange *flah*!' Well,
one thing led to another, including tears from the Viola. I tried
to help matters by saying, 'Listen, darling, it could be worse.
Try to think of it in a more positive way—I mean, as long as
they've got sidewalks, you've got a job, right?' It didn't quite
win her over, but she did laugh.

"While I had their attention, I sallied into my rap about
boys as Elizabethan heroines, whereupon I was challenged to
do better than the girl—and of course, I did, imitating not
badly mother's gift for empathic-emotive portraiture, right
into the video camera. Steve was amazed at my 'as it might
be . . . were I a woman.' For a moment, he said, I became one;
but then, if you remember, when I took him to MoMA for the
Orphrey Whither retrospective and he first saw *Avenged*, he
went crazy over Mother. Wonderful, in a way, to have confirmed what I'd always suspected—that she is my primary
erotic rival.

" 'It's no mystery I do the part so well,' I said, 'having been
conceived during a run of the play out on Long Island while
Avenged was also being shot.' I did *not* mention in the same
breath the fact that my scene goal involved positioning *him* as
Orsino in my sight—handy as he was being just then just there.

"I then, amid what you might call the general consterna-
tion, sat down and played a little of Father's *Willow Cabin
Suite*, declaring it really ought to be played on lutes and bom-
bards, shawms and sackbuts, and discoursing—the actors had
all taken a little break—on the willow tree oracle: how it reveals one's female side and is particularly sacred to people born
in February.

"The director came over then and asked was I available to

play the music during the run. I said I'd make them a tape. The Hell's Angels all roared off down Broadway, and Steve and I went back to our burritos, whereupon I lay the tree oracle on him—and more.

"Well, to cut to the chase that wasn't, I went home that night alone—Steve and I had been staying up together night after night and then going for breakfast down on Delancey Street and I knew it was because he couldn't face staying in Gramercy Park in the same room with me and trying not to fall asleep until I did, which I wouldn't, out of longing. And so I wrote—I copied it out of a book, naturally,—'Don't sit up with me again. Do not show me so much goodness, if you have decided not to show me more,' and in view of the fact we were to be separated in the fall, 'Could you not remain just a few weeks more as you were—what are a few weeks at the price of a life?'

"Which was idiotic, of course, because he *was* being the same, *I* was being different. I was starting to tell myself that he'd never really liked me, only Mother—and Grandmother, who owned a copy of everything Verve ever put on vinyl—that had kept him coming back to Gramercy Park. And now I'm having the unkind thought that both our mothers, yours and mine, were not only women but female impersonators too, but whereas yours impersonated conflicted women at the top of her voice, mine went in for glamorizing fucked-up tramps who mumbled. I've become vicious—no doubt about it."

(Maev said, "Steve told me they went from Madison Square into Gramercy Park. There was a full moon, and while doing the tree oracle Tristan said 'I love you,' and Steve said 'I love you too, dude,' and T. said 'No, I *love . . . desire* you.' 'Oh, *shit!*' Steve said, and sat silent a minute, and then said, 'Whizzer, we gotta go to a therapist.' 'My grandmother is a psychoanalyst.' 'Whatever.'")

As Tristan told his uncle, they'd each gone home, saying

"Call you tomorrow" as they had every night for the last two years and always followed through upon waking, but neither did. Tristan then knew that Steve would stay away on some pretext from the party the Friends senior class was having the next night. Tristan arrived alone, was rude to everybody, got drunk and stormed out.)

"Well, I remember reading in a book somewhere that if you have three days in front of you on a Saturday in August, the best thing to do is stay where you are. Seasonal stress. I had just that—three days—before Steve and I were supposed to go down to D.C. to do another signing. I couldn't think of that— I couldn't go forward, so I went back, first to Tower—the Tower Struck by Lightning, as Astarte might put it."

At Tower Records the next day, Dickweed was signing their hit single "No Good at All." Tristan retraced the previous days' steps, thinking to undo the worst of things, tarried at the Village Idiot, then arrived at the Friends party, where a classmate had begun to read out loud from *On the Road* while Tristan sat across the room strumming.

" 'It was drizzling and mysterious at the beginning of our journey. I could see that it was all going to be one big saga of the mist. "Whooee!" yelled Dean. "Here we go!" And he hunched over the wheel and gunned her; he was back in his element . . .' "

" 'What country, friends, is this?' " Tristan had begun.

" '. . . leaving confusion and nonsense behind and performing our one and noble function of the time, *move*.' "

" 'And what should I do in Illyria? My brother he is in Elysium.' "

" 'We flashed past the mysterious white signs in the night somewhere in New Jersey—' "

" 'Perchance he is not drowned.' "

" '—that say SOUTH (with an arrow) and WEST (with an arrow) and took the south one. . . . From the dirty snows of "frosty fagtown New York" as Dean called it, all the way to the greeneries and river smells of old New Orleans at the washed-out bottom of America. New Orleans! It burned in our brains.' "

"More like burned *out* their brains, such as they were," Tristan snapped. He stopped strumming his guitar, got up, and went over to the reader to inform him that unless he ceased interrupting Shakespeare with the adolescent rant of a closet-queer hustler—

"You don't like Kerouac?"

"Bent over and whimpering, while that razor-tongued jerkoff speed freak he worshiped got busy cutting him a brand new asshole, I'd doubtless have liked him a lot. Enjoyed listening to *The Lone Ranger* on the radio with him and telling him inside stuff, like how 'kemosabe' means cocksucker in Navajo. Phat chat like that."

("The gang was shocked," Maev said, "because T. never used such language—he's always been detached, ironic, sophisticated, and rather formal. I heard him from where I was standing, and the next thing I knew he was next to me. A few of us had been talking about *Cymbeline*. He suddenly came out with 'For a smart girl, my sister makes a lot of mistakes—for instance, she thinks *Cymbeline* is greater than *Blade Runner*.' ")

"I'm afraid that did it. She walked out of the place, but not before schooling me. 'It's about time,' she said, 'you got your histrionic discharge. You know that test you give people? You should take it yourself—you're good at tests.'

" 'You're right to refuse to be intimidated,' I then assured the Kerouac reader, 'by my short-suffering indignation and easy command of competitive invective, but would you on that account have me read out of meeting for questioning? When I came in here I did dig it that the vibe was chill, and in that line I did bring my blunt and was ready to bob my head in the seriously fine peer teen lineup—but, well, just between us hookers in the powder room, has it ever occurred to you one may be artificial by *nature*? What has happened, I'm afraid, is that my strengths and weaknesses have suddenly and quite inexplicably changed places in the contradance that is my life—that ring chimes with anybody here?'

"Stendhal's Octave had asked his cousin Armance, 'Am I fated to live without friends?' She replied, 'You furnish the people who do not like you with pretexts.' "

"Another parable. One wishes to come to know a young man, handsome and attractive, who appears to be concealing a secret. Is he issue laden—perhaps gender-dysphoric? It would be indelicate to pry—and, after all, as the masters avow, the first step toward higher learning is to limit your intake—but not perhaps maladroit to inquire has he a sister whose character and nature could to some small extent betray his own?"

("The others left," Maev concluded, "but not before hinting about Steve's absence. Then T. freaked out and ran, leaving Steve a note, 'How'm I gonna keep myself away from myself?' ")

"You'd probably like the whole story," Tristan offered, warily, "plethora of jumbled detail stripped, sieved, and sorted. You must, however, be satisfied with a few perhaps edifying truths. A detached, ordered, and self-contained exploration of personal experience that hopefully also dramatizes a sense of life as an elusive process whose depths resist interpretation. Here goes."

The story Jacob later told his brother (the boy's father, after all) was this.

At Port Authority, he'd gotten on the first bus going out to Atlanta. "There is no truth but in transit," Tristan declared. "Emerson. Also, psychoanalysts take note, the city of his mother's birth. There were buses departing regularly for other cities, but he chose Atlanta, thinking of Clayton, Warwoman Dell, and Tallulah Falls, where he thought he might keep some appointment with destiny—for time was, for him, as much as it had been for Neal, of the essence. Greyhound buses. Robert Johnson, who died raving like a mad dog, poisoned by a jealous homicidal peer in a shit hole in Mississippi, sang, 'You can bury my old body by the highway side, / But my evil spirit will get on that Greyhound and ride.' "

After a couple of hours on the New Jersey and Pennsylvania turnpikes, looking out the window at heavy silver-bodied transport vehicles outlined against the night by borders of red, white, blue, and green lights—like enormous tinsel-wrapped Christmas boxes—he started reading *Sir Gawain and the Green Knight.*

" 'By a mount on the morn merily he rides / Into forests full depe that ferly were wilde.'

"I kept thinking, one of the things I've never done is go jousting on an Appaloosa. I'd also brought along Melville's *Pierre.* Most people in fact or fiction are other people, and I'd been Pierre ever since doing a fast-track entrance essay calling it 'a fable about castration anxiety and the Orestes complex moving beyond the superficial evidence of stylistics to the realm of deep interpretation of the human body and its world,' which caused a stir at school, as most were writing about *The Red Badge of Courage*, *The Catcher in the Rye*, and *Gatsby*. I'd been reading Otto Fenichel, and besides, I felt I'd lived it—that summer.

" 'Most melancholy of all the hours of earth is that grey one which to the watcher by the lamp intervenes between night and day; when both lamp and watcher, overtasked, grow sickly in the pallid light; and the watcher, seeking for no gladness in the dawn, sees naught but garish vapors there; and almost invokes a curse upon the public day that shall invade the lonely night of sufferance.' "

. . .

At the end of the first night out he'd gotten off the bus for breakfast—call at a truckers' stop on Backlick Road ("at the foot of Purgatory Mountain, in Breece D'J Pancake country"), leaving his guitar stashed overhead. He'd wanted to encounter real Christian snake handlers, with their hypnopompic hallucinations and apocalyptic scenarios of rapture and retribution on a date certain, singing in tongues and dancing naked—because Satan had put on the serpent—with adders fanged as a garment draped loosely over their limbs. No luck.

"In another place next morning" (Tristan continued) "after breakfast—there was so much food, family style, and when I asked if they had any pokeweed to go with the fried ham, biscuits, and grits, nobody knew what I was talking about until one old black woman said, 'Baby, folks don't eat *pokeweed* no *more*—nor *dandelions* neither!' Whoever said, 'Life is old there'? No more.

"Anyway, we staggered away from the table, already behind schedule, and the driver went casually off to the can, and two kids pulled joints out of their pockets and skulked behind one of those awful God billboards saying DON'T MAKE ME COME DOWN THERE AGAIN! as the light fell from the long stretch back east all over everything. Somebody boarding came out with, 'Ah don't reckon Ah give a shoot in a boot whether Ah'd be received in Graceland, but Ah shure would feel real put out to be turned away from *Dollywood*!'

"I was standing aside watching these two truckers hosing down their rigs—a big Mack and a Peterbilt—with the same loving attention their predecessor American heroes showed to styling their palominos and paints. Scrubbing and polishing the grilles as if they were their own torsos, when all at once a local Johnny Reb got into a brawl with a tourist who barked that after the fall of Richmond, Jeff Davis was apprehended in a South Georgia swamp: 'a little old piney wood rooter dressed up like a woman.' "

Enrapt by the brawl, he missed the bus's last call and it left with his guitar on board. The Mack truck took off after the bus but was stopped at a weigh station. ("In *Way Station* Mother played a tramp. I was playing son of a tramp, and Pierre.") The truckers told him the only thing to do was head for Dallas, the Greyhound headquarters lost-and-found. He stayed with them across Tennessee until Memphis, where, leaving him at the bus station downtown near the Great Pyramid, they headed south into the Delta.

The mirror melodrama started when he was sitting in the right front seat watching the bus pass Christmas-packaged truck after truck and one white eighteen-wheeler called Cove-nant Transport (driven by creatures of indeterminate gender who looked zapped by aliens).

"I thought 'transport' as in the Rapture, but also as in kid-napping runaways and holding them prisoner in the trucks, which I never saw open in the daytime, or idled any-where either. The interiors I imagined as little chapels, where sedated white children of the American middle passage were made to sit in neat rows and sing 'How Many Stars in My Crown' and 'There's a Land Fairer Than Day.' And suddenly, instead of Christmas boxes, I saw them as immense Fabergé eggs on wheels, depicting all-male sex scenes inside, and then I started feeling every bit the prisoner—like Pierre.

"I suppose as I was being this someone else when they offered me a joint—this was somewhere in Arkansas, where they also have stone circles, I was informed, but we were at a Hardee's—I just took it, and unlike our President, I inhaled. And no sooner had we gotten back on the bus, it seemed, when we were stopped as for a roadblock, and I thought, This is a bit extreme, but what had happened was that a van—not Covenant Transport, but Arkansas Department of Corrections—carrying juvenile offenders had had its tires shot out by a car speeding past and nearly caused a pile-up—and getting high fitted right in the picture."

He described the boys let out, manacled and in foot chains, one sporting new Nikes with the chains around his ankles ("Very *Sullivan's Travels.* Mother's always had a Veronica Lake quality") and then Alice in Chains.

"When I'd fallen asleep against the driver's shoulder in the cab of the semi, I got an erection, naturally, and now, sitting at the long window opposite the bus driver—the place called in cars the suicide seat, remember?—I kept getting one after another."

The window seemed to be devouring the road.

> *"Look out*
> *the win*
> *dow cluck:*
> *it's real,*
> *it's there,*
> *it's life."*

"The road—the terrible road that leads simultaneously to perfection and nothingness . . . and to Santa Monica. I moved across to the seat behind the driver. His back rest against the glass separator created a perfect mirror: in it I saw everybody behind me outlined in the semi-dark. One reading light was on: a kid with a long yellow pencil stuck behind his ear was examining rock samples with a kit. I thought of Rock Formation as we rolled across America in our omnibus rock-away. The light kept bouncing along the yellow pencil; the detail made me salivate."

Tristan said he could see himself as a member of the audience, and—still high—split in two, performance self and mirror self disassociating, while free-associating. As if he were in the mosh pit of his own longed-for big number at a gala performance.

> "*Mirror, mirror on the bus,*
> *Who's the most fucked up of us*
> *As in frugal fugal flight*
> *We barrel down the road at night?*"

"A guy got on at Texarkana, taking the seat I'd left; we got to talking across the aisle. 'People in this country are pathetic,' he said, 'hooked in no particular order on sex, work, security, personal expression, entertainment, and spiritual fulfillment. Ludicrous. The whole point of living is to become perfectly lonely, to follow, in the spirit of the perfect surgical incision made in sterile conditions with the absolutely steady hand, the canons of mechanical drawing: severe utility, simplicity and directness of action, the fewest possible parts, resistance to intrusion of outdated arrangements.' I thought, truckers hold with that."

They were at a rest stop in Texas. The company had coalesced into a unit, everybody headed for California. They were listening to the song "What if God was one of us / Just a stranger on the bus, trying to get home?" and a voice called out, "Girlie, you tell that God if he's with us he's on the *wrong fuckin bus!*"

"I thought of Southern Culture on the Skids—Southern Comfort on the Rocks, as I call it—and their lyric 'Doesn't matter if your pants are shiny / If your dick is big or if it's tiny.' I thought of Iris De Ment's *My Life* and I wanted to start singing out loud the song from *Greenwillow* I used to love so."

" 'The Call'—you always called it 'Born to Wander.' "

"Yes. You know what they say. A kid has to wander, starting about two years old, in the supermarket. There is no why, there's only how-it-is-that. 'Born to wander till I'm dead.' "

"Yes, well, you nearly just were."

"You don't mince words. No second opinion, no request for a set of confidence limits around official estimates?"

"There wasn't time."

"Or world enough without one. Who was it said, 'Whoever falls for marching songs, as for toy soldiers, to him opens the door on the irrevocable'? You know what the etymology of 'adolescent' is, don't you—becoming sadder by degrees. You know, at one point I told El Matador, 'Wittgenstein was my great-grandfather's lover.' 'The guy that made the monster?' 'You could say that,' I replied. Anyway, it's a curvilinear world."

"Over which a rectilinear grid pontificates."

"Maybe. But it is the heart and not a dancing master that teaches refinement and dignity. My mind, like Melville's, is random, but lynx-eyed, formed by a varied scope of reading, little suspected by friends."

"I question," Jacob declared, "the notion of little-suspecting friends; moreover, you are not everybody."

"Or everybody's . . . or anybody's? All right. Well, as Melville has it 'Pierre was not arguing Fixed Fate and Free Will now; Fixed Fate and Free Will were arguing him, and Fixed Fate got the better in the debate.'"

"Listen, what if I went under to discover the secret knowledge of the loser?"

"What if God were one of us?"

"My initial self-diagnosis lay somewhere in a triangle between hysterical psychoneurosis, paranoid-schizophrenic reaction and sociopathic personality disorder, passive-aggressive subtype. I was the good guy, but there was one bad guy out there impersonating me, and I had to go get him. Then something reminded me, in Latin, that entities are not to be unnecessarily multiplied—and that made me decide that yes,

it's simpler than that: the whole deal is Kerouac's sullen revenge from the grave, pivoting on El Matador's appearance at El Paso—risen up like a dirt devil or, more, like a Slurpee on a summer's day. I was driven off course by a blast resistless and the aching need to feel another beating heart."

"You keep on calling him El Matador. Why so? He didn't—"

"Succeed? Maybe not in killing me, just something. . . . Anyway, he called himself that, and he did look, if not exactly lethal, at least *sidelong*—you know, *el aire tenebroso más excitante*—as I watched him getting off a bright blue bus from Ciudad Juárez wearing black, carrying, as it turned out, Che Guevara's motorcycle diaries and nothing else. Pan in on the cleared dance floor."

"Are you sure he was Mexican?"

"And take down my statement, Officer: *Bajo el azul de su misterio, el bolero fue mi ruina!* Well, he came over the bridge in a blue bus with all the Mexicans. He didn't look like anybody getting a Hollywood divorce."

"So you said. Was he much like Plácido?"

"Maybe not a lover sighing like a furnace, but undeniably hot. Plácido? He was nothing like Plácido—but Plácido dances the paso doble around the house all day, singing 'Granada' and 'Siboney.' Anyway, he said he was on his way to join the Unarians at El Cajon, to wait for the thirty-three ships to land in the Great Landing at San Diego, and if by any chance that didn't transpire, to the deserts of the Coachella Valley, near Fontana, where they hold all the outdoor macho queer sex jamborees."

"We don't believe he was Mexican at all."

"You think he posed as a Mexican—what for?"

"That we don't know. But according to eyewitnesses, he was, for one thing, older than you seem to think."

"Aren't they all."

"And then the costume profile." Jacob took a piece of paper from his pocket and read. "The double-breasted black leather French Highway Patrol jacket, the lace-up thermal undershirt, the intense leather hip-hugger jeans, with the cool-update braided details and the side stud-snaps, the leather chaps, the Road Warrior trapunto-tongue boot with boot wallet and metal bar details."

"The things you remember," Tristan rejoined, "and the things you don't. You think he was on a hot trot to cut a caper in Balboa Park? Gearing up to audition in full faggot fig for *Sex Garage: The Musical*? Or maybe that the truth is even darker—that knowing one for who one was, he was out on a little excursion into home movies and blackmail?"

"Something like that."

"*Qué lástima*—because when he removed the reflective aviators, excitement blew out of his stoked eyes in stabs of fiendish light as in the glow of the Burning Man. As for me, I practically had tattooed on my forehead the sign gluttons love most: Avail Yourself."

Jacob nodded. "Also the accessories—the alchemy pewter skull wristlet—the silver-bullet atomizer. Was he allergic to pollen or something, or was that for his cologne?"

"For his amyl; he disdained cologne. I forwent my scented custom until he left, saying, 'Querido, I have liked you very much; it is too bad.' Then I slapped it on like a Tijuana whore. Musil says all the fine actions of the mind are only like droplets of scent whose exquisiteness lasts only an hour or so."

"In any case, all items available mail-order from International Male in San Diego."

"All of you think he was the outcast son of the second-best weasel killer in Sugar Land, Texas, don't you, and that he saw me coming down the Interstate, a little piece of live hot stuff, as it were, among all the blown-out tires and the roadkill—had me all formulated in his mind, or thought he did, even before

I thought I saw him coming across the Rio Grande in a blue bus in the insane sunlight in the blistering heat. You think he took one look at me then and thought, This one I can destroy."

"Why would he want to do that?"

"Search me—I seem to remember they did when I arrived."

"Did it—with him—make you feel good?"

"I can't say I liked it tremendously, although he was endowed beyond anything Mattie ever told Hattie. I liked the view in the morning better, from the La Bajada Overlook on the Camino Real between Albuquerque and Santa Fe—but, as the French say, *il fallait que je sache*. And if it was ugly— penetration's sacred pain is no great joy—it was also easy and fascinating, and I knew I'd do it again. It was already, the first time, exactly that: something I was doing again.

"So, to go back to the beginning in El Paso, I must have been devouring the hawk in question with my eyes—from under what Gary Indiana calls antic yoo-hoo eyebrows— suggesting something fork-tender, for minutes anyway, before he popped the question. 'So anyway, how old you are?' Sounded Mexican, so I thought. Of course I lied. We went into a bar. He ordered tequila; I followed suit. Shadrach says Rumi says share a cup of firewater with your new best friend."

"A loose translation, I would think."

"As befit the situation. Unpacking the most beautiful tooled-leather pistol case, he said, 'I decided to come in through El Paso and pick up the wheels on the white side, with white plates on them.' "

"I have to tell you," Jacob interrupted, "we find the pose unconvincing. It doesn't fit the description from Bolsa Chica."

"Well, he may not have been brilliant, but he wasn't some Todd's of La Cienaga–Colt Studios–gym-buff-generic retard either, not some big, ripped, beefed, buffed, shredded, juiced, and chiseled Bad Boy Ballroom offering in white three-in-one zip-off nylon techno pants and turquoise microfiber eyelet halter top, all from Nerve Ends in the Beverly Center—*that* one might not live down. And on Bolsa Chica he said my eyes were 'como dos ventanas que miran hacia el mar.' Call me naive, I found it more exhilarating than Steve's 'Lookin' good today, Whizzer'—not to mention the prospect of iris scan for personal identification at banks, airports, and nightclubs in the twenty-first century.

"Of course he lied from the beginning. I found out soon enough his story of shooting gray wolves in the Apache National Forest was quite untrue: the pistol case was for his works, but until I did I suppose I found it erotic simply being with an armed man. By now he was calling me 'chico de la Frontera.' And later, after the tequila in the cantina, I followed him, unbidden, into the Harley showroom, where he bought a new Heritage, with an enormous amount of chrome dressing, just like that, with a platinum American Express card.

"The trip to San Diego was put off, and we headed north-west on the Harley, to Albuquerque, then Santa Fe, then curving back down into the Arizona desert and up again into Nevada at night, bound for Lovelock and Reno, and then across and down through Wayfaring country to L.A. and Bolsa Chica. We didn't quite tiptoe around each other like heart-breaking new friends. He said when he first saw me his fantasy was fucking me out in the middle of the empty Estadio Azteca under a full moon.

"He said, 'If I fuck you, chico, that's a sin.' 'Oh, well,' I said, 'hate the sin, love the sinner.' 'No, chico—eres el pecado.' I was the sin. I rather liked the sound of it. Whoever said that in human contract formation one capacity, the detection of cheating, is developed to exceptional levels of sharpness and rapid calculation was full of shit. I should have known it wouldn't, couldn't work. The scripting—arrogance and patronage on the one side, weakness and gratitude on the other, the latter disposition being at the lazy mercy always of the winds, frets, and gentle fingers of the former—can make for no foundation for a satisfactory adult relationship, however transitory.

"But speaking of the full moon, he went on to say he'd come into the U.S. for two main reasons, San Diego and the Burning Man Festival, and so it was we went out into the middle of the Hualapai Playa at the edge of the Black Rock Desert with a platoon of topless females, the Space Cowgirls, circling around on misshapen multicolor bikes from a place called Pedal Camp, while a record number of freaks were crash-testing TVs—the cross-dressers, not the sets. Somebody said sixteen thousand, dancing and drumming all through the night, stoned on ecstasy, crystal, and bong in double lungfuls; licking cherry syrup from a huge ice sundial holding clocks and watches. Neon skeletons and other unearthly, chancelike apparitions of life coexisting with re-creations of the Sumerian cult of prostitution and yakuza love-death victims, all seeking the solace of spliff oblivion in fierce landscapes. Concessions called Alien Abduction Camp, Fat Frat-Boy Camp, Pervert Scout Jamboree, Sailor Parlor, Los Muchachos de Entonces, Toxic Amphibian Lounge, Cult of the Jolly Green Convergence, and Environmental Disaster Camp—and everywhere freaks out to impersonate sperm fertilizing a giant egg, covering themselves with mud from the hot springs nearby. Then, while we were watching the Burning Man mambo, I remembered Ahab in *Moby-Dick* ordering a man from the ship's blacksmith. 'Make him fifty feet high in his socks, with a chest modelled after the Thames tunnel, then legs with roots to 'em, to stay in one place, then arms three feet through the wrist' . . . like that. And I told him Melville believed in a parallel world of beings on this planet whom we could not perceive, with whom we could not communicate. His answer was, 'Faggots-who-want-to-get-fucked-and-don't think that. You know, Montezuma ate young chicos for dinner—and fed them to the conquistadores.'

"Well, whoever said the desert is no place to meander and fatal to innocents—but love or the imagination of same has the curious capability of turning a place like the Black Rock Desert into springland Vivenza. Then in the morning a bitter taste is left in the mouth, right at the base of the tongue, one not even tequila and Dr Pepper can erase when two tongues wrapped—"

"Tequila and *Dr Pepper?*"

"I invented it. He thought it was disgusting too, and without gaining a sense of humor laughed so hard he got me laughing too. Then he stopped and said, 'Tu risa es preciosa, chico.' "

" 'Your laugh is lovely . . .' " Jacob repeated. "There's a poem of Sappho's, 'The man sitting facing you looks like one of the gods, / Listening carefully to what you say, and to your lovely laughter.' "

"I really must learn Greek," Tristan said, smiling. "Especially now. Well, there we were, god and mortal, tongues wrapped around each—I've shocked you!"

"Maybe just a little around the edges."

"I get that. He sure got around my edges, and twiddled my chakras to boot—or you could just say, if you like, that if I take a deep breath I can still feel him."

"Tell me," Jacob interrupted, "exactly what happened—if you can . . . more or less."

Tristan did so, beginning in El Paso. They were at the bar in a cantina there and the visitor asked why, did Tristan think, God permitted things to evolve in such a way that the two *más gordas* American places—Texas and California—ended up just north of—and cast their ugly shadows over—two of the poorest districts in Mexico, Chihuahua and Baja. Tristan answered, "Search me."

"And then he took my arm—'With your permission, chico, I will do that.' And so he did. Listen, all this happened to

Rimbaud during the Franco-Prussian War. Did he complain? Did he pull a Pierre and crawl under a convenient Terror Stone? No. If ever a good little soldier stood to attention at death's door . . . ! And his story, as distilled in exquisite French verse and prose, is widely regarded today as a gorgeously textured metaphor for sexual identity and freedom, a shining vision—contains nudity, violence, obscenity, and date rape; parental guidance suggested—that continues to burn long after the forces of fear that would have snuffed it out have met their match.

"And if Rimbaud were alive today he'd meet his, in this Melvillean who's experienced cannibalism in savage climes and survived—who's been *taken* in an abomination of desolation known as a national sacrifice area: who's done his bit. You know, Napoleon said a soldier ought to know how to overcome the grief and melancholy of his passions, that there was as much true courage in bearing mental afflictions as in remaining unmoved under fire.

"Anyway, when I asked him his name, you know what he did? He first punched his left open hand with his closed right fist and then his open right hand with his closed left fist and said, 'Paff! Paff! Otro nacout por El Matador!' Then he reached into his pocket and pulled out a packet of See's candies—*caramelos*, he called them—and offered me one. He ate them the whole time we were together. Later in the trip, on the way down from Lake Wayfaring, at West Covina, I said I didn't want to go into Los Angeles, but he said we had to, to go out by the airport and get a new supply. He said everybody in Lomas de Chapultepec grooved on See's caramelos; he'd grown up on them."

("Hmm," Astarte later remarked. "He was never Mexican—that Great Landing business isn't at *all* Mexican; it's typically Californian. First Mormonism, a big hit in the twenties—Moroni at the autumnal equinox—but many other revelations have followed hard upon, particularly in earthquake country, along the major faults.")

" 'With your permission,' " Tristan repeated. "And he gave me to understand that everything is decided forever—happens at once, more or less doing away with the romance attached to thresholds."

"You still hold that?" Jacob asked.

"No . . . but I'll probably always remember that I once held it. And that Albuquerque is without question the weirdest place in America. And even if it turns out he was just some butch-accoutred pedophile out to bury his rage with a boy half his age—well, remember that Bresson picture—the one that ends up in Père Lachaise?"

"*Le Diable probablement.*"

"Yes—imagine that: *probably*! The scene in the church with the would-be suicide and the heroin addict who eventually murders him. They're lying together with Monteverdi on the record player—one of the parts that isn't very talky—well, I thought of it, lying out there in nature's cathedral under the stars."

"With the heroin addict who—"

"Nearly murdered me. As was pointed out to me, he had his ways. Well, I don't call it love, even if the Lord doesn't mind, but I'll always be grateful to him for the way he . . . managed it. It didn't hurt so very much, really; he said I was a natural. And the way he kept saying 'querido' all the while. Even if he was lying, I'll always—well, love is injustice, says Camus."

"That's horseshit—the horseshit opposite of 'Love is never having to say you're sorry.' "

"You want me to say I'm sorry. What if he taught me something?"

"Such as?"

"I don't know—some technique? Not costume technique; some *morceau de réception* of the gifted newcomer in the art of—"

"Seduction?"

"Attraction. Belonging. Investing one's erotic interests with the power of an identity. Of course, even as it was going on I was having a whole separate—his voice, murmuring 'querido' with that macho, *de afuera* accent that makes everything sound all at once fated and matter-of-fact, reminded me of the voice on the Talgo—calling out the stations: 'Próxima parada Zaragossa . . . Reus . . . Barcelona' . . . like that. I kept thinking, people are getting fucked on the Talgo all the time— it's why you can never get into the can when you need to.

"I mean, I did *not* feel, and I *would not claim*, to be reenacting the ecstasies of those 'who let themselves be fucked in the ass by saintly motorcyclists and screamed for joy—' "

The boy fell silent, unable to finish.

"Tell me, did he—did you—use—?"

"Proper protection? Oh, absolutely. Glove love. I didn't keep the evidence—I didn't think it fitting . . . anymore. It certainly wouldn't've fitted me."

Jacob didn't say anything.

"I told him there wouldn't be another full moon for a couple of weeks—and then for the second time I asked his name. Again, 'Paff! Paff! Un otro nacout por El Matador!'

"And then, as politely as I could, that as I had never been fucked, I wasn't sure it was near the top of my wish list, although I had heard, in Spanish, that if it went well, the earth moved.

" 'Tortas y pan pintado,' he said. Easy as pie—a greased shoot. We were sitting there in the middle of the New Mexico desert, after a night of turning on and looking for UFOs in the sky, and now listening to all this looking out at the waves of dawn light bouncing off the sand, he asked me, 'Le gusta esta jardín? La rosa sin saber por qué florece, porque florece.' Then he nuzzled me, whispered, 'Bailamos, compañero,' and declared that just as tequila was the drink of the mystical marriage of fire and water, so we were the food of the mystical marriage of air and earth. I was that air. Did I know what happened when air married earth? I said no, what? Then he did something I may never forget. He reached over and jiggled the frames of my glasses so the world jumped up and down, and he cried out, 'Terremoto!' For such gestures you fall in love forever—or for the time being, whichever lasts longer—longer than a drop of scent.

" 'Para tí, pan y cebolla, muchacho,' he said, sitting out in the open in the middle of a stand of Joshua trees, for which I knew no oracle. Instead, after he told me all about Hollister in 1947, I laid out my Stonehenge theories. He seemed charmed: said they were a relief from his exposure to the incessant rantings of Mexican politics. I'd described Stonehenge as a great geomantic orgone box trapping sun-moon rays, focusing them on initiates in the inner sanctum, so *then* I had to explain what an orgone box was. This warp seemed necessity, as Melville says. Talk about egging on! It was the terrifying Nevada desert—the great dead ocean floor honeycombed with mineshafts that billow radioactive silt all the way to Reno in the Burning Ring of Fire grand tour. Reno, where Marilyn comes out of the courthouse with her decree in *Misfits*."

"Do you believe it was the places?" Jacob asked.

"Well, Texas and Nevada between them. Kerouac said Texas was undeniable.

"You know, in my opinion, the narrative in this family—in which, it would seem, there are no forbidden stories—has been weighted in favor of the women."

"I wonder what your sister thinks about that?"

"My sister is fair-minded—that torments me."

. . .

"Well," the doctor reported, "we now have the full report of the trackers on the Internet. The passenger getting on at Dallas watched the boy come out of the baggage area through a pass gate carrying his guitar, which he held upright in his lap, and knew right away who he was."

"*Is*, Doctor," the boy's grandmother corrected.

"Er, yes. The passenger, on his way to Phoenix, knew right off who the boy is, but pretended not to. They talked about the Kennedy assassination, which the boy attributes to sexual gluttony."

"As you undoubtedly realize, Doctor," Mawrdew Czgowchwz advised, "justification scenarios are a routine and quite indispensable part of the adolescent's panoply of defense mechanisms."

"Indeed," the physician replied, stiffly. "In any case the boy indicated he was traveling to Los Angeles, so when he failed to reboard at El Paso, the concerned passenger contacted the Web."

"As Johnny Cash sang in 'Jesus, I Don't Want to Die Alone,' 'My love wasn't true, and now all I have is you.'"

"Make that 'you' plural," Jacob advised.

Tristan looked out the window. "'The friends who come to see you and the friends who don't,' the poet wrote. Of course if this was New York . . . I'd be in Payne Whitney too, and I too could say, 'Give my love to—oh, anybody.'"

"You could—but would it be smart?"

"Have I been smart? *I* have been good—sort of—at writing myself—and now what? I look and listen around and it turns out *everybody's* title track finds them marveling at the vast complexities of life, pondering an incalculable number of simultaneous events and trying to seize a fleeting moment of time. And everybody seems to have a flair for writing about obsessive behavior—whether relating to cars, sex, substances, or self-loathing. That in itself ought to be enough to drive anybody with a brain back to 'Plaisir d'amour.'

"I always wanted to be somebody else. *She's* made a career out of it. She has said about acting, 'If all else fails, substitute.' Well, guess what? 'If all else substitutes, *fail.*' "

"Who once substituted what for you? Tell me."

"It's a fantasy of mine that Mother in making love to Father thought of her brother, Jack, and so I've ended up being him."

"That's from Goethe's *Elective Affinities.*"

"Gay old Goethe. You know all learning is about getting neurons to fire more readily on a second or third try than on a first, until finally you're gunning them all down like Billy the Kid in the streets of Laredo. Until you run out of slugs—or the property department does, because it was all for show—and you end up, on the streets of Laredo, mindless, toothless, and dickless, carrying a tin can. As for me, and maybe a propos twins, a double dose of nothing isn't something; I figured that out—speaking of sustainable yield.

"Well, back to El Matador and me. We came down the Sierra Nevada to Lake Wayfaring, through Hollister and the high chaparral to Bakersfield, Marilyn's birthplace, and Jimmy Dean's death intersection at Cholame. Then south to West Covina, avoiding L.A., looming like the Emerald City, a dream out of the past. You know, if the problem for the actor playing entering a strange place is to simultaneously establish with conviction that he belongs on the stage *and* convey the impression he has come to a new environment, the problem for the Angeleno arriving in Los Angeles is quite simply the reverse."

. . .

"There's nothing to *look at*," a voice had been complaining, "on Bolsa Chica. Look around—nothing but a lot of dead-ass beach crud degenerates wasted on downs, looking out at a dead-ass surf that pounds and pounds in dull dead-ass hammer blows."

"Up the *coast*," the first voice keened, "there are surfers gliding on boards and skidding through the bore . . . but who can undertake the move?"

Nusrat Fatah Ali Khan was singing in Old Persian, and somebody was saying "Yeah, Rita Hayworth was Mexican; so was Lupe Velez—they called her 'the Mexican Spitfire'—and Dolores Del Rio, who slept all day long and only went out at night and never grew a day older until the day she died."

"Orson Welles," the first voice declared, "took Rita Hayworth up the coast to Nepenthe; fucked her senseless day and night."

"What," Shadrach speculated, "*was* a nice pretty boy like him doing with a *maquinista* like that?"

"Yeah," Crystalman chimed in. "Who was that masked man anyway?"

"The Prince of Darkness," a voice called out.

"*Miles* was the Prince of Darkness!" another contradicted.

"What was the *appeal*?" Shadrach, persevering, demanded.

"The appeal?" El Sabio repeated. "The untamed brilliance of the flashing eyes, and the facial semblance, on which the wind and sun had left becoming furrows of encroaching age and the tint of an Aztec warrior, all proffering the devil's own spurious form of adscititious custody . . . and he got the boy very drunk."

"Yeah," Crystalman concurred, "shitfaced—then shot him up."

"A terrible creature," El Sabio bullied on, "who, for all his works and pomps and all his prowess steering that terrible machine was quite unable to skid around the corner from self-regard to an imaginative view of the world."

"And men go," Crystalman keened, "to admire the high mountains, the vast floods of the sea—"

"Surfing off Point Concepcion," Shadrach put in.

"—the huge streams, the circumference of the ocean and the revolutions of the stars . . . and desert themselves."

"The time, the place, the lover," El Sabio declared, "all together in a land where oranges bloom: the Land of Smiles and of Paraphernalia—get the whole set: Accepting Transactions on the Next Business Day—consecrated to the culture of manifold data increase, technological enterprise, and engineering precision—exemplified by that departed motor vehicle and its deceiving rider: twin instructors in all that is dark and unknowable in another, tragic about any future, and malign about the cosmos. It *riles* me that such a complex, quality boy should be cozened into enacting the role of bagman to a single-strand synthetic-fiber type like that.

"Is it any wonder," El Sabio concluded, "they end up here, like this boy, in their droves, to go forth into oblivion?"

"The Land of Paraphernalia," Crystalman repeated, looking down at Tristan. "It's all worth it if it brings you to your wave. Suddenly your life is this long stretched-out wave; you're removed from the past, everything on your mind has become immaterial; you feel completely removed from the world. Nothing matters any longer but you and the board and the wave and this instant in time."

"That isn't a surfboard you're straddling now," El Sabio said; "it's a length of bleached driftwood. Let us pray for this boy.

"Love is baffling," El Sabio declared, "but betrayal is a snap. Well, we've taken him down to the water and rinsed him. I hope the kid makes it; I really do."

"To the smooth, complete, and rapid salvation," Crystalman repeated, "epitomized by the Japanese proverb 'Tora ha yoku ichi nichi ni sen ri wo yoki, sen ri wo kaeru' and by the serene and celestial music of Nusrat Fatah Ali Khan."

"But wasn't he Mexican?" Crystalman asked. "On the major Harley?"

"In a pig's eye! Only another of those American sociopaths annually promoted to the nationally televised Most Wanted List, baring the nation's own truth to itself, dishing out the abuse, anguish, and final annihilation it most deeply craves."

Tristan said then, "Listen, I know where he's gone—to Fontana. It's where the original Hell's Angels was formed by a bunch of Harley-Davidson freaks in the late forties."

"I know all about Fontana," El Sabio declared. "The question is not does it concern that place or another. The question, in two parts, is this. Firstly, why does nature create the best sort of human being, only to seem to turn him into a dupe barely a quarter of the way along; and secondly, how does God plan to compensate for the black moon that shines in the bright white sky, for indignities like those suffered by this boy, injured by accumulation regimes and Satan's new weaponry?

"An adolescent woken from some rubble-walkthrough nightmare an hour before dawn by the perception of a sound that descends overpoweringly upon him may never cease to await the return of what he heard for the split second between sleeping and waking."

"This," Tristan said, "I remember thinking I should pay attention to—also to the fact that each of them seemed in his whacked-out way to be praying for me. Then the last thing before the church bells out the window: one guy was holding the syringe full of saltwater up and another was using my belt to tie me up, saying, 'Yes, then Rita Hayworth married Ali

Khan.' I heard Mae West in *She Done Him Wrong* drawling, 'Oh, hello, Rita.' Then El Sabio saying, 'Wake up, sad boy, there are two suns in the sky!'

"And finally Crystalman urging, 'Hang on, man, hang *on*—NASA's got a spacecraft in the *pipeline*—to determine by the year 2005 whether Andromeda is gonna plow head-on into the Milky Way or *sideswipe* us.' Then I saw the chopper coming down, and heard Crystalman plead, 'You gotta hang *on* and find *out*!' And in the background, 'Inn-A-Gadda-Da-Vida'! Then I went into chordal ideation: 'Mein armes kind' / 'Eres el pecado, chico' / 'No vale nada la vida' / 'Oh, hello, Rita.' "

As the chopper landed, and the medics jumped out and began to work on Tristan, El Sabio declared, "And now, there descends out of the heavens, like the white angel Albion, the new winged cradle of El Niño—for although that brutal dago called the boy *cabrito*, I shall always remember him as El Niño."

"El *Niño*," Crystalman chimed in. "El *Niño*!"

El Sabio nodded gravely. "El Niño, whose depressive activities created such atmospheric furor on both coasts and in many place in between. For although weeping endureth through the night, in the morning cometh joy—or more to the point, medics in rescue choppers." He then began to recite "On the Beach at Fontana."

"There is no beach at Fontana," a voice cried. "Fontana is in the middle of the fucking *desert*, all the way down there near El Cajon; it's where idiot stoners go to die!" But El Sabio persisted, as the medics prepared to remove Tristan to the hospital, and a voice crooned, "And then we'll all go off to sweet life, 'cause now is the time and we all know time!"

"There is," Mawrdew Czgowchwz said, "some theoretical bolstering for the idea that after a glut of experience, over-rich, dystonic, there is a call to deep rest, an attempt to get distance, to regroup one's imagined forces for belated mastery."

"Gluttony," Kaye said. "These women I've played so many of—gluttons for punishment. Maybe I *transmitted*—"

"Is that how you thought of them—when you played them?"

"It's—how they were written."

"By men—but is that how you've always played them?"

"But we're talking about me; this isn't about me, this is about him. Unless it's *always and forever* about the mother. Is it?"

"Yes and no—more no the longer life goes on."

"Please, God, let his life—let my son's life go on. In the meantime," Kaye Wayfaring said, "his guitar has been returned."

"Well, what happens now," Tristan asked, leaning back. "More analysis?"

"Not, I would think, right away—not at any rate until you've found the new place where the kids are hip, and defined your territory."

"*Territory* again! Well, it isn't Bolsa Chica beach, that we know. You know, don't you, what Bergson said about time? He said it was either redemptive or . . . now I don't *remember*!"

"You will; it will come back to you."

"As I lie here. It would be so nice, you know, to lie here and say nothing and see what happens. Probably nothing would."

"Hardly. If time is redemptive."

"Like acceptance. Acceptance is—that we know. If I were to lie here and say nothing, you'd sit there and accept my silence."

"And that would leave you unsatisfied; I know."

"Maybe I should just quit pretending to understand all the advanced shit like Bergson and stick to Patsy Cline's 'Faded Love' and things at my own level."

"You aren't composed entirely of water—you may seek another level."

Tristan said, "You think I'm manipulating."

"I don't mind. You know, the guitar has been returned."

"Yes. Kind of restores my faith in mankind—somewhat. You know, there was a Trinity on Bolsa Chica. El Sabio, Shadrach, and Crystalman. Who would the mother have been then?"

"The sea."

"That's nice. El Sabio was reciting a poem about a beach at Fontana, and I thought Ali Akbar Khan on sarod would go nicely with it—so would Martin Denny and the Hollyridge Strings, or even Wayne Fontana and the Mindbenders.

"When I was on Bolsa Chica, freezing with the saltwater in my veins, I just lay there remembering the snowman on the beach at Santa Monica that time, and grandmother telling us about Tir na nOg."

"I remember."

"All that was in my head was that El Matador, as soon as the moon had begun to set, had said, 'Well, that's it: when the moon is down, the game is over and it's time to move on. Adiós, querido gringo—no vale nada la vida. No la tomes a pecho.'"

"How did you feel about that?"

"The great psychoanalytical question. I suppose I ought to have felt like shit—I had, after all, opened myself to the Other, whose unattainability induces weeping—but I didn't. I had begun to go all numb and felt nothing—probably fortunate, one of the negative aspects of chaos being the exponential divergence of trajectories. I never mentioned Grandmother—I can't think why.

"Then this morning I heard the church bells, a peal of three, and thought of Marilyn on the casting couch listening and wondering what denominations they were, and I thought how nice to have some butch priest who looks like Spencer Tracy cuff me and declare, 'There's no such thing as a bad boy.'"

"With both Mae and Marilyn looking out for—"

"From their ghostly widow's walks? Well, I'm ashore—a sacrifice that somehow has lived on—better than claiming to be resurrected; I believe they still put you into Camarillo for believing that. Then they inject you, stopping, or decreasing, ego functions, the withdrawal intended to prepare a fresh start for the reconstruction of the collapsed equilirium.

"But it was a peal of three, a trinity: Mae and Marilyn and—Norma Jean, I guess. Norma Jean and Marilyn were hung in the same belfry, but always rang in split seconds apart: it's what finally drove . . . But no more driving—not for now."

Lying back on the pillows, he looked up at the ceiling.

"Look, I'm throwing in the towel—crying uncle. It turns out I wasn't more powerful than pain. Am I more than the sum of my wounds? Or is this nothing more than background for an acoustic-driven compilation of contemplative whispers and husky regrets?

"I remember Mother bringing home fabulous strawberries dipped in white chocolate on that same afternoon—the one when it snowed at the beach.

"You know, I'm terrified of being queer."

"So was I, quite terrified. Who wouldn't be?"

"But you're all right—you're married to Uncle Dee."

"In the realm of the spirit, yes."

"Is there another realm? There's Waimea—with Crystalman and Shadrach in the Pipeline. Where men are men, all wet, all the time, but men. Omnivores with webbed feet, but the male of the species anyway. Yes, you're married—clearly; as they say, all the good ones are."

Sitting up, he looked out the window again.

"El Sabio asked whether it was love that brought me to Bolsa Chica on the motorcycle. You're saying nobody around here will object that I'm queer, either."

"Nobody we know, no."

"All I've done is pig out on what passed for life."

"Don't be so hard on yourself—you were hungry."

"Thinking of El Matador just now, I wonder only one thing. Would I find it speechless sweet to murder him?"

"What do you think?"

"I think I'd have to tell the world—and be set free. I'm terrified all the same—of being queer."

"I was once too."

"Although I do remember taking heart once at something I read about gay life. 'This was what he had in mind: a vision of intense conversations, of shared wardrobes, and seasons by the sea.' You don't think love means never having to say you're sorry?"

"More likely never having to say you're there. We all love you."

"Isn't that what her fans told Judy Garland? Now they tell you, until you can love yourself."

"They must mean it. There is simply no way at all that anybody around here is going to reject you."

"Well, it seems no amount of love people feel for you can prevent misfortune."

"Listen, you know who called and sent flowers—Mexican bougainvillea? Desiree Von G. Why don't you read the message."

Jacob went to the large spray and unpinned the note.

" 'Hon, *Bolsa Chica*? Glad you're back. They'll be telling

you to "keep coming back." I have a better idea—stay. Pig out on love—and music, the food of. Go out the food door on it. I'll be seeing you in all the soon-to-be-familiar places. Hugs, Desiree.' "

"Listen," Tristan asked, as Jacob pinned the note back on, "tell me this—what are the instrumentalities along the way? 'He'd shared everything with his partner—not only the beginning and the end, but the instrumentalities along the way.' "

"I'm not absolutely sure."

"I'm crazy about you—and Father too—and *all* the men."

"I don't know the way out, either. Do I study lieder and learn to sing the 'Erlkönig,' even though my real ambition is to grow big balls and blow the roof off with the Prologue to *Pagliacci*? Or do I get really serious and become a cognitive philosopher?"

"Must you worry about all that at your age?"

"Apparently. Philosophy—'the celebration of certain impassioned failures.' The *great*-grandfather, they say, was one. Philosophy seems to spawn fewer epigones—or fewer recognizable ones."

"If you do write philosophy, I'll read you."

Then Steve was standing in the doorway—a worn-down yellow pencil nestled behind his ear.

"Hello, Sluggo," Tristan said.

"Hello, genius—you know you left something turned on back home?"

(I will not, the boy thought, say what I could say.)

"Someone sent me a card signed 'Me'—was it you?"

"What with so many—you come out on the first flight?"

"Yeah. I thought we could do lunch."

"Too bad you missed me in ICU."

"Listen, Whizzer, I need help with this new song."

Tristan sat up in the bed. "D'ya ride up front?"

"Yeah."

"Good. Trouble with the hablaz or with the music?"

"You've always been the music man."

"There's a title?"

" 'Come Back.' "

Tristan looked out into the white noon sunlight.

"One word or two?"

"Two. Emphasis on the second."

"Yeah? I see they gave you the stick to bring in." He turned to his uncle. "Sometimes a guitar is just a guitar—that right?"

"Absolutely."

"When there's music." He motioned to Steve, "OK, bring it over, but don't be surprised with what we get out of it—God only knows where it's been. You have to go back soon?"

"No."

"Excellent. We have time on our side. Bergson said time was either redemptive or it was nothing. Meanwhile, you know what the weirdest place in America is? Albuquerque—absolutely. And, man, those Zuni shalakos—"

Leaving his nephew's room, Jacob thought, *the instrumentalities along the way.*

Yes, they'll be all right. Ought to be . . . for a time.

Driven Woman

"THEY REALIZED," the publicist announced, "they could never call it that."

"They could have," the boyfriend challenged, looking at the Pacific, "conceivably."

"No, they couldn't. Leland knew that, if Orphrey didn't—so they called it what they did."

"What's in a name?"

"Sometimes everything, and sometimes nothing else."

"I'd've called it that—*Nothing Else*."

"Negative leads in a title are felt to be catastrophic."

"Oh, really? I call suicide a catastrophe—especially when you throw yourself off a cliff, into a roaring river, to be swept along the cataracts down over a waterfall."

("Without question," the *L.A. Weekly* had declared, with conviction, "*The Undertow* is not only O'Maurigan's most austere script, but also Orphrey Whither's most uncompromising foray into auteur sadism. From where else but Hyperion—a reconstituted Hyperion tucked under the condor wing of legendary buck-bang veteran visionary synergist Leland de Longpré—could a feature without build or the slightest hint of backstory [directed by the one man left in the Industry for whom the very suggestion of video-assist is an obscenity] unleash such a succession of perturbing images and inescapable situations [check them out: story boards and frames at www.undertowhyperion.com] which neither have nor require any justification beyond the histrionic intensity of the driven woman's relation to the rearview mirror?")

"You know," the boyfriend added, "many found Wayfaring's performance a little evasive."

"Really?" the publicist countered. "You know, according to the most reliably attested opinion in esthetics, the effect on the spectator of the awareness of form is an elongation, or a retardation of the emotions, a mesmerizing counterpoint of equanimity and menace. Look, take a memo: Wayfaring does not put by, she puts *out*. She was once asked by Bunny Mars what was the difference, did she think, between her and her contemporaries, nearly all of whom were saying the same things in what was then called the Last Hollywood Roundup. You know what she said? 'Maybe it's that I mean it!' "

"You do want her to win very badly, don't you," the boyfriend noted, with obliging concern. "Maybe you ought to do puja."

"The son, currently in turnaround, in the good sense, is somewhere up the coast doing puja, even as we speak. You and I serve better doing what we know best, which is lunch."

"I miss *Buzz*—*Buzz* would've had a preview feature on Wayfaring sitting it out on the patio in Silver Lake."

"I miss it too," the publicist avowed. "It may have been the last truly authentic Los Angeles voice that gave a shit. 'The File on Kaye Wayfaring' was one of their definitive pieces. 'In *Avenged* she is everybody: anhedonic, bitter, driven, insane without a plan for survival.' "

"And now," the boyfriend sighed, as if suddenly betrayed, "In *The Undertow*, she's her own mother."

"They say it had to happen."

"Which is just what the *Hollywood Reporter* and Rough-

Cut.com are saying about Oscar. 'If not now, when? If not her, who?' Well, you must admit," the boyfriend declared forthrightly, "she's—what is she?"

" 'Unprecedented' is, I suppose, the proper term," the publicist concluded. "Entirely, like cinema itself."

"And when did you start calling it 'cinema'?"

"When I got worn out calling it what it is."

"And the envelope, please. . . .

"And the winner is—"

Kaye Wayfaring broke off daydreaming.

Do I want the thing? What's not to want? Don't ask.

On the terrace overlooking the Lautner pool and the "hanging gardens" she thought of what was to come in spring, the bougainvillea, jacaranda, manzanita, hibiscus; tree camellias, lanai, both pink and white oleander; two trellises of morning glory, masses of honeysuckle. Meanwhile a row of cypress held sway along the high white wall, a few stray eucalyptus, a cluster of tulip trees, a stand of the ever green and always dusty California oaks, another of grevillea trees, another of larches, a long row of royal palms.

The Santa Ana winds had been blowing, bending the larches back and forth, whipping the royal palms' fronds around, and canceling the herbal aroma in the warm afternoon. Some broken palm fronds lay on the terrace amid swirls of leaves off deciduous trees, blown all the way to Silver Lake from the New England section of Forest Lawn (where Bette Davis lay). Plácido had just finished cleaning them off the flower beds, the patio, and the surface of the pool, remarking as he did so, "You know, Miss Wayfaring, what palm branches all over the place reminds me of? The entry of El Cristo into Jerusalem on Palm Sunday."

"Uh-oh."

"Exactly. This is why I am getting rid of them pronto, because in not long now we are supposed to start out."

We might, she thought, looking over Silver Lake. The crater of a dormant volcano, ringed by pretty hills, so the place looked to her. Fabled Silver Lake, veritably Umbrian, so they once insisted (some of them; others called it Glendale's ratty bolt-hole, a lay-by for Hollywood derelicts). Orphrey Whither in particular—from high in his Whither Park fastness—had been—still was—in the habit of, as O'Maurigan put it, slagging the storied enclave through clenched teeth.

"*Umbria*, for instance! Oh, indeed—don't miss the many correspondent features: the priories, the castellated dwellings, the *mottes* and hanging *gardens!*"

But she loved it.

"And the tone of the place!" (Orphrey would go on taunting them.) "The whole intellectual *irrigation* of the district in the nineties would put you in mind of Urbino, surely, with the added proviso, in the age of communication beyond telepathy, of instant access, instant replay, incessant peekaboo."

She loved it still, and you could turn switches off.

The Horizontales: Mae West as example. Not lazy, simply industrious in an unapparent manner. For instance, Mae's comment on Freud: "I didn't exactly read him myself, dear, I had him read to me—I found it relaxin'."

Watching Plácido at work, with a single California poppy stuck in his gorgeous black hair, she imagined herself—a Dorothy, not a Diana—asleep in the field of them, unwilling or unable to stir. She remembered the very day Plácido had driven her back from Vartanessian's and she'd decided to employ him. It was the day it snowed in Los Angeles. Would it snow again in Los Angeles to rouse her from her lethargy, send her to the charlatan wizard for the award (the task, retrieval: not of a broomstick, but of a little gold-plated statue of a eunuch), then home?

She looked now across to the towers of downtown Los Angeles and thought of a country preacher in Georgia: "And Nimrod built a tower in Babylon." And then of the de Longpré party, taking place in the tallest green tower over in the Wilshire Corridor. Emerald City.

The de Longprés' pre-Oscar cocktail was held in the penthouse living pavilion in the Wilshire (wraparound view of Beverly Hills, West Hollywood, Hollywood, Los Feliz, Silver Lake, downtown, Culver City, Santa Monica, Pacific Palisades, Brentwood, Bel Air, Holmby Hills, Whither Park, and Westwood).

The superbly coiffed and coutured hostess, looking down over Westwood, was, in her own mind, simply explaining herself (rather than, as her most mistrusted guest—a restless, insecure, skeptical generative liaison grammarian from UCLA—was busily telling himself, putting into negotiable words the profound and pulseless apathy generated by the paradox of inaccessible elevation) the while the sound machine in her rose bedroom emitted reassuring sounds from nature: the plash of Pacific waves, wind chimes rustling in the redwoods, and rain beating against windowpanes. (To the highly controlled Fortuny-Bennison tranquility of this sanctum, walls embellished with California adaptations of late French baroque frescoes: all florid, tumbling putti, writhing women, swollen clouds, and plunging horses, she, Livonia de Longpré, wrapped in a vivid pashmina shawl, would, once Leland had left for the ceremony, retire together with a few intimates, disposed around her in various French-upholstered baignoires, to watch the goings-on from an enormous Second Empire bed decked out in yards of dusky-rose silk and guarded by gilded sphinxes and harpies.) Meanwhile, until such time as she could feel free to unburden herself of her many long-held, more subversive opinions, the former B-picture star and Academy nominee held forth in general terms.

"Yes," she declared, "we got out of Los Angeles after the riots, but life up in Trancas was a little *too* uneventful, really. Now things have calmed down, and as it was a little soon for us to consider upscale senior campus living, it only made sense to take to the wide-open skies of the Wilshire Corridor. I get a great big kick out of watching the local buzzards wheel and swoop down."

Leland, surveying the flats, the hills, the canyons, the beach, the works, kept his counsel.

The restless, insecure, skeptical (and mistrusted) UCLA generative grammarian/film liaison agreed with Livonia. (For, seized at that very moment with an inexplicable and shaming stab of nostalgia for articulating windows, he was determined to show his powerful and, he felt, more-often-than-seldom sinister hosts that he was sensible both of the weight of what he called, in the privacy of his own calculating mind, Leland's "old guard vaticinations" and of the privilege of being received in what he knew to be, by any Los Angeles standard, exalted company cavorting in a prime real estate corral, complete with Venetian tile flooring, French antique pewter bar, so much eclectic contemporary furniture it looked like half a dozen competing emporia on Melrose Place had been emptied of their stock, and everywhere masses of Mexican bougainvillea in malachite vases.)

Leland, looking down at the surrounding strata of Greater Los Angeles (representing so many stages of fragile stability in the overall process of collapse, and so surely constituting, he thought, essentially a particularly grotesque and clear-cut case of the foredoomed planet) seemed passive, detached and resigned (qualities the academic simultaneously envied and deplored: were he to have indulged in the luxury of assuming them, he realized, he'd still be living in a ranchette in El Segundo, lecturing at Irvine on story / substance / style, pimp-rolling down classroom aisles with his *Yo*-cultic white-rapper routines, making a "mad guy" event statement out of racing home after class on his black Yamaha Virago to water his ice plants, and pulling down a little extra stash doing home delivery for Lupe's Azalea Ranch).

"Reflective," Hyperion's prince regent began sternly (as if from nowhere, a trick of rhetoric he'd mastered at green-light meetings), "of the prevalent lentor, the general *accidie* and the industry's current predilection for stories without spine.

"Drugged by the embrace of nature into what we call most natural in us, our sleepiness and our sexual desires—at once a pleasant and unhappy fate, available even to the socially disadvantaged, who go in for black tar heroin.

"But what is it, after all," he demanded more forcibly, "that pictures have taught people—bored people, lazy people—to do, except attempt to restore their equilibrium and their putative propadeutic leverage not by possessing an object, but by violating a spectacle?"

"Is *accidie* the term, really?" Livonia questioned. "Or is it really not more a question of the diminished-capacity defense? Is it really a question of laziness with these actors, when, apparently intent on affirming their own silly little bottle-rocket self-appraisals, they become quite suddenly capable of such disarming feats as throwing their arms up into the air in mixed company and loudly shouting 'Wow!' Or, for instance, of hitting the Hollywood to Harbor to Santa Monica interchange doing an even seventy as if they're thinking of putting in for flight pay?

"Vain, yes, utterly self-infatuated and obsessed with upping what they insist on calling the 'happy ante,' they are certainly victims of compression and of rotational fatigue resulting from one-sided activities. You wouldn't call any one of them in as a percipient witness, and if you were to file a discovery motion, you wouldn't dredge up much that would cross over from conjectural to inferential. But *lazy*? I don't know."

"UCLA law school," Leland countered, "was not wasted on you, darling, even if, speaking of suspicion of *accidie*, you have declined to practice."

"I have declined to practice, darling," Livonia cooed, "because the very thought of my starting up in some go-to litigation boutique for Hollywood liberals on the skids made you, shall we say, nervous. Otherwise I might be at Hyperion right now—right down the hall from you, running legal. Call it a suppression motion, if you like."

She turned to the liaison grammarian.

"I will allow their belief that they are preapproved does seem to betoken sloth, as does their peculiar idea of subsistence chic, which seems to combine distributed denial of service ambitions with haphazard dressing from consignment stores."

"Sloth," the liaison grammarian responded eagerly (as he attempted, vaingloriously, to tamp down the adrenaline exuberance of his terribly rich and powerful hosts with that aggressive and mendacious sincerity which in Los Angeles stands in for adversarial tact), "in which a self state is *stored* in an object present at the time of the ego's investigation, is now increasingly referred to as an adaptive-preferential *solace*—a defense against the menacing idea of further necessary forays into the information field."

"I've heard that said," Leland drawled (with, as the grammarian later reported, a certain edge), "and of course cake is rarely seen anymore in the best of houses."

The liaison grammarian looked down at Westwood,

whence he'd lately come, and, feeling his way along the Wilshire Corridor, expanded his argument.

"But Wayfaring, now, surely is something else."

"Just so," Leland concurred. "Wayfaring's allure lies precisely in convincing her audience that what happens to her in a picture always *reminds* her, moment by moment, of something *else*—and not only something else, but something more momentous than what's happening just then."

"*Huh?*" asked a fascinated guest, one of Livonia's contract-player colleagues from another era, a stalwart of the Hollywood Dress Extra and Contract Players Classical Theater Repertory Company on Highland (by invitation only).

"Which reminds me," the liaison grammarian persisted (beginning to show the strain of the long game as he surveyed the room through the leaves of a very large potted dracaena).

"*Really?*" Livonia cut in, like a cross-examiner. "What of?"

Biting his lip, he looked away quickly, then turned back.

"Of the fact that her interior world is always consistent in gesture and expression—juxtaposed, rather than superimposed on the script. A salient characteristic that marks her a true Gemini. And of course internally consistent worlds when juxtaposed make a completely inconsistent composite world, one that with its jagged rhythms gives an air of brimming over with an excess of its own situation. In a word, her performances are ergodic."

"Oh?" the former contract player asked, unsure.

"Yes, illustrating perfectly the proposition that the mean of observations of a single individual over time is equal to the mean of observations of many at a single moment over an area."

"In her case," Leland cut in, "an area that stretches, metaphorically, from Silver Lake to the beach."

"Oh, that's *so* true!" the contract player exclaimed.

"But concerning sloth," the generative grammarian continued, boldly, sure of his footing, for the moment anyway, "it would seem to be built into the very nature of posing for pictures—passivity inversely aggravated to sloth. The very earliest pictures had to be posed for in long stretches—"

"Yes," Leland confirmed, "and in pictures taken of crowded city streets where people were moving, the people disappeared."

The liaison grammarian acquiesced.

"Because always and everywhere," Leland resumed, "in troubled times of hesitation, of transition, various trashy types appear. The test for us as a tribal society is to extend to the spiritually afflicted the courtesy time immemorial prescribes."

"Despair is stupid and lazy," his wife persisted, "and had I been given to either, I'd never have landed *you*, darling, in spite of the memorable caution Miss Tuesday gave on that back lot when she let Elvis know 'it needs a man to go to hell with.'

"*God*," Livonia went on, "you know, when we all first came out here, we were ambitious certainly, but we didn't *lose our essential selves*. We didn't, in spite of rivalry, suspicion, gossip, hangovers, upstaging, missed cues, delays, overtime, rumors, deadline pressure, or sexual jealousy, end up turning into these *creatures*! Of course—" she paused, dramatically, then concluded—"they are, like the coyotes, just wild things lost in the dark."

"Ugly, withholding rationers of enhancement," the generative grammarian urged, to solidify his ground. "Cut back by abatement, containment, and exclusion. They live for the spotlight; when the lights go out, so do they. Like the illiterate and unskilled peasants turned by the Russian Revolution into industrial robots, what they live in greatest fear of is the accusation by ruling cadres of bourgeois spontaneity and locomotive advantage."

. . .

Looking back on the early days of *The Undertow*, Kaye Wayfaring had told Astarte and Mawrdew Czgowchwz, "I couldn't seem to come to terms—locate—the designated victim—"

Astarte said, "Until Tristan—"

"—until Tristan nearly died. Then every ambition of mine, every notion—well, who was it said fatigue was ever the basis of virtue. Still, I didn't know if I could find the invalid—or attract the feeling that would engender it. Except as the victim of success and celebrity, and that was *so* outworn—a fact that came gate-crashing when those other people offered me the part of the older woman—"

"Voni de Longpré's old part," Astarte interrupted, "in that terrible television remake of *Avenged*—what was it called? It died the death of a bad, bad Saturday-night special."

"*Getting Even.*"

"And anyway you weren't—*aren't*," Astarte insisted, "a victim of success, celebrity, or any other distraction."

"And yet," Mawrdew Czgowchwz nodded, affirming her daughter-in-law's insight, "the difficulty is terribly real."

(Thus the requirement for the film actor was the very opposite of the stage actor. "No, darling, *look*, don't just do something—*stand* there!" Stella said. "Just because they cry 'Action' on the set doesn't mean you have to *do* anything—except remember something you did and what it made you do next.")

"Then a sign I'd once seen on the Hollywood Freeway, THE BEACH BOYS SAVE—and the song 'God Only Knows' running through my head, brought back the whole past.

"And now Leland wants me to seriously consider *The Long, Lonely Life of Mary Miles Minter*, set entirely on the day of her death during the 1984 Olympics. Sees it as a cross between *What Ever Happened to Baby Jane* and *The Lady from Shanghai*.

Maev, when I told her about it, came out with, 'Sounds tired to me—like the Rita Hayworth story. People said Rita Hayworth had Alzheimer's because she forgot ever having been Margarita Cansino, but she was a drunk.' I said, 'You shouldn't speak that way about a woman who gave so much inspiration to soldiers, who was so incredibly beautiful.' 'Did I say she was a *mean* drunk?'

"I was right here in this house the day Mary Miles Minter died, having lunch and watching the Olympic women's marathon while they were tearing down the house next door. Then we bought the property and put in the gardens and the pool. Well, I don't think I'll do Mary—too much like a nightmare of ending up here in Silver Lake, decayed beyond recognition, alone, after the earthquake, living on rodents and sewage, madness and whatever."

At the awards ceremony, while Tristan Beltane and Jameson O'Maurigan were sitting out front, Jacob Beltane was sitting backstage reading his nephew Tristan's e-mail dispatch from a retreat house in northern California.

The Boy-Who-Lived, postquam rearrived through ragged heaps of lost innocence, crusty outcropping of old guilt, and sticky tar pits of shame, greets you, dearest uncle, from this place on high ground at the horizon—not unlike, really, a big Georgian box bathed in the serene supernal light of the West-of-Ireland countryside, or Duino, and one could envision a party in the place, full of Irish eccentrics out of The House by the Churchyard, *and ghosts, like Central Casting Central European vagabonds and gypsies, or like a murder weekend acted out by a gang of out-of-work Hollywood types.*

Here by the cliffs of northern California ("caught up," as the poet says, "in the crotches of sharp hills") amid the fumaroles of supposedly extinct volcanoes, where no skelp of loud laughter is heard to rend the fabric: put you in mind alternately of Machu Picchu and indeed of Holy Ireland's coast itself, looping in and out of the coiling mists, between a rock and a soft verge, or as we used to say on the road, on the lam somewhere between Loose Chippings and Dangerous Bends.

I have not swerved from thy testimonies, O demi-progenitor, while but one small voice whispers sit still, count your change and ponder the requisites for successful progress from genotype to phenotype to leadership in a higher station, another wonders, what for?—as, treading the minefields of our times, I amid sorrow sit on a fin of ancient Pacific sandstone. (Excursions to the countryside or to the shore, far from affording a pure romantic solace, present their own form of emptiness and loneliness.) Making sea bird noises on long blades of grass and trying to learn to love the fallow way and gather in the patient fruits (though no longer drowsed with the fume of poppies, for late summer has passed into what passes for early spring in northern California).

So, a sloth among so many soft-spoken Schedule D's, former students of shamanism, virtual reality and the botany of the Amazon; biofeedback dropouts and escapees from the clutch of Excite! At Home, plus adjudicated burn-outs from the Red Cliff Ascent Outdoor Therapy Program for Wayward Teenagers who couldn't make it trekking through the Escalante. They have dark, razor-sharp senses of humor and genuine rhyming skills, and busily exert themselves doing watercolors and differential equations, collecting wild mushrooms, polishing gemstones and, while awaiting to be milled into spiritual adepts (capable of amortizing their sleep debt and thus made whole, of finding God in deepest Nod), they masturbate with an eerie, prophylactic pleasure in contemplation of the violent raptures of the Promised End as figured in the eroticized images of children with which mainstream print advertising in this vitiated time hot-wires the hopes of a desperate people to unattainable bliss.

Then relaxing in the evenings with a Popsicle (nourri, vita-
miné, rassasié, manicuré, rasé, bichonné, cravaté, parfumé,
comblé, garé, massé) *grooving on God's given thrust.*

*Of course the Sirocco and the Bora were insufferable at
Duino—although not a patch on the Santa Ana when it scours
Malibu Canyon—but what could be? And who can deny that*
Walden *remains, despite superficial popular characterizations,
an extraordinary document of reflection on the extent and nature
of personal responsibility for common things? Not I.*

What is it the slothful get up to in Dante's Purgatory?

*However, whatever of that, up here it's quite another moun-
tain landscape. A land of profusely grassy wildflower-perfumed
mountain meadows and silver-mirror icewater tarns nestled in
windless, rocky, goat-frolic hollows over which in a listless sky
drift tattered clouds like sheets torn into strips by chronic depres-
sives in art therapy class at Camarillo. Like Arcady or Illyria, or
maybe Idle Valley.*

*You know me for a good student of nice differences—those
for example obtaining in tea ceremony among the Senke, the
Enshu, the Uraku, and the Hayami. So have I been trying in a*
gedanklich *mood and in spite of the fact that, as Bill Evans
wisely pointed out a long generation ago,* suibokuga *equals 'So
What?' to work out the nuances of Endtime belief in the inter-
val between the defeat of Antichrist and the Second Coming
(given over to the repentance of the apostates and the refreshment of the saints) and even—on a subject allied to that of the
rental units, and before it's too late, how the child is father to
the man.*

*But has anybody but me ever asked, "Then what? Who's the
mother?" There's only one answer so far as I can tell: the adolescent. This is not because my mother was an adolescent when my
father was a child, quite the reverse, I look at adolescence in the
scheme the poet has set in train: i.e., coming* later, *and therefore*
younger—*to the memory of the man, where it's all happening,*

right? As Marlowe says, in Hollywood anything can happen, anything at all (although the rumor casting Mother and me together in a Sally Marr–Lenny Bruce biopic was, well, silly).

I once asked Astarte why is California so laid back? "In California, darling, abreaction *is the result of meltdown midriff workout. The most reliable clue to the narcoleptic tenor of life in Los Angeles is what does not happen." And lately, if you look, that's what it is: some version of the Bardo of Dharmata: a persistent vegetative state (self-denial as self-indulgence; disorderly wanderer tamed by judicious, compassionate dispensation of the appropriate indicated S.S.R.I. No more hot sex in the edit room, dive time curtailed to the point of extinction. You might as well go all the way and take up residence in the abandoned lifeguards' quarters in Zuma Beach. Withholding is not the same as sloth, is it, or unilateral disarmament? I mean, pace Browning,* should *a man's reach exceed his grasp? Perhaps not).*

And so here I am out in Russian country, near Sebastopol, wanting badly to live to be something that eschews plot, rather than being chewed up into slutty mush by it, something to whom what is happening page by page outweighs any interest in what must happen in the end, result of neurasthenic cholerine brought on by nervous strain, moral shock or compound thought.

The high moral ground is terribly lonely. So's Wyoming in winter.

And on the Magic Mountain, doesn't it snow!

But not up here, where one wide double door opens to a hundred little single ones, behind so many of which like the Buddhas in the twenty-nine caves of Ajanta sit the purposed and sibilant, fed up, or fucked out from a life of forced marches and brooding in base inns, telling their beads, chanting the Heart Sutra: cute-hoor chancers here on spring break side by each with adepts up all night clutching kyosakus, on rattle watch against their fleshly demons, resisting with everything in their spiritual arsenal the irresistible siren song, in retro late-70s disco beat, of

the worldly whiplash dancing master, "tour, battement, jeté,
révérence" *(and the untoward visions he brings of oral sex in
the Oval Office . . . or oval sex in the Oral Office . . . whatever).*

*Steve and I have come to an agreement—we are leaving
all our adolescent anguish to Korn (as Heine says, tendering
bruised hearts rueful comfort,* "Krankheit ist wohl der letzte
Grund / Des ganzen Schöpferdrungs gewesen"). *Coming
from Bakersfield they can not only handle it, they and their
assigns can process it. I retain however (lest they should fall into
the irreverent hands of the Buzzcocks, Elastica, and Imperial
Teen) the rights to certain sentiments expressed for example by
Pablo Neruda, such as* "En mi interior de guitarra hay un
aire viejo / seco y sonoro, permanecido, inmóvil / como
una nutrición fiel, como humo."

*In some old Indian myth or other, some woman asks some old
god or other for only two children—but that they shall be more
beautiful and powerful than any thousand others.* "You shall
have one and a half," *the old fuck answers. So he grows up, this
half-ass, asking such otherworldly gravamen-laden grievance
questions as* "Am I made of something else than syllables?" *Then
his mother tells him a thing or two.* "You are my son—and you
were born to ransom me. Children are born to ransom their parents. And there is only one way I can be redeemed—by giving the
soma to the snakes. You will find the soma in the skies."

*May I tell you, I identify with neither woman nor god, but
with the punch-line half-offspring in a tribal creation myth
made of God knows what else but syllables. (For that matter, do
I exist apart from my self-reporting?)*

*Maybe if Mother gets the Academy Award, that's the
ransom? I hope she does, if only to not have to listen to anybody
crying,* "Oh, I love everybody here!" *and* "Thank you,
Providence—thank you, Consequence—thank you, O silent
working of the Secret Ballot . . . and thank you, thank you,*

thank you, *all my lovely bright gold angels!" Because I know absolutely that Mother in her acceptance speech would be so free of any such rectitudinous industry need I wouldn't even have to watch to ratify.*

Although I intend to try. Yes, I intend to do what Marlowe does when he finds himself in one of those shambolic old piles out in Bay City—or up in the hills—those battered, pocked-white eroded clapboards wrapped by wide porches; places with port-cochères and parquet floors and stained glass windows, like the Wayfaring house back in Clayton. Places full not of the walking wounded (who after all, nurse psychic exit wounds, and espouse exercise) but of the immobile disabled (who have suffered the worse indignity of psychic splat wounds). Places in which he's forever getting zapped by goons and/or injected by defrocked dope doctors. I intend to leap over the wall in the stillness of the after-noon and make it, if not down to the port, to look for driftglass, et cetera, then at least as far as the trailer park, to stand at a window and watch them sitting there on bargain mud cloth, burning frankincense, given over to the voluptuous passivity of the higher faculties, toking on spliffs, watching it happen—because it's got to happen; it's bound to this time, isn't that so?

Tristan's twin sister, Maev, and her grandmother, Mawrdew Czgowchwz, were at that moment seated together in the observation car of Amtrak's *Coast Starlight* on their way back to Union Station, Los Angeles, from a visit to the retreat house.

As they had ridden down through northern California—Wayfaring country—Maev remembered tales of private rail-way cars, star passengers from the East getting off at Pasadena.

"No," Maev declared, "I don't like him anymore."

"Really?"

"Not at the moment, just at present; all right?"

"It hasn't to do with 'all right.' "

"I know—I needn't have permission to feel—in spite of the fact that T. may be right in saying that one's truest feelings cannot be provided with respectable derivations. Fine, in that case I don't like him at the moment, just at present—especially when he writes me e-mail addressed to Jordana Leavitt—that's from *Hollywood Kids*—and signs himself Woot the Wanderer—that's from *The Tin Woodman of Oz*. He's the little boy transformed by the giantess into a green monkey."

"Yes, I remember reading it to you both."

"Yes, well, if you'd ever read *Hollywood Kids*, you'd find poor Jordana driving around in a Porsche all day long, always home alone at two a.m., awake and at loose ends, not reading a book of any kind, listening to music, or even looking at an old movie, after what she calls bitterly 'another scintillating night in the City of Angels.' Moreover, she's in love with her dead brother who jumped out of the window at twenty. He even quoted one of the brother's lines: 'You know, Jordana, the world is full of married men, and only one of them is our father.' I mean, really!"

"I see your point," Mawrdew Czgowchwz admitted.

"For the first while, in his recovery, he'd been writing to me as Tammy, Princess of the Visigoths. Then as Hermione and signing himself Harry and referring to you as Professor MacGonagall coming downstairs in a funny tartan bathrobe and hair net to tell us all to go to bed. He talked about starting his career in enchantment at eleven, as Bankei Yotaku had, and complained of feeling drained and strangely empty, even though he was so full of chocolate. He declared that although Draco Malfoy pretended to hate him and wished him dead out loud, it was quite clear to everybody he only wanted to get into his pants, and kept referring to the game of Exploding Snap. All transparently adolescent, but as I understood it, that was regression.

"Then, for a time, he was calling me Daria, from the cartoon show all the kids watch now. She's a funny, smartass redhead in glasses at the high school; has a weird thrust—and asking my advice on how to play it when he came back home."

"Not terribly uncomplimentary, that."

"Well, I'm glad we went to see him and I wish him well, but if twinship is the occasion for an extreme of fellow feeling, then he frightened me terribly with that drug thing. I know about the long-dead cousin T. is supposed to resemble so—though I don't see it myself in the pictures—and it's no fun. Why should a person have to think about somebody dead they've never known, even a relative? I mean, I never mind thinking about Marilyn—Mother makes her come alive in the most attractive way—for instance, singing 'Look for the Silver Lining' and 'Someone to Watch Over Me' when she came over to baby-sit. And I don't at all like thinking about my other grandmother, movie or no movie; you are more than suffi-cient. And anyway I think of you in some measure, rightly or wrongly, the way so many others do, as a great diva who, in the end, brooks no rivals. Although I will say Mother is sensational in the picture—the best yet. I can't imagine playing—but then I'm no actress, and never will be."

"Not as such, no."

"And I really hated his calling me Orfamay Quest—I did. And the way he referred to the Oscars as 'wake amusements'!"

"Yes, that was untoward."

"In a word. And I didn't care, either, for the mother-maiden-crone remark, or the business about this being the final story. I haven't heard you say you're ready to pack it in; I don't think Mother is, either, in any real sense; and as for me—anyway, that triple goddess thing is nothing but a paranoid male fantasy."

"He is a male," Mawrdew Czgowchwz assured her grand-daughter at once, "and that means that if a circumstance seems at all unsuspecting of him himself, he in turn cannot conceive of it. Then too, the desire, once glimpsed, of replacing millennia of the fear of prosecution by God the Father into its inverse, contempt for the injudiciousness of the almighty Mother . . . you understand."

"I'll buy that. By the way, about that expression—*as such*, I realize it's characteristically Irish—I remember I used to love it."

"No more?"

"Perhaps not just at present—yet one more thing."

"They do pile up."

"As we determine ourselves."

"Yes."

Let me tell you about the characters in my dreams—or rather the character. He's called Delete Sentry, and he stands next to a big black car under a streetlight—down the block away from the taxis, on a midtown street in what must be New York: you can smell the river. Maybe it's Rutherford Place. He wears a big black Italian overcoat with a high collar turned up against his ears, his hat—it's a big black fedora—pushed down. I wake up thinking I must have enemies. "Only the finance company," a voice snaps.

Symbolic, huh? Smart, fast, and funny, if you like 'em that way—and I do, even if I seem to have become inert, like the body locked in the trunk of that car under the streetlight away from the taxis, destination come dawn, the river—

Of course Lois Magic's not in the phone book.

A trailer park is a universal place. If Oscar viewing is the Te Deum of the American religion of hope-to-die fantasy and star-struck optimism emanating from Los Angeles and taking place simultaneously on the Universal Plane of Earth and on that other plane among a sacred band of pure witnesses in a distant land, from whose heaven the dove descends . . . et cetera, then a trailer park (the halting site, the nestling village neath the gloomy chateau) assumes the centrality of a sacred grove, a Stonehenge: full of gleaming streamlined mobile homes you could drive to Mexico, each with a swept red-dirt front yard done up with a seashell, rock, and garden-hose water feature, interspaced with cast-off-timber lean-tos swathed in Insulbrick and propped up on truck wheels that you couldn't roll down the hill.

So whether Mother wins the Oscar or not, I must a while longer sit it out up here in this asylum on the cliffs—a vexing cross between the Chateau Marmont and the Chateau d'If, wrapped in the redwood fog-dripped Pacific mists. Fugies inaudax proelia raptor, *in a state of eerie and mellow fatigue doing fuck-all and attending lectures on the seven essential stages: innocence, pain, knowledge, understanding, vigor, vision, and aloha.*

Question. Why, when the French Revolution instituted holidays for Virtue, Genius, Labor, Opinion, and Rewards, did they not call one up for Bone Idleness? Or to put it another way, why is Carnival always frenetic and never just a lazy afternoon?

Anyway Maev said that in all the years she now looks back on she never remembers hearing me say exactly the same thing twice. So should I start? Or stop? I mean, I could learn to raise my head, and flash my eyes—making decisions pertaining to constant compassionate regard toward the human element. Others on the beach have done so.

So many long double-glazed windows, so many sliding glass doors, so many mirrors, reflecting the outdoors. Different back east, she thought; there people still preferred to live in caves and cover their walls with pictures of places. They sat in rooms from the past, spread with thick carpets and clogged with heavy furniture, the views out their windows shrouded in portieres.

("The mother," Astarte had reminded Mawrdew Czgowchwz, "read the Bible incessantly and painted landscapes, and left stacks of them—heavy gouaches, forbidding things apparently. I mean, they were called landscapes, but they were all of the same dismal swamp—some lowland Georgia place, it seems, from the woman's childhood. And she had the habit of telling anybody who would listen how greatly she preferred magnolias and water lilies to all other cultivated plants; she'd laugh and call them shiftless, because they lack most of the specialized, industrious parts found in what she called the more 'mod'run' flowers."

"There is such a place," Mawrdew Czgowchwz recalled, called just that. Dismal Swamp. One heard stories of it at Willows, Thalia Bridgewood's place in Westchester. Thalia said the way her willows hung aslant the Bronx River always put her in mind of the eerie bald cypresses and the Spanish moss hanging down off the river oaks jutting out from the subtended riverbank.)

The light was falling anyway; it was already half past six. The award for art direction would have been announced by now.

Art direction . . . music . . . then best supportings, best original screenplay . . .

I've just come from a visit to a solitary neighbor down at the trailer park—a contingent of hip locals has dubbed him "Foul Ole Ron"—rumored to be a veteran of the Air Force's Man High program, who once rode a hot-air balloon to the very edge of outer space and who, in contemplation of the timeless meaning of the human condition celebrated yearly at the Cowboy Poetry Festival at Elkton, Nevada, has long since run out of sympathy or regret. I love him: he has no heart (although the tattoo on his shoulder reads UNEXPLODED ORDNANCE and the sweatshirt he wears-and-washes-and-wears—its faded legend, I WAS GOOD AND DID JUSTICE, he will not explain—speak of something). Wolfing down with relish his own canned peaches and homemade cottage cheese, he holds forth on solitude, fallen friends, Western values and (with the petulance of a small mouth set in a heavy chin) tenders such pronouncements as "All experience is an arch through which the vision of the road untraveled appears in the same perspective always, diminishing to vanishing point at a horizon never to be reached" and "What the movies teach us is that not all the repeated events of our lives, merely by recurring, serve the szuzhet *action or help us construct a* fabula *line." (Did I tell you this was Russian country?)*

The publicist and the boyfriend had nearly reached the contentious stage.

"Driving by."

"What do you mean driving by? Driving by as in 'drive-by shooting'?"

"It could be done."

"You mean you think she's not just afraid to show?"

"Nothing of consequence," the publicist announced loftily, "to do with a personality of Wayfaring's caliber can ever be considered that simple—despite the glass-smooth moves and captivating confidence habitually on view. Billowing like silk with those long arms and that arched eyebrow, she'd make anybody think she had the ability to walk through walls. And after all, the fear system is not, strictly speaking, one that results in the experience of fear, but rather one that, having detected a danger, produces responses that maximize the probability of surviving a dangerous situation."

"Oh," the boyfriend responded.

"William James believed man's ascendancy over the

beasts is most clearly evident in the reduction of the conditions under which fear is evoked in humans. He never knew Hollywood."

"Or Wayfaring—who operates on her bets."

"Well," the publicist insisted, as if challenged, "why should she sit there in the auditorium all night? It's a matter of record she never looked at the dailies. She wasn't at the premiere. Why should she even drive by the place if she wins? No, wait, what is this, a pitch meeting? *When* she wins. They could send it over by messenger in ten minutes, right to Wayfaring at Waverly in Silver Lake."

"Yeah," the boyfriend cracked, "with a media crew. We know how she'd finesse that—'Slip it under the door.' But, listen, maybe she doesn't drive by. Maybe it's more complicated than that, worked out like clockwork. Maybe she's got it timed so the minute she drives up—"

"Excuse me, that's the minute she's *driven* up."

"Whatever. That's when they announce it—and out she steps like it was the premiere, only it's the back door, because she knows all about back doors."

"And what's the motivation?" the publicist demanded.

"You mean why is she doing this?"

"No, not at all. What makes Wayfaring different from all the others is that precise blend, in her life as in her performances, of the reminiscent and the current. You consider, as she works that room for points, not so much, or hardly at all, Where is she going? or What does she want? but only and always Who *is* she and where *does* she come from?"

"Well, maybe," the boyfriend allowed, thinking it through. "But maybe also she doesn't want to make a scene walking right down the center aisle—people would say it was the seventies again and she was having hysterics in the front office or shooting up in the can."

"No chance," the publicist declared, now getting into the game. "The way it's been choreographed, with all the nineties Wayfaring gravity and grace, she barges right in the back door, past all the VIP backstage admits, through the wings and onstage, right to the podium. Remember the Bette Davis quote on acting she gave Bunny Mars for the *Herald-Examiner*? 'The first and most important thing is you must always hit your marks.' "

"Wearing what—silk pajamas? Top hat and tails?"

"I don't think so."

"Well, I don't see anything in reassuring earth tones. I see something iridescent, with shoulders."

"Whatever she puts on would be that—Wayfaring *is* Hollywood's shoulders—Hollywood's shoulders and expensive night energy embodied. Want to know what of the night? Ask Wayfaring. So, do you mean you see her *barging* in, as you delicately put it, all gravity and grace, in Bob Mackie or Thierry Mugler spatial-Amazonian Hollywood-diva power drag?"

"Well," the boyfriend answered hesitantly, "something with some kind of authority."

" 'Wrapping her strong white shoulders in the gorgeous stole Athena wove.' Something along those lines?"

"Why not? Driven-woman battle dress, tall, strong silver heels—a flash of *luxe*—and carrying an absolutely overwrought Judith Leiber bag. And hair and makeup too—I remember she had that fabulous consultant."

"Cégeste; long gone."

"Home to God."

"Wayfaring would say so. I see severe hair, very little makeup—very pale, with a light blush—and she enters wafting Sudden Midnight—or maybe, if she can get hold of any from some old bag in the Hollywood Dress Extras Club,

Schiaparelli's Shocking. The mother drenches herself in it in the picture, remember, to go to funerals. Yes, wearing that beige brocade suit and that beige veiled pillbox. She might . . . but, no, that's the kind of indulgence she's never been guilty of."

"Well," the boyfriend concluded, "the gods impel all things to success."

"Really. Publicity campaigns have a lot to do with it too."

(She had decided, in a conversation with her brother-in-law, what to put on that night. "I thought perhaps the layered smoke organza—it takes the light." "And gives back what?" "Nothing to speak of." "Perfect.")

Now, about the empty pistol case full of works he—El Matador—left behind on the beach (which the Bolsa Chicas had the presence of mind, having used them one last time to rinse out one's derelict veins, to deliver to the undertow*), which case came back to me along with the guitar. Yes, concerning it and the empty pockets in which the pistols had some long time lain in the 69 position, abrading the crushed red velvet—such a provocative outline: what I did was fill them full of my best old marbles, and I bring them now (like some significant-exculpatory-materials kit) to the common room here, where in front of a roaring fire of birch logs and mesquite we unwind of an evening over a game of Chinese checkers. (Even the holy guys play—and play to win— to the end, apparently, that the lazy and the vagabond may be rebuked and the truly contemplative more readily welcomed and extolled. Cometh the hour, cometh the iceman—and strange is the state of men's minds in the End Zone, in which the lapping tongues of Pentecostal flame quite melt the product, if not the deliverer.)*

.   .   .

"Let the story tell itself," the publicist declared, approving the Pacific. "Whether it has love and buried treasure in it and is therefore likely to appeal to a wide public, or is intended for generations yet unborn, and likely to remain so, it should be made to move on—action-figure toys and all. The ballots are in and counted. 'On the Sabbath he rested.' "

"Today's today," the boyfriend said. "For Christians, anyway—which, considering, is pretty—oh, never mind, he *who?*"

"Price Waterhouse. You know, the great Lisbon earthquake of 1755, it was said, marked the beginning of the end of the Christian faith's hold over Europe. It remains to be seen whether the Big One will do the same to our religion of passive imagination occasioned by the motion picture."

"I never knew Price Waterhouse was actually a guy."

"We beat back rumors to the contrary—sent him out on the breakfast circuit. Beverly Boulevard, et cetera. Beverly put him on opposite Miranda Fuerte. We tried the mall-appearance thing too, but Price ankled—there's just too much paranoia in people away from their televisions. Of course, since then, there's been a merger, and now he's Price Waterhouse Coopers Somebody."

"Oh, like Gloria Vanderbilt."

"So tonight people at their televisions—"

"See Wayfaring win, and be vindicated."

"They start believing in the Oscars again?"

"It's been a long time—your lifetime, probably."

"The light isn't everywhere; there is a source." Cordelia had taken to declaring the principle in almost any connection.

And now the long windows, darkening, had turned into long mirrors. Time to get dressed.

The publicist had left the beach house and was speeding downtown. The boyfriend sat in disintegrating light, watching *The Undertow* on the wall-sized television, while on the wall opposite he had turned on the virtual aquarium system, a Japanese-made computerized display featuring an array of Pacific Rim marine life, which the publicist had had installed. (It reminded him, he said, of the Manitoy Bar back on New York's smart East Side, since torn down.)

"You know, Plácido, how I've always liked driving the car myself."

"Not tonight, Miss Wayfaring."

"It's why I'm so glad you like the garden so much, and grateful to you for making so much of it, too."

"The garden is the garden, Miss Wayfaring; the car's the car."

"All I mean is after working in the garden all afternoon—"

"The sun goes down, things stop growing—the night-blooming jasmine comes out."

"You're a philosopher. My husband and my brother-in-law are at the ceremony."

"The way you say that, Miss Wayfaring, sounds like a funeral."

How was what she, Cordelia's daughter, had been going about doing—being driven, for example, to the studio or to some location in the early morning, all made up, or to all those premieres and award ceremonies over the years—so very different from what her mother used to so disturb them all by doing, attending all those anonymous funerals?

What perfume? She concentrated.

"Anyway," Plácido continued, determinedly, "I'm supposed to bring you, they said."

"Take me."

"Excuse me, Miss Wayfaring?"

"Nothing—a technical point."

"They said bring you so you could take the Oscar yourself instead of them having to bring it home to you. Understand?"

"I understand almost nothing anymore."

"Don't say that, Miss Wayfaring—you're very smart."

"I'm afraid not, Plácido. It's true my children are very smart."

"Well?"

"Available is not quite the same as smart."

"That's true of English, Miss Wayfaring, not true of you."

"Astarte," Livonia was telling the French cineast, "goes all the way back past Rhona and Radie to Hedda and Louella, to Adela Rogers St. John. She's epic."

"I think you mean 'epochal,' " Leland advised.

"I mean," Livonia snapped, "she knows her shit."

"Well . . ." Astarte demurred, somewhat.

"Excuse me, darling," Livonia declared, "it's my nerves. These parties we keep on giving—I don't know a tenth of the people who come—or who get in—and they nearly all behave like Bolsheviks. The way they dress!"

"Bolsheviks are a little out of fashion," Leland observed, not unkindly. "Although I'm sure it's perfectly true that a great many of the party-shuttle samples on display here this afternoon, while perfectly willing to eat our food and drink our wine, think of us, even as they without compunction sate themselves into stupors, as representative of everything in Hollywood that is limited, dull, pompous, and dead, of our habitat as a recycle bin of folded careers, and of themselves, of course, even as they slither like eels through the swamp that passes for society in this town, as passionate, militant, resistant, and self-assertive Remonstrants. Progenitors of—something advanced certainly."

"Living as they do," Livonia summed up, "in their own *fabulous* world of fashion, counterfashion, industry coyotes, and imposter trash."

"I have never seen," the French cineast excitedly exclaimed, "these coyotes! It is said they walk freely in the streets of Hollywood!"

"They do," Livonia laughed, "and wander into the canyons at night to prey on unguarded household pets—the terribly expensive ones, like the Lhasas kept by all those filthy-rich, barbaric, and defensive enthusiasts of the so-called avant-garde in Hollywood. And how they do love crash-diving Oscar parties and playing arch word games!"

"Nothing more," Leland agreed testily. "Yet they consider the Oscars—like everything else connected with the industry—part and parcel of a naked, unchecked discourse of power, born of spite, bred in frustration and nourished by vengeance. Manners are viewed nowadays as conventionalized survivals representing former acts of dominance."

"*Vraiment?*" the cineast barked, looking alarmed.

"Absolutely. The spite of the powerful for the powerless, the frustration of the brutally rational against the gifted intuitive, and the vengeance of the orthodox against the nonconformist. A lot of them go to my wife's songa in Encino, where the idea of the pre-emptive strike is, of course, work stoppage before the temptation to so much as begin work sets in."

"Which does *not* mean," Livonia insisted, "apart from the fact that my husband's analysis of spiritual ambition in Encino is, to say the least, skewed, that one invited these people here!

Does Ralph Von Gelsen—speaking of niche conformity, *autres couches sociales*, second-round picks, and back alleys off Santa Monica Boulevard—get them too? I'd like to know."

"Undoubtedly," the generative grammarian interposed, "as they are known to live rudely and rovingly shifting from place to place according to their exigencies, never confining their rambling humors, as it were, to any one set circuit."

"Ralph's, they say," Leland interrupted, "is where the Chippendales go to sit on Chippendale. And the burned-out, discontented, and restless are anything but a lazy sect."

"Those terms describe just about everybody one knows," Livonia countered combatively. "The Von Gelsen daughter, perhaps not exactly a Bolshevik, is at any rate as *democratic* as it is possible to be in Los Angeles. 'Equal-opportunity maladjustment' is, I believe, a favorite term of hers and her fellow covenanters. She's also responsible, apparently, for the new decor, which just happens to be featured in the *Los Angeles Times* on this very Oscar Sunday. Lots of fusion with nature: use of linen, stone, and wood. Teak floors throughout. Natural woven sea-grass carpet in the bathrooms—that kind of shit.

"Oh, and vibrating massage chairs in the lounge. 'I think people are interested in *honesty*,' quoth the decorator. 'I think America and Hollywood are interested in *honesty* after everything that went on in the nineties.' *Honesty*! Vibrating *massage* chairs—can you *believe* it? And *what*, exactly, went on in the nineties? Well, if I *really* need to know what goes on over there, it's all bound to be on www.partydigest.com."

("She's just jealous," the somebody nobody knew whispered to a spy, who'd hooked an invitation to the Wilshire Corridor through Voni's hairdresser at Cheveux. "All Hollywood knows the new Von Gelsen decor is Selma Havenhurst's latest, most masterful, and *beyond-expensive* incident. The teak floors throughout are sufficient statement by themselves, but the slender date palms growing at seemingly random intervals *through* the teak floors—they are *beyond bonsai*. And as for the guest list, it is just *imbedded* with fascinating, beautiful people, in and out of the industry, many of whom Ralph tape-records for posterity.")

"And after all," Leland concluded, "they may have some sort of point. Undeniably the collective hot flash of the Great Age of Cinema has succumbed to the Second Law of Thermodynamics. All the same," he tweaked his wife, "I would have thought it was trying for you, an Academy fellow, to have to sit here at home, in no matter what degree of relaxed comfort, and watch televised the very ceremony you could have been assisting at, like it or not, amid your own, in the damned auditorium."

"I wouldn't be caught dead in that zoo!" Livonia sniffed. "And not merely because the Bolsheviks—including, I'm afraid, many of your made men in the new Hyperion—regard it as the pathetic campfire ritual of a lot of diminished-capacity geriatrics."

Leland addressed the cineast again. "I fear you are hearing the butt end of a very long story. My wife, as you may know—"

"Was once nominated. Yes, I do know. It is an honor—"

"It *was* an honor in those days," Livonia countered.

"I mean, madame, it's an honor to *be here*."

"You're a gentleman, monsieur, and not a Bolshevik. But it was an honor in those days to be nominated. Now they send them out—the nominations—to random addresses marked Occupant." She tossed her head the way she'd done on the screen. "Vous savez, monsieur, à tous ces gens de bas-étage— and they hope somehow to arrive at . . . I don't, of course, mean tonight, but tonight is another very long story. Vous voyez, monsieur, que les acteurs me préoccupent encore. J'aime suivre leurs traces et vivre avec eux leurs découvertes. And there's a reason. Actors tend to invest in the very same corrective-vengeance scenarios that Bolsheviks spring for; it is their particular *déformation professionelle*—even at Hyperion, despite the fact that on a Hyperion shoot everybody from the line producer right down to the begging grip is the recipient of *very encouraging* money."

"A very long story," Leland remarked, "that will certainly arrive at a conclusion. That is if—"

"If Wayfaring wins!" the French cineast exploded. "But she *must*!! Must she *not*, madame?" He turned to implore Astarte.

"I believe she must, monsieur—unless my sins abuse my divination."

(The cineast regarded her solemnly, as he did so much to do with the industry, much to the amusement of his colloquotors in France, more than one of whom had declared of the seer's social cachet, "Mais c'est ridicule, cette pithonesse!" But he knew her ascription of the entirety of memory to the pictorial order of the zodiac according to the ancient design of Metrodorus of Scepsis was one of hidden Hollywood's credential absolutes.)

"Yes," the seer decided, looking around at the de Longprés. "Yes, Voni's hit on it: Hollywood has gone Bolshevik. There are few distinct minds on display, the sloth of fools has reached its zenith, and anybody can say anything without fear of being shown the door."

"Which does *not* mean," Livonia concluded, "that I favor catered-site public housing or need a Web site of my very own."

"Say what you will about Bolsheviks," the somebody nobody knew declared, "one must concede one thing: they have looked into the abyss."

"The abyss of their own making," the liaison grammarian chanced.

"Not really," Leland drawled. "Bolsheviks are too fucking

stupid and too fucking lazy to perform the necessary evacuation. Abysses are born, not made—born out of major earthquakes, actually. What Bolsheviks do, essentially, is piss into the abyss—that is the whole extent of their existential participation."

The boyfriend was immersed in *The Undertow.*

In a room full of long mirrors the woman, having put aside her Bible, sat alone looking first into one (the French *verre églomisé*), then another (doubling the effect, the viewer noticed, of the impression rendered throughout the picture by the large number of close shot-to-shot graphic matches). And as she did, behind her, a sequence likely to frustrate deciphering progressed, resembling (the viewer thought) a succession of foci racked to the moon: a collage of split-field diopter lens takes and highly evolved background plates (in fact Orphrey Whither's first foray into computer-generation: a new optical rendition of an Italian silent-film technique in which cameras remained odd-angled but fixed while simultaneous actions flashed on receding planes). One time a single figure, another time a little scene—around a table, outdoors in a rose garden, in a backyard where a stage had been set up upon which another little scene was being enacted . . . and the woman would reach out to what was being depicted in one long mirror and then another, and as she did each time the tableaux as it were suspended in glass bubbles behind her image would dissolve, and she would turn away from her own image and from the remembrance.

And in the swamp, overhanging branches of bald cypress and the cone-shaped knees of their submerged root system radiating upwards through cool green water, all reflecting strange primordial shapes in cerulean blue, white-streaked skies.

"The son, they say, is such a ringer for the brother he could play him."

"The story of the brother," Astarte assured the questioner, "elaborated beyond that one sequence, would have proved too distracting. He was, as was his cousin Gabriel Wayfaring, a wild boy with a streak of melancholy that seemed in those days an even greater art than screaming, whose legend did not die with him."

One story begets another.

"They'd somehow gotten hold," Leland was saying, "the friends of the deceased, of a compilation of Irish wake amusements, proscribed by the church in rural Ireland, but which flourished all the same, and devised out of it a kind of second wake and funeral, like something out of the *Iliad* or *Beowulf,* held in the old clubhouse cabin they'd all shared, a fairly exact equivalent, in size, of the archetypal Irish country cottage. No thatch—roofs in the South are tar or tin—this one was tar, and it collapsed, burned, in the fire the wake set off. They'd been singing, 'Can the circle be unbroken, by and by, Lord, by and by,' and getting drunker and drunker, pouring lustral moonshine over the body and chanting Cherokee prayers to the north wind and the west wind to ignite the funeral pyre of this fallen beauty—until finally the place went up in flames.

"No notice would have been taken of an old cabin burned down in the woods—but at the wake held in the cabin, and focus, or target, of virtually all of the raucous, profane, and even obscene rituals enacted there, there was a kind of body— almost certainly that of a big dog, although the awful rumor was that the boy's body itself, in his army uniform, had been stolen in the night out of the funeral home in Clayton and the body of the dog left in the casket, discovered, and in some versions hastily removed, and in others, because there was no time, and the army chaplain was outside waiting, closed up in the coffin and buried, but either way of course not before the mother, Cordelia—"

"But suppose that," the contract player interrupted, "was what finally drove the mother mad?"

"It was thought," Leland assured her, "that grief alone had sufficed. In any case, none of it was ever really credited. The funeral took place as the cabin burned, on the Chattahoochee River bank. And the body, whatever it was—we used a straw man—was carried on a burning catafalque over Tallulah Falls."

"Plácido," Kaye Wayfaring asked, "did Dolores Del Rio ever mean anything to you?"

"Not to me, Miss Wayfaring, no—but to my mother, next to La Morenita, and maybe Maria Feliz, she was the most important woman in Mexico."

(She was very moving in *Flaming Star*. Can I say that?)

"I never saw her," Plácido offered, "in the movies; I don't believe so, anyway."

"She slept a lot—did you know that?"

"Oh, everybody knew that—to stay beautiful. But La Morenita is more beautiful still, and she never sleeps; she can't—somebody is always praying to her."

"You arrived here," one of the due-diligence rectified pedophiles—tamers all of riotous youth—taxed me the other afternoon, "driven in a vehicle of European make, without a trailer hitch, and you hunt alone like Mowgli in the forest." (I'd come in from a night out under the redwoods, back to this world of appearances from the realm of truth.) "Your strange beauty is intensified by a quelling look of grave intelligence, but I fear you will confuse the issue all the same." Not playing the game (fetch)

was the clear implication of this one, who strides the earth here like St. Peter in the Brancacci frescoes, healing cripples will they but kneel in his shadow. Being shirty, like, while everybody else is dedicated to being undershirty. Makes you think more than ever, in defiance, that you've wandered into the Ancestral Hall of the Exalted Brave, that home for distressed eunuchs (Those-Without-Shadows) of the lost Empire. I wanted to say, "Listen, fuckwad, eat my leftovers. You seem to think I ought to look up to you as toward virtue, from below, whereas the only way I can picture you is down on your knees whimpering please." *But I did not. (Better not shout, better not cry, better not pout, they'll all tell you why. Seems you must just be good for goodness sake.)*

"Only for a season is the flesh perfect," the old buzzard actually said to me. I wanted to answer "You speak a great truth, O King Flat Devil of the Higher Realm, in your snazzy-dude cargoes, and each of us begins to die when the organism becomes too puzzled to go on." (You know I revere elders, but geezer *chic?* Too Melrose Avenue.)*

There are long windows everywhere, and doors made of teak like at 47 Gramercy—in fact, as you may know, the whole joint is tongue and groove—hmmm—not a nail in a board. Of course (with a single exception) no carpets, and nothing significant on any of the mantelpieces. I keep wondering, what could it have been like here—what all took place—before the beaverboard and the gongs, the shoji screens and the little jami-chunatra *spirit houses they make out of matchsticks and Crazy Glue.*

I made the mistake of saying something to one exercitant about the kind of breath a holy man uses vis-à-vis the kind of breath the singer uses. I was informed in no uncertain terms by this fretful, ursine type with pivot-issue chops that no holy man uses breath. *"Breath is not a* utility; *breath is a* possession, *yet we do not* breathe: *we are breathed in, breathed out." (I connect: but if it's true there is no me, what must I do? It seems that properly understood, life is a stationary state—anchor out; stern high on the shingle—in which one need do nothing at all but sing one's own deep song of the loon. And what of it? Will we ever be able to distinguish between mystical visions and mental illness? Should we even try, now that the American Psychiatric Association has officially recognized the religious or spiritual as a normal dimension of human life, and many practitioners are seeking new ways—bless them—to acknowledge the legitimate role of spirituality in their patients' experiential profiles?)*

And another time, "This is not a retreat house; one doesn't come here to bargain for conditional manumission from enslavement to the world of things, much less to repent of sin—which is only a kind of gloating over one's promiscuity." (Yes, all taint, every residue of horizontal translative religious practice and egoic petitionary prayer—not to mention intimate relationships and/or questions pertaining to the future—must go, in favor of in-store signage submission to . . . whatever. You couldn't accuse any of these ones of promoting a society whose overall group ethos aids eccentric behavior patterns or reciprocally stimulated personality differentiation—a.k.a. schismogenesis.)

"Not, it must be allowed, that you, young man, seem to do either. Indeed you never talk about yourself at all—not about your past, nor about who you are, nor of your plans for being made whole."

The young hero, I heard myself not say, never discloses his holific plans; they evolve in primordial tone in the dark. As if reading my mind, he said, "We must try to think beyond the dark, into the morning. Why is it that, when while we sleep, the morning always comes on its own?" (Certainly solves the problem of the hurdle of the baccalaureate, does it not? I mean, if the deal is no pain, no gain, what the hell, I'll take it.)

Almost unendurable, having walked down the Infinite (polished) Corridor, knocked and been noticed, to wait to be received by the Preceptor. Yet one's will is tied, having left one's book behind (unseemly to be caught reading as if one were waiting to go in for a filling) and imagines, for no reason, one has in fact dropped it somewhere in the labyrinth of the empty corridors leading back to one's cell.

At length the unseen figure opens the communicating door; a light snaps on, revealing a pressure weal across his forehead. "I understand you speak Irish and German." "Not both at once, and not all the time, but yes." "Won't you sit down—and not, perhaps, behave like some sort of suspect under caution. There are no suspects here"—and then he smiled—"at any rate not of the usual kind."

There was, besides the roomy (I decided Russian leather) chair he sat in and the little straight-backed one he offered me, one other just like it, and against the far wall a stack of eight gilt ballroom chairs. (Only, there's no room in here, I thought, to dance, or even to arrange more than two or three of them at most.) I asked somebody later did he have savvy-seating group sessions there—maybe move back the enormous inlaid Biedermeier desk? "No, those stay exactly where they are, always. Some conjecture they're meant for all his previous avatars when gathered to laud his progress in this appearance." (In which in the combat zone of negation and transcendence he is, one supposes, the angle bearer. I have an idea they look at Baywatch *reruns together and dish cyberspace.)*

"You have come here, it seems," he said, from behind the desk, "hungry for justice—to know more truly what justice may be. Plato suggests that the need for justice arises from the individual's experience of inner conflict. You appear to be invested with such need. Morality, Plato says, enters as a negative force prohibiting unworthy desires. I use Plato as the entry point, for in the world from which you have come, there is, or soon will be, no such thing as an unworthy desire." (No more things you just don't do. I took his point.)

"Whereas here in the world you have entered, there is no such thing as a worthy one. We are not much interested in out-

standing warrants or other workings of procedural justice vis-à-vis conflict resolution. Nor in psychoanalysis, which in our view is nothing but lullabies."

(I couldn't help wondering was he or was he not of a mind that an omelette pan ought never to be washed, or that the social moment matters still.)

"We leave all that to the outside world, to preference utilitarians and to the velocity of cheap evangelism, which has obliterated the very concepts of time and space that once had a calming and dissipative effect upon its political passions—with the unfortunate and uncontrollable result that the very rending and coercive forces they sought to mollify now coalesce by instantaneous communication with intensifying effect."

He said a lot more, including the admonition that the sluggish must be spurred on, for they are loath to put to use, when it is given back to them, the energy of their rebirth, but I couldn't help feeling that no matter what he said, what he was thinking *was, "For all his intelligence, station in life, looks, complexion—his unmerited rewards in this our life—this boy will never see God."*

"You may go now." "Back to my room?" "To your room, to that world." "Whatever?" "Whatever is a corruption; you may go." (Control tower to pilot: flight of the alone to the alone: advisory directive: sunt lacrimae rerum.*) A worse outcome, however, having knocked and been seen, would be to have been dismissed. Is it possible to attract, almost simultaneously, both an extreme attention and a benign neglect?)*

As to the single exception in the matter of the carpeting—deep-pile saffron thick-shag wall-to-wall, and the enormous ring of keys, all absolutely identical, on the desk . . . next time.

"Voni is devoted to Jackie Collins," Leland admitted.

"Jackie Collins knows Hollywood," a guest declared firmly.

"I so agree. Her characterization of the typical aspirant—two tits in a trance—is radical."

"Magnetism," the somebody nobody knew put in, "the magical faculty which lies dormant in us by the opiate of primitive sin, stands in need of an excitator, which may be good or evil, and often by some previous pignoration or compact with witches."

Another suspect came forward to declare, "All this reliance on the occult in California—santos and crystals, astrology and whatnot—is nothing but a bunch of spiritualist baloney!"

"Spiritualist perhaps," snapped a waiter offering hot hors d'oeuvres; "baloney, perhaps not."

"I myself," the first guest sniffed, passing on the little empanadas, "so much prefer world peace through corrective diet."

"Really?" the waiter said, smiling sweetly. "I prefer lead out trumps."

"And I," the neutral suspect mused in conciliatory tones, "the old idea of a consoling God. You know the saying 'He is nigh unto them that are heartbroken.' "

"So are we all," the lingering waiter offered, "five mornings a week: the captive television audience."

"The news. But you can beat the rap if you have the technology to deconstruct the information later. Taking the images of world leaders, for instance, transcribing them at high resolution into time-series protocols and comparing them with samples from identical operations done on the images of, on the one hand, notables in the media, and on the other hand, a random selection of the ordinary populace in curbside interviews."

"Or," the waiter (his sudden window of opportunity seized) continued, "if you're like me, a vampire with elevated taste, not up for Joey Buttafuoco on cable or going online to eavesdrop on the sighing, giggling, sobbing, drooling nothing-burger landscape of the American night—the bump and grind, the endless pointless 'I'm like, you know, blah-blah-blah, da-da-da'—you can groove on that female deejay on midnight classical FM radio."

"Oh," a voice crowed, "I know *her*—she's now *famous!*"

"That she is—for heavy-breather renditions from the tormented lives of great composers—breathtaking details of ecstatic self-deceptions and low-down betrayals—culled from diary entries, love letters, testimonies of biographers and other codependent agony freaks brimming with articulate compassion and grisly relish—these collections not available in stores—followed by cuts from the masters' heartfelt output—like she's auditioning for the remake of *Play Misty for Me*. Whenever there's a news break she becomes especially urgent. 'Stay tuned, there's more refined programming coming up on this station, including a radical debate between Women Up Against It and Girls in the Life on the politics of the invaginated eyeball.' It's like she's selling Frederick's of Hollywood lingerie—it's a scream."

"I don't know," the first voice returned, "what is meant by 'the invaginated highball,' but the way you said 'grisly relish' on top of 'nothing burger' made me think of all those drunken Malibu Colony cookouts Voni used to have with the *first* producer husband. The food was absolutely execrable, but the *highballs!*"

"Not *highballs*," the waiter corrected, "*eyeballs*. It's vaginated *eyeballs*."

"Yes," the somebody nobody knew continued, "we are a captive audience, both representative of and victimized by the American obsession with beauty, celebrity, and the transmitted image, in both the active and passive modes, both coming and going."

"Really? Well, *I* am neither active nor passive, I am simply sitting still. This is an occasion I've been awaiting for too many years. Usually I am as ambivalent as it is possible to be without having a breakdown in the turning lane, but tonight I feel that if this award is not correctly bestowed there will be an unruly commotion in the streets!"

So this other adept, a sleek white anklet-diamond sutra fashion plate, takes me aside and says, "You know you have the aura of a fallow deer." This one, I said to myself, is not just making a move, he's making a movie. Demobbed soldier male finds young convalescent in old sanitorium—a demure boy whose vacant, troubled eyes peer into dark shadows in every corner. Detects not anguish but only, with the steely gaze of a Hollywood hack writer, turn into second act. Boy humbled, seized from death's jaws (but harried still by his demons, by Nishkala Shiva, and feeding like a diligent insect on the humiliation of his downcast state). Prey to the many temptations of his own lively and impetuous character, thrown suddenly into his warder's bare, open, manly arms, he trades up. Sort of like More of a Man, *but emphasizing the authentic cry of the soul for help.*

"Listen," he continues, "why must we go downstairs to that awful dining hall? They microwave everything, you know, which at the prices being paid to keep us here really is an outrage. (Ça c'est vrai, rien ne plaît; ni les vins ni les mets.) *"Why must we mix with all those awful, ugly, not exactly fragrant people from who can say what background?*

"Why not have our meals up in my room? I keep a stock of quite superior sous-vide *comestibles sent up from Tasajara— I'm attracted to sturdy items; everything is absolutely organic— and a little electric stove. I mean, I am not offering you peanut butter." Tasajara! (Or, as Uncle Dee would say,* Tasajara-how-are-ye!*) Why not Spago; why not Vernissage?*

"I find people in the dining hall supportive," I said, "and doesn't the Buddha say one of the many ways in which awakening can come about is in hearing the gong strike for dinner?"

Silence, at first, and then he almost wailed, "There must be a place after death where great artists foregather, away from the daily grillings, the praises, lies and ridicule, where nothing matters and where living is an easy thing." (Yeah, in summertime. Gosh, talk about the plucked tension between limit and nothing!) It's indecent, one's being imagined the target of such lobe-grater rote garble, such smarmy freeze-dried lust (no fuss, just a little casual-hummer nembutsu *with you) camouflaged as a pre-emptive strike against yearning? And really, why wait until after death, when right here and now you might don nineteenth-century costume (people do) and ride around on bicycles, or sit in garden chairs bandying idle nothings and investigating the possibilities of joy at the postconventional level? And what about Sony Glasstron wall-screen television with virtual-viewing glasses?*

"You know," he then said, "the world will either break your heart or turn it to stone." (The Cistercians have the same notion.) "These people up here and their doctrine are, from the point of view of civilization, slovenly." Pause. (He does want me to know he gives till it hurts.) "On the other hand, what, in sum, has civilization given us, apart from offensive clutter, the population explosion, and more efficient torture?" Pause. "This country has brought nothing to the world—taught the world nothing, has contributed not a single original great idea—and don't try to tell me about the Declaration of Independence, the Constitution, or the Bill of Rights—all fatuous hobby horses of the landed Virginia rich who liked to assume French manners."

*What could I say—*on yer bike, Moriarty? *Or quote Tom Paine to the effect that while government promotes happiness only negatively, by restraining our vices, society does so positively, by uniting our affections? I said, "All the same, I think I should give it a shot."*

"Perhaps I'm a coward," he sighed. "They say the only way

to find out is to spend a lot of time among your enemies. I'm a
person who needs to be on the cutting edge in terms of visioning."
(I'm not making a single word of this up.) "Do you," he then
asked, pointing to a board covered with black and white thumb
tacks, "play Go?" (We got game? I thought not quite—in fact
quite not. This one, I told myself, is not in this place on retreat—
not on your, my, or anybody else's life; on the very contrary, he's
bivouacked in harness, the sulky-remote performance a blind.)
"Only," I replied, "if when I pass it, I get two hundred dollars."

("He wrote to me," Maev said, "saying that we two 'like
two billows of the Irish sounds, forcibly driven with contrary
tides,' meeting in midstream, 'back rebound with roaring rage'
and so 'divide the doubtful current into divers ways.' That's
from *The Faerie Queene*, which he knows I love.

"And I do have to admit I sometimes get a big kick out of
listening to him—especially when he's on his high horse at
somebody else. That time years ago at Friends—we couldn't
have been further along than the fourth grade, when he was
rehearsing a Schubert song in the music room, and somebody
on the faculty asked him did he plan on doing a gig with you—
you hadn't officially retired—and he announced, 'My grandmother, who, under the auspices of the most important music
managements in the business, has filled *engagements* in virtually *all* of the world's important concert halls and opera houses,
does not *do gigs!*' ")

"Maybe I shouldn't call Maev Jordana, or rag her that way.
Maybe I merely wished to indicate she'd never been Ophelia.
Nevertheless. After all, is she a young twentysomething who
drinks too much, gets involved with married men, is unable to
get her life on track, and spends a lot of time staring out win-
dows at the night—who then rises up at noon to spend her after-

noons sitting in Fred Segal shades at Campanile, sporting a two-hundred-dollar faux-sun-bleached Dirty Girl crop top cut to look like something that cost ten bucks and was done in Downey, draped in soft shades of black, crossing and recrossing her legs every two minutes to relieve the weight of precarious four-inch block-heeled slides? Does she—while watching hordes of remnant wanton Baytan-and-body-gloss Eurodrek in terrible eight-hundred-dollar Manolo Blahnik steel-heel slut pumps, fresh from shopping full retail at Prada on Rodeo Drive, pass by slurping high-tech rainbow fro-yo—brood on the ironic discourse by which she subversively assumes the oppressive images of Brazilian bikini-waxed women found in white patriarchal society, then clomping like a Clydesdale—the Angeleno, not the Eurodrek—over to the top-down ass wagon and gunning the engine down Sunset to Silver Lake (the desperate shout line "a girl in her Porsche against the world" pounding in her temples, tears streaming down her face with the a.c. jacked to meat locker and Kurt Cobain—dead in pain, but not in vain—on the tape deck) to nasty, dark, crap-can middens of depravity full of teen glueheads in Converse All-Stars patched with duct tape—"We own the night!"—their numbed ears grooving on illbient trip-hop and progressive techno house bonding emotive synthesized melodies to locked rhythms while in even darker more discreet corners splotchy echo-boomer tongues lap up K residue off chipped-formica tabletops?

No, she does not. Rather she spends her afternoons at the University of California, Los Angeles, in Westwood, examining the moral necessity of the passionate pursuit of the real. In addition (if it may be so put and stay nicely meant) she does not seek requited love from carhops, neither is she easily flattered in retail emporia. Plus which Maev hates stiletto heels. "When you think of all those beautiful marble floors in Italy," I heard her say to mother, "destroyed by the steel rods in stiletto heels!" (I remem-

*ber thinking, there are marble floors in the entry hall at Payne
Whitney, too.) Nevertheless I feel competition between us is
robbed of significance, girls being different: the playing field is
uneven. If there had been a brother, a real victory might have
been possible, and a real defeat delicious.*

The boyfriend was watching the son's funeral with the sexy
backwoods boys, enjoying fantasies of what he'd missed by
growing up in Sherman Oaks in the eighties, when the most
exciting adventure was camping at Lake Arrowhead and spy-
ing on the schizophrenic survivalist "hill people" destined, he
thought, for varieties of mass suicide along the lines of the
Heaven's Gate mob.

"They tried," Livonia announced, "to get you-know-who for
the Colonel, but it was a no-go—and of course, the size of
him! Imagine having all that talent and money power to do
whatever you like, and doing nothing but lying in undisclosed
locations like a beached whale, in apathy and resentment."

"They say," the former contract player offered, "it's
because he's sickened by the applause of admirers who persist
in attributing his achievement to a love of truth. Whereas he
thinks of it alternatively as dumb luck and as the working out
of a deep mystery quite at odds with ego function. Also he says
he realized all the trouble in the world comes from the exer-
tions of busy people, especially in the industry."

"That *is* desperate—go that route, you end in hell."

"It's said we must never impute damnation to a living
soul."

"Did I do that?"

"It's a great life, they say, if you don't weaken."

"Really. But whether you do or you don't, what it comes to

at the end is boxed billing and then oblivion. Of course you'll still have those Hollywood teeth—if you had the good sense at Christmas to put in for more than your two front ones."

I dream of going down to Tehachapi and having breakfast (hash and eggs, coffee and sweet rolls) with the hard driven women immured there: old deferentialists, new cynics, prisoners all—and wardens too—of tough love, listening to their diverse invectives and talking philosophy with them—game theory and Parfit's prisoners' dilemma, whereby, as a result of no reciprocity, if both confess it would be worse for each than if both kept silent. Anything but more tofu and green kelp tea with the adept.

One thing more than any other is true of the place. If you arrive, awakened from the first deep sleep of shocked and wearied youth, with a whole lot of fresh ideas—musical or otherwise—if you think you're in a life situation as pregnant with possibilities as anything in Homer—the rage of Achilles, the travels of Odysseus—what they've got here is a whole range of abortifacients. For them, as a result of their own enclosed experience of bhav *and the esthetics of Ahnava Gupta, the closely guarded assumption is that inasmuch as the universe is a battleground between two tendencies, and repulsive gravity is winning—pass it along—it is sufficient for a human life to simply mark its own wandering course (exclusive of all natural phenomena and human exchange) to a fixed end.*

Stay long enough and you won't have a clue. (This is not good; as Gordon Merrick says somewhere, "You can't let me become myself without looking at the danger.") Never mind as to who done it, as to if it was really done. You'll leave no wiser as to old-hat Truth or Consequences than you were when you arrived. (If you ever indeed get to leave, because they really like it if you tell them that rather than starting all over again in uphill ways in some other place, you'd like to stay, praying long and alone, at liberty in the labyrinth: the tantalizing state of advancement-evasion—drawing a veil over the compensatory tendency to develop the nocturnal habits of the montane vole— for as long a time as the residential bursary is routinely main- tained, nasty microwave cooking notwithstanding—for as Homer insists, no matter how wracked we are by devastating sorrows, the belly is a barking dog that will be filled. And there are no such things *as the finer instincts.)*

I'll take Manhattan, thanks. You sit there on the park bench, minding your own business, watching a little get-up neighbor- hood ball game, and right at the moment when the cutest kid you've yet seen that day is gloving a hot grounder, some old what's-his-nuts comes along carrying a scrapbook; sits next to you. Picks a topic—say, brooding doves and the brutality of men—and after expatiating for a time, turns to you, holds out a thermos, offers you a little sip of his awful coffee, and asks, "Would you care to have a look-see at these personal notices?" "Not only would I care to, it would be a privilege. And did you know that my paternal grandmother, fleeing from the Irish Civil War, was sent by the Blue Nuns to the great Bohemian diva Destinn, whom my maternal great-grandmother, having seen as Aida in Atlanta in 1912, *opposite Caruso and conducted by Toscanini (whom she, Destinn, had been fucking in the train on the way down) proclaimed the greatest singer she'd ever heard?"*

All of which means either *no film, gang, or at the very least (situational ethics must, I would think, come into it somewhere)* closed set.

This just in. Quote of the week. "To live another day, if only to jump to reset a sail during an off-wind leg."

She looked down to the tracks along the Los Angeles River and saw the Amtrak train making its way to Union Station.

·   ·   ·

Leland, just before leaving for the ceremony, was telling the room, splashed incandescent now by the russet sunset, why Orphrey Whither had never sold Hyperion's product to television.

"The moron esthetic of the American TV sitcom is intended to arouse the appetitive instinct of the viewer while simultaneously sedating the aggressive drive. Only in this conflicted position can the unconsciously sedated couch potato be microwaved—can the sucker born again every minute be serviced with advertising. Big-screen esthetics so modified can only thereby conform in all ways—close-ups, zooms, etc.—to the esthetic of television.

"Whereas on the loading-zone level of dispensation the art product is commensurate with any industrial output unit, at the storyboard level of conceptual disposition it is radically opposite. The profit motive is fundamentally antithetical to the motive of artistic negotiation, which is more like one-to-one relationship marketing. Very like a hustler operating without a john, isn't it? Risky, but the new Hyperion has become interested in it. The Sherwood Oaks Experimental College on Hollywood Boulevard is giving seminars in it at the Roosevelt Hotel, and weekend screenwriters' retreats in Santa Barbara, too."

"Leland's remarks," a voice declared, as the host departed (and anxious faces began as the sun dipped further to figure the next move), "are as usual right on the button. Everybody you know is going off on some kind of retreat or other, to let the graze wounds heal. You really have to in a town where underneath the facade of smiling alliances and the pretend conviction that life and work are twin hurdles best approached with a little ingenuity and a sunny outlook there is such a dense web of motive, circumstance, needs, and longings whose origins are primal."

"And that's exactly," another declared, "why we had primal

scream—it was honest! What we have now isn't honest in the least. Minor celebrities decked out in major jewelry—how can that be honest?"

"I had a dear friend back in the eighties—I forget the name—whose hairdresser's mother was cured of an enormous tumor by Rosalind Bruyere at the Convention Center."

"Oh, yes—'Razzle-Dazzle Roz'—I remember. She lived in the Valley and rode a Harley."

"Lawrence LeShan's psychic workshops . . . Jim Berenholz's Cahuenga-shaman wisdom . . . the Korla Pandit revival: salamanders in the fire. Important questions were raised, such as 'Which is more pervasive, the denial that leads to cancer or the cancer that leads to denial?' All forms of government and corporate secrecy were going to become obsolete due to people's enhanced awareness of surveillance and their acquired ability to beat it back."

"Yes, indeed," another remembered. "We were going to learn to find our moment and grow mega-vegetables in the sand and the snow using our minds, like in Scotland. Entertainment was to be wholly reconfigured, throwing the industry into chaos. What ever happened to all that?"

"The majority proved to be too lazy—probably just as well. I mean really, darling, when most people in this very room look on thinking hard as something like sustaining a blunt trauma to the head, preferring to a woman-man endless-summer variations of high-glamour, low-maintenance self-delusion and the intellectual equivalents of laser vaginal rejuvenation, you can hardly suspect them capable, now can you, of psychic Krav Maga."

"There was that Brazilian psychic painter—remember him? All those newly channeled Renoirs and Van Goghs,. Degas and Modiglianis painted by the hour with his hands and feet? He was anything but lazy—and they looked *real*, or so people said."

"I heard that guy finally fritzed out on speed."

"I heard he switched to downs, started doing white-on-whites, and that was the end of him."

"I heard he was greatly assisted by the La Cienaga mafia."

"But wait a minute, *is* there an intellectual equivalent of that laser vaginal whatever? If so, it can't be a bad thing."

"It all depends, I suppose, on your definition of it all."

"Rather. You know what they say, in New York two and two makes four; in Los Angeles it makes two-point-two."

"I suppose there must be a point to that remark—one I don't get."

"We all live in spite of the world—of what it may up and do next . . . the Earthquake . . . whatever."

"Just remember, culture follows money—west."

"Pictures," the generative liaison grammarian stressed, "tend to be addressed to lazy minds. When we are exasperated with someone for not understanding what we say, we say 'What, do you want me to draw you a picture?'

"In our beginning was the word. The only high civilization based on pictures is the Egyptian. The oldest of these was carved in the rocks above the Second Cataract five thousand years ago. The Egyptians lay about for thousands of years just waiting for the Nile to rise. Of course *slaves* toiled, but the rulers—people like us—sat looking out the window for long periods—only there weren't, strictly speaking, any windows—watching the lazy progress of the sun, moon, and stars across the heavens."

"In Nacogdoches," Livonia was saying, "the sunsets were blazing like in *Picnic*. 'The sun putting up a big scrap to keep the night from creeping on.' In Los Angeles the tired winter sun slinks into Santa Monica Bay like an old whore. That sky is the color of an old whore's lipstick. Moonrise, though, is another thing altogether. Los Angeles has always come alive at moonrise—why we so loved going to Ciro's, Mocambo, the Cocoanut Grove."

A partial moon was rising in a cobalt-blue sky over the royal palms. The view over the reservoir was all pinpoint lights. Kaye remembered an adage. "It used to be said in Hollywood if you were going to be a star, it was just as well not to play a mother—or if you did, not the mother of anybody too interesting."

On the other side of the wraparound room, they were looking at the Hollywood Hills. Somebody pointed out Ralph Von Gelsen's place—the Lautner spaceship—reminding somebody else of the rumor of Orphrey Whither's impending "last" picture: the escape-from-earth one with the cast of thousands.

"All celebrities."

"They're probably playing Celebrity over at the Von Gelsens', sitting under the date palms in vibrating chairs."

"Ever played Celebrity here? Voni's a killer. Know who Vera Vague was? Probably not in the phone book anymore, but Voni can give you the address of her star on Hollywood Boulevard."

"Maybe to make the game interesting for Hollywood," the former contract player mused, "it should be renamed Nonentities."

"Also, the first of the great labyrinths was Egyptian—located by Pliny in Lake Moeris. A labyrinth is an architectonic structure, apparently aimless, of a pattern so complex that, once inside, it is difficult-to-impossible to escape."

"I get it—and yet I don't get it at all. The picture you draw of us lolling along the Los Angeles River or in Echo Park Lake looking up at billboards while we wait for the next inundation doesn't exactly represent the, to me, enormously strenuous struggle of our day-in, day-out passage from unspoiled youth to renewed youth to eternal youth."

"Of course, if in ancient Egypt there were no windows, then there were no window treatments, or window dressers, either!"

"Window dressers aren't called that anymore—they're now called visualizers."

"I know someone," the someone nobody knew said, "who has the New York skyline computerized from sundown to sunrise on his wall for when he goes crazy out here."

"What there *were*, however, were decorative *tiles*. This was a civilization eons removed from the requirements of mere shelter and therefore into the first and surest of advanced culture's primary markers, decorative tile."

". . . standard signifiers, phonetic values . . ."

" '*Nobody*,' he said, 'is going to exploit *me*!' 'You are *so* right,' I said. 'It takes missionary enthusiasm to be exploited; you haven't a prayer.' Know what? He agreed."

"All this talk of Egypt reminds me of *The Egyptian*—it was my favorite allegorical picture of the fifties."

"*The Egyptian* an allegory? What of?"

"Ambition, California, rough trade, antiques. Curtis Harrington said that at the time of the original release, at a party at Samson de Brier's. Somebody else said he was full of shit, that the destiny of Los Angeles was foretold in Apocalypse 16, when the angel pours the vial of God's wrath into the Euphrates and the river dries up and the Satanic hordes teem in along the dried-up riverbed."

"Symbolic. Remember, in the fifties, when everything, but *everything*, was symbolic?"

"I liked symbolic thought; it framed the concept, thus avoiding libel, false light, invasion of privacy, and slander complications."

"Look, whatever you remember, remember, it's still *now*."

"That sounds to me like lying down on the job."

"Who doesn't know about *that* in Hollywood!"

"Too true; it is oxymoronic to talk of the *dynamic* of the industry. You want a definitive existential definition of Hollywood? Irrelevance in formaldehyde. Virtual particles do not *seethe*, they *slump*."

"Well, the Egyptians knew how to infuse the statues of their gods with cosmic and magical powers—in other words, *how to make gods*. Hollywood does the same—relentlessly."

"*Utterly buffet?*"

"A *leap* of *faith*."

"Articulation was always a problem out here, even before the hearings, but did we ever think the day would come when 'Can we talk?' would become a serious crisis question, or that the answer to it would become, more and more, 'Let me get back to you'?"

"Hollywood is one history that has not survived its own fulfillment."

" 'We are sorry,' the message read, 'but we do not support that ability at this time.' This, I told myself, is the voice of the Beginning of the End!"

"Face it, technology is a crock of shit."

"I'll grant you this, if life *is* a tale told by an idiot, full of sound and fury, signifying nothing, then movies are becoming more lifelike every year."

"And then we're dead—and that's *it*? I don't think so."

"Excuse me, but I *do* think so."

"Well, then, you're just giving *in*—just taking it lying *down*!"

"Talk about passive, lazy, and stupid—to turn yourself into a walking array of *logos*! It was the end—you can't even say everything else followed, because nothing follows the end. Nothing *happens* after the end—and anybody who thinks *anything* is happening *now* is *fucked*."

"You're right, it's past the end, and that is exactly when it started—when everything started turning into shit—when they started putting the *labels* on the *outside*, and people, instead of saying 'We don't think so,' said 'Oh? OK.' "

"They do *not* say that the meaning of life is doing little or nothing, a crude paraphrase commensurate with misstatement. What they *say* is whatever the meaning of life *is*, it is to be found on a road that leads *in the opposite direction* from whatever you mean by your latest *transaction*. They point to the fact that Aristotle, Aquinas, and Newton all believed that the *substratum* of reality—First Cause, Prime Mover, ether—existed *at rest*."

"Yes, even Einstein and the quantum physicists believed that. It's my idea of heaven too, sleeping in with the cell phone off—and I don't care how passive-aggressive they call it."

"Can I ask someone—what on *earth* is a *vaginated eyeball*?"

"I haven't any idea—have some more caviar?"

"It's true—Rin Tin Tin died in Jean Harlow's arms."

"...!"

"Meanwhile, what will she say? Wayfaring, I mean."

"*Say?*"

"When she *accepts*. I mean, she's a genius at press conferences."

"Oh, I think she'll say something historical."

"Really? 'Four score and seven years ago . . .' What?"

"Well now, let's see, how about this. 'Four score and seven years ago, D.W. Griffith made *Birth of a Nation*, and a young girl in the Deep South . . .'"

"Or what about, 'Although I am going back to New York next week to appear in a play, do not think for—'"

" '—a moment that I am leaving you.' That's good."

" 'How could I? For my heart is here in pictures.'"

"That's good."

" 'I'll be back to claim it—and soon—on *Hollywood Squares*.'"

"That's *very* good."

"But is she really—going back to New York?"

"You hear rumors—a revival of *Phèdre*, for instance—in *French*!"

" 'Miss Wayfaring, have you anything to say to Los Angeles before going back to New York?'"

"In twenty-five words or less."

" 'I might.'"

"You ready, Miss Wayfaring?"

"Plácido, how am I going to do this?"

"Miss Wayfaring, you could do this in your sleep."

"Do you think so?"

"I'm sure of it."

"In that case, would you wake me when it's over?"

The sun had set with a Pacific splendor.

Miss Wayfaring, have you anything to say to Los Angeles?

I think I have.

They had reached the entry ramp.

There's really nothing to it—a door opens; you go through

it; they're there; that's it. Otherwise you might as well—no offense to anybody.

The herald voice, charged, breathless in the big moment, was broadcasting over the car radio.

"And the winner is . . . of *course*—"

Of course. Los Angeles lay lustrous in the clear night air.